A nerdy hero, a dashing villain...

And an interfering auntie.

Life's complicated for Seema Rawat, cyberspy.

One Monsoon in Mumbai

by

Anitha Perinchery

Copyright © 2019 by Anitha Perinchery

Publisher's Cataloging-In-Publication Data
(Prepared by The Donohue Group, Inc.)

Names: Perinchery, Anitha, author.
Title: One monsoon in Mumbai / by Anitha Perinchery.
Description: [Second edition]. [Anitha Perinchery], [2019] | Series: [Indian summer series] ; [1]
Identifiers: ISBN 9781733798624 (paperback) | ISBN 9781733798600 (ebook)
Subjects: LCSH: Women spies--India--Mumbai--Fiction. | Cyber intelligence (Computer security)--India--Mumbai--Fiction. | Aunts--India--Mumbai--Fiction. | Man-woman relationships--India--Mumbai--Fiction. | LCGFT: Romance fiction. | Thrillers (Fiction)
Classification: LCC PS3616.I546 O54 2019 (print) | LCC PS3616.I546 (ebook) | DDC 813/.6--dc23

Cover: www.EBookorPrint.com

www.AnithaPerinchery.com

Table of Contents

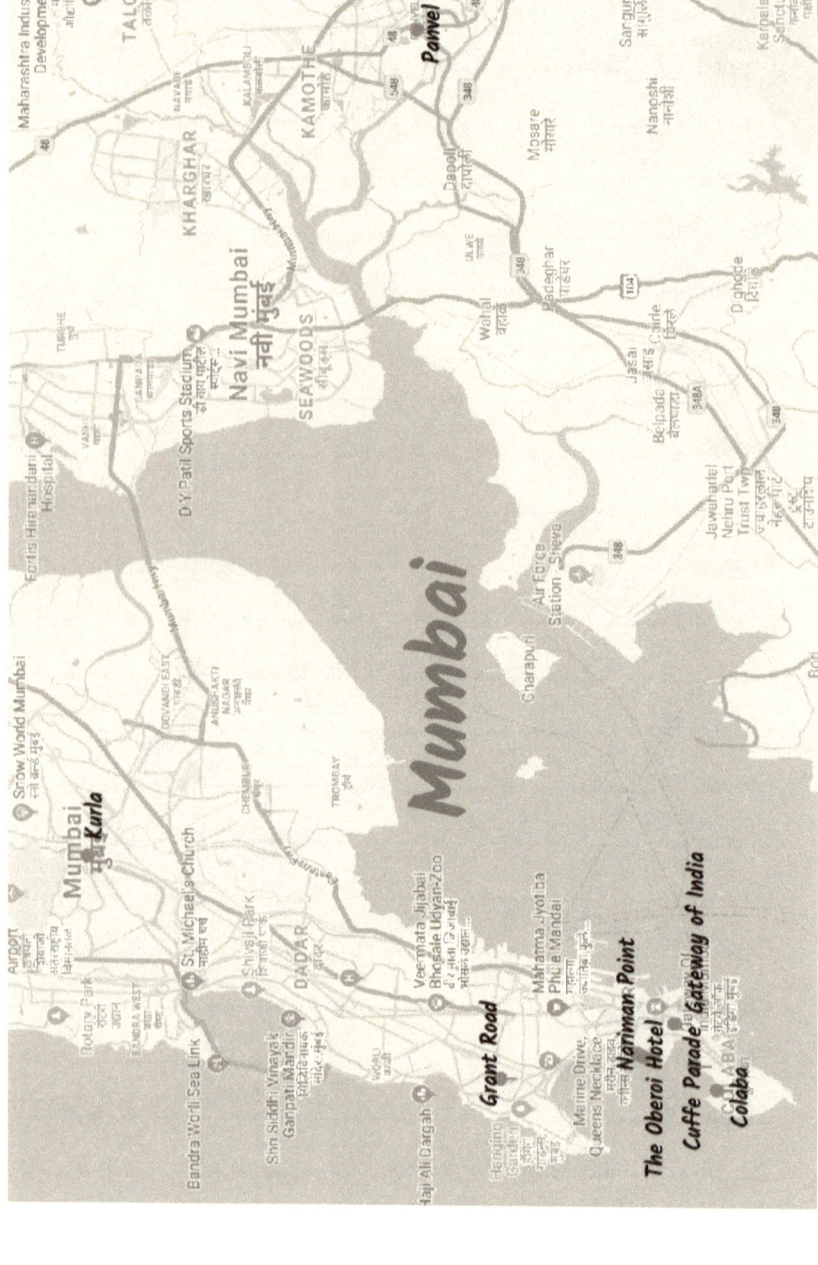

Chapter I

Mumbai, a puzzle of a city, put together with jagged pieces of wildly fruitful dreams and shattered hopes. Here, some gambled for fame and fortune, some looted, some cut throats. They called it business. The successful crooks coveted an address along Queen's Necklace—the C-shaped Marine Drive extending between the magnificent houses on Malabar Hill and the gleaming office towers of Nariman Point.

From the backseat of the speeding taxi, Seema Rawat grinned at the urchins jumping along the black tetrapod rocks which protected the boulevard from the tidal waves of the Arabian Sea. High-rises lined the road on the other side. A warm breeze whistled in through the partially open window of the cab, ruffling Seema's curls.

"We're here," announced the driver, pulling in front of the building housing Imperium Technologies' Indian office on its twenty-first floor. Speaking in coarse Hindi, he added, "Fifty rupees. Hurry up, madam. Lunchtime is peak time. I don't want to miss another fare."

Seema dug into her large, black tote for cash, but a volley of barks had her looking up. The tan stray dog she'd often seen walking this block was right outside. With playful leaps at the passenger window, he obstructed her way.

"Open the door," suggested the driver, impatiently. "Once it thwacks him in the head, he'll move."

Rewarding the man with a glare, Seema exited through the door on the driver's side. She counted out the fare and glanced briefly towards the small crowd at the entrance of the building. "Oh, crap," she muttered. In the centre of the group was just the fellow she didn't want to see.

With the shrill blast of an air horn, a Bullet bike tore down the road, perilously close to the parked taxi. The thug riding pillion hollered, "Hey, hey. Hot piece of ass."

1

Barely avoiding having her foot run over, Seema squeaked and jumped closer to the taxi. She lost balance and fell on her bottom. *"Bastar—"* She had to swallow the rest of the curse. If she could, she would've chased after the bike and shoved her elbow into the thug's puny chest. Unfortunately, she needed to stay put and stay silent or risk blowing her cover.

She crouched on the road and squinted through the windows of the taxi at the office building, trying not to breathe in the exhaust fumes from the succession of vehicles cruising down the road. The heat radiating from the asphalt had her drenched in sweat within seconds.

"Aey," exclaimed the driver. "Are you crazy or what? You can't sit on the street. Some poor fool will hit you and have his licence taken away. Get up, please. And gimme my money."

"In a minute," Seema muttered. The crook she was supposed to be covertly investigating was at the entrance. If she paid now, the taxi would take off, leaving her exposed.

"I *told* you it's lunchtime—that's it. You now owe me two hundred."

"What?"

"Waiting charge."

Seema hissed. "Son of a—"

"Madam," said the driver, shaking a finger. "Watch your language."

Heaving in an angry breath, Seema said, "Fine. If you're charging me extra to wait, I'm waiting inside."

Without delay, she tugged open the passenger door and scrambled back in. The dog was still there, barking at her taxi. The silver-haired man in the white kurta-pyjama—the knee-length tunic and skinny pants favoured by Indian politicians—was also in his spot at the entrance. The nation's finance minister. The target of Seema's investigation.

He was conversing with the tall, leanly muscled man in the light-blue shirt and red power tie. Adhith Verma, the minister's only son and Seema's supposed boyfriend. Adhith was the assistant manager at the office where she was currently assigned. She'd been sent to Imperium Technologies to investigate the father-son duo for looting crores from the taxpayers.

Thank God she'd decided to go out for lunch, or she'd have had no excuses to avoid meeting the minister. She had to wait in the cab until he left. If Adhith introduced her as his girlfriend, the old man would run background checks on her. The whole plan could fall apart.

Someone in the politician's entourage twisted around to glance in the direction of the barking dog. Seema ducked. *Damn.* She hoped the noisy animal didn't give her away.

Dusting the dirt from her denim leggings, she asked, "Can you at least turn on the AC?" Two hundred rupees entitled her to some degree of comfort.

The driver peered at the crowd. "Is the old man your boss or something?" He hadn't bothered to keep up with the who's who of Indian politics, it seemed.

"No, my father-in-law," Seema snapped. "What is it to you?"

"Oh, your *father-in-law,*" said the driver as if missing her sarcasm. "No wonder you're hiding." He twisted around and ogled her chest.

The sweat trickling down her cleavage had made the polyester tunic cling to her boobs. The outline of her best bra was visible through the navy-blue fabric. "Hey, keep your eyes in front." Seema clutched her purse to her breasts. "Or my cousin will pay you a visit."

"Your cousin?" jeered the driver. "Is he the police commissioner or what?"

Head swivelling one way and the other, Seema leaned forwards. "He's with the underworld," she lied, smiling beatifically.

The leer on the driver's face vanished. "Get out of here."

"*Bhai* is best friends with the don," she insisted, prepared to elaborate on her non-existent cousin who worked for the imaginary mafia boss.

"I meant, gimme my money and get out of my taxi. Your *father-in-law* is gone."

After a quick look at the entrance to make sure the driver wasn't lying, Seema threw the cash into his extended hand and jumped out. When she raced into the blessedly cool lobby, the lift doors were closing. "Wait for me," she screamed, galloping over. With a muttered apology, she squeezed herself in. She'd make it before Adhith. He had a habit of jogging up the stairs all the way to the twenty-first floor.

Catching a glimpse of her reflection in the metal plate where the buttons were lit, she scowled. She'd *better* make it before him. Her curls always got mad frizzy in humid weather, and with the mascara smeared around her light brown eyes, she closely resembled a feral cat. There were damp patches on the carefully selected tunic. If Adhith saw her in this shape, all her hard work of the last two months would go to waste.

By the time he sauntered in through the swinging glass doors, she was walking out of the staff bathroom, long curls clipped back into a neat ponytail and eyeliner once again crisp. Closing the door on the sharp smell of disinfectant, she tossed a shy smile at him.

"The men in your town must've been crazy," Adhith said, his warm voice holding a teasing note. "Or they'd have never let a cutie like you leave."

God, the cheesy line! It was enough to make a girl barf. Seema somehow managed to keep the coy smile on her face, batting her eyelashes for good measure. Until the mission was successfully completed, she'd have to maintain the village belle persona. Seema Rawat, former urchin from the slums of Mumbai, would have to remain the innocent from the hills of Himachal Pradesh, arrived in the big, bad city a few years back.

A shrill sound interrupted her thoughts. Digging into her tote, she found her phone. Before the caller could utter a word, she hissed, "I'm with my boss."

"Heh?" asked an annoyed female voice.

"You know," Seema whispered. "My *boss*. The assistant manager at Imperium."

Adhith looked on, the expression on his face amused. With his clean-cut appearance, he was what they called a *chikna munda*—someone boyishly handsome. Seema had never been able to figure out the appeal of such men.

"Well, get rid of him and call me back," snapped the voice from the other end. "I need an update." Before Seema could say another word, the line cut off.

"Problem?" asked Adhith.

"My auntie," explained Seema, tucking a stray strand of hair behind her ear.

Her auntie, otherwise known as The Woman Who'd Hauled Her Niece out of Her Drunk Father's Home. The Mumbai director of The Income Tax Criminal Investigation Department. Seema's actual boss.

The digital clock on the wall flashed 2:00 PM. Lunchtime was done. A hundred-odd people swarmed in through the doors, entering the cubicle maze. There was no opportunity for more chitchat with Adhith.

As soon as she sat at her tiny desk, the phone rang a second time. Turning off the ringer, she muttered to herself, "I'm twenty-friggin'-four. Can you please trust me to know what I'm doing?"

If Seema had actually said it to her auntie, she'd have been subjected to such looks of immense disappointment words wouldn't be needed to remind her of every bad deed she'd ever committed. Thanks to some do-gooder women, her auntie had escaped the slums along Grant Road at the age of fourteen, and after making something of herself, she'd shown up to snatch her drunk brother's only child from him. She had a court order, and there was nothing the drunk could do.

***

Twelve-year-old Seema had *not* been grateful. She'd been on the roof of the two-room shed she called home in the middle of a deluge when her auntie came wading through the grey-green water flooding the narrow lane, clad in a dark raincoat. She was accompanied by a couple of government-type men.

Shuddering violently from the needles of cold rain stinging her back through the torn cotton chemise, Seema was trying to weigh down the plastic sheet covering the hole in the asbestos roof with a couple of bricks. She could barely see the visitors through the torrent and the wet tendrils of hair hanging in front of her eyes.

"Crazy people," she muttered, not sparing the group more than a quick glance. Only the insane would venture outside in this thunderstorm. Thousands of men, women, and children were crammed into the dilapidated buildings lining both sides of the street, but with lightning crackling across the darkened sky every other minute, there wasn't a single soul to be seen even on the balconies circling the upper storeys.

When the group bellowed her name, curiosity had her leaping from the roof to the top of the plastic water tank two feet away. From there, it was an easy scramble to the flooded street where she listened to the woman shout over the downpour to introduce herself.

Back inside the two-room shed, Seema tossed out the dead rat which had floated in with the dirty rainwater. The woman who claimed to be Seema's auntie wrinkled her nose at the putrid odour.

Rubbing herself dry with an old shirt of her loser father's, Seema tried telling the visitors she was happy with her life, thank you very much! Going to school only when she felt like it, stealing coins from the temple collection box, smoking dope with the other kids from the colony... her mother had eloped with a lover the year before, and her father was usually too drunk to care what she got up to, but Seema had her *bhai log*—her peeps. They'd kept Seema out of the redlight part of the slums, where girls either died young or grew up to be madams.

The neighbourhood gang had admitted Seema as an apprentice pickpocket. The boss, whom the members called *Usthaad*—their teacher—fed her most days and personally supervised her education in lockpicking and key casting. There were tears in the one eye he had—the other having been incinerated in an unfortunate accident with a propane torch—when he announced he'd at last found a worthy heir.

The cops from the local station had caught Seema a couple of times, but the judges at the children's court always let her go with warnings. Her large eyes and trembling lower lip served her well. Her principal warned her she'd end up in reform school, but Seema didn't care.

A frozen expression on her face, the woman listened for a while before reaching out to twist Seema's ear as hard as she could. Seema was dragged through the dirty water in the streets all the way to the waiting taxi. The government men on either side made sure she couldn't jump out until they got to her auntie's two-bedroom prison/flat in Panvel.

Seema tried every trick to escape the prison. Smashing dishes, kicking, biting, scratching... unfortunately, the woman possessed a belt of some colour or other in karate. Seema also ended up sporting a few colours. On her backside. She tried a hunger strike, but her spirit wasn't strong enough to resist the aroma of butter chicken and basmati rice. Abetted by her loser father, she ran away twice. There was no third time. Seema spotted the pimp the loser had waiting for her and escaped in the nick of time. When she got back to safety, her auntie arranged for the loser to be beaten to a pulp.

Finally, Seema and her auntie shook hands over a peace deal. Seema would stay and follow all the rules. Once she got herself a college degree, she could leave. *If* she wanted.

What followed was sheer torture. Seema was kept at home for a year, being taught how to read and write, how to bathe, how to dress, how to keep her nails clean. How to defend herself.

When she was finally allowed to attend school, she'd been strictly warned not to mention her background to anyone. Seema marched in, determined to flout the warning. She wasn't ashamed of who she was, by God.

At the end of her first week at the all-girls institution, one of her classmates lost her silver anklet, and a giant search was organised. The principal called Seema into the office and told her if she returned it right away, there would be no consequences. Seema's vehement denials were not believed. At lunch, Seema eyed the cliques hanging out together, whispering behind their hands. She squared her shoulders and stared into the distance, pretending to be unaware of the tears rolling down her cheeks. Before the end of the school day, the anklet was found in the craft room—the one place Seema had not been to. She loathed basket making.

It took one week for Seema's auntie to enrol her in another school.

"You have only two options," said the auntie. "Give them a plausible story and fit in or mind your own business. You don't have to lie, but you don't need to tell them anything, either."

Seema breezily lied, cooking up the story of a childhood in Himachal and how after the death of her entire family in a landslide, her auntie adopted her. Picking her up on the dot at last bell, her auntie dutifully corroborated all the falsehoods, but there had been disappointment in her eyes.

Her auntie didn't think she knew how to stay out of trouble, so Seema wasn't allowed to hang out with the other girls after school. When her friends chattered excitedly about going shopping together or attending a wedding, all Seema could do was glumly decline. She'd agreed to stick by rules, and she'd do it. Even if she totally *died* of boredom.

It wasn't all bad. Sandwiched between school and self-defence lessons were the Sundays she and her auntie spent at the movie theatre. When they chose to stay home, they danced madly to Hindi songs from the black-and-white era. Seema preferred the more modern songs they could flop around to. But hey, whatever. Slowly, "the woman" turned to "family." Still, every minute of Seema's day needed to be accounted for.

Unexpectedly, she discovered a love of numbers, something else she shared with her auntie. Patterns fascinated her. A degree in mathematics from Mumbai University was the outcome, followed by four years at the Indian Statistical Institute in Kolkata doing two master's degrees—first in math and then in cryptology and security.

In both cities, Seema had been excited to live in the hostel with the rest of the students. The first time she stayed past curfew, her auntie dragged her out of the Santa Cruz campus of MU, telling her she could commute to classes from home. Seema's group of friends explained to the French girl who was there to study yoga how young Indian women were always expected to toe the line. Thwarting the unwritten rules of society would bring heaping doses of condemnation on the culprits and their families.

The Kolkata episode when Seema was completing her postgraduation had been worse. Before she could even *think* of committing an infraction, her auntie got herself transferred to the city, and they were back to sharing a flat.

No matter. The day Seema got her spanking new degree in cryptology and security, she planned to declare independence. Unfortunately, employers who seemed so excited at recruiting events sent polite rejection letters after background checks. Juvenile records were supposed to be sealed, but Seema was convinced her early years in the slums prompted more in-depth searches than usual. Six months of futile job-hunting later, she accepted a position with her auntie—now back in Mumbai—working to expose tax fraud.

While Seema considered herself to have matured, her auntie didn't agree. Even at work, Seema was watched with an eagle eye. Whenever there was a murmur about nepotism, she ended up assigned to the most mind-numbing of projects. Which in an income tax office could get excruciating!

When the Verma investigation came up, Seema pushed her way into this undercover assignment in the middle of the meeting to discuss it. With their superior from Delhi watching, there had been nothing her auntie could do to stop her without endangering both their jobs—except, of course, call twenty times a day, demanding "updates."

*⁎⁎

Forget all aunties, Seema scolded herself. She threw a glance at the far end of the large hall, where the manager and assistant manager had their own rooms. Oh, yeah. Adhith Verma and his thief of a father were going down, down, *down.* This cryptanalyst was going to destroy them. She was going to prove herself to the world, to her auntie, to whomever was remotely interested. Then, she'd proudly proclaim herself a free woman.

It was another couple of hours before Seema found the time to return her auntie's call, but she needed a spot where she wouldn't be overheard. The *chaiwalla* was making his afternoon rounds, selling little glass tumblers of sweetened tea and chilli *pakorey,* the deep-fried green pepper poppers. Seema scanned the hall holding the hundred-plus employees of the cybersecurity firm's Mumbai division. Leaving the office before the end of the business day was out of the question. The security guard at the entrance would snitch. The staff bathroom next to the front door had no privacy, whatsoever.

For as long as Seema had been in the office, the manager's room had been empty. The holder of the title had been in San Jose for the last six months, training for higher and better things. Adhith served as manager as well as assistant in the interim, but his boss was expected back in Mumbai the following week.

Seema hadn't yet met the man. She *had* previously made acquaintance of his room with its nice, *clean* loo. The first time she used it, she'd found the office accountant waiting outside, telling her the room was out of bounds. After the rebuke, Seema sauntered all the way to the entrance to the office and used the space between the last row of cubicles and the wall to get to the room without drawing attention. The door remained unlocked. Apparently, the accountant trusted the employees of Imperium to do what they were told. Not that there was anything there to steal besides furniture. Anyway, Seema was only interested in the privacy she'd get in the loo.

This time, she found the chaiwalla barring the door, a thin towel wrapped turban-style around his moustachioed head. "Hold on," he said. "You're not allowed in the manager's office."

As though he were the CEO! "I need to use the bathroom in there," she pleaded. "The staff latrine stinks."

"Doesn't matter," said the chaiwalla, heartlessly.

Eyes darting in both directions, Seema leaned forwards to whisper, "Lady troubles."

The chaiwalla flushed. "Maybe, this once," he mumbled. "Be careful to leave everything as it is. If Vikram *saar* finds out, he won't like it." As far as Seema knew, the chaiwalla had been delivering snacks to their office for years, but he still used "saar"—the South Indian version of "sir"—instead of *"saab,"* the Mumbai version.

"Vikram saab is in San Jose," said Seema.

"I know." The chaiwalla preened. "My wife's cousin lives there." Face turning stern, he admonished, "Go quickly and get back to your seat before anyone sees you."

***

The Directorate of Income Tax (Intelligence and Criminal Investigation) had been aware of certain companies making sizable contributions to a couple of charities—all perfectly legal and tax-exempt. The finance minister ended up purchasing properties for a pittance from the board members of said charities. Companies which made the original charitable contributions got their projects through the finance ministry without much fuss.

While auditing the companies, the DCI recognised the pattern for the bribery it was, but the courts would demand solid proof. Weeks of diligent research by the department's brightest cryptanalysts yielded no evidence of online criminality.

"Off-grid transactions," said the team leader. The other possibility was that the digital security was so good the department's cryptanalysts had been tricked into thinking there was nothing to see. The prime suspect was the minister's son, Adhith Verma, graduate of the Indian Institute of Technology in Mumbai and the assistant manager in the India division of Imperium Technologies, one of the world's largest cybersecurity firms.

The team requested a warrant to seize Adhith Verma's personal and work devices, but the minute they approached the judicial system, the minister would shut down the investigation.

"Time to contact the CBI?" the director of the Mumbai division asked the director general from New Delhi. "Unfortunately, they're going to run into the same problem we did. If they try to get a warrant, the minister and his cronies in the government will find out and force them to cease operations."

"The Intelligence Bureau can do a lot of things without needing a warrant," mused the director general. "Some of those so-called charities have been accused of funding terrorist activities. We can make a case for involving IB."

"No way," interrupted the leader of the analysts, a sneer on his face. "What's IB going to do? Have someone steal the data? We can do that ourselves."

The director rocked back in her leather chair. "Don't be ridiculous. Covert operations are best left to the cops."

"I'll pit any of my men against them," insisted the team leader. "Any day."

The director eyed the young people arrayed behind the leader—baby-faced, earnest. "Right," she said, dryly. "Who's going to volunteer?"

"I will," piped up Seema. With everyone in the room turning towards her, she carefully avoided the thunderous gaze of her auntie, the Mumbai director, and focused on the big boss from New Delhi.

Her auntie ground out, "Your enthusiasm is remarkable, but there are legal issues to consider. The income tax department is not allowed to do warrantless searches. We *have* to hand the case over to IB."

The director general held up his palm. "Hold on. Miss... Rawat, right? If I'm not mistaken, you're the one who first alerted the director about the minister's pattern."

Squaring her shoulders in pride, Seema nodded.

A middle-aged man with a skinny moustache, the director general smiled. "It's only fair you get to continue your work on the case, but as our Mumbai director said, there are legal issues. After all the effort, we don't want our evidence getting tossed out of court. However, I have a solution. I'll talk to the director of IB and ask them to take you on deputation."

Enthusiastically, the team leader nodded. "It will work. Seema is the best man for the case."

The look on her auntie's face was priceless.

Seema went through several interviews with officers from the white-collar crimes division of IB. There was a battery of tests she had to pass. The officers were surprised to find her skilled in self-defence and adept at handling a gun. The years of torture/training her auntie had put her through in the name of safety paid off. Seema was accepted on deputation and assigned to the team attempting to break into the systems at Adhith Verma's cybersecurity firm, Imperium Technologies.

By then, IB's field agents were covertly investigating the charities and businesses that had come to the notice of the income tax department. The bureau even installed a mole in the minister's office. Adhith Verma's role was suspected of being limited to electronic security, so the plan was to get him from the safety of cyberspace.

The digital tools available at IB's disposal nearly made Seema's eyes pop out of their sockets, but neither technology nor skill helped them penetrate Imperium's devices or even Adhith Verma's personal gadgets. Oh, Seema got in, but the information she encountered was so bland and benign she had to be in a decoy server.

"We could force our way in," Seema ventured. They possessed the digital equivalents of cannonballs in their arsenal. "But they'd know."

"No," snapped the SSP—the senior superintendent of police—assigned to the project, pulling her printed hijab more securely over her head. "If it were that easy, we could've simply asked Imperium for help. We didn't because we can't risk any of them alerting Verma. We're not breaking in, either. There are field agents deployed, investigating all those charities and businesses connected to the minister. Once he knows there was an infiltration into his son's stuff, he'd definitely suspect something, and our agents might get outed. The whole mission could fall apart. For another, we're not talking about some two-bit company. If word gets out the Indian government hacked into Imperium, it will become a PR disaster for the nation. Multinationals will think twice about doing business with us. We can't tank the economy to get one corrupt bastard."

Physical break-ins to access Adhith Verma's devices were also out of the question. The bureau could conduct warrantless surveillance only electronically, but they weren't beyond faking robberies to get evidence. Still, their current suspect was the goddamned finance minister. He had the money, the political clout, and the media savvy to turn the tables on IB by accusing them of illegal practices. The case would get tossed out of court. IB would also lose to the politician in the court of public opinion. If Verma retained his position, the bureau and its officials would pay for their audacity. Of course, the second they tried to get a warrant to make it all legal, Minister Verma would hear of it and cover his tracks.

Finally, the bureau decided to send Seema undercover as an employee of Imperium, hoping she could get Adhith to grant her access to his devices. The SSP commented, "Rawat is young and presentable enough to attract Adhith Verma's attention and skilled enough to extract data from his machines."

Just what every twenty-four-year-old woman loved to hear about her appearance. "Presentable enough." And *skilled* enough? She was the best even among the IB team!

"Be careful, Rawat," warned the SSP. "Don't do dumb shit. The only reason we're sending you in is you have an unusual level of talent for breaking into digital systems. It's all we expect you to do. Nothing more. We have experienced officers handling the rest of it."

Nevertheless, Seema was thrilled. This was her chance to prove her mettle. If she got evidence implicating Adhith Verma, his father would automatically fall. The proof collected by the "experienced officers" might not even be necessary. Once the bureau presented Seema's data to the president and the prime minister, there would be nothing the Verma duo could do to slither out of trouble. As Seema later announced to her auntie, she—the former pickpocket—would infiltrate the criminals' lair and catch them.

IB didn't even have to squeeze anyone out to create a job opening. With a whitewashed résumé, Seema answered an ad on Naukri.com, and in less than a month, she was hired. The day after, IB issued her a clean phone—a device which could not be tracked—and a brand-new Glock 26, with a couple of options for holsters.

She'd now been at Imperium for two months. During the time, she'd managed to infiltrate not only the digital systems but also the manager's private loo. A clean space from where she could use the clean phone.

✻✻✻

Seema closed the lid on the toilet bowl and sat, biting her tongue to hold back the blue streak of curses hovering at the tip. When in boss mode, the auntie always had that effect on Seema.

"Come home," came the low, measured voice over the phone. "You've had two months."

It wasn't enough time. Cybersecurity at Imperium was superlative, almost impossible to breach from the outside. Adhith was not the architect of the digital fortress. The manager—currently in California—had added the modifications protecting Imperium's systems. The same product established them as the leader in the cybersecurity market. Seema spent some time admiring the manager's handiwork before getting down to business. Breaking into the internal systems hadn't been easy even from the inside, but she'd graduated top of her class at the Indian Statistical Institute. Unfortunately, her search yielded zilch. Zero. Nothing.

"You're not going to find anything you already haven't," continued her auntie.

"I can do this," insisted Seema. "The bureau believes I can. Why won't *you?*"

"Because there's nothing else you *can* do."

"What I need is a chance to check Adhith's personal devices."

"If he doesn't trust you—"

"He does. He asked me to his flat a few times." Where his computer would be. Where she could also sneak a peek at his personal phone.

There was silence from the other end of the phone line for a couple of seconds. "And?"

Seema hesitated, wondering how much she dared divulge. With Adhith, it was never a simple invitation to spend time together. The expectation of sex had been clear. She shuddered. "He... umm... wanted me to stay over."

"No," snapped her auntie.

Flippantly, Seema insisted, "He's young and handsome." Not to mention fashion-conscious. She'd never seen Adhith Verma less than perfectly groomed. "Why not?"

"Who do you think you are? Some kind of super-spy? Get your backside home. *Now.* I'll have the director general talk to IB."

Heat rushed into Seema's head. "Don't. You. Dare."

"You're fired."

"Oh, yeah? You can't fire me. I'm union." Glaring at the phone, Seema hung up.

It wasn't as if she'd been serious about jumping into bed with Adhith. No. She wasn't going there. The nation could only ask so much of her.

Seema fumed. She couldn't reveal the conversation to anyone, but she badly needed to vent, or she'd rip the head off the next person she saw.

Unfortunately, her personal phone had been left in her auntie's flat to minimise chances of being tracked, and the contact list on her clean phone was limited to those she'd met on her mission. Any calls between her and her superiors—including her auntie—were automatically and permanently erased. The company-issued phone listed only Imperium's numbers on it. *I'm a pathetic loser—not a single person to confide in.*

With a groan, Seema slumped back. Her head hit the toilet tank. The flush handle, to be precise. Rubbing her sore scalp, she glanced around the spotless bathroom and reluctantly grinned. She couldn't say this assignment didn't have its perks.

She had a private loo—at least, until Monday, when the manager, Vikram Joshi, returned from California. And there was the—

Seema brightened. There *was* someone she could call.

***

Vikram Joshi was back in Imperium's Mumbai office. The tap-tap-tap of hundreds of keyboards, the steel labyrinth into which every man and woman disappeared when the clock struck nine, the stink of the dirty latrine on the left...

Home, sweet home, he mused, eyeing the maze from the entrance. Well, office, sweet office, at least. The manager's room at the far end *would* be home until he found a new flat to rent.

Before flying back, he'd contacted his former landlord through WhatsApp to see if his old one-bedroom in Andheri were still available. In a response filled with emojis, the wheezy *buddha*—the old man—said Vikram must be crazy if he expected the flat to be kept vacant when he'd declined to pay rent for the months he was away.

Vikram hadn't cared. He could always crash on Adhith's sofa for the weekend—or for the rest of the month. What were best friends for? Especially, when they were employed by the same firm. Except, Adhith hadn't answered his calls. Hot nights with the new girlfriend, no doubt. Adhith must have talked her into moving in—which meant he wouldn't want Vikram around.

Desperately needing to throw his luggage somewhere and take a long nap, he finally called his mother from Mumbai airport's noisy lounge. The five-bedroom duplex in the upscale neighbourhood of Cuffe Parade had enough room. Only, the apple of his parents' eye was visiting. The son-in-law of their dreams. The super-achiever neurosurgeon. The arrogant dumbass who knew exactly how to put down a mid-level manager at an IT firm.

Nope. Vikram would rather sleep on the footpath than sit through a family dinner with the dumbass brother-in-law.

There was no way Vikram was forking out cash for a hotel. Every extra rupee in his wallet was going towards his dream. Towards the day he'd open his own cyberprotection and cryptanalysis business. He'd both destroy walls and build impenetrable ones. His name would be on the cover of *Forbes,* whispered with the same reverence afforded men like Bill Gates and Steve Jobs. The Joshi family would finally have to open their eyes and see their own son. Until then, Vikram refused to be under the same roof as the dumbass.

So he'd come straight to the office. The manager's room would do until after the weekend when the dumbass left the family home. Fortunately, Vikram's direct supervisor, who was stationed in Singapore, wouldn't know what the newly returned manager was up to. Unfortunately, Vikram hadn't showered in two days and smelled rank. Sweat glued the olive-green T-shirt to his chest, and the jeans had seen better days. Also, he needed a haircut. *A shave, too,* he mused, scratching the stubble on his jaw.

Hoping to get to the room without encountering any of his subordinates, Vikram hauled his black suitcase and backed in through the glass doors. The security guard dozing on the chair by the entrance woke with a start. Vikram put a finger to his lips.

There was a narrow gap between the wall and the last row of cubicles on the right. The back wheel of the suitcase was squeaky. Cursing profusely in his mind, he lifted it an inch off the floor and squeezed through the space. It wasn't easy when he was six-foot-two with frame to match. Not to mention the bulk of the luggage he had to manoeuvre.

The thirty-two-kilogram weight of the bag didn't bother him. If there was one thing even his parents had to acknowledge Vikram possessed more than the dumbass, it was muscle. Otherwise, the super-achiever was movie-star handsome, while Vikram was... well, no one had yet run screaming at the sight of him, but unkempt hair, thick, slashing eyebrows, and a nose broken in two places courtesy of a childhood fight didn't exactly make him silver screen material.

Phew. Made it. Vikram shut the door behind him. At least, the company hadn't rented the manager's room out to someone else simply because he'd been away six months. Thank God it came with an attached bathroom, shower space included. Dropping the suitcase by the door, he sank into the big, leather chair behind the desk and kicked off his sandals. Once the employees left for the day, he could slip out and get something to eat from the South Indian restaurant a few streets down. *Soft* idlis *with spicy* sambar... eyes drifting shut, he daydreamed of the rice cakes and sour vegetable stew.

The toilet flushed.

Sweet, cool coconut water. He hadn't had any in a long time.

A female voice cursed, using words fouler than the ones he'd heard at the men's hostel in his engineering college days.

Vikram sat up. Someone was using the latrine in the manager's office? *His* latrine? Whoever it was would die today.

The door squeaked open. A hankie in one hand, the girl was wiping her face and speaking into the phone—something about her auntie.

Who *was* this? Vikram couldn't yet see her face, but he didn't remember any female underlings with precisely this physicality. Five-foot-five and decent curves. Her black platform sandals and denim leggings showed off long and shapely limbs. The navy-blue kurta featured pink flowers embroidered all over. The faint echo of a soft, floral perfume reached Vikram's nostrils.

Turning to shut the door, the girl swore to whomever was on the other end of the call, "I'm going to kill her."

There was an unintelligible squawk from the phone.

"You haven't met my auntie," the girl exclaimed, her tone clear and light. "She's not your average bitch. She's a *criminal* bitch—" The girl turned. Her eyes snagged on Vikram. Mouth opening in shock, she froze.

A few dark curls had escaped her loose ponytail, framing even features and enormous, light brown eyes. Vikram finished his cataloguing. *Mmhmm, not bad.* He especially appreciated the toned calves.

An ear-splitting shriek.

He leapt out of his chair, pulse thundering at his temples. "Stop," he ordered, and took a step towards her.

Eyes widening, she screamed even louder. There were alarmed noises coming from the phone and shouts from outside the office door. A thud. The unlocked door swung open. A large form rushed in, tripping over Vikram's suitcase and tumbling to the floor. Following him in were four or five men, all of them Vikram's subordinates. The one on the floor was the rotund accountant.

The second man in skidded to a stop. "Vikram?" exclaimed Adhith Verma, Vikram's best friend and assistant manager. "Bro, when did you get here? Why's Seema screaming?"

"Seema?" echoed Vikram. The foul-mouthed latrine-trespasser, wannabe murderer of criminal aunties, was Seema Rawat, the shy cutie from the small town of Sarkaghat? Adhith's new girlfriend?

Chapter 2

Ever since he landed in Mumbai as a seventeen-year-old bound for the Indian Institute of Technology, the neighbourhood of Colaba called to Adhith. Its multitude of colours, the never-ending sounds of the city, the fragrance of everything from luxury perfumes to the egg masala at the coffee house... the streets percolated with youth and life.

Tonight, Adhith was staying in, making do with takeout Chinese and Kingfisher beer. He had important business to discuss with Vikram—namely, the strange behaviour of one Miss Rawat.

The TV in the living room was muted. On the reality show, the contestants vied to outweird each other, but neither Vikram nor Adhith paid any mind. Vikram was on the sofa, busy tuning the acoustic guitar he'd stashed in the flat before leaving for California. The instrument he inherited from his maternal grandfather counted as one of his most cherished possessions.

"You and your fixation with bathrooms." Carrying two bottles of beer, Adhith seated himself on the other end of the couch. He set one bottle down on the coffee table within Vikram's reach. "It's the only reason you're pissed at Seema. She's not going to kill her auntie. Even *you* must understand hyperbole."

"Fine," said Vikram. "What about the cussing?"

"She was talking to a girlfriend. Women have been known to cuss."

"*Adhi, meray bachchey...*" Mockingly calling Adhith a mere boy, Vikram reached over the guitar and grabbed the beer. "This wasn't your ordinary cussing. She has a *PhD* in it."

"When did you turn into such a bloody prude, bro?"

22

Objection aside, Adhith was annoyed. Her soft smiles, the sweet voice, the shy curiosity when he'd hinted at sex... in twenty-eight years of life, he'd had plenty of experience avoiding fakers, but he'd still been taken in. Hell, there were people who'd say *he* was a fake. Him *and* Papaji, his father.

***

The name "Verma" conjured images of power and grandeur, but Papaji manoeuvred his way up from union leader in rural Uttarakhand—then part of the state of Uttar Pradesh—to union minister in New Delhi. He felt no hesitation in strong-arming opponents, but smooth talk and media spin were his preferred weapons. Even the name "Adhith" was the result of forethought on his part about his son's place in the rapidly urbanising India.

From what Adhith had been told, the village priest bestowed the name Uday Kumar Verma on him. Not long after his mother passed away from a fever, he'd been enrolled in primary school, and Papaji wrote down the fashionable "Adith" instead of "Uday." The five-year-old hadn't cared; "Adi" and "Uday" sounded much the same to his ears.

"Appearances are not everything, but it's exactly one half of whatever you do in life, *betay*." For as long as Adhith could remember, Papaji never used his son's name. It was always "betay"—literally, "son." Reknotting Adhith's uniform tie after *Daadima*—his grandmother—made a total mess of it, Papaji continued, "People judge you by how you look. The way you talk. How you make them feel. Let them first believe you're important, and they're important to you. You'll have them eating out of your hand in no time."

"The other half?" the five-year-old asked, trying to push the tip of his tongue through the gap in his teeth.

"Intelligence. Understand what people want, not just what they need. If you can't deliver it, get them to believe what you have is what they want. Or let them believe they can manipulate you into doing their bidding. It almost always works."

"What if it doesn't?"

23

"You cut them off at the knees."

Daadima aside, there was no one else around young Adhith to express contrary opinions. Papaji never remarried. Talk was he was still grieving his dead wife. Adhith harboured a suspicion—in fact, he was certain—Papaji shamelessly used the image of the grieving widower with a young son to melt the hearts of a few thousand female voters. Enough to win him his first elected position. But then, there had been no romance in Papaji's life Adhith could remember. It was always the two of them. Father and son, both spiffily dressed, graciously manoeuvring their way through all the complications in their path.

Daadima patted herself on the back for Papaji's victory. A few months before the state went to the polls, she'd taken the advice of the local numerologist and made a minor adjustment to her grandson's name. Adith Verma became Adhith Verma, and with the stars ruling their destiny having changed with the name change, Papaji became an MLA. Merely a state government position, but it was only the beginning.

Sadly, Daadima forgot to ask the heavens to let her live long enough to see Papaji become the leader of the party in their home state and eventually, the finance minister of India. The oil portrait of her which had hung in the living room of the stone-roofed, whitewashed house in Bhikiyasen—their village—was now in Papaji's ministerial residence, next to Adhith's mother's likeness.

The years spent in New Delhi after Papaji moved up the political hierarchy only confirmed for Adhith his father's philosophy. When the minister's son first arrived in the nation's capital, he had no idea what a finger bowl was. For him, Red Hot Chili Peppers were what you put in curry. His classmates' posh speech left him muddled.

It took him one year to spin his rural background into something exotic. His vacations back home were painted in hues of wild adventure, something every boy in the class dreamed of being invited to. Girls openly sighed over the trace of an accent he'd retained. To his surprise, Adhith found he enjoyed the whole process, not merely the adulation. The getting-to-know-them part. At heart, they were kids like himself with high hopes and big dreams.

Unfortunately, most tended to judge by appearances, so Adhith was forced to continually maintain the aura of mystery and glamour. Adhith ended his time in the highly acclaimed educational institution as the school captain and the captain of the science club, as well as the off-spin bowler on the cricket team.

Papaji approved of Adhith's desire to study engineering. The degree would help build the image of a technocrat, someone well equipped to take India through the new millennium, an opinion Adhith shared. If only they'd known what would happen just months into the future.

Bombay had become Mumbai in 1995, but the Indian parliament never got around to amending the IITs Act to rename the nation's premier engineering colleges. IIT Bombay remained what it was, and in 2008, it granted admittance to the finance minister's son.

Within days of moving into Hostel I on the Powai campus, Adhith challenged Vikram—merely a grouchy roommate at the time—to hack into Papaji's computer. If the cups lined up on his desk were any indication, the grouch had won several hacking contests. Adhith only wanted to tweak the grouch's tail; he never expected the grouch to be successful. The numbers scrolling down the screen left both young men in shock. With the kind of money Papaji possessed, he could own a small town. Sweating, Adhith backed away from the computer.

"It all looks perfectly legal to me," Vikram said, voice hoarse.

"Legal?" Adhith parroted.

"He did purchase all of it."

Urged on by Adhith, Vikram continued to search. At the end of two weeks, Adhith heaved a sigh of relief. He wasn't obliged to snitch. Papaji did the job he was supposed to, and there was no evidence he'd stolen from the taxpayers. Papaji truly bought all those properties on the up and up. There was nothing to snitch.

Except, it all looked peculiar with businesses donating to charities which invested in the properties eventually sold to Papaji. Plus, when the same businesses got their projects signed off by Papaji, the whole damned mess emitted a foul stench.

Bribery. Adhith hadn't wanted to put a name to it, but he knew what it was. Or he wouldn't have caught the first flight to Delhi that weekend, making a production of checking his father's computers now that he was an engineering student. Casually, Adhith mentioned to Papaji how North Korea's systems were the world's most difficult to spy on since they were off-grid.

Back in IIT, Adhith watched as Vikram tried another attack, unsuccessful this time. Smiling in relief, they bumped fists.

Neither Vikram nor Adhith talked about it afterwards. From that night, Vikram Joshi became the second most important person in Adhith's life, the best friend who'd stood by him when no one else in his acquaintance would've had they known. Vikram understood Adhith couldn't rat out the father he loved.

He also accepted Adhith for what he was—with and without spin. Vikram knew damned well Adhith gagged at the sight of sushi and when drunk, slipped into the coarse Hindi of rural India. There was still a tinge of admiration in Vikram's voice when he groused about how Adhith managed to fit in everywhere.

Their coffee-fueled study sessions were followed by midnight trips to the omelette shop and *daaru*—the local moonshine—on weekends. Getting high in the privacy of their room, they rocked along with the rest of their classmates to the psychedelic tunes strummed by Vikram. They even lost their virginity on the same night to a couple of girls they met at the Brabourne Stadium while cheering for Mumbai's cricket team, the Indians.

Vikram dragged Adhith to the gym on a regular basis, where they bench-pressed and leg-pressed and perspired on the treadmill until their vices oozed off along with sweat. This was how Adhith developed an interest in boxing. He routinely sparred at the club, and he watched all the matches from those of the greats to the ones live-streamed on digital platforms.

Amongst all this, Vikram managed to graduate with honours. Adhith didn't do too badly, either. While both were courted by technology companies, Adhith wasn't planning on a future in engineering. When he confided to Vikram he saw himself living in the prime minister's residence in twenty or so years, they toasted their bright destinies as the masters of the universe. Before their dreams could come true, there was the small matter of getting started.

Imperium had been looking into opening an office in Mumbai, but it was planned as a satellite centre to the Singapore office with less than a dozen employees, including Vikram and Adhith. Within months, Vikram made modifications to the original software, and the appreciative company leadership put him in charge of expanding the India division. In the seven-plus years he'd spent as Vikram's assistant manager, Adhith fielded several questions on why he didn't feel bitter about working for his best bud. For one, their personal equation was strong enough to withstand any awkwardness. For another, what was the point in resenting it when his true destiny was in politics? He was merely waiting for the perfect opening. He'd been mulling a couple of possibilities when he ran into Seema.

Her glamour quotient wasn't up to par with the women Adhith dated thus far, but her hill state background struck a chord in his heart.

***

Gulping a mouthful of frothy beer, Adhith pondered the mystery that was Seema Rawat.

"I'm not a prude," Vikram objected. With his left hand, he strummed a few chords on his guitar. "In fact, I'm impressed."

It took Adhith a second to remember they'd been talking about Vikram's take on Seema's cussing.

"Also, a little surprised *you* didn't already know," Vikram continued. "Last I heard, you were going to ask her to move in with you."

"That was the plan," Adhith muttered. "She never gave me a chance to bring up the subject. I haven't even managed to talk her into spending *one* night."

"Oh?" Vikram smirked. "If you weren't busy having hot sex, why didn't you pick up my calls? I could've avoided hearing about the dumbass's latest visit."

Adhith grinned. Whenever Vikram talked about his parents and the ideal son-in-law, he sounded like a petulant three-year-old. The neurosurgeon *was* a dumbass, though. After he went on and on about how *he* would manage the finance ministry, Adhith was highly tempted to sock him one. "I'd turned off my phone," Adhith explained. "Papaji's secretary has been calling. A party meeting they want me to attend. They cornered me at work, anyway."

"Yeah? I'd think you'd be jumping at the chance."

Adhith would have, but there had been so many conflicting thoughts about getting onto the same merry-go-round as Papaji he wanted to pause and reflect. "Don't know, bro. I've been... I just don't know."

"Losing your touch?" Vikram teased. "You haven't gotten the girlfriend to put out and now this."

"Give it another couple of weeks, and Seema *will* be living here," Adhith bragged.

"In that case," Vikram said, morosely. "I'd better move in with the parents. *After* the dumbass leaves."

Forget the penny, Vikram didn't spend an Indian *paisa*—which carried less than one-fiftieth the value of the American coin—if he could help it. When they first started their jobs at Imperium, they'd thought of sharing a two-bedroom. But Vikram refused to budge on his budget, and Adhith refused to consider anything outside Colaba, exorbitant rents notwithstanding. Now, Vikram had lost even the shabby place he used to rent before his trip to California. Until he found another flat he deemed cheap enough, he'd suffer the indignities of living with the senior Joshis, *sans* the brother-in-law.

Vikram's *kanjoos* attitude—his miserliness—wasn't limited to his living conditions. All the entertainment in his life had to be strictly within budget. There would be no fine dining, no expensive holidays, not even cable. Strictly, no women.

Unlike him, Adhith enjoyed everything the city offered a young professional, including the soft warmth of feminine arms. Except for Seema's arms. Everyone thought her his girlfriend, but she never let him get anywhere. With each bashful rejection, he'd become more and more convinced she was holding out for wedding vows, something very common in rural India. The hill town she claimed as home certainly qualified as rural as did Bhikiyasen, where Adhith spent his early years.

Still, Adhith had been an urban creature for close to two decades, not someone who'd want—much less expect—a virgin bride. Strangely, he'd found Seema's coyness amusing. Charming, even. He'd vaguely considered offering her exactly what she wanted—the title of wife. After all, he was old enough, and married men fared better in politics.

Was it all a charade? To what end? Grimly, Adhith smiled. Whatever her intentions, he possessed the one weapon on his side she'd have no defence against: the man currently sitting on his living room sofa. "Do me a favour." Adhith swallowed a mouthful of beer. "Put the guitar aside and help me do some digging."

They started with their company's HR records. She'd responded to a job advertisement on Naukri.com and in Vikram's absence, interviewed with Adhith and the office accountant. They'd verified her college degree from Mumbai University but not what came before. Vikram now went through city birth and death records. The one red flag he found was she'd gone to high school in Mumbai, not Sarkaghat as would've been the case if she'd grown up there. They moved onto other data stored by the government not supposed to be accessible to the public—benefits, census, criminal records.

The television stayed on. Muted. The reality show changed to late-night TV. Reruns. Soaps. Movies. Meals were delivered—chop suey, pizza, sandwiches. The guitar rested against the side of the sofa, a silent witness to their labours. By Sunday night, Adhith and Vikram were exhausted and shaken.

"She didn't want to admit she grew up in the redlight district," Vikram muttered, closing the laptop. His tone still held shock.

"That's all," Adhith agreed, quietly.

"Her family *was* originally from Himachal Pradesh." Decades back, her great-grandparents moved from Sarkaghat to Mumbai. After Seema's birth, all the elders died in quick succession. Years later, her mother eloped with a lover. Soon after, the father lost custody of the child to an auntie. Both niece and auntie were working as accountants in some private firm no one had ever heard of when the younger woman applied for a job in the multinational corporation.

Adhith stared holes into the top of the computer.

"She was trying to save face." Vikram collapsed back into the sofa. "No criminal history... you think she might have been trying to trap you into marriage?"

Though the thought indeed occurred to him, Adhith dismissed it. "How? If things got as far as marriage, I'd have found out."

"True," Vikram mused. "You know how it goes. She started with one lie and got caught in it."

There was a gloominess in Adhith's chest he didn't need to analyse. Seema might not have been trying to trap him into marriage, but marriage between them was not likely to happen. Not if he wanted a career in public service.

Former residents of the Mumbai redlight district didn't make good political wives.

***

It had been a week since Papaji visited Adhith at his workplace, insisting on his presence at this meeting at the Sahyadri Guest House in Malabar Hill. The conference room held a long table with all the politicians looking expectantly towards the foot where Adhith sat. Even the hum of the air conditioner was tinged with anticipation.

"What do you think, betay?" asked Papaji. "Opportunities like these don't come up all the time. It's not often one of the retiring MPs has no preference in heirs. It *is* a central government position, not state, but the party executive command is agreeable to letting you run."

Appearances, Adhith muttered to himself, taking a sip from the glass in front, letting the ice-cold water soothe his insides.

Papaji didn't know it, but his son was complicit in his dishonesty. Adhith didn't regret it one bit, but he'd thought about it a lot. He'd concluded he didn't want to operate the same way as his father. There were so many things he wanted to do—knew he could do. If he took the offer currently under discussion, he'd be beholden to the same people and stuck in the same rut.

But he couldn't undermine Papaji's position with a public rebuff, not to mention the hurt the old man would feel. Time. Adhith needed to buy time until he found a way to strike out on his own *while* leaving Papaji's feelings uninjured and reputation untarnished.

"I thank all of you for thinking of me." Adhith smiled at each of the *netas*, the leaders of the party. He'd known most of them since he was a mere boy. Thanks to Vikram's hacking skills, Adhith knew more *about* them than their respective spouses.

In Papaji's database, there had been little notes stickied to the names of his colleagues. Starting there, Vikram and Adhith tracked all of them. They'd also followed the activities of all the charities and the companies who'd done business with Papaji. If one thread were pulled, the entire network would unravel. The trouble was Papaji would go down with the rest of them. Still, the information was sure to come in handy at some point. Adhith kept the data stored partly in his brain and partly in notes written in code which no one else would understand.

The bald uncleji on his right nursed a weakness for voluptuous servant maids. The clean-shaven man at the middle of the table who was proclaimed the most vice-free politician in all of Mumbai possessed shares in two cannabis cafés in Amsterdam as well as a couple of brothels in Bangkok. The lady in the cotton sari was currently the mistress of one of Papaji's colleagues.

"There's someone I have to talk this over with before making a decision," Adhith continued. "My future wife."

Seema, the girl from the slums. Once Papaji heard the details, he wouldn't want to advertise this utterly unsuitable relationship and ruin his son's political career before it began. He'd prefer to wait until Adhith was over the phase. There was no way Adhith could marry Seema *and* keep his political career, but he could use her name to escape Papaji's plans.

Surprise, curiosity, concern—a gamut of emotions ran over the faces at the conference table. Papaji's eyes were wide open in shock. "Future wi—"

On cue, Adhith's phone rang. The caller ID flashed. "Excuse me," Adhith said, an apologetic finger raised. Injecting the most besotted tone he could muster into the words, he crooned, "Hello, darling."

"Huh?" said Vikram.

Chapter 3

Leaning against the doorjamb, Vikram eyed the cubicle maze.

The chaiwalla was doing his morning rounds, eliciting murmurs of gratitude at each halt. "Excuse me, saar," he said, skirting Adhith, who'd been pacing the carpet with his phone glued to his ear.

Instead of letting him pass, Adhith tossed the phone into a cubicle and engaged him in small talk, accepting the *samosa* and *chai* at the end of five minutes. Biting into the potato pastry, Adhith finally continued his rounds between desks. He'd been doing that since the office opened at 9:00 AM sharp. He was extremely busy coordinating tasks before the presentation to the EU client. So busy he hadn't picked up any of Vikram's calls over the weekend. The watchman of the posh building in Colaba had said Adhith would be out of town until Monday morning. Even today, he hadn't popped into the manager's room yet. Adhith was avoiding his best buddy. No question about it.

Then, there was the perturbed call from Adhith's papaji five minutes ago. Papaji was set against Adhith marrying Seema. Vikram's jaw dropped. Marriage? Adhith surely knew Seema was not appropriate wife material for an up-and-coming politician. It did explain the strange phone conversation on Friday. Adhith had been pretending Seema was on the other end. The "why" of it was apparently something he was unwilling to explain. Hence, the avoidance.

"Saar," called the chaiwalla.

"Thanks," said Vikram and accepted the refreshments. He took a sip and hid a grimace. The tea wasn't sweet enough. It never was, but there were packets of sugar stashed in his room.

The chaiwalla was staying put, an eager grin on his face.

Had the expression of gratitude fallen short of expectations? Vikram added, "Thanks very much."

The grin faded.

Now, what?

"The baby is doing well," said the chaiwalla.

The baby? Oh, right. The daughter had been pregnant. "Congratulations on becoming a grandfather."

"Father," corrected the chaiwalla, clearly annoyed. "My *wife* gave birth."

"My mistake," said Vikram. "Wasn't your daughter pregnant, too? I think I saw her here with you last week."

The annoyance on the chaiwalla's face morphed into outright hostility. "She," he said through clenched teeth, "was my wife."

Vikram gawked in silence. There was a snicker from the nearest cubicle. As the chaiwalla stalked off, his spine stiff and vibrating with insult, Vikram eyed the glass tumbler, acknowledging glumly this would have to be his last cuppa from this particular tea seller, or he'd risk downing spit along with the brew. Unlike Adhith who knew what to say when, Vikram kept adding to the list of establishments which were off-limits to him.

Adhith was nowhere to be seen. Since he wasn't *in* the office, he couldn't pretend to be busy. Back at his desk, Vikram thumbed out a message on WhatsApp to Adhith's personal device. The corporate office strongly discouraged the use of company-issued phones for personal purposes.

Code Master: We need to talk.

The clock on the wall ticked. Tick-tock, tick-tock, tick...

Code Master: Do I need to remind you we're still within work hours?

It was an old joke between them, a sort of SOS from Vikram to his friend's personal number, requesting emergency aid in awkward social situations. When they'd first found themselves as manager and assistant, Adhith only half-comically suggested putting the alert down as one of his official duties. He'd be pissed at the current subterfuge, but he could either be pissed or deal directly with his father. The old man sounded agitated enough to march to the office to confront the prospective Mrs Verma.

A minute passed.

A. Verma: What can I do for you?

Huh? Not "what's up, bro?"

Code Master: Your father had called.

Again, a minute.

A. Verma: Sorry about that. I'll make sure it doesn't happen, again.

What the hell?

Code Master: It was about the girlfriend.

Another pause.

A. Verma: My father shouldn't have involved you in my personal life.

Okay, this was beyond weird. Either someone had done a brain transplant on Vikram's old roommate, or this wasn't Adhith.

Vikram peered through the open door, studying the cubicles. Adhith could've lost the phone, but the device he'd been using before the chaiwalla interrupted him was his personal one, not the company-issued brand. The girlfriend's desk. That's where he'd tossed it to grab the snack.

Vikram grinned. So Miss Seema was trying to make sure her beloved didn't get into trouble with the boss for not answering messages. Picking the phone back up, he thumbed, again.

Code Master: Your papaji's wondering what you're doing with someone like her.

A. Verma: What do you mean "someone like her?"

Code Master: You know, considering you used to date (Vikram paused) Deepika Padukone.

Given a chance, both Adhith and Vikram would've worshipped at the feet of the film star, but neither had been within a mile of her. The closest either ever got to a celebrity girlfriend was the aspiring actress who'd dumped Vikram for the lead hero in a TV show.

There was shocked silence from the other phone for a few minutes. Then...

A. Verma: She's married!

Code Master: Dude, you don't have to hide it. Her husband's not going to care you used to date before they met. From *her* to Seema. What happened to you?

An annoyed moment later...

A. Verma: Seema may not be as good-looking, but she has other attributes.

Code Master: Name one.

A. Verma: Seema's honest.

Riiight.

Code Master: Deepika is well known for calling a spade a spade.

A. Verma: Seema likes children and old people.

Code Master: Deepika is a (Vikram paused, thinking) UNICEF ambassador (He had no clue if it were true, but it wasn't as though his lie would hurt anyone). Last year, she gave polio vaccine to thousands of children in Ethiopia. With her own two hands.

Ethiopia sounded good. Kids starved there, didn't they?

A. Verma: Ethiopia has been polio-free since 2001. India has had polio more recently. Why did Deepika have to go all the way there? Why couldn't she do it at home?

Damn.

Code Master: I might have gotten the country wrong. The point is Deepika is a humanitarian.

A. Verma: Seema could be, too. Anyone could be with enough money.

True.

Code Master: Sure. She could be a great beauty, too.

As soon as Vikram hit "send," he wished he could take it back. Scratching his cheek, he waited for the response. And waited. The landlines rang, the clerk from accounting brought in papers for him to sign, notifications popped up on the computer. Mussing his hair, Vikram eyed his phone. Finally, after half an hour...

A. Verma: That was mean.

Mean? If she were going to pretend to be a dude, the least she could do was sound like one.

Code Master: What are you, a girl or something?

Another offended silence.

A. Verma: You're a sexist bigot.

Code Master: You forgot homophobic.

A. Verma: You didn't say anything about gay people.

Code Master: I called you a girl, didn't I?

A. Verma: But I'm not gay.

Code Master: Whatever. Does the girlfriend know?

> A. Verma: What do you mean does she know? He's not gay.
>
> A. Verma: I mean, I'm not gay.

Vikram's abdomen was hurting from the effort to hold back laughter. Going to the latrine, he turned on the tap in the washbasin and laughed. He guffawed until tears came to his eyes. Regretfully deciding he had to put an end to it, he returned to his desk.

The bad angel on his shoulder had other plans. Sputtering with mirth, Vikram typed.

> Code Master: I can't believe you're still pretending that night didn't happen.

There was a thud outside. He hoped she hadn't just succumbed to a seizure. *Nope.* It was one of the other analysts, dropping a pile of folders onto the carpet. Why they needed paper records in addition to digital ones was beyond Vikram. *Oh, shit.* There was Adhith, a few steps away from the glass-doored entrance to the office.

> A. Verma: What night?
>
> Code Master: Since you're right outside the front entrance, why don't you come into my room? I'll remind you.

Seema scooted her chair back to gape in the direction of the entrance, then scooted hurriedly back inside.

Vikram fervently hoped she possessed the good sense to delete the entire chat before Adhith got to her desk in search of his phone.

At the sudden rise in chatter, Vikram glanced at the clock. 1:00 PM, already? The presentation to the EU client was due the next day, and he'd wasted almost two hours on the phone.

Adhith was at Seema's desk. They were both looking in Vikram's direction, the expression on their faces urgent. He bit back a groan. It never occurred to her to delete it? There was no way he could explain it away as momentary insanity.

Striding into the room, Adhith announced, "We have a problem."

Vikram cleared his throat. "I have no excuse—"

"We're not going to have the presentation ready for review by three."

"It was stupid—huh?"

Seema appeared at the door. "I'm sorry, sir," she mumbled, staring wild-eyed at the two men as though expecting them to pounce on each other in torrid passion.

Vikram was tempted—oh, so tempted—to twirl his friend into a dip just to see what she'd do. He gritted his teeth to keep the laughter from escaping.

"My fault, entirely," said Adhith. "Seema was having some difficulty with her reports. I should've remembered she's new."

Coughing mildly, Vikram agreed, "You should've at least answered calls. Did you even have your phone with you? Your personal one, not the company device." He paused until he heard the satisfying gasp from the door. "Things happen. We'll do some overtime and make it work."

"Sure will," Adhith promised, tone more relaxed. He didn't even ask why on earth he was expected to answer work calls on his personal phone.

Seema, on the other hand, was repeatedly opening and closing her mouth, no sounds emerging. As Adhith continued talking, she took a couple of gulping breaths, eventually settling for shooting a murderous glare in Vikram's direction.

***

"Jerk," Seema hollered, hurling the dart onto the board on the kitchen wall. On the ledge outside the small, barred window, the orange-and-white stray cat stopped washing himself and meowed in alarm. Vikram Joshi was a jerk. A *criminal* jerk. Seema imagined his mug shot on the dartboard.

"Yaar," said her sort-of-new flatmate, calling Seema her friend. Stirring chickpeas and tomato slices in the wok, she smacked the spatula sideways against the edge of the vessel. The metallic clang made Seema's teeth ache, but she sniffed hard, enjoying the tangy aroma spreading through the room. Clucking, the flatmate continued, "Bosses are always jerks. It's a job requirement."

The flatmate worked for a digital magazine. Since the job didn't make her enough money to rent a two-bedroom in the middle-class neighbourhood of Kurla, she'd advertised for a second renter. In two days, Seema stood at the doorstep, luggage at her feet.

Her auntie hadn't been able to do a single thing. The Verma case was high profile enough to warrant monitoring from the IB big shots in New Delhi. Seema was an income tax officer on deputation to the bureau, and Verma was the *finance* minister, the boss of all bosses in the income tax department. Crores were involved, each about 150,000 U.S. dollars! With the bigwigs watching, her auntie reluctantly agreed to minimise any contact the Vermas had with Seema's real background.

While Seema didn't expect to stay around long enough to trigger any sort of investigation from them, enough dead ends were created. She'd never been to Himachal Pradesh, so the bureau thought it safer to create a lie which could be explained away if she were caught in it. Seema could claim she'd been so ashamed of her actual past she'd made up the story of moving to the city sometime in her teens instead of growing up there.

Part of her history was left as such with Seema using her own undergraduate records for the job application. As far as Imperium and Adhith were concerned, she'd earned a degree in mathematics from Mumbai University and basic certification in cybersecurity. They knew nothing of her master's degree in cryptology. The accounting company she listed under "work experience" was a sham. As an extra measure, her auntie's role in the income tax department was also buried under layers of bureaucratic nonsense. She was listed as a mid-level employee in the same sham company as Seema. IB also buried Seema's juvenile record with the Mumbai police department so deep it would take supernatural powers to bring it to light. But better safe than sorry. Hence, the move to the flat even before she started her "job."

Seema smiled warmly at the other girl in the kitchen. She adored her flatmate. Gayathri liked to cook and eat and was so happy with herself that everyone who met her was charmed. All her colleagues ran to her for advice.

Gayathri was the only one who'd come to Seema's mind when she was searching through her contact list in the manager's loo, needing to vent about interfering aunties. Gayathri didn't know anything about her investigation, but she always knew the right thing to say. She didn't even mind Seema's cursing.

Gayathri asked Seema why she didn't cut off contact with the auntie if she were such a bitch. Of course, Seema wouldn't do that. They were family. Ignoring the sudden shame at her own bad behaviour, Seema doubled down on her condemnation of her auntie.

Precisely then, the jerk entered the scene. Her first instinct was to draw her gun on the dangerous-looking stranger who'd turned out to be the manager. Thank God she hadn't, or her cover would've been blown. *Instead, I had to scream for help,* Seema muttered to herself, face heating in embarrassment. *I looked like a damned fool.*

Karma visited Seema for badmouthing her auntie to an outsider. The jerk *had* to have said something to his buddy about the cursing and carrying on he'd heard. They *had* to have figured out she came from the slums of Mumbai, or Adhith wouldn't have been maintaining a distance. He wasn't even giving her a chance to explain away her lie. All her hard work was now down the drain. The idea of adopting a persona different from those of his usual lady friends, the nauseating giggle... all wasted.

Seema had been racking her brains for a Plan B when Adhith forgot his phone on her desk. Logged in, to boot. She'd stared at it, hardly able to believe her luck. Then, it pinged. She shouldn't have bothered to respond, but she'd been afraid the jerk would go looking for Adhith, and they'd both realise the phone was with her. She needed to buy herself a couple of minutes to upload some spyware. Then, the jerk said something about her, and she saw red. She'd uploaded the spyware, but she'd also picked a quarrel with Vikram Joshi.

"For *two* hours," Seema mumbled. "What a waste of time." She even needed to pretend she didn't know how to do those simple reports. Her! The topper of her class at the Indian Statistical Institute.

"The jerk wasted two hours, too," consoled the flatmate. Gayathri believed Seema had only been trying to keep Adhith out of trouble with the boss for being incommunicado.

Shaking her fist at the dartboard, Seema vowed, "I'm gonna get you." The jerk wasn't a suspect in the Verma investigation, but she'd get him. For *something*. The government couldn't possibly mind if one of its cryptanalysts put in some personal time to take out the jerks of the world. She entertained herself with the image of Vikram Joshi being dragged away in handcuffs, sobbing and pleading with her for mercy.

"Supper's ready," Gayathri sang. Curried chickpeas with *batura*, the wheat bread.

"Gimme a minute." Opening the freezer, Seema took two pieces from the sardine stash and deposited them in front of the orange-and-white cat.

"This is why it sits outside your window," Gayathri admonished. "At least, it stopped spraying urine."

"The trip to the veterinarian did the trick." Seema shook a finger at the cat. "You heard what the doctor said, young man. Neutered cats live longer, healthier lives." Ignoring the outraged meow, Seema returned to the dinner table.

As usual, the batura was impossibly soft and fluffy, and the chickpea masala carried the perfect blend of tanginess and spice. Yet all Seema could taste was the embarrassment from the morning.

"Damn him," she muttered, scratching her collarbone. The flat did not have air-conditioning, and the combination of humid weather and spicy food had her sweat glands working overtime. She longed for monsoon to hit Mumbai. At this point, she was prepared to do a rain dance in the middle of the street to tempt the heavens into opening.

Gayathri clucked. "The Jerk? Forget him. Focus on The Boyfriend."

Otherwise known as The Fashion Plate Felon. "My life sucks," Seema mumbled, fanning herself vigorously with an old magazine left on the kitchen table since she'd moved in. "*I* suck." Or she'd have known Vikram Joshi was close enough to his friend to pick up on her impersonation even over cyberspace. For God's sake, he'd said the senior Verma called him. *She* should've picked up on how close— Seema frowned. "Tell me. I'm not bad looking, right?"

"No! The jerk said you look bad?"

To Seema's horror, a tear came to her left eye. She dropped the magazine and reached for her glass of water. "*He* looks terrible. You should've seen him when he first came in. Dirty T-shirt and all those muscles. His hair was all over the place. Like... like a *lion* or something. Except, it's really black and thick."

Piece of bread held to her lips, Gayathri arrested. "Go on."

When Seema screamed, he'd leapt from the chair, advancing in her direction. "He doesn't walk. He *stalks.*"

"He did just find a stranger in his bathroom," Gayathri pointed out.

"I'm not talking about that episode. He came to work all last week like other people. *Normal* people. Shave and haircut and decent clothes." Even a tie.

"Uh-huh."

"Cologne, too," Seema muttered. "Some kind of woodsy smell." She'd caught a whiff when he walked past her chair once.

"Smell is important," Gayathri agreed, tone grave. "One of the first things I notice about a man."

"Yeah... he still looked like an animal. He's got these black eyes, and his nose is crooked."

Gayathri coughed. "His nose, huh?"

"I'll bet you my next paycheck he broke it in a fight."

"Interesting."

"That guy..." Seema's voice broke. "*That* guy thinks I'm not pretty enough."

"Aww." Pushing her chair back, Gayathri rushed around the table to envelop Seema in a warm hug.

"I'm okay," Seema mumbled. It wasn't as though she wanted the jerk to like her or something.

Once she was back at her plate, Gayathri remarked, "Men—no matter how awful they look—always believe they deserve the hottest girl on the planet."

"What are the rest of us supposed to do?"

Gayathri shrugged. "Act like we *are* the hottest girl on the planet. Confidence goes a long way. You'll have him drooling in no time."

"I don't want him drooling," said Seema. "I have Adhith." The thief she was supposed to catch.

Nodding sagely, Gayathri concluded, "Jus' sayin'. Want some ice cream?"

Chapter 4

Morning sunlight streamed through the large windows at the end of the room, drenching the three occupants of the dining table, but the silent air conditioner mitigated the heat. The aroma of freshly brewed coffee permeated the air. Stirring in a spoonful of sugar, Vikram flipped through the newspaper. Election results, the latest royal kerfuffle in Britain, the unusual pairing of pineapple and clams offered by a celebrity chef... there it was: Wal-Mart and its e-comm strategy.

In the chair next to Vikram's, his mother was busy on the phone, chatting with old college friends. His father sat across the table, typing on his own device. In unison, they giggled. "Look," said Mom, fluttering fingers at her husband. Her eyes were still on the screen. "Everyone loves your poem."

Ah. They were in the same group. Unsurprising, since they'd met as classmates at the Grant Medical College back in the 'eighties.

"You're my muse," crooned the bald poet. "The wind beneath my wings. With you by my side, I could leap tall buildings."

Mom's hair had been hennaed for years, so if any grey existed, the world didn't know it, but there was no hiding the plumpness of age. Whatever the changes wrought by time, Vikram's father had eyes only for her. And Mom—

Typing out her response, she muttered. "My superhero. I could drown in your eyes."

"Hey," said Vikram, grinning. "Children present."

Neither parent looked up. Shaking his head, Vikram rolled up the newspaper and grabbed the coffee mug. As soon as he was done caffeinating, he'd head out. He'd be fifteen minutes ahead of schedule, but he preferred to spend the time walking to the next bus stop than sitting at the breakfast table as the spare tyre. He'd put up with enough of their indifference in his childhood.

45

Vikram's first memory of school was of needing to pee. He was in the principal's office with Mom and Anjali, his big sister. They were busy discussing Anjali's upcoming musical performance with the rest of Class Two. There were only two chairs across the principal's desk, and Vikram had to stand.

***

Crossing his legs, five-year-old Vikram wiggled in place. Their appointment was set to end at six, but the needles on the wall clock were going so slowly. Did clockmakers set them that way on purpose to torture kindergarteners?

"Mummy," he whispered, holding up a little finger.

"Anju's been training with a classical guru," Mummy continued, her eyes glinting in excitement. "He says her tone is perfect."

In the second chair, Anjali preened. Everyone always said she was perfect. In every way. The school day had ended, but her hair was still in two perfect braids, her tunic was crisp, and her shoes were unmuddied.

Vikram's brand-new shoelaces were frayed, his white shirt was half out of the navy-blue shorts, and the matching tie was stained the orange of the curried green peas from lunch. Any second now, his shorts were going to be drenched in pee.

"Mummyyy." With the same little finger, he jabbed at her shoulder. "I really gotta go."

Shifting in her chair, Mummy continued talking to the principal. "Anju's dad wants her to focus on her studies. So do I. The Joshi family has always been interested in fine arts, but academics take precedence."

The Joshi family. Vikram nearly wept. Now, she'd *never* stop talking.

Mummy was the daughter of a simple housewife and a guitarist who'd worked for one of the music directors in the city, making songs for the movies. Naniji—Vikram's maternal grandmother—had died when Mummy was still in school. According to Nanaji—Mummy's father—it was a blessing because the day their daughter met her husband, she started being ashamed of her roots.

The Joshis got the final say over good taste. Any interest in music needed to involve classical music, or it didn't count. Above all, every member of the family was expected to excel in school. They were bred to be doctors. Once Mummy started gushing about the perfect Joshis, it would be days before she stopped.

Vikram took a slow step to the back. In a few more, he was at the door. The watchman nodding off on the stool outside didn't even open his eyes when Vikram took off at rocket speed, heading towards the latrines at the far end of the empty hallway.

Pulling down the zipper on his shorts, he tugged at the doorknob. And tugged. *Locked? No!* He was going to explode. Wildly, he wheeled around. There was an open window, looking out to the volleyball court where the sports teacher was yelling at the big girls. Right below the window was a flowerbed.

Vikram leapt onto the sill and pulled his shorts down in the nick of time. The pink flowers danced under the stream. "Ahh," he sighed, blissful tears spurting from his eyes.

The giggles from the volleyball court alerted him to his audience. His ears heated in embarrassment, but he couldn't stop. By the time he finished, even the sports teacher spotted him.

Keeping his eyes averted, he pulled his shorts back up and raced towards the principal's office.

"...the chief cardiologist, so his recommendation carries weight." Mummy finished, shooting a benevolent smile at the clearly grateful principal. "You can send the bio-data with Anju tomorrow."

Oh, good. They were done. They passed by the volleyball court on their way out. More giggles erupted. Mummy flicked an irritated glance at the team. "You need to be careful with your appearance, Vicky. People are laughing at you." She continued, holding Anjali's hand securely in hers. Gaze firmly fixed on the ground, Vikram trailed along.

The next week would forever be etched into his memory. The hallways and the playground rang with the nickname "Teapot." The big kids snickered when he walked by. The other kindergarteners refused to play with him. When he trudged to Anjali's classroom during lunch recess, she pretended not to know him. Vikram counted minutes until the weekend when he could visit Nanaji, his maternal grandfather.

"So what?" hollered the old fellow. "If they don't need you, you don't need them, either. You gotta learn to defend yourself, though. Don't let any of those bullies at school get you."

Nanaji was right. There were a couple of Anjali's classmates who cornered Vikram at the age of eight, checking out his "teapot." This time, he didn't seek refuge with his sister. The bullies both lost a few teeth, and Vikram broke his nose in two places. All of them got suspended for a week, but not a single kid ever laid a hand on Vikram for the rest of his school life. Nor did any of them ever again utter the nickname around him. Even if the kids didn't say anything, Vikram knew they remembered him at the window, peeing into the flowerbed. He was well away from all of them. As Nanaji noted, neither party needed the other.

The Joshis had no use for their son, either. They didn't understand his penchant for taking things apart to see how they worked. His father didn't appreciate it when he hacked into the family computer. His mother showed no interest in the awards he won with his guitar. They didn't care he spent his weekends with Nanaji and his stunt director friend in the *chawl*—the working-class tenement building the old men rented rooms in.

Nanaji and his friend regularly took Vikram to the gym, making sure his muscles matched his large frame. There was also the retired background

48

dancer who lived next door to Nanaji and taught Vikram how to dance. She said it would impress the ladies when he grew up.

Vikram was left to his own devices at the Joshi family gatherings and the social events attended by Mumbai's elite. Not that he cared. The kids in the crowd his parents hung out with loved the gadgets Vikram invariably carried on him, but the minute he started muttering about languages and programming, they wandered off, glazed looks in their eyes. Some would initiate contact and ask questions. If he made the mistake of answering, they'd elbow each other and laugh. Red-faced, Anjali would whisper pleas for him not to indulge them. Once Vikram entered his teens, he refused to subject himself to any more of their mockery.

Afterwards, his parents didn't insist on his presence at any of the shindigs. Why would they? All that mattered to them was their precious Anjali with her Hindustani music and oil paintings and the acceptance letter to India's most prestigious medical college—the perfect daughter with her perfect life and perfect reputation.

"Someday," a fifteen-year-old Vikram grunted, hurling the cricket ball at the far wall of the gym. He wasn't any good at the sport, but he played it every chance he got. "I'm gonna make them care."

Nanaji cackled. "As long as you don't act smart and classy like the rest of the Joshis, your mom's going to pretend you don't exist."

"I'm smart," Vikram muttered. His eyes teared. Mortified, he blinked away the moisture. "I'll show them I'm as good as Anju. I'll do it my way."

He did. With near perfect scores in the board exams. For once, his parents were pleased, but when they learned Vikram had no intention of following their footsteps into medicine, they again lost interest.

Two weeks before he was to start his first year at IIT Bombay, Nanaji's stunt director friend called. The old man had passed away—in a brothel of all places. He was quietly cremated by his mortified daughter and son-in-law with no gathering of friends and family to remember the colourful life he'd led. The only people openly sobbing at the funeral were the stunt director and the retired background dancer.

Nanaji left few earthly possessions. Just his guitar and a few thousand rupees in his current account, the entirety of which he willed to his only grandson. Vikram was also the sole beneficiary of the contents of the bank locker. According to the stunt director, the pile of papers in it was an attempt at a memoir. Vikram took a quick glance at the first couple of pages and threw the whole thing into the back of his cupboard. It was less a life story and more the wishful thinking of a bit player in Bollywood who boasted of having bedded half the divas of the silver screen. The old man was forgotten within days, deliberately erased out of the minds of everyone except his grandson.

The seventeen-year-old took the guitar and soon moved into Hostel 1 at the Powai campus. He'd been determined to leave home even though Powai was only a few kilometres away.

Mind full of misery, Vikram was in no mood to put up with the antics of the energetic roommate who'd charmed everyone in the whole damned place from the janitor to the director. All he wanted was for Adhith Verma to shut up. If Vikram needed to hack into a minister's computer to be left the eff alone, he'd do it.

To this day, Vikram wasn't sorry he did it. One look at Adhith's starkly pale face was all it took for Vikram to recognise the thought running through his roommate's mind. If the information came out, Minister Verma would be ruined. Just as Nanaji had been, Adhith's father would be shunned by society.

They'd both known it was bribery but chose to close their eyes. Hell, Vikram even helped Adhith cover it up. Together, they'd dug up dubious connections between politicians and corporations, between legitimate businesses and shady enterprises. But if they tried to prove any actual wrongdoing, Adhith's father would've been among those who went down. So they did nothing.

In turn, Adhith forced his way through Vikram's initial surliness and offered friendship. Every student on campus knew the two roommates were best buddies. Anyone who wanted to make the acquaintance of the well-liked Adhith needed to acknowledge Vikram, the nerd. For the first time in his life, Vikram enjoyed a set of friends to hang with. The only thing irking him was the lack of his own latrine.

Thinking back, Vikram knew he should've been scared shitless of what Adhith and his father might have done to him. At seventeen, the idea hadn't even occurred, and thanks to the stupidity of youth, he found himself a brother.

Not a moment too soon. Within a year, Anjali brought home the perfect boyfriend. At the end of her final year in medical college, she married the dumbass. He became the son the Joshis wished they had, and he never ever missed a chance to remind them what a misfit Vikram was in their perfect little paradise.

Vikram was left without a place to go on his breaks from college if the dumbass and his wife were visiting Mumbai. Most vacations were spent with Adhith at his old home in Bhikiyasen, Uttarakhand.

They might have decided on different living arrangements after graduation, but Vikram could always rely on his best buddy and his Colaba flat. Until the arrival of Seema Rawat in said buddy's life, that is. Thanks to her, Vikram—at the age of twenty-eight—was back in his family's bosom. He *did* have his own latrine.

***

Surprised to find himself still in his parents' dining room, Vikram gulped sweet, creamy coffee. He *shouldn't* have been surprised. Disappearing into his thoughts was a routine occurrence for him in his childhood home. The flat was decorated according to both Feng Shui and Vastu Shastra, the ancient Chinese and Indian philosophies of architecture. Everyone's *ch'i*—their life force—was perfectly aligned with the aura of the duplex, but Vikram still had nothing to do there except daydream or play his guitar in the upstairs bedroom.

The doorbell rang. None of the occupants of the breakfast table paid any mind. Kusum, the housekeeper, would deal with whomever it was.

"Hey, Mom," sang a familiar voice.

Vikram gagged. The coffee went down the wrong way, making him cough. The dumbass? What was he doing back here? He wasn't alone. Mrs Dumbass was with him—Dr Anjali Joshi, Vikram's big sister.

With exclamations of surprise, the Joshi parents stood.

"We have news," squealed Anjali. A coy smile on her face, she whispered something in Mom's ear.

Mom clapped a hand to her mouth. "O. M. G."

"What?" asked her puzzled husband. "Everything okay?"

"Everything's fantastic." The dumbass clapped his father-in-law's shoulder. "You, sir, are going to be a grandfather."

Vikram's father stared. There was a hint of moisture in Dr Joshi's eyes when he placed a benedictory hand on his daughter's head.

Shoving his chair back, Vikram stood. "Congratula—"

"We need your help," the neurosurgeon said to his mother-in-law. "The obstetrician we like has a waitlist of three months."

"I'll make a call." As the chief of obstetrics in one of the nation's best medical colleges, she had the clout to make sure her daughter was allowed to cut the line.

"Anju," called Vikram. She looked up, her face genuinely happy. "This is great news—"

Their father hugged her from the side and dropped a kiss on top of her head. "You two are going to be great parents. This baby's going to be one lucky fella."

"Could be a daughter," said Dr (Mrs) Joshi. "Doesn't matter. But you must prepare well for its arrival. Every detail is important."

"Of course," said the dumbass. "We have all the prenatal vitamins, but Anju hasn't been able to keep much down."

Mom clucked. "You *are* a little pale, Anju."

Was she? Vikram thought she'd never looked prettier. Her eyes were shining. "Are you feeling all right—"

The dumbass interrupted, "I have chewable vitamins on special order from the U.S." All around Vikram, his family chattered, planning for the baby's arrival. Not only obstetricians, the dumbass already had nanny candidates lined up to interview. He even pulled out a list of exclusive kindergartens from his pocket. "The right school is important. The right company, the right attitudes... or..." He shot a glance towards Vikram.

Or the baby might end up like his uncle.

"I've got to get going," said Vikram. "Don't want to be late."

"Vikram," exclaimed Anjali. "He was kidding."

"Of course, *saale saab*," said the dumbass, calling Vikram "Mr Brother-in-law."

"We all know how good you're at..." Mom glanced at Dad. "...at... ahh..."

"Computers," finished Vikram's dad, tone triumphant.

The senior Joshis always made sure to mention the dumbass couple's credentials to new acquaintances, their son's accomplishments abbreviated to "he's a software engineer."

Vikram held both hands up. "We're all good. There's a presentation coming up this afternoon. I have to get going." Laptop bag slung over his shoulder, he got to the front door.

"Wait." Anjali came hurrying. "You're not going to congratulate me?"

As though... Vikram bit back a retort and parroted, "Congratulations."

"Thanks," she said, catching one of his hands in both of hers. "You're going to have responsibilities, you know."

"Like what?"

She tossed a glance over her shoulder to the dining room, where their parents were still chatting with her husband. "Like stopping the rest of us from completely messing up the child."

On a short spurt of surprised laughter, Vikram repeated, "Congratulations, Anju."

"And," she went on, "I want you to teach her to play the guitar."

Startled, Vikram said, "I didn't think you liked my playing."

"Are you kidding me? I always wished I—"

"Hey, Anju," the dumbass called, tone nauseatingly sweet.

"Coming." Before she reached her husband, she twirled and shot Vikram a mischievous wink.

For one moment, she was the big sister he'd longed for, the friend he'd always wanted.

***

The pleasant feeling stayed with Vikram all through his bus ride, dissipating when he saw the familiar figure ahead of him, walking into the office. Seema. He owed her an apology. Not only because the company bigwigs would have a fit if they knew what he'd done. There had been no need to embarrass her.

When she reached her chair, she took off the rose-coloured hippie sunglasses, and her gaze swept to the side, arresting as she saw him. *Damn.* She did have gorgeous eyes. Light brown and enormous, prettied up with something pinkish on the lids.

Turning away from Vikram, she tugged down the hem of her tunic before settling deliciously rounded hips into the chair. The clingy material of the blouse stretched over perfect breasts. Sweeping her long tresses into a loose topknot, she secured it with a sparkly clip. *Hmm.* There were streaks of a lighter brown in her otherwise dark hair. A few curls escaped, dancing along her nape.

Vikram had to try hard to stop himself from gawking at the shapely neck. Clearing his throat, he shifted the laptop bag to conceal his crotch. He must have been more tired than he realised the day he returned to Mumbai to have thought her merely "not bad." She was downright stunning. Plus, there was a glow about her as though her cells radiated pure energy.

Settling into his office, he considered calling her in to render his apology. If he were to keep the rest of the office from overhearing, he'd have to close the door, and the latest missive from HR strongly recommended never doing that with female colleagues. The *#metoo* movement kept upper management jittery. Gossip in San Jose was a couple of the bigwigs did deserve public thrashings for the stunts they'd pulled, but the belated and self-serving feministic zeal from corporate made life difficult for poor middle managers like him.

Going into the personnel files, Vikram pulled up Seema's info. Only the company device and one other number were listed. Cell phones. No landlines. Not an unusual occurrence among tech employees. She lived in a flat in Kurla. The emergency contact listed was a friend, Gayathri. The address was the same as Seema's. *Flatmates?* Vikram frowned. From his research, Seema's only family was her auntie. Why didn't they have *her* contact info in the database?

Absently, Vikram clicked through folders, coming across phone numbers of other employees, addresses, activity log... *what the hell?* There had been unusually high levels of activity recorded on the company's systems over the last few weeks. If Vikram were to buy the number currently flashing on the screen, he'd have to believe his employees actually worked twice as hard in his absence.

Quickly, he checked for malware, signs of spying. Nothing. However, a skilled hacker would use operational activities to conduct reconnaissance.

Vikram typed in commands. In thirty minutes, he rocked back in his chair, ignoring the squeak. Someone had been reviewing the employees' internet habits. What would a hacker do with the information? Surely, it was the overzealous HR department back in California. He needed to have a conversation with them about unnecessarily hassling the staff over minor infractions. Too tight a rein made for unhappy employees. He'd need Adhith's help talking to the—

Adhith was outside, making his way towards his own room. First chance he got, Vikram was going to have a conversation with his former roommate. Adhith couldn't possibly be serious about marrying Seema. Her background made her unsuitable for the role of a politician's wife. Vikram had to stop Adhith from making a mistake. What else were best friends for?

Before cautioning Adhith, Vikram had to apologise to Seema and preferably, when Adhith was not around to see the messages.

For the next couple of hours, Vikram kept an eye on his buddy's movements. Unfortunately, Adhith stayed within earshot of Seema, giving Vikram no chance to text her.

Around eleven, Adhith walked out of his room and towards Seema's cubicle. "Finally," Vikram muttered. Leaping out of his chair, he strode to the maze, only to be stopped by the rotund accountant. "Later," Vikram said, sweeping the man aside.

Adhith turned, ready to pace in the other direction.

"Adhi," shouted Vikram. "I gotta talk to you." Jogging to his friend, Vikram flung an arm around his shoulders. "Let's step outside for a couple of minutes. I want to get something to drink."

"Krishnan will be here soon," said Adhith.

"Who?"

"The chaiwalla," Adhith clarified.

"I knew that," Vikram muttered. He simply didn't have names and faces at his fingertips.

"It's *Vada Pav* Day."

Vikram loved the local version of veggie burger. "I can't take the risk," he explained, glumly. "Krishnan might spit in my tea."

There was a chortle from the direction of Seema's desk.

On a long-suffering sigh, Adhith asked, "What did you do?"

"There's a coffee place I want to check out. Let's go there, and I'll tell you all about it."

Instead, they decided on coconuts from the street-side vendor. Leaving Adhith to pay, Vikram dug his phone out. He paused a second before thumbing out a message. He was her boss, and she might feel pressured to respond.

Code Master: xxxxx-xxxxx. Vikram Joshi.

His name and phone number. No explanations. If Seema wanted, she could text him back. *Although...* Vikram cursed in his mind. This wasn't right. If Vikram wanted to apologise, he should've done so to Seema *and* Adhith. Going behind his back like this... also, Vikram had no business interfering in Adhith's love life. It was his right to decide whom he married.

Numbers Girl: Taking him outside and texting me your number. You're a jerk, mister!

"Here you go," said Adhith, balancing coconuts in both hands, straws stuck on top.

A total jerk, Vikram admitted, eyeing the trusting smile of his friend. He tucked the phone back into his pocket and took the proffered drink. "Adhi, we gotta talk."

"You want an explanation for the call."

"Heh?" Oh, the phone call where Adhith pretended it was Seema on the line. He didn't know his father had already talked to Vikram. Adhith didn't know Vikram had done much worse. Dammit, Vikram needed to apologise to *Seema*, first. He wasn't just her boyfriend's buddy. He was her boss. Then, he had to admit what he'd done to Adhith. "I..." Vikram started, frantically searching for an explanation for having dragged Adhith out of the office. "Did HR contact you?"

Adhith frowned. "No. Why?"

"They've been running scans on employee activity." It *was* a real issue they needed to deal with.

"What do you mean?"

"High activity levels in the operations systems." Vikram recited the numbers he'd found while looking for Seema's contact info. "Got to be from California."

Eyes suddenly alert, Adhith asked, "Could it be a hacker?"

"Intrusion was my first thought, but I didn't see any signs of it in our product-related applications. Why would a hacker monitor our daily operations?"

"True. As you said, it's probably HR. How did you find out?"

"I... uhh... was looking up a phone number and happened on the activity log for the last quarter."

"Last quarter?" Adhith asked, tone dismayed. "Dammit. *I* was in charge. I should've caught it."

Vikram shook his head. "It's not like we regularly keep track of what the staff is up to. Also, you wouldn't have had time for anything other than the ongoing projects."

On a typical day, Adhith shared the responsibility for technical management with Vikram, leaving office administration to the accountant. With Vikram in San Jose, Adhith handled everything. "Still..." he muttered.

Dismissively, Vikram said, "Forget that part. We need to talk to California."

"We will," Adhith assured his friend. "I'll shoot an email over to HR and set up a conference call for the morning. Vikram, I do need to talk to you about *my* phone call... and Seema."

"No time right now," Vikram said, hurriedly. "We need to finalise things for the EU presentation."

Adhith nodded. "Tell you what... let's meet at our old place in the evening."

Vikram would have to fix things with Seema before then. "Sure."

The old place was a tea stall on Grant Road, where the slums were. Where the redlight district was. Where Seema grew up. Vikram suppressed the twinge of discomfort in his chest. He and Adhith stumbled upon the tea stall in their first year of college, courtesy their weed contact. They'd returned for the food and the "special" rum-laced tea served to favoured customers. Frequent visits to Grant Road notwithstanding, Vikram never bought sex. He didn't believe Adhith had, either. Now that he'd met Seema, Vikram was profoundly grateful for the fact.

Her face floated to his mind—the lively eyes. God, the childhood she must have endured! No wonder she'd lied. Helpful auntie or not, she certainly possessed incredible will to have broken free. Her spunk was evident even in her text messages. She deserved all the good things the world could offer, including a husband like Adhith, who'd treat her like a queen.

Vikram needed to clear things with Seema. Once he'd done so, he'd have to come clean to Adhith about the messaging. Back in his office, Vikram typed again.

> Code Master: Look, I'm trying to apologise for yesterday. Nothing else.

Minutes ticked by. No response.

> Code Master: But you're right. I shouldn't have done it. I *am* sorry for both times.

Still nothing.

> Code Master: Can we start over?

He grimaced. Somehow, the message sounded wrong.

> Code Master: By that, I only mean can we pretend we didn't have these conversations? Adhi's my best friend, and you're his girlfriend. Also, you both work for me. I don't want things to get awkward. I'll let Adhi know what I did.
>
> Numbers Girl: Fine. Starting over.

Phew.

> Code Master: Thanks.
>
> Numbers Girl: You're welcome.
>
> Numbers Girl: Only because I don't want to mess up things between you and Adhith.
>
> Code Master: I get it. Thanks, anyway.
>
> Numbers Girl: Also, since the conversations never happened, please don't tell him about it. It's more drama than I can handle.

Oh? More drama than threatening to kill her auntie? More drama than pretending to be her own boyfriend and texting his boss?

Code Master: On a scale of one to ten, how dramatic do you think you— (Vikram cursed, erasing the words. He didn't need to be any pettier than he'd already been). I won't bring it up unless you do.

Numbers Girl: Cool.

Code Master: Cool.

Later in the afternoon, they video-conferenced with the EU client. Vikram and Adhith presented their parts, followed by the accountant. The bigwigs from California were also online, watching the proceedings. Around the conference table were all the staff members who'd worked on the project. Eyes partially closed, Seema's head jerked forwards in a nod. Vikram took out his phone.

Code Master: Wake up. They can see you.

With a start, she glanced at the message. There was no response, but he hadn't expected one.

Much later in the evening, Vikram was on his way to meet Adhith at the teashop. The phone vibrated in his back pocket.

Numbers Girl: Thanks. You're still a jerk, but you're a decent jerk.

He grinned, thumb hovering over the response box. Emojis lined up. He paused over the wide smile, his eyes drawn to another one on the right—the kiss emoji.

Need surged, incredibly physical, to have her in his arms, to devour all of her. Vikram froze. With a foul curse, he tucked the phone back into his pocket.

Chapter 5

Cars and motorised rickshaws crawled under the bright streetlights, honking at pedestrians who paid them no mind. Singing an ode to the motherland, a group of young men stumbled along on their night-time adventures. Prostitutes in glittery tops and tight minis posed at the doorways of the shops, shooting come-hither looks at passers-by.

Inside the tea stall smack in the middle of the redlight district, Adhith chewed on roasted mushroom and observed the girls. One of them sported a black eye, not entirely hidden by the layers of makeup on her skin. How old was she? Fifteen? Twenty-five? Hard to tell. Smoke swirled from the cigarette between her lips, sending the sickly sweet smell of tobacco into the heat and humidity of the night air already thick with the scent of spices.

The tea stall did brisk business in the hours between twelve and six in the morning. Despite the crowded tables, the owner headed straight to the two men, the large bottle in his hands ready for his "special" customers. He poured a generous helping of Old Monk rum into the tumblers of hot tea in front of Adhith and Vikram.

"Thanks, *bhaiyya*," said Adhith, calling the owner his brother. "You're the best. How's *bhabhi's* back?"

The owner launched into an account of his wife's hospital stay, concluding with a complaint about the bribes he had to pay. Once Adhith promised to look into it, the owner left, all smiles.

"You're meant for *this* sort of stuff." Dipping a cookie into rum-laced tea, Vikram popped it into his mouth. "Not IT."

"Yes," Adhith admitted. "Don't get me wrong... I do enjoy my work at Imperium." He hesitated. "Bro... about the phone call..." The call where Adhith pretended it was Seema on the other end, not Vikram.

Tone morose, Vikram said, "Your father called me. He said you want to marry Seema."

"I did say it," Adhith acknowledged, trying to gather his thoughts. He knew he couldn't marry her, but had he ever wanted to? Sure, he'd thought about it, but if his heart was truly in it, shouldn't he have been more upset at her deception? Did Seema want to marry *him?* When he'd believed her to be from the small town of Sarkaghat, he'd thought she was acting coy *because* she wanted marriage. But she was a city dweller, not a village belle, held back by social restrictions. So why had she...

Adhith shook his head. None of it mattered. As soon as he realised there was no future in it, he should've broken up with her. Instead, he'd used her name to get out of trouble. Thank God she didn't know. She'd *never* know. He couldn't lead her on that way. He needed to ease out of the relationship *while* keeping Papaji in the dark. Still, the whole bloody business left Adhith with a bad taste in his mouth.

Vikram shifted in his chair. Pounding his fist lightly on the table a time or two, he glared at his drink. "You like her; she likes you. You're going to get married. I have to congratulate you." He took the tumbler and tipped the contents straight into his throat.

Vaguely noting his edginess, Adhith said, "Let me talk to her and see what *she* wants. I'm not even sure what *I*—"

"You're not sure?" Voice rising, Vikram leaned forwards. "You haven't talked to her? How can you make announcements to your father without talking to her?"

Adhith's face heated. "Stupid mistake."

"Mistake?" Vikram yelped. "Mistake is when you pick the wrong item from the menu. Not when you pick the woman you want to marry."

"Why are you getting so angry, bro? I'll get it sorted out."

Vikram's fist thumped the table. The plate containing the mushrooms jerked, tipping one of them over the side. "You should've sorted it out *before* calling dibs."

"Heh? Calling *dibs?* I was the only one around."

"Poor girl."

Adhith studied his old friend. "Did you start drinking before you got here?" After all, the dumbass had visited in the morning with news he could procreate. Junior dumbasses! The thought was enough to drive a saint to drink.

Hands on the tabletop, Vikram hauled himself to his feet. "If I'm a jerk, you're a son of a bitch."

"What the hell? Why are you overreacting... someone called you a jerk?"

Not bothering to answer, Vikram announced, "I'm going home."

"I'll get my car." Adhith stood and flicked off a crumb on his blue tee before digging into the pocket of his khaki shorts for his wallet and keys.

"Don't bother. I'm calling a cab." With his index finger, Vikram jabbed at the air an inch from Adhith's nose. "I don't want to see your effing face."

"Hell must have frozen over," snarled Adhith. "You're going to pay for a cab."

Flipping him the bird, Vikram stalked off.

By God! What the hell is wrong with me *tonight?* "Bro, I'm sorr—" But Vikram was already out the door. Adhith plonked himself back down and raised a hand, signalling the waiter. "More rum-tea, please. Skip the tea." Plucking the phone from his left pocket, he thumbed out a message to the manager at his gym. They'd be closed now, but he needed a sparring session.

As soon as the waiter brought fresh tumblers over, a voice from behind parroted Vikram's words, "Poor girl." A female voice.

Enough. He'd had enough. Twisting around in his chair, Adhith snapped, "Mind your own busi—"

The woman—on her own at the table—pushed her hoodie back. Later, Adhith would be thankful he didn't embarrass himself by doing something ridiculous like gasping. Or drooling. Or both. Perfect oval of a face, almond-shaped dark eyes behind square-rimmed spectacles, straight, glossy hair in a high ponytail. Not a trace of makeup, but she didn't need any. His eyes involuntarily drifted over the rest of her.

The black cotton hoodie and skinny jeans and fabric slip-ons did nothing to enhance her figure, but it didn't need embellishment. Adhith could easily see her as the centrefold in a men's magazine. She was—quite simply—the hottest woman he'd come across.

"Madhubala," she introduced herself, leaning closer. Her hair shifted. A sweet, intoxicating fragrance wafted around her.

"Adhith," he said, finding his voice. "Adhith Verma."

"I know," she said. "I recognised you."

"Huh?"

"I'm a... journalist. *Political* journalist."

Oh, crap.

Noting his dismay, she laughed. "I don't do gossip, Adhith Verma. Your love life will remain your secret. Plus, I feel sorry for the girl. She doesn't need your ambivalence splashed all over the tabloids."

"Why's everyone—you don't need to feel sorry, okay? I like her. There are complications, but I *am* going to... I *will* talk to her. She deserves as much from me. What she doesn't deserve is to have her name dragged through the mud by unscrupulous 'journalists.' Write whatever you want about me. Leave her out of it."

Madhubala eyed him up and down, from the top of his head to his brown loafers. Then, she shrugged. "I told you I don't do tabloid work."

Adhith didn't entirely believe her, but there wasn't much he could do about what she'd already overheard. "Which paper do you work for?"

Waving a dismissive hand, Madhubala said, "It's too small to have come to your notice."

"No such thing as too small," Adhith immediately said. "I try to keep up with what the media says about my father. If you've done a story on him, I've probably seen it, Miss Madhubala..."

"Let's stick to first names," she said. "A little mystery is good."

"You know *my* last name."

"Life isn't fair."

"Are you on a story? Did you follow me here?"

She smirked. "Full of yourself, aren't you? No, I'm not here on a story. You're not important enough."

"Not yet."

That managed to surprise a laugh from her. "Not yet," she agreed.

"If you're not here on work—" Adhith hesitated.

"That's one way of asking what's a nice girl like me doing in a place like this." Her expression brooding, she glanced the young prostitutes waiting for customers by the door of the teashop. A cab stopped in front, and one of them sashayed over, disappearing into the darkness of the back seat. The girl with the black eye was still there, teetering on six-inch heels. Tone meditative, Madhubala said, "I'm not a nice girl. I used to be one of them."

First, it didn't register. Then, he gaped.

"It was a long time back," she continued. "I was fourteen. My second customer broke my knee."

66

Adhith didn't know what to say. "How did you get out?" he finally asked.

"My pimp refused to take me to the hospital. There's an NGO with an office around here. I crawled all the way there. The ladies gave me another option. If I wanted, they could help. I didn't even have to think. That was twenty-two years ago."

Which put her at thirty-six, eight years older than Adhith. "Why are you back?" he asked, genuinely curious. "I'd have thought you'd want to forget the whole damned place."

"I did," she agreed, nodding. "But I've been back before. Twelve years ago, I heard from the director of the NGO my old pimp had his eye on my niece. He'd negotiated a price with her father. I got her out."

Her childhood in the redlight district, the niece, the interest in Adhith's conversation with Vikram...

"Madhubala *Rawat?*" Adhith asked. "Seema's auntie?"

***

"Madamji," interrupted the waiter's hesitant voice. "Your kebab." He set the plate before Madhubala, the skewers holding sizzling mutton cubes. Continuing in a curious mix of locally spoken Marathi and pan-Indian Hindi, he asked, "Anything else? You should try our biryani. It's excellent."

"Some other time." Her eyes glinted with sudden alertness. Her hand was on the large tote on the chair next to hers, as though she were getting ready to bolt.

Disappointed, the waiter turned to Adhith. "What about you? Only rum-tea?"

Adhith didn't take his gaze off the woman. "Bring me some biryani. Extra spicy."

As soon as the waiter left, Adhith stood, spinning the red plastic chair around on one leg. He settled down facing... Madhubala. For the life of him, he couldn't imagine thinking of this woman as "auntie."

Her right brow rose. "I don't recall inviting you to join me."

"I do recall asking if you were following me. You lied. Guess what? I get to sit here with you."

"I didn't lie," said Madhubala, eyes still watchful. "I only said I'm not doing a story on you. Which I'm not."

"How could you be? You're an accountant, not a journalist. But a lie is a lie is a lie."

"How did you figure out Seema's my niece? Also, you seem to know a lot about me. How much did Seema tell you?"

"Seema didn't say anything." Adhith hesitated, wondering if she'd be offended at having been investigated. "Hell," he muttered. "You're here to investigate *me*."

Her hand slipped inside the tote. "You had my niece investigated?"

Did the woman have to keep on saying "niece?" When Seema mentioned her auntie, Adhith immediately imagined someone grey and disapproving. Not hot and sexy Madhubala Rawat. She *did* have the disapproval down pat. "There were some... discrepancies in how Seema behaved," he said. "Once we figured out she was from *here,* everything fell into place."

"That's how you knew who I was," Madhubala said, tensely.

He shrugged. "Everything fit. I wouldn't have thought any less of Seema, but I understand why she did it."

"Do what?"

"Lie about it. Like you, Seema got out and made something of herself. She works for one of the world's biggest cybersecurity firms, and you have your job with the accounting company. Both of you should be proud."

"Ahh." Madhubala's shoulders relaxed.

Adhith asked, "Did you get what you came for?"

"What do you mean?"

Grinning, Adhith said, "Oh, c'mon. Don't pretend it's not why you were following me. You wanted to make sure I'm not the kind to ditch Seema once I got to know her background."

Madhubala skewered him with her eyes. "Aren't you? You said there were 'complications.'"

Damn. He'd been so busy trying to impress her he'd forgotten what he'd done—toss aside the idea of marrying Seema.

With a scornful chuckle, Madhubala said, "I don't believe we have anything else to talk about. Return to your perfect little world, Verma."

"Things are not always black and white, Ms Madhubala Rawat," he returned, tone equally nasty. "There is this thing called nuance."

Her face darkened, her lovely eyes wide and shooting sparks. Mentally, Adhith cursed. First, his best friend. Now, this gorgeous woman who had a perfectly valid reason to question his motives. Was there going to be an end to the number of people he pissed off tonight?

The waiter arrived, carrying the plate of fragrant chicken biryani. Adhith smiled his thanks at the cheerful lad. "What's happening with your attempt to join the army?"

Twisting his waiter's cap around in his hands, the boy admitted he'd again failed his tenth-class exam.

"You *keep* doing this." Adhith's hand itched to smack the back of the boy's head. If Madhubala weren't watching, he'd have done it, too, but he didn't need to give her any more reasons to dislike him. "Can you at least get minimum marks? You have the height and the weight, and you're healthy."

"Next time, bhaiyya," the boy promised.

"You'd better," warned Adhith. "In another couple of years, you'll be aged out."

After the boy left, Madhubala commented, "You seem to know all the people in this place." Her tone was calm, collected. There was none of her previous rage on her face.

"Some. Vikram and I used to come here almost every week. Back when we were students."

"Then, what? Graduated to finer dining?"

"Not really. Vikram doesn't—" Adhith stopped. His friend's *kanjoos* attitude was no one's business. "He's been busy. *I* try to make it down a couple of times a month."

With a fork, Madhubala separated a cube of mutton from the skewer. "Tell me about nuance."

"The dictionary definition?"

Near her full lips, the sliver of meat trembled on the prongs of the fork. Her hand arrested. She glared across the table.

"Okay, okay. I know what you mean." How did he even begin to explain what was going on? To Seema's aun—to Madhubala, no less. "When Seema first started," he began, "I thought she was cute. Educated, intelligent, good company... she got my jokes."

"How sweet," said Madhubala, pleasantly. "You can write her matrimonial ad."

"Sarcasm is not a good look on you."

"Snobbery is not a good look on *anyone.*"

Adhith shouted, "I'm not a—" Noting heads swivelling in their direction, he broke off. The usually smooth and articulate Adhith Verma had been provoked by a snide comment into making a spectacle of himself. This situation with Papaji and Seema was messing up Adhith's game. Lowering his voice, he said, "There are things I've always wanted to do with my life. I still like Seema, but if I married her, I'd have to give up everything I ever—"

"I don't need to hear any further. You're not good enough for my Seema." Madhubala stood, all five and a half feet of her stiff with insult.

"Yeah?" Adhith said, goaded. "It's not for *you* to decide. Seema's a grown woman, and you're not her mother. Thanks to you, her father's also out of the picture. Whatever relationship we choose to have is solely up to her and me."

"Relationship? You're not planning to marry her, but you want a relationship?"

Adhith snarled, "Even if we shack up, you don't get a say."

"We'll see about that." Digging into her tote, Madhubala brought out a wad of notes and slapped it onto the table. "Have a nice life, Verma."

She was leaving? Shooting out a hand, Adhith caught her wrist. "Where are you going?" Even as he was asking the question, Adhith was horrified at himself. He might as well have worn a loincloth made of animal skin and swung from vines.

"None of your bloody business. Let go of me."

"I hope there's someone waiting to escort you home. This is not a safe neighbourhood for women." *Idiot. As though she wouldn't have known.*

A blur of movement. A black shape. The gun in her other hand.

Releasing her, Adhith jerked back in his chair, his eyes peering down the cavernous barrel of the weapon. He didn't dare make a sound. All noise in the teashop came to an abrupt stop.

"Safe enough," she said, striding out.

Not a soul in the place moved an inch until after she left.

Chapter 6

Seema paused at the front entrance of the office building and tucked her red retro sunglasses into her tote while glaring at the giant billboard of the latest Bollywood release. Clad in skintight jeans and minuscule shorts, the two heroines clung to the beefcake hero. They all looked disgustingly healthy, whereas Seema's nose dripped, her eyes burned, and head pounded. She'd tried calling the accountant to get time off, but the unsympathetic moron oversaw staff requests for casual and sick leave, and he firmly reminded her of the EU client.

Squeezing her way into the jam-packed lift, she saw a couple of her colleagues but limited herself to a vague smile. She would've loved to get to know them, especially the Bengali girl who was right now at the back, her nose buried in a book. She worked one row down from Seema. Except for having to live with her auntie, Seema had enjoyed her stay in Kolkata, the capital city of West Bengal. The food, the festivals, the movies... but mostly, the food.

A tickle started in her nose. Frantically, she dug into her purse for the hankie. "Ahh... ahh... ahhchoo." Finally finding the already sodden piece of fabric, she honked into it. "Sorry," she announced to the other occupants of the lift. "Bad cold. Hope it's not the flu or something."

The lift shuddered to a halt on the fourth floor. The crowd rushed out. When the cage continued on its way, the only people in it were Seema and the Bengali girl.

"The flu?" asked the girl, grinning. "You don't seem to be doing too badly with it. *I* had the flu last year. Couldn't even get out of bed."

"Hey," Seema said, hoarsely. "I didn't actually say I *have* the flu. It's not my fault if other people decided I did and ran out of the lift." Thus Seema and the Bengali girl were riding up comfortably, instead of being packed like fish in the six-by-six space.

"I'm not complaining. The uncle in front of me was... er... passing gas."

Seema wrinkled her nose. "Eww. Thank God I can't smell anything."

The Bengali girl laughed.

"I'm Seema, by the way. Seema Rawat."

"I know who you are. Everyone in the office knows who you are."

"Really?" Their office had more than a hundred employees. Given the nature of her presence there, she'd talked less and listened more to her colleagues. Or more accurately, eavesdropped on their conversations every chance she got. She didn't realise they harboured any interest in *her*.

"You snagged Adhith Verma," the girl exclaimed. "Of course, we all know you."

Yikes. "Umm... I haven't snagged—"

The girl clucked. "Men. Always afraid of commitment. He's never dated anyone from work before, so we all thought... Seema, don't let him get away. He's the most eligible bachelor in the whole building!"

"I... umm..."

"Now they know he doesn't mind dating within the office pool, there will be dozens trying for a chance," the girl warned. "Everyone thinks he's super cute."

"Do they?" Seema asked, trying to keep the doubt from her voice.

"Yeah," the girl enthused. "He's always *so* stylish. Plus, he's super nice. He helped me fill out my tax forms last year."

With a loud ping, the lift stopped on the eighth floor. A couple of middle-aged men got in, arguing over IPL teams and jabbing impatiently at the buttons. Their entry gave Seema time to collect her thoughts.

Even if *everyone* didn't think Adhith Verma was hot stuff, *one* person clearly did. Miss Kolkata was in the throes of a full-blown crush. Seema wouldn't have been surprised to see golden stars and pink hearts flying out of her eyes. And *tax forms*? He was a felon! Used to robbing the taxpayer. No wonder he knew how to fill out the forms. "We're all busy with the EU project," Seema finally muttered.

"I know. Isn't it super exciting? I hope I get to go to Brussels with the site team. Hey, maybe, we'll both get to go."

Super. They could gush over Adhith, the felon's cuteness and niceness.

"I've always wanted to travel," the girl continued, dreamily. "Last month, there was an ad from Air India, looking for cabin crew. It would've been a great job, flying city to city. I didn't even apply."

"Why not?"

"The usual. Family objected. So I'm still here, stuck to a computer."

"Family," Seema said, feelingly. "You don't like this job?"

The girl shrugged. "It pays well. What about you?"

The lift stopped on the fifteenth floor, letting the men out. "I like working with computers," Seema said. "I've never wanted to do anything else. But..." If it hadn't been for her inability to find a job on her own, she wouldn't have dreamed of working for the income tax department. This project was interesting, but what would happen after?

"There are always 'buts.' You could go anywhere in the world, *but* you're a girl, so you can't. You could do whatever you want *but* make sure it's safe... and boring."

"True," Seema agreed, glumly.

"That's why I love reading. When I'm in the middle of a story, I *can* be anything I want." With a giggle, the Bengali girl waved the book in her hand under Seema's nose. "This one's about a woman who disguised herself as a boy and stowed away on a pirate ship."

Hmm. Seema revised her opinion of the Bengali girl. There was more to her than her one-way love for Adhith Verma. Who hadn't babbled insanely about a crush one time or the other? Even Seema had prattled on about Vikr—she frowned. She'd been *venting* about Vikram Joshi to her flatmate. Big difference. Out loud, Seema said, "We have a lot in common, but I prefer movies to books." Scowling, she added, "I was planning to stay in bed and watch Netflix all day."

"Why didn't you? You have a bad cold."

"Fever, too, but the henchman wants to see me dead."

"Huh?"

Seema ptchaaed. "The accountant."

Grumbling about heartless monsters who refused leave to deathly ill employees, they got to the twenty-first floor. The Bengali girl walked through the office doors ahead of Seema. "We should get together after work. It will be super fun."

With a friendly nod, Seema went onto her cubicle. Unexpected tears pricked her eyes. She couldn't socialise with anyone at the office. Not without compromising the investigation. Except, she already had—even before the conversation in the lift. Damn Vikram Joshi and his WhatsApp messages.

Her gaze flew to the manager's room at the end. The door was only partially open, but there was movement inside. Most days, Vikram was already in the office when the rest of the staff ambled in for the morning. What time did he get there? At the crack of dawn? Didn't he have a life outside of work? No one keeping him at home? Snuggling into his warm chest, refusing to let him leave? Tempting him with kisses all across those killer pecs and abs?

Her eyes snapped open. She hadn't even realised she'd shut them. God, she was sweaty. Her heart was pounding hard like she'd run a marathon.

Seema was in the staff break room and grabbing an ice-cold bottle of mineral water from the fridge when the Bengali girl hurried in. "Are you all right?"

"Yeah." Fingers slick with moisture from the bottle, she wiped her face. "Just thirsty."

"The fever must be breaking," said the Bengali girl.

"Must be," Seema agreed, tremulously. That's all it was.

***

Seema glared at the accountant. "A memo?" An actual typed-up memo, ordering her to find solutions to certain questions brought up by the EU client before she called it a day. What was wrong with Vikram this morning? Instead of calling her into his office as he did with the rest of the staff, he'd sent this brusque note with his henchman.

The accountant shrugged. "He probably didn't want to catch your cold."

So Vikram knew how she was suffering? He was still giving her extra work? Her first instinct had been correct. Vikram Joshi was a total jerk who put his job over everything else. "Heartless," she muttered. "I could be dying."

The accountant rolled his eyes. "Just get the work done."

Seema had no time for anything else the rest of the day, not even to check on the spyware she'd loaded onto Adhith's phone. She peeked in the direction of his room. Where *was* he?

Numbers Girl: Hey. What happened to you?

A minute, fifteen minutes, an hour. Seema's gaze kept going to the device next to the keyboard. No answer.

At eleven, Krishnan chaiwalla came around with hot tea, and she paid him extra to have lunch brought to her. "I don't care what as long as it's hot and spicy." Her sinuses were so full, her head was going to explode any minute. She needed something to help her breathe.

"Vikram saar is in a bad mood," Krishnan whispered.

"He's a jerk is what. He gave me extra work when I'm—" After a second, she asked, "What did he do?"

Head swivelling up and down the row of cubicles, Krishnan made sure the coast was clear. The tumblers clinked in the stainless-steel drink carrier as he set it on the floor. "I heard him talk to Adhith saar on the phone. They were arguing."

She gestured at him to go on.

"Adhith saar wanted to visit his father, and Vikram saar wanted him to come to work."

Which explained Adhith's absence. "And?"

"Vikram saar said the EU client was demanding all the details of the project by the end of the day. I think Adhith saar said he'd work from his papaji's home and email Vikram saar. Trust me, Vikram saar was not happy."

Seema waited for the rest. And waited. "That's it?"

At having his news fall flat, Krishnan's eager expression turned to one of disappointment. Nose stuck in the air, he said, "I'll be back with your lunch."

He was already two cubicles down when she rolled her chair back. "Listen, bhaiyya. Can you get me something for the cold? There's a medical store not too far from here."

After Krishnan left, she resumed her work, but her mind kept wandering. Adhith was visiting his father, which meant they might be discussing something relevant to her investigation. Adhith could even be using his phone. Thanks to Vikram, she didn't have the time to check on the spyware.

On cue, the phone pinged.

A. Verma: Out doing personal stuff today. Will talk to you tomm.

That was it? From her supposed boyfriend? *It's all the jerk's fault,* Seema fumed. Since the day she'd run into him, Adhith Verma stopped being easy to manipulate.

Precisely at one, the rest of the office staff streamed out for lunch, leaving only the handful of employees covering the hour eating at their cubicles. Most preferred the dining hall on the second floor where they could mix and mingle. A few went home to eat or splurged on restaurant food.

"Seema madam," a voice shouted from the entrance. Krishnan, squeezing past the crowd headed in the opposite direction.

Gratefully, she took the tiffin carrier from him, opening the steel containers to inhale the aroma of piping hot rice and *dal,* the curried lentils. There was even mango pickle to go along with it and *pappad,* the deep-fried crackers. All of it looked homemade. The money she'd given him was in the plastic bag with the cough syrup. "Thank you. I'll name my first-born after you."

"Light food is best when you're sick," he said, gruffly. "And thank my *wife.*"

"I'll name my kid after *her.*"

"Phoolan Devi Stalin," Krishnan supplied the moniker, chortling.

"Your wife was named after a *bandit?*"

"*And* a dictator," said Krishnan. "My in-laws were communists; they thought it was a fine idea."

"Give your wife a nickname, and I'll use it. Agreed?"

"Agreed." Solemnly, they shook hands over the pact.

"No dacoits or dictators," Seema warned. "Or the deal's off."

Guffawing away, Krishnan said he needed to return to get working on the afternoon snacks.

Watching his departing back, Seema sighed. She was going to miss him when she left. The Bengali girl, too. Even the mean accountant. The one person she was *not* going to miss was her boss. The jerk didn't even care his sick employee would have to work through lunch. She glared in the direction of the manager's office.

The door was wide open. Vikram hadn't left for lunch, either. He was still at his desk, fingers on the keyboard, eyes boring into the monitor. The thick, dark hair was unusually neat, as was the pale-yellow shirt, with grey and blue tie perfectly in place. Seema craned her neck. No signs of a packed lunch. By God, did the man *live* to work?

Spoon in hand, she bent over the food, prepared to pour the dal on the rice. There was so much of it. Krishnan's wife surely imagined Seema was pregnant or something. With quintuplets! Leaving the steel spoon in the thick, creamy dal, she picked up her phone.

> Numbers Girl: We could share lunch. I have enough food for twenty people.

Through the open door, she saw Vikram pause his typing and pick up his phone.

> Numbers Girl: I haven't touched it yet. You're not going to catch my germs.

Phone in hand, Vikram rolled his chair back and stared in her direction.

> Code Master: What germs?
>
> Numbers Girl: You told the accountant you didn't want to catch my cold.
>
> Code Master: I didn't say anything of the sort. I didn't even know you had a cold.
>
> Numbers Girl: Why were you sending me a memo? Everyone else in the universe got to talk to you.

Code Master: What's wrong with sending a—you know what? This is absurd.

Leaping from the chair, he strode out. Pulse pounding erratically, she watched him get closer. His slacks were a deep grey and creased to perfection. Black shoes were polished to a gleam. Vikram was unusually well-dressed today. He was probably wearing that woodsy cologne of his, too. Was he meeting someone after work? A woman?

An elbow resting on top of the partition between her cubicle and the next, he studied her. "You look terrible."

"Thanks a lot!" Her nose might have been bright pink, her eyes puffy, and her curls sticking out in a hundred directions, but he didn't have to point it out! Especially, not when *he* was looking like a million bucks. Her own clothes were nothing special. She'd opted for the comfort of khaki slacks and a soft shirt in dark red. Her well-manicured toes were hidden by an old pair of flat pumps. "This is the second time you've been mean about my looks."

"Huh? Oh, the text."

As though he hadn't compared her disfavourably to the reigning queen of Bollywood. Over her teen years, Seema had come to the sad realisation she was never going to be a ravishing beauty, but she didn't need to be constantly reminded of the fact. "There *are* people who think I'm cute," she mumbled.

"Don't be ridiculous," said Vikram. She was about to toss the rice and dal into his face when he added, "You're more than cute. Lovely, to be honest."

She was? "Maybe, when I don't have a cold," she allowed, biting back a goofy grin.

"Why did you come to work if you're sick?" Vikram asked.

Seema couldn't help it. She bared her teeth and hissed. "Your henchman told me the EU project would fall apart if I didn't show up. When I got here, you gave me extra work!"

"I didn't know... do you want to go home?"

"Now? I'm halfway done with the client's requirements. If I give it to someone else at this point, it will take more time."

Agitatedly mussing his hair with a hand, Vikram asked, "Will you be able to handle it? I don't want you fainting."

"I'll be fine," Seema said, softening her voice. "Krishnan brought me some cough syrup."

"Who?"

"Krishnan, the chaiwalla," Seema reminded Vikram. "He got me lunch, too."

Tone envious, Vikram asked, "Really?" His eyes went to the open containers.

Seema turned to the food, and with the spoon, scooped small portions into one of the lids. It looked delicious, but she didn't think she'd be able to keep much down. Pouring dal over the remainder of the rice, she handed the box to Vikram.

He pulled a chair from the cubicle across the aisle and sat, commenting, "You're left-handed."

"Yup. You superstitious?"

"Super—" He chuckled. "I only asked because I am, too."

Seema was absurdly pleased at the titbit. "Oh, yeah? In that case, we should stick together." She could've bitten off her tongue. What a stupid thing to say.

Absently, Vikram agreed, "Lefties of the world, unite." His gaze was on the food. Within minutes, he polished it all off and set the steel container back on the table. "I didn't realise I was this hungry."

Seema loved messing around with computers, but she never ever lost sight of priorities as he did. Food always came first. Today, though... her whole mouth felt cottony. Aimlessly stirring her small share of rice, she asked, "How can you possibly not realise?"

"I started working, lost my sense of time..." He shrugged.

"You really enjoy what you do," Seema commented.

Even in school, she'd relished taking apart digital systems, but she'd never paid much attention to the business side of it, and her auntie never let her hang with any other hackers. She'd never heard of Vikram Joshi before she started the job. It was only with this project she discovered he was the architect of the fortress within which the company housed their systems. After their WhatsApp encounter, she did some checking into his background.

By the age of nine, he was already a superstar in Mumbai's hacking circles. "Security researcher" was the official term used by the companies which ran the contests. He'd been considered extraordinarily gifted by his professors in IIT.

"I heard you were the one who made the modifications to the original product," she said. "I love it."

Slight puzzlement on his face, he asked, "You do?"

"The firewall algorithm has a nice beat to it. Musical."

"I play the guitar." His tone was tentative as though he weren't sure of her reaction.

"I don't play anything," she said. "But I love to dance."

"What kind?"

"Heh? Oh... I never took lessons. If I see it once, I can follow along."

"*I* took lessons," he admitted.

"Seriously?"

"Seriously. My nanaji had a friend who—long story. She taught me all kinds of dancing. Tango, samba, Marathi folk, even breakdancing..."

Inside Seema's body, her unruly hormones jerked to attention. Suddenly, she had a vision of a shirtless Vikram, swaying in time to—hurriedly blinking away the image, she said, "No wonder the firewall sounds like a song."

"I wanted to call it 'Firesong,'" he confessed.

"I can see why." Thank God he didn't know what was going through her pervy mind.

"You're the only one who does. Except for Adhith, I mean. I don't think he understands, either. He just doesn't look at me like I have a screw loose. Everyone else does."

"No, they don't," she said, promptly. "They simply don't know how to react to genius. Everyone who works here thinks you'll eventually open your own firm."

"I plan to someday."

"What's the holdup?"

"The usual. Money."

"Can't you get a bank loan?" She licked the hot and sour mango pickle off the spoon.

"Funny thing about banks," he said, eyes crinkling. "They won't give you a loan until they're convinced you can pay it back. Adhith offered to have his father talk to them, but I want them convinced by the merit of my proposal, not political recommendations."

"How do you intend to make it happen?"

"By putting my own cash into the project. I've been saving for it since the day I started this job." Leaning forwards with an eager expression on his face, Vikram elaborated on his plan. Even with a bank loan, he wouldn't have enough funds for a big splash, so he'd start with small clients—standalone department stores, schools, those who couldn't afford the bigger cybersecurity companies. He'd have to make up for the lower charges with the number of hours he worked.

Incredible. Talk in the office was he came from money. Add to it the degree from IIT and the job at one of the world's largest cybersecurity firms. There was his best friend with political connections. Even with everything going for him, Vikram was determined to strike out on his own.

"I'm going to get there," he finished.

"You are," she agreed, smiling helplessly at his enthusiasm.

For a couple of seconds, he stared at her in silence. A red flush spread across his cheekbones. "Did I bore you?"

"Not at all. I was thinking... this is the first time we've talked. Face-to-face, I mean." She'd heard him speak, but his lovely baritone hadn't registered until today. His voice was manly, like the rest of him. *Down, girl,* she admonished herself.

"We've talked before." He waggled his eyebrows. "Remember the day we met? And after you pretended to be Adhi?"

She stuck out her tongue. "You can't count those as real meetings."

"Can, too. I learned some new words from you."

She let loose with a stream of curses, making him guffaw. Still laughing, he asked, "Why were you pretending to be a prude? This is the twenty-first century. No one would've held your childhood against you."

Of course. He'd looked her up. "Not everyone thinks like you." Her supposed boyfriend obviously didn't. She shoved Adhith and the Verma project out of her mind. She was on personal time. A few moments here and there were not much to ask for.

Although... the friendship between Adhith and Vikram ran deeper than former roomies. Seema kept in touch with her college buddies and had faithfully attended half-a-dozen weddings by now, but she didn't have anyone she couldn't do without. Even her colleagues at the income tax department were kept at arm's length. Her current flatmate was the first one who knew some of her past, but as soon as the Verma investigation was done, it would have to be "buh-bye, Gayathri."

There was a trace of envy in Seema at Vikram and Adhith's friendship. They were more like brothers, destined to always be part of each other's lives. Here was Seema, chatting one up while working on tossing the other in prison. An itch started in her chest. *Go away,* she crossly ordered her conscience. It had a habit of popping its head out at the most inconvenient times.

The itch became a tickle rising to her nose. Nope, not her conscience. She was going to sneeze. A humongous sneeze right in front of Vikram! Seema set her food on the desk and frantically reached for the box of tissues. "Ahh... ahh... ahhchoo." She wiped the snot off her face, daring a quick glance at the soiled tissue. *Yuck. What a revolting green.*

"God bless you." He scooted his chair close to place a cool hand on her forehead. "You're warm."

"You'll catch my cold," she objected, fighting the urge to nuzzle his palm like a contented cat.

Vikram reached beyond her to pick up the bottle of cough syrup. "You'd better take some." Reading the label, he frowned. "This is going to make you sleepy."

Seema sighed. "Why did you have to turn back into The Jerk?"

His mouth dropped open. "What did I do?"

"'This is gonna make me sleepy,'" she quoted, feeling thoroughly disagreeable. "You're worried I might not be able to do any work."

He scowled. "Nuh-huh. Not what I meant."

"Okay, what *did* you mean?"

"Only that you're going to need someone to take you home... tell you what, if you can wait, I'll drop you back."

Seema was getting angrier by the second. He was obviously dressed for an evening out. Did he seriously expect her to wait until he waved goodbye to his lady friend?

Vikram continued, "The EU client's local representative is coming by after five, but the meeting shouldn't take more than half an hour. An hour, at the most."

Client meeting? No wonder he'd been upset Adhith hadn't turned up to work. Everyone in the office knew Vikram delegated customer relations to his friend. Feeling idiotic, Seema muttered, "Oh... umm... fine. I'll wait for you."

He grinned. Her heart skipped a beat. "Am I still a jerk?" he asked.

"My flatmate says bosses are always jerks. It's a job requirement. *You* are a nice jerk."

"Thank you," he said, his humble tone setting them both off. There was a scuffling sound from the glass door at the entrance. The morning security guard was up from his seat, making room for his afternoon colleague. "Lunch hour is done," Vikram said. "I'd better get back."

He hadn't taken three steps before she called, "Hey."

Vikram turned back, a question in his eyes.

"Fix your hair before the meeting."

"Fix my... oh, right. I always mess it up." Like she hadn't noticed. "Hair's the least of my worries," he grumbled. "I wish Adhith had shown up. Usually, he does the talking."

"You'll be fine. Just imagine them all naked."

Vikram grimaced. "Won't work. Not in this case."

"Why not?" she demanded. "That's what all the advice columns say."

"I'm sure," he agreed, snorting. "Those columnists have never met our EU client."

She was still laughing when he reached his desk and settled into his chair. The rest of the staff trickled into the office. The trickle became a deluge. All around Seema, a sea of humanity toiled. She was on a rock, a safe place, tendrils of something she dared not name anchoring her to the man in the manager's room.

Chapter 7

The scooter cruised across the airspace between the roofs of two skyscrapers. "Woohoo," shouted Seema, one hand keeping the helmet on her head.

"Hold on to the bars," said someone.

Startled, Seema looked left. Her auntie was sailing through the air, superhero style, red cape fluttering behind. "I didn't know you could fly," Seema said, wonderingly.

"I can dance; I can fly," sang Madhu. "I can dance while I fly." Twirling in mid-air, she executed a perfect hip thrust.

"Dance and fly," crooned Seema, swaying her shoulders. "While we verifyyy... tax retuuurns..."

"Seema," said a voice.

"Seema," the traffic policeman called from her other side. With the usual white shirt and khaki pants, he was wearing a navy-blue cape. Ballpoint pen in hand, he scribbled in his notepad. "Dancing while flying a scooter is illegal."

"How do you know my name?" she asked.

"We work together." The voice sounded amused.

A hand landed on her shoulder. Who was this new fella? "Go away. Can't you see we're busy?"

"All right. We'll sit here and wait until you finish whatever you're doing."

Seriously? Didn't this person understand crime-fighting was important business? She tried to open her eyes, intending to tell the intruder off, but her lids were so heavy. Gritty. With a great deal of effort, she managed to pry them apart enough to see a blurry form. She wasn't dreaming. There was a man in front of her. Her hand instinctively darted to her waist, to the side

88

where the Glock was concealed. The blurry shape sharpened into Vikr—

"Vikram?" Seema withdrew her hand.

A second voice—also male—said, "I'm sorry, Ms Rawat. *I* insisted on an introduction."

She turned her head and somehow managed not to scream. A ghoul. A freakishly pale man who looked like he'd stepped off a "how-not-to" magazine on plastic surgery. Fashionably skinny, blond, and skin stretched so tightly over his cheekbones the outer angles of his eyes were nearly at his hairline.

The fog in her head dissipated. She was curled up in her chair, not on the scooter she'd owned in college. She'd fallen asleep, waiting for Vikram.

"Mr Peeters," introduced Vikram, smile apologetic. "You've been emailing back and forth with him all day. When I told him you'd stayed to finish the work despite being sick, he wanted to meet you."

The EU client's local representative.

Smoothing back her hair, she uncurled herself and stood. Except for them, the office was empty. One of the good things about Imperium was their schedule. Unlike the other IT companies in India, Imperium assigned employees around the world to the same projects, so except for those in charge—like Vikram—no one was expected to work unreasonable hours, covering the clients. This kept the governments and the unions across the planet happy with the company.

"I told Vikram I wasn't leaving without talking to you," said the client, tone jovial. "Not when you were right here."

Ever think of being considerate? Biting back the retort, Seema smiled. "It's good to put a face to the name." Despite being hoarse from the cold, she kept her voice as polished as the British queen's.

Vikram's expression changed from wary to amazed. What did he think she was going to do? Curse at the ghoul for disturbing her nap?

In the ten minutes it took them to hustle the client out, night was already falling on the city. The tan stray dog who'd claimed the block bounded to them, whining. Peeters eyed the new arrival warily, his sigh of relief audible as a taxi drove up to the curb.

Climbing in, Peeters said to Seema, "I hope you visit Brussels with the rest of the site team. Take a couple of days off after work is done. I'd love to show you around my country."

Was he hitting on her? Seema couldn't tell.

Vikram's possessive arm settled around her shoulders, his thumb pushing aside the strap of her purse to rub circles on her sleeve. "We'll see what we can do."

What the— There was a light warning squeeze on her deltoid. *Ahh.* She got it. Vikram was making it easy for her to reject the ghoul's advances. *If* it were an advance. Seema moved closer to Vikram's warmth. Since his laptop bag was slung over his other shoulder, it was easy for her to rub her cheek against his chest.

He muttered under his breath, saying something about "overacting."

Eyes darting between them, Peeters coughed. "I'll get going. Don't want to miss the flight."

The dog barked in agreement.

As soon as the taxi drove away, Vikram removed his arm. Seema held up a fist. "Not bad, Mr Joshi."

They bumped knuckles. "We make a good team, Ms Rawat." Digging into his laptop bag, he came up with a couple of biscuits and tossed it to the waiting dog. With an embarrassed smile, Vikram added, "It's become something of a ritual."

"There's a cat near my flat I feed," Seema said.

"I'm a dog person, but I don't mind cats."

Foolishly, they grinned at each other. Her heart thudded. Were *they* flirting? She'd never been able to tell where friendly conversation ended and the banter of romance started. Did the delight in his gaze when it landed on her mean something more than casual amiability? What about his hand cupping her cheek to check for fever? The arm he'd wrapped around her shoulders? Was she gonna have to wait until he initiated a liplock to be certain? Could *she* plant one on him? What if he ran, screaming in horror?

When Seema got home, she was going to have a heart-to-heart with her flatmate. Gayathri always had the answers to such things.

Vikram's eyes darted to the end of the street. "There's *our* taxi."

Sliding sideways into the backseat, Seema settled her purse on her lap. "What happened to your car?"

Vikram set his laptop bag by his shoes. "I don't have one."

"A bike?"

"Not even a moped."

"Why not?" Seema demanded. "Don't they pay you enough? I thought your family had money."

"You're nosy."

"I know," she preened.

"It was *not* a compliment," he said, severely.

"I know that, too."

Laughing, he raised both hands and bowed in surrender.

"Address, please," chimed in the driver.

Once the car was speeding towards Seema's flat, Vikram said, "Yeah, they pay me enough, and no, I don't take money from my family. A vehicle is an unnecessary expense at this time. Not merely the cost. I'd have to pay for petrol, maintenance... can't afford it."

"Can't affor—right. You're saving up for your business. How do you get to work?"

"Like thousands of other people in Mumbai, I use the bus."

Tonight, he'd splurged on a cab. For *her. And* he thought she was more than cute. Something inside her chest turned into mushy goo. Thank God for the half ounce of sense left in her brain, or she might have slobbered all over him and blown her cover. "Man, you're disciplined."

"Not kanjoos?"

"Miserliness is when you refuse to spend for no reason at all. *You* have an excellent reason. Your future."

With a pleased smile, he said, "Once the EU project goes through, I'm supposed to get a bonus. The cash will help. Everyone in the team is supposed to get a little extra with the paycheck."

She hadn't known that.

They chatted for a while about the EU project. "You *will* probably need to go to Brussels with the site team," Vikram said.

Would she? As soon as Seema got what she needed from Adhith Verma's devices, she'd return to her actual job. Pushing the thought into a dark corner of her mind, Seema said, "Yeah, your henchman told me to get a passport when I first started the job."

"Poor Britto. Does he know what you call him?"

"Poor, my—he made me come to work when I was sick! I could've died!"

Vikram deserved credit for not rolling his eyes. "It gave me a chance to talk to you," he argued.

Her pulse skittered. Calling her lovely, acting possessive in front of the client, the melting smiles, the cab ride, the pleasure in her company... Vikram *had* to be flirting. Flirting meant romantic intentions. Well, to Seema, anyway. She might not be a village belle from the hills of Himachal, but she was a middle-class Indian girl. When they weren't involved in covert operations, middle-class Indian girls took flirting very seriously. Like happy-ever-after seriously. Only, Seema *was* involved in a covert operation.

"Also, you made quite an impression on the EU client," Vikram continued as though he hadn't made her spin a thousand dreams in a couple of nanoseconds. "I'm sorry I woke you, but he wouldn't take no for an answer. I wasn't expecting him to hit on you."

"It's fine. It wasn't like you could refuse when he could see me sitting right there. He's not going to chat me up, again. Not when he thinks I have a macho boyfriend."

"Mach—me?"

"Yeah, you. I almost expected you to thump your chest and growl 'mine.'"

Vikram guffawed. "I never thought of myself as a... a..."

"Caveman?" she teased.

"I don't know. What's better? Caveman or jerk?"

"Both are better than ghoul."

"Who?" asked Vikram.

"Duh. The client. Doesn't he look exactly like a ghoul?"

Vikram stared for a moment before going into fits of laughter. "I'm going to be thinking of it each time I talk to him. Hope I don't say it out loud."

"Oy," Seema said. "There goes our bonus."

"There goes my future," he agreed, mock-dolefully.

Seema snapped her fingers. "Pfft. You're going to make it with or without the ghoul."

An incredibly sweet smile softened Vikram's features. "Thank you for the vote of confidence. What about your plans? What do you want to do with your life?"

"*My* plans?"

"Don't tell me you don't have any," he teased. "I got to see your downtime research from the last couple of months. It's why I asked you to work with the EU client."

Seema flushed. One of the nice things about her fake job was the policy they had in place which actively encouraged *all* employees, and not only those hired to do research and development, to work on projects that interested them. She'd been tinkering around with a few ideas of her own in the time allotted.

"You have a brilliant mind," he enthused. "I'm sure you have something planned for your future."

Outside, a bus honked and sped past. Lights from the shops and streetlamps melded into one continuous stream. Through the partially open window behind Vikram, the dusty smell of the city filtered in.

This was the second time today someone asked about her career plans. What *did* she want from her future? Did she see herself continuing in the income tax department? Her current assignment was interesting. If she succeeded in bringing Minister Verma and his son down, bigger and better things waited around the corner. Promotion. Better salary. Autonomy from Madhu. Was that all she wanted from life?

"I want to prove myself," Seema said. "Beyond that..."

"Prove yourself to whom?"

"My auntie."

"The one who brought you up?"

Seema grimaced. "She thinks I'm still twelve. I need to show her I can do it on my own without having her hovering over my shoulder, double-checking everything."

"Do what? The job? You should introduce her to the ghoul. He was impressed."

Seema shrugged. "Numbers and patterns are easy."

"You simply have to figure out the vantage point," Vikram agreed. "*I* was more impressed you didn't cuss him out."

"I don't cuss at clients," she said, nose in the air.

"Only at bosses," he said, laughing. "Hey, if you *had* given the ghoul an earful, you could've stopped him on your own."

"Hmph." Shuddering, Seema added, "Nope, not introducing him to auntie. She'd beat him up and order me back home. Once I refused, she'd apply for a job with you just so she could keep an eye on me."

Morosely, Vikram said. "Be happy you have someone who cares. I bet my parents couldn't tell you which company I work for."

"What do they do?"

"They're both doctors. My sister, too. And the dumbass."

"Dumbass?"

"My brother-in-law."

"Oh... *that* kind of brother-in-law."

He nodded. "You have *no* idea."

"Family of doctors."

"Yes. The Joshis used to be astrologers in the old days. My father says his great-something-grandfather became a physician in Chhatrapati Shivaji's court. After him, the line of sons going into medicine was unbroken... until me."

Wow. The emperor Vikram mentioned lived in the 1600s. The Joshis had been doctors since then. "What did your parents say when you decided on IIT?" Seema asked.

"My father went to the hospital where I was born to make sure I was actually theirs."

Seema's jaw dropped open.

"Kidding," he said, laughing. "I thought it might appeal to your sense of drama. He sat me down and asked me to reconsider. When I refused, he said to my mother—and I quote—'doesn't matter; we have Anju.'"

Anju had to be the sister. Seema waited for him to detail the angry scenes following. When he showed no signs of going on, she asked, "That was it?"

He shrugged.

"Oy," Seema marvelled. She tried hard to picture a similar scenario in her own household. They wouldn't have quarrelled over the degree she'd chosen for herself. As long as Seema could support herself, Madhu wouldn't have cared. Yet when it came to things she believed in, it was her way or the... actually, only her way. "Cool parents," Seema mused. "You're lucky they let you do what you wanted. I mean, you're their only son. Lots of families would've insisted."

Vikram's brows drew together, forming one thick line above his eyes. "Yeah, it's why the dumbass is 'our son-in-law, the neurosurgeon,' and *I'm* 'oh, he does something with computers.'"

The grumpy look on his face was so adorable Seema was highly tempted to pinch his cheeks.

"Anju's pregnant," he announced. The tone was bemused, but there was a thread of excitement running through the words.

"Your sister?"

"Yeah. My parents are thrilled." From the glint of enthusiasm in his eyes, so was the prospective uncle.

Loud honks sounded all around. The car came to a screeching halt. She peered into the night. "Traffic jam," said the driver. "We're only a couple of blocks from the address. Walking distance."

"We'll wait." Vikram's gaze darted to Seema. "Unless..."

"We'll wait," she agreed, tucking an unruly curl behind her ear. She couldn't bear to leave. Not yet. "So that's why you're working so hard. You want to rub your success in the dumbass's face."

He shook his head. "The thought crossed my mind a time or two, but I also want it for myself. Like you, I want to do it all on my own."

"So no car."

"No car, no holidays, no eating out, no wom—" Vikram broke off, leaving a sudden silence inside the vehicle. Awkward, uncomfortable silence. His gaze ricocheted around the car before returning to her. His mouth parted as though he were surprised to find himself with her. "I don't want you to misunderstand. I'm taking you home only because you're one of my staff."

A jolt. The joy inside Seema shrivelled into nothing. Humiliation slapped her across her face.

Ears turning a dull red, Vikram looked away.

To save her face at least if not the mission, Seema knew she should laugh off the awkwardness. Instead, she snarled, "Maybe you were away from India too long. Or maybe you're not used to middle-class women like me. In *my* world, you don't share a girl's lunch, flirt with her, put your hands on her, and take her home if she's *just staff.*"

"Seema..." Vikram's eyes darted meaningfully towards the back of the driver's head.

"You're not just a jerk," she said, her tone wild. "You're a jerk-*face.*"

"I'm not—what the hell's a jerk-face?"

From the front, the driver hazarded, "Maybe a jerk worse than other jerks? She's right, saab. You shouldn't have led her on and broken her heart."

Vikram howled, "But I didn't—"

"Driver," Seema called, trembling in anger. "I changed my mind. I'm getting out here. Jerk-face will pay full fare."

"Wait," Vikram said, a light hand on her forearm. "I didn't mean to make you angry."

Purse gripped tight, she opened the door next to her and slipped out.

"Seema, stop," called Vikram.

A hand on the roof of the car, she did pause for a couple of seconds, allowing the surroundings to steady. The pleasure of bantering with Vikram had masked the dizziness from the cough syrup.

She stumbled between halted vehicles, ignoring the honks and the shouts. At the footpath, she skirted the beggar with the scraggly beard thrusting his aluminium dish under her nose.

She stepped on something squishy. Her foot flew out from under her. The pavement rushed up to meet her face. She screamed. With a hairbreadth of space left between her nose and the road, a pair of hands hauled her upright. The universe seesawed around her.

"Slow down," said Vikram. "You don't want to fall."

She shrugged off his hold. "Go away."

"I will. As soon as I make sure you're safely inside your home. You're too ill to make it back on your own."

"Why do you care?"

"As I said, you're one of my staff."

"Really?" she asked, throat hurting. "Jerk-face. Bloody, *cheating* jerk-face."

He goggled. "Cheating? *Me?* You're *Adhith's* girlfriend."

"'Adhith's girlfriend,'" she mocked. *"You* told him I was cussing. *You* made sure he ditched me. I'm no one's girlfriend now."

Vikram's face twisted into an ugly snarl. "I wish I *had* talked him into ditching you. Instead, he's making plans to *marry* you."

"What?" The noises of the street went on. Vikram continued his tirade, saying something about Adhith talking to his father about Seema. Her thoughts whirled. Adhith wanted to marry her? "I... I hadn't intended... oh, my God... what am I supposed to do?" She'd never imagined things getting this far. She'd never intended to get Adhith so emotionally involved as to propose marriage. "I... I..." Seema turned and limped away, needing to think.

"Where are you—slow down, please." Vikram jogged to her side. Thankfully, he stayed silent until they got to her building. Inside the lift, he asked, "Which floor?"

"Fifth."

The ancient box moved up, lurching side to side. "Okay," he said, tone pleading. "It wasn't because you're part of the staff. We started talking, and I got caught up in it. I didn't remember I'm supposed to be off... Seema, there's no space in my life for women. I have no time or energy for another person. Dammit, I didn't even *think* of Adhith. I should have."

"Did you make it up? About Adhith wanting to marry me?" Desperately, she prayed for Vikram to admit he'd cooked up the whole thing. She didn't want the guilt on her conscience.

"No." He sighed. "Adhith does want to... he's one of the good guys... uhh... generally."

"Is this where you encourage me to marry your best friend?" she jeered.

The bell pinged. They were on her floor. They both got out, and a hand blocking the lift door, Vikram waited for Seema to let herself into the flat. Her fingers were shaking. After three attempts to put the key in the hole, she ignored Vikram's offer of help and stabbed at the doorbell for her flatmate to let her in.

"Get this straight, Seema," he said, vehemently. "You and Adhith would be a terrible match."

"Now, you show your true colours," she said, a tearing pain in her chest. "What was it you said? 'No one's going to hold your childhood against you'?"

When the sounds of the lock being clicked open filtered out, he slipped back into the lift. "It's not because of your... you and Adhith won't gel, all right? *And* I don't know if I can handle seeing you as his wife."

The lift doors slid shut. "Oh, yeah?" she screamed at the closed door. "It's not *your* decision to make."

***

All Seema wanted to do was crawl into bed and have herself a good cry. Except, Gayathri, her flatmate, blocked her way. "Who were you screaming at?"

"Nobod—I don't know his name. Who cares, anyway? He's gone. Let me in, please."

A finger to her lips, Gayathri jerked her head sideways.

"What?" asked Seema. Her legs were wobbly. "If you don't let me walk in right now, you're gonna have to *carry* me in."

Tossing a furtive glance back into the living room, Gayathri hissed, "Auntieji is here."

"Auntieji—*Madhu?*"

"*Shh.* She looks upset."

"*She's* upset? She's not even supposed to be here!"

Leaving Gayathri making squawking noises, Seema stumbled in. On the sofa was her auntie clad in her customary cotton hoodie and jeans. Drop-dead gorgeous, as always.

Jiggling a foot, Madhu said, "You look terrible."

The same words Seema had heard from Vikram right before he lured her in with sweet talk and a tender smile, only to toss her aside by the end of the day. A monster roared in her brain. "Go back home, Madhu."

"Seema," exclaimed her flatmate. "Don't talk like that to Auntieji... you call her by her *name?*"

"It's not a big deal," said Madhu. "She's always done it."

The refusal to acknowledge their relationship started during Seema's rebellion against being taken from familiar surroundings. The child psychologist Madhu brought her niece to recommended ignoring the small act of defiance if it gave the girl a feeling of control.

Gayathri continued, "She said there was some kind of family emergency she needed to discuss."

Logical excuse, since Gayathri wasn't aware of the investigation. Seema's flatmate knew about her Grant Road background and about the prickly relationship between Seema and her auntie but no more. Seema wasn't gonna keep up her coy girl persona at home, so she'd come clean on her childhood. Plus, Gayathri wasn't likely to encounter anyone at Imperium and blow Seema's cover. It didn't matter since Seema had partially blown her own damned cover.

"Oh?" snapped Seema, not taking her eyes off the woman on the sofa. "Calling to check on me every hour wasn't enough? You decided to tell my friends how useless you think I am?"

Madhu stood, her gaze sweeping over her niece. "You're ill. Have you seen a doctor?"

"No, I haven't. I was too busy doing my job. The one you think I'm so bad at?"

"Stop it," said Madhu, tone low and firm. In a couple of strides, she was next to Seema, a hand cupping her cheek. "Not much of a fever."

"I took some cough sy—" Seema swept aside Madhu's hand. "Why am I bothering to explain? You're not supposed to be here!"

"Oh, yes, I am. We need to talk." When Seema refused to respond, Madhu softened her voice. "Please? It's important."

In the privacy of Seema's bedroom, Madhu did a 360, taking in the tidily made single bed, the laptop on the desk, the chargers with their wires neatly tied up. There was a vase with fake roses on a small table next to the bed. "Perfect." Another thing they had in common. Neither could abide clutter.

The window on the right overlooked an alley. As usual, there were kids on the street, playing cricket, shouting, screaming.

Seema turned on the ceiling fan and paused only to place the Glock on the side table. She collapsed into the bed, not even bothering to kick off her shoes. Her legs were too weak to hold her up, and anything Madhu had to say could be heard equally as well from the mattress.

"Where's the cough syrup?" Madhu asked.

"In my purse." The blades of the fan circulated warm air in the room. Shivering, Seema tugged one of the pillows to her chest and curled around it.

In two minutes, a capful of the pink liquid was thrust under Seema's nose. "I'll take you to Dr Deshpande and get you antibiotics. But his clinic doesn't open until nine."

With a sound somewhere between a laugh and a groan, Seema said, "Deshpande is a paediatrician. I'm twenty-four, Madhu."

"He knows you best. He's been your doctor since you were twelve."

He knew best, she knew best... "Theme of my life," Seema muttered, sitting to down the medicine. Why did medicine always have to taste so... *medicine-y?* She frowned, hoping she didn't overdose or something. It was barely a couple of hours since the last dose, but the headache was excruciating. Her throat felt so tight and swollen it was a wonder she was still breathing. "Why are you here?" she asked.

To her surprise, Madhu's gaze skittered away.

Seema tossed the empty cap to the side table. "What did you do?"

With a rueful sigh, Madhu sat next to her on the mattress. "Look, Seema. You're young—"

"I'm the same age you were when you dragged me out of the slums."

"My life was different. I'd been on my own for years before I got you. I tried my best to protect you. Unfortunately, it left you naïve in a lot of ways. About men, especially."

Seema yawned. "I'm ill, Madhu. And sleepy. Not in the mood for a recap of my own life. Just tell me what you did."

"I met Adhith Verma."

For a few seconds, Seema stared. "You did not just say that."

"Seema, I—"

"You met with the suspect I'm supposed to bring in? The suspect in a *covert investigation?*"

"I was afraid you'd stopped seeing him as a suspect."

"What's that supposed to mean?" Her shout came out squeaky, but Seema didn't care.

"Something you said... men like Adhith may be attractive, but they use their charms to fool people."

Attractive? Okay, the Bengali girl from the office said the same thing, but Madhu was too smart to fall under the spell of some smooth talker. "Tell me everything," Seema snapped. "I hope to God you haven't completely compromised the investigation."

Madhu detailed her trip to Grant Road, tailing Adhith Verma. She recounted every minute of her reconnaissance, starting with the argument between Vikram and Adhith.

Seema flushed. Madhu did see Vikram. She didn't seem to have paid much attention to him, though. Thank God. Seema didn't need her auntie interfering in her... what, exactly? Vikram already made it clear there would be no romance.

Yawning again, she tried to focus on what Madhu was saying. Her voice echoed, but Seema caught enough words here and there to know there was plenty of reason to be livid. "You told Adhith who you were," she accused, none of the outrage she intended in her tone. "What a damn fool thing to do. You're..." The room tilted. Seema blinked hard, trying to bring everything back into focus. "You're supposed to be the *director.*"

Red colour stained Madhu's cheeks. "I didn't tell him. He IDed me because he already had some of the information on you."

Which Vikram only thought of looking for because Seema gave herself away, cursing and carrying on in his loo—something Madhu didn't need to know. "Doesn't matter," Seema said. "What matters is you went there and made contact when you were not supposed to. You compromised the investigation. I'll have to let IB know."

Eyes angry, Madhu said, "I was trying to stop you from compromising your *safety.*"

"How?"

"I was trying to get proof he cannot be trusted. Chocolate boy looks and a tennis player body don't mean anything if he doesn't have a moral compass. Tall and handsome translates to hero only in the movies."

Vikram's face was arresting, and he had a better build. He was also taller than his friend by an inch or so. Adhith's warm voice was pleasant, but Vikram's lovely baritone caused every hair on Seema's form to stand and sing *"Ang laga de re."* Like the heroine in the song, Seema was ready to beg Vikram to touch her body with his. He was super smart, *and* he had a moral compass. All in all, a gorgeous specimen of masculinity. Except...

"None of it means anything," Seema muttered, "if he's not into you."

"You already know?"

"Know what?" Seema asked, flopping back onto the mattress. The light was so bright. Too bright. She closed her eyes.

"That he doesn't want to marry you?"

Seema didn't need any reminders of her disastrous evening with Vikram. She frowned. Madhu wasn't talking about Vikram, was she? "Who're you talking about? The jerk?"

"It's exactly what I've been trying to tell you. He *is* a jerk."

"He's nice when he forgets to be a jerk," Seema mumbled. "What you see is what you get."

"Oh, my God. Have you heard *anything* I've been saying?" Madhu asked, despairingly. "Seema, Adhith Verma is not the right man for you."

Vikram's words. How many people were going to tell her the same thing? Sputtering, she asked, "Why? Because you couldn't handle seeing me as his wife?"

"What the hell's *that* supposed to mean?"

He didn't tell me, Seema tried to say, but her tongue wouldn't cooperate. Leaving Madhu to her tirade, Seema sank into sleep.

Chapter 8

Leaning against the balustrade, Adhith kept his gaze fixed on the green lawn below. On the grass, a pair of slate-coloured pigeons battled over an overripe mango, circling each other with guttural coos and flapping wings. Like the birds, Papaji kept his voice low, but frustration was evident in every word.

Adhith's trips to the Sahyadri Guest House when Papaji was visiting Mumbai were always cherished by father and son. Normally, they would've sipped ice-cold sherbet and debated the pivotal moments in history leading to the metamorphosis of Malabar Hill from rocky jungle to one of the world's most expensive pieces of real estate. They would've quizzed each other on the various governors who'd ruled Mumbai, obsessively tallying scores to the bemusement of the minister's staff.

Today, Papaji was not in the mood to talk about anything other than his son's bizarre plans for his future.

"Seema is not a topic open for negotiation." Adhith scratched the back of his sweaty neck. The air was so thick with humid heat it was hard even to breathe. He wished he could've ordered beer instead of the fruity beverage. Unfortunately, not when his father was around. Oh, Papaji knew his son enjoyed an alcoholic drink here and there, and so did anyone else who cared to know, but to imbibe in the presence of a parent was considered bad form. Disrespectful.

No one—not even staffers—could be allowed to think Adhith Verma was anything but a model son. His current disobedience would be dismissed as the foolishness of a young man in love, but open rebellion would not only create personal hurt, it would destroy their public image as ideal father and son. Appearances needed to be maintained.

Papaji sighed. "Betay, I've always encouraged you to be your own man, but as your parent, I'm also duty-bound to intervene when I see you making a life-altering mistake. We need to talk about this girl."

Which meant they wouldn't be talking about Adhith contesting in the bypoll to replace the retiring MP. Silently, Adhith begged Seema for forgiveness. He wasn't proud of himself for using her like this, but she was his best bet for getting out of this conundrum.

Adhith would need another excuse to extricate himself from his father's network of colleagues and supporters and strike out on his own without hurting Papaji personally or politically. The unsuitability of Seema as Mrs Adhith Verma could be used to delay things until he found such an excuse. He had no plans to marry her, but he could use her past to further his future.

"You're not good enough for my Seema," hissed a female voice from his recent memory.

According to Madhubala Rawat, Adhith was the unworthy one. *Auntie, my ass.* Madhubala looked like no auntie he'd ever seen. Not with her gorgeous face and sexy body.

The woman bothered him. In one meeting, she'd judged him and dismissed him as wanting. After leaving the tea stall, she'd have hot-footed it to Seema's flat. Adhith meant to slowly break things off with Seema while keeping Papaji thinking the opposite, but once Seema heard from Madhubala Adhith had no intention of offering marriage, his initial gambit wasn't going to work. He needed to figure out a way to get Seema to play along. He'd stayed away from work for three days to avoid running into her until he came up with a fix to his problem.

Unfortunately, he still didn't know what he was going to say. He liked her well enough but wasn't prepared to offer marriage? And by the way, could she continue to be his girlfriend until he got what he wanted from his father? Afterwards, she'd have to quietly go away. Adhith tried to imagine the scene. Madhubala would take a front-row seat to gloat.

Dammit. The woman occupied too much of his mind. Her snooty attitude still grated. She was old enough to understand marriage was a big step, to be entered into with a lot of care.

"Seema won't fit into your life," Papaji continued.

It took Adhith a couple of seconds to drag his thoughts from Madhubala to Seema. "She fits in well enough."

"Into the life of an IT professional, yes," Papaji conceded. "It's not all you are. You're *my* son. Someday, you'll be a statesman in your own right. You'll be mingling with presidents and prime ministers, ambassadors, and business magnates. Do you believe a girl like her will be able to handle all it would entail? You'll be embarrassed, and *she'll* be miserable."

"You and I didn't come from wealth, Papaji. Until I was ten, all I knew was the convent school back home. When we moved to Delhi, neither of us even knew how to eat with cutlery. *We* managed."

"There's a difference between not knowing and knowing all the wrong things. Especially when your history is public information. Plus, not everyone's like us. We had the drive to learn."

"So does Seema."

"You have a great deal of confidence in this girl."

"Yes, I do." Adhith blinked, grasping with some surprise he did have confidence in her. Seema might have been pretending to be a village belle only because she was ashamed of her roots, but she'd pulled off the act. If Vikram hadn't overheard her in the manager's private bathroom, no one would've been the wiser. What she needed to learn was co-opting the truth was better than lying. Taking a sip of the sherbet, Adhith reflected, "It will take some doing, but the slum origins can be turned into a net positive." In a detached sort of way, he realised his statement was one hundred per cent accurate. Seema's story could be spun in the media. *If* he wanted to marry her.

"Hmm," mused Papaji. "You might be right. Tell you what. Prove to me she can do it."

"Huh?"

"I meant to ask you. Vikram's parents have invited me to The Oberoi for their anniversary dinner. I assume you're going?"

The dumbass would be there, so Vikram wasn't going. Adhith didn't plan to, either. He made a noncommittal grunt.

"Bring the girl there. Let's see how well she functions in the upper-class milieu."

Shit. This was getting complicated. "Are you going to scare her off?"

Impatiently, Papaji said, "Don't be ridiculous. I don't use such crass tactics. Also, if she can prove she won't be a liability, why wouldn't I want a girl with emotional investment in you?"

Adhith chuckled. "I think the word you're looking for is 'love.'"

Even as he said it, he wished he hadn't. There had been tenderness in his heart for the lost little soul from Sarkaghat. The foul-mouthed girl from the redlight district would've felt just as lost amid the young and fashionable crowds of South Mumbai. Still, after he learned of Seema's deception, there should've been anger. Oh, Adhith had been gloomy, but there was no... *heartbreak* for want of a better word. Instead, there was a disconnect. The awareness marriage between them was unlikely did not bring on the pain it should have.

He should've broken things off with Seema right then and there. Instead, he'd ended up blurting out her name to foil Papaji's plans. When Adhith met his best friend at the tea stall on Grant Road, he'd meant to talk about it. Vikram stalked out before Adhith could say a word, and Madhubala aimed her gun at his heart.

Adhith bit back a growl. The judgemental woman was driving him nuts even four days after their meeting. He needed to focus on Seema and Papaji's unexpected suggestion of bringing her to the dinner party. Adhith had only meant to use her name, not seriously present her as potential wife to his social circle.

Although... the solution he'd stumbled upon... he might be able to marry her as he'd originally intended. If Seema met expectations at the dinner party, even Papaji could be persuaded to accept the match. Yeah, that would still leave Adhith with the problem of evading Papaji's plans in favour of his own, but spinning Seema's story in the media could potentially take a year or two, buying him time. Funny how detached he felt about it.

"It won't be a fair setup," Adhith finally said. "Any woman would be nervous about meeting a prospective father-in-law, especially when he's a minister."

"I'll stay away," Papaji said, promptly. "Dr and Mrs Joshi should be able to tell me how the girl fares."

Adhith couldn't find any other objections to raise. Things were working out better than he'd hoped. Once everyone agreed on the match, and all details were planned out, even Madhubala Rawat would have no choice but to take her delectable backside off to some other corner and sulk. So why was Adhith attacked by this sudden urge to pound a punching bag?

***

"Hear me out, Vikram," Adhith pleaded, settling his hip on one corner of the desk. His eyes went to the cubicle maze outside the manager's office. He'd arrived at work early so they could have a face-to-face conversation without any of the staff overhearing. Without *Seema* overhearing. At 8:00 AM, the only other person around was the morning security guard.

With Papaji insisting on the dinner idea, Adhith needed his friend's help. Vikram still had no clue about Adhith's not-so-straightforward motivations, though. Vikram believed Adhith was only trying to see if Seema would fit the role of Mrs Verma.

"No," Vikram repeated, face thunderous. He paced the room, hurling a balled piece of paper into the wastebasket. "Firstly, I don't want to go to the damned dinner. Secondly, you show up to work after one week—"

"Three days. The rest was the weekend. Five days in total. I *was* working from home."

Vikram ground his teeth. "You knew the EU client was going to be here, and *I* had to ask HR to stop monitoring staff activity. The woman said she'd look into it."

Adhith bit back a smile. The HR director in San Jose preferred not to deal with Vikram. He was not as suave as she would've liked. "Bro." Adhith held both hands up. "I did know all this, and I'm sorry for staying away. I'm trying to tell you why."

"When you do show up," Vikram continued as though Adhith hadn't spoken, "you ask me to attend a dinner you know damned well I don't want to attend. Thirdly, I will not help you set up this stupid experiment to test Seema's worthiness. How could you put her through—you should be the one—" He made a vague gesture with his left hand. "You know."

"What?"

Vikram's face turned bright red. "Battling the world for her or something."

"Battling the—" Adhith guffawed. "What do you think this is? A costume drama? In the real world, we must take into consideration things like family and society and future plans. It won't be just her undergoing the test. *Madhubala* will have to decide if my lifestyle's something she can handle."

"Who?"

Hurriedly, Adhith corrected, "If Seema agrees to marry me, Madhubala will have to live with the decision." Yup, that's what he'd meant.

"Again, 'Madhubala' who?"

"Her auntie." The gun-toting temptress.

Vikram paused in his pacing, his shoulders slumping. Tone oddly strained, he asked, "Seema introduced you to her family?"

Scratching the back of his neck, Adhith debated coming clean. Not only about his encounter with Madhubala but also about his initial plan to use Seema as a weapon to break free of Papaji's political network. With Vikram's current belligerence, they were sure to have a replay of the argument at the tea stall. Only, a hundred times amplified.

Briefly, Adhith said, "Madhubala's the only family she has, and I just met her once." One meeting had been enough. Each time he remembered the gorgeous eyes shooting angry sparks at him, every nerve cell in his body fired up.

"It had to be after I got back to Mumbai," Vikram brooded. "Until we dug up Seema's history, you didn't even know anything about the auntie."

Vaguely, Adhith waved a hand. "A couple of days back."

Vikram's eyes narrowed. "Really?"

Adhith embellished, "Now you know why I needed to work from home. I had to make arrangements. You know, impressing future in-laws and such..."

Shutting the door to the room, Vikram returned to his chair. He hooked an ankle over the other knee and leaned back, glaring at Adhith.

Silently, Adhith stayed put, his hip on the corner of the desk, merely turning his head to return Vikram's stare.

After a minute or so, Vikram asked, "So in the five days you were off—"

"Three."

"—you made arrangements to meet Seema's auntie. Without a word to *me*."

"Bro, I planned to tell you. I wouldn't leave my best buddy out of one of the most important decisions of my life. Still, I wanted a one-on-one, first."

"Just you and the auntie?"

Annoyed, Adhith said, "Can you *please* stop calling her 'auntie'? She's not related to you or me. Plus, she's too young for it. Only thirty-six. Her name's Madhubala."

"Whatever. You met her? Just her?"

"Seema, too, obviously," Adhith lied.

"The three of you met?"

Adhith rolled his eyes. "Yeah, the three of us met."

"When did your papaji come up with this dinner plan? Before or after the meeting?"

"Papaji hasn't met Seema or Madhubala yet. He's not going to be at the dinner, either. He's planning to ask your mom to see how Seema does."

"In relation to his visit to Mumbai, when was your meeting with Seema and the aun—Madhubala?"

Irritated, Adhith asked, "What *is* this? An interrogation? Seema introduced me to Madhubala. Afterwards, I met Papaji to discuss the matter."

"Since your papaji was in Mumbai the entire weekend, your meeting with the auntie—sorry, *Madhubala*—had to have been during the workweek."

Ahh. "Bro, people have personal lives, and managers can't hold it against them. Besides, I worked the entire time, and Seema still showed up at the office."

Nostrils flaring, Vikram commented, "Must've been tough. Putting in a full day of work before rushing home to introduce her boyfriend to her auntie."

"But she did it," Adhith said, injecting effusive pride into his voice. "She's amazing."

"She sure is," Vikram commented. "Even the EU client was impressed."

He was?

"I'm sure she told you." Vikram continued.

Adhith added another lie to his already long list. "She did."

"I'm going to have to fire her."

"Huh? Fire her for *what?*"

"For not showing up to work a couple of days last week under the pretext of being ill."

Shit. Adhith racked his brain for some kind of explanation.

"She put on a good show, too." Vikram uncrossed his legs and gestured with his hands. "All the coughing and the sneezing in the office. The green snot was a nice touch. She even got me to take her home. Then, she called the chick from Row Four... what's her name... she always has her nose stuck in some book."

"Payel," Adhith supplied, automatically. "Payel Biswas."

"Yeah, her. Payel told our accountant Seema would need medical leave until she was 'back from the brink of death.'" The last part was said with air-quotes. "Now, if she were well enough for an evening out, she should've been well enough to get herself to the office."

Adhith eyed his friend. He couldn't think of a way out of this.

"Green snot," Vikram repeated, gleefully. "With brown flecks... dripping into her lunch—"

"Stop," Adhith shouted, throwing his hands up. "You don't have to gross me out. I admit I lied."

Guffawing hard, Vikram rocked back into the leather chair. "Adhi, meray bachchey. Out with it. What's going on?"

"I ran into Madhubala at the tea stall," Adhith confessed. "After you left. I think she was checking into me." He decided not to divulge any of what

Madhubala said about her own past or about Seema's father trying to sell her to a pimp. Adhith didn't think Madhubala would appreciate having the information broadcast.

"Makes sense," Vikram said. "But why did you lie to me about it?"

"Because we—she overheard us. You and me, I mean. She got angry."

"Can you blame her? You *were* saying you weren't sure about Seema."

"Well, we ended up arguing. She... I needed some time to figure things out before talking to Seema. I didn't want to tell you because we'd argued about the same thing."

The mirth on Vikram's face faded. "Sounds like you've finally made up your mind. I would congratulate you... except, *you still want her to pass your damned test.*"

"Shh." Adhith took a look at the wall clock. Not yet nine, thank God. No one would be in the office to overhear. "I got myself into deep shit, okay?" It came out. His desire to keep himself out of the swamp, the unexpected offer of a parliamentary seat, his unthinking use of Seema's name... "She's a nice girl," Adhith muttered. "If there's a way around the slum thing, I wouldn't mind marrying her. *And* I'd get to delay things with Papaji."

Vikram stood and walked around the desk. "You wouldn't 'mind marrying her.' Even if you did, you have to play along with your papaji's idea, or he'll smell a rat. Whether or not you get your father's approval on the bride, you *will* get the delay you want."

His voice... the threatening note in it... warily, Adhith nodded.

"Get up," Vikram ordered.

"Why?"

"So I can beat the shit out of you."

"Bro—"

"Don't 'bro' me." Eyes wild, Vikram accused, "You're planning to break her heart, and you want *me* to help—"

"Heh? How am I planning to break her heart?"

"She's a... a..." Vikram clutched at his hair with both hands. "A middle-class Indian woman."

"What in God's name does that have to do with anything?"

"She'll start getting expectations," Vikram warned. "If you're just leading her on, she'll get badly hurt."

"How am I leading her on? All I'm going to do is ask her if she'd like to attend the party as my date. I'll tell Papaji and your family I haven't brought up the marriage issue with her. If your mom gives Papaji a bad report, I'll keep arguing until I figure a way out of my actual problem. Afterwards, I'll break it off with Seema. *Gently,* I assure you. If all of them do approve of her, I'll bring it up with her, and she can decide. If she says no, I'll spend some time persuading her until I get out of my other problem. Whatever happens, I'll have my delay. *She's* not going to get hurt, either way."

Vikram didn't seem soothed by Adhith's perfectly reasonable explanation. "You're one cold bastard," Vikram snarled. "Seema deserves a lot better than you."

"God, what is it about some people?" Adhith snapped. "First, Madhubala. Now, you. Can't you get it through your heads it's not *your* decision to make? If Seema doesn't want to marry a 'cold bastard' like me, *she* gets to say no. You don't get to say it *for* her, and you don't get to interfere with *my* plans. *Samjha?*" They'd all *better* understand. Adhith had about had it up to here.

Vikram snorted, dangerously resembling a bull ready to charge.

"Madhubala has the excuse of being related to Seema," Adhith jeered. "What's yours? You went nuts in the tea stall, accusing me of calling 'dibs' without thinking it through. When I come up with a solution, you want to fight me over her? You met her only a couple of weeks back. Don't tell me you fell in love."

Without responding, Vikram glared. In a couple of seconds, he deflated, the rage on his face replaced by angry resignation. "I can't afford to fall in love."

"So what's the problem?"

"I... uhh... I... nothing, I guess. It seems unfair. But you're right; it's up to you and Seema, no one else." Vikram returned to his chair. "What do you want *me* to do?"

"I need you at the party. It will look strange to Seema if I'm there, and you're not. Also, Madhubala would've said something about what she overheard. I'm sure Seema thinks I've dumped her. There's a way out of it. I'm going to say I was simply talking things over with y—"

Vikram's face was back to being bright red.

"*You* said something, didn't you?" Adhith asked.

"I'm sorry," Vikram muttered. "I told you I took her home when she was sick. We were talking about... uhh... future plans... I said something about you wanting to marry her."

Adhith frowned. He'd followed office policy before asking Seema out on their first date, which is to say, he reported it to his immediate supervisor—Vikram—and assured him there would be no violation of the rules of professional conduct. If they worked in the company's American division, workplace romance would've been out of the question no matter what assurances the involved parties gave, but corporate didn't care what their Indian employees did as long as no one made waves. Vikram still insisted on being kept updated on any potential personnel problems.

Surprisingly, *he'd* forgotten office decorum and blurted out things he shouldn't have. What the hell had been going on in the last one week?

"Vikram," Adhith started, carefully. "Is there anything else you and Seema talked about? Anything I need to know?"

"No," said Vikram. "Nothing at all."

***

A. Verma: Hey.

Phone in hand, Adhith walked up and down the cubicle rows, slowing to chat with colleagues and check for updates on the ongoing projects. Out of the corner of his eye, he watched Seema.

She dug into her purse, coming up with her phone and staring at it—staring at his message.

If he hadn't heard from Vikram about her cold, Adhith wouldn't have known she'd been out sick. She looked as pretty as she always did. A ray of sunshine dressed in a Punjabi suit with a bright yellow tunic and floral bottoms. Her eyes were neatly lined, cheeks lightly rouged, and lips glossed. If he got close enough, he'd be able to smell the soft, flowery perfume of hers.

Not intoxicating like the fragrance Madhubala had worn in the tea stall. The scent had been her only adornment. There had been no makeup, whatsoever. She already possessed perfect features and a figure designed to drive men mad even in a shapeless hoodie and worn jeans.

Adhith shook his head. The annoying woman popped into his thoughts at the most inconvenient moments. Seema, on the other hand, took forever to... Adhith frowned. Responding to a simple "hello" shouldn't take so much effort.

He'd dealt with two other analysts *and* the accountant when his phone pinged.

Numbers Girl: Hey, yourself.

A. Verma: I owe you an explanation.

A. Verma: For the silence, I mean.

Numbers Girl: 🙂 Ya think?

A. Verma: 😁 I know, I know. Lunch today? I'll apologise, properly.

Seema tossed her phone to the desk and turned back to the computer, her spine stiff with displeasure.

"Adhith." The accountant hurried over, huffing and puffing. The man recited numbers, droning on and on about staff members who'd called in with requests for medical leave. "It's that cold Seema brought in," he said, darkly. "Right when the EU project is due. Thank God, Vikram didn't catch it, or we'd have been in soup."

"Happens," Adhith said, keeping his eyes on her. "Whoever's left will have to do overtime." He glanced at the manager's room. Vikram was hunched over the keyboard, as usual. Not paying any attention to what was happening in the cubicle maze. Not even looking in Seema's direction. Adhith shrugged off the idiotic thought. Vikram had no reason to gape at *any* of the analysts. Or to avoid gaping. "We'll discuss this at the staff meeting," Adhith said to the accountant.

Returning to his own room, Adhith thumbed out another message.

A. Verma: We both gotta eat. Might as well be together. Gimme a chance, pls?

After a minute...

Numbers Girl: Fine. The Italian place. I'll meet you there at 1.

Adhith blinked. She was determined to make him pay. Literally. The restaurant was one of the pricier ones in Mumbai, and the bill was sure to be in the thousands.

A. Verma: Are you sure about the place?

Numbers Girl: Take it or leave it.

A. Verma: I'll take it.

He slipped the phone into his pocket, wondering which Seema would show up at lunch. The sweet, shy girl from the mountains or the assertive woman he'd just talked to. The village belle or the city slicker?

✸✸✸

Chatter hummed, punctuated by the clatter of cutlery. Uniformed waiters hurried between diners, serving pizza and pasta and wine. In their booth, Adhith forked grilled chicken lasagne into his mouth, relishing the burst of garlic and tomato on his tongue.

In front of Seema was a different explosion. Chocolate truffle, chocolate fondant, chocolate mousse... with a side of hot chocolate. Strange order for someone determined to eat Italian for lunch unless she were trying to make up for her intransigence by eating cheap—or as cheap as she could in this place.

Eyeing the dishes, Adhith teased, "You could get diabetes just by looking at it." God, he could *see* her struggle to respond to the pathetic joke. The battle to stop her eyes from rolling, the smirk she was forcibly stretching into a smile... *Idiot,* he chided himself. He'd actually fallen for the act before Vikram entered the scene. "It's all right, Seema," Adhith said out loud. "You don't have to find everything I say incredibly interesting."

The mild pink of embarrassment washed into her face. "Oh, no. It's not that I didn't—"

Taking a sip of his sangria, Adhith shot her a bland look.

Seema's shoulders slumped. "Fine, you caught me. Is that why you didn't talk to me after... you know?"

Perfect opening. "You did use... ahh... unusual language, so I was a little confused," Adhith admitted. "That's not why—"

"Vikram didn't ask you to dump me?" she demanded. Vikram. Not "your friend, Vikram." Or Vikram sir. Or the umpteen other ways she could've referred to her boss.

"Why would he?" Adhith countered. "In fact, he's very supportive." There was surprise on her face, swiftly hidden. Was there a tinge of hurt behind the puzzlement? Adhith went on, "I get why you did it. You didn't want any questions. Then, things snowballed."

"More or less," she said, quickly. "You're not holding it against me?"

"Not really. When Papaji and I moved to Delhi, I... ahh... was a total hillbilly."

Seema scoffed, "You were also the son of the finance minister."

"There was that," he allowed. He remembered the initial loneliness, the struggle to communicate with classmates who seemed to speak an alien language. "I'm trying to tell you I understand why you... ahh..."

"Lied."

"Created a story," he corrected, grinning. "But I needed a few days to think things through."

"Now that you have?"

"I'd like to get to know you. The *real* you."

With the stainless-steel spoon, Seema scooped out chocolate fondant and brought it to her mouth. "The start of a beautiful friendship?" she asked, her tone wary.

"If you want," Adhith said, nonchalantly. *"I'm* looking for something more."

Her eyelids fluttered. "Like?"

"I know Vikram said something to you."

She tossed the spoon into the bowl and grabbed her napkin to wipe her mouth. If Adhith hadn't been observing, he'd have missed the slight trembling of her fingers.

"Then, Madh—your auntie, I mean."

121

"We talked," Seema said, her words tripping over each other.

So Madhubala *had* gone to Seema, carrying tales of how unsuitable Adhith Verma was. Didn't the woman have better things to do than interfere in his love life? She was gorgeous. There had to be men waiting in line, pleading their case. He couldn't believe she wasn't— "Is she married?"

"Excuse me?"

Goddammit. He'd blurted out the question. Picking up his glass, Adhith gulped sangria. "Just wondering how her husband could've sat on his hands while she wandered around the redlight district."

"I'd like to see how any husband would've stopped her from doing what she wanted," Seema said, her nostrils flared. With the spoon, she stabbed at the fondant. Brown cake splattered.

"Why wouldn't he be there, guarding her back?"

"Madhu is plenty badass on her own. She doesn't need any man to guard her."

"No, I meant—" He needed to stop before he got himself any deeper into doo-doo. "*If* there's a husband in the picture, he should've damned well helped out."

Seema's eyes widened. All she needed were clouds of steam puffing out of her ears, and she'd be the perfect cartoon cutie.

"Or a wife," he added, hurriedly. "Partners for life, etcetera. I'm not putting Madhubala down. Swear to God."

Seema's gaze held his for a couple of seconds before she relaxed back into her chair. "No, she's not married."

Adhith hadn't thought so, but it was good to confirm. Information was key to success in politics *and* in love. He frowned. Madhubala's marital status would have a bearing on *his* love life only as far as her husband's clout in vetoing her niece's relationships was concerned. "You're very protective of her," he commented, setting his glass down.

"Madhu is my family," Seema said. "I'd take a bullet for her."

"I respect the sentiment," Adhith said, noting she called her auntie by name. Surprising, even with the age gap between them being a mere twelve years. "I feel the same way about my father."

Seema blinked once, her face suddenly draining of all expression.

"Something wrong?" he asked.

"I was wondering what your father's going to think of me."

"I'll talk to him when..." He hesitated. "Madhuba... your auntie misunderstood me. What I said to Vikram about marriage still stands, but I'd like us to get to know each other first. Without any pretend modesty. Let's see where it goes."

Seema's eyes remained impassive, but she didn't summarily reject his proposition.

Phew. His strategy to thwart Papaji's plans for his future hinged on her cooperation.

"What are you suggesting?" she asked.

"The usual. Dinners, movies, hanging out. There's a party I'd like us to attend with a few friends of mine."

She shifted in her chair. "Wouldn't it be better to decide where we're going before we meet each other's friends?"

Not if he wanted Papaji not to smell a rat. "You already know them," he urged. "Well, *one* of them. It's Vikram. His parents are celebrating their thirty-second wedding anniversary next weekend. The party is at The Oberoi."

The cup of hot chocolate held to her lips, she glared into the beverage. "Vikram is okay with this idea?"

Vikram, again. No, Vikram Joshi was not okay with the idea. Evasively, Adhith said, "The Joshis always invite me to their events. They invited my father, too."

"No way," Seema said, tone horrified. "I can't—I mean, it's too early to meet your father."

She sounded like she expected Papaji to have his guards shoot her at sight for daring to date his only son. But then, Papaji was not just a prospective father-in-law, he was also a union minister. "Papaji won't be attending," Adhith soothed. "There's no reason for you to be nervous. The Joshis are nice people."

"It's not just them. What if *Vikram* doesn't want me there?" The melancholy on her face...

Keeping his eyes on her reactions, Adhith asked, "Why wouldn't he? He knows you're my girlfriend."

Seema's hand shook. The hot chocolate hovered at the edges of the cup, threatening to spill. She didn't sip the drink, but she didn't put it down, either. Something *had* to have happened. Something neither she nor Vikram was willing to talk about. Something that could destroy Adhith's plans.

"You and Vikram seem close," she finally commented, morosely.

"We were roommates in college. Most people in the office know about it."

"I have no idea where my old roommate is these days," she muttered. "Although I stayed at the hostel only a few weeks. After that, I moved back in with Madhu."

Adhith smiled. "When I met Vikram, it was like finding a long-lost brother. We lived together for four years. He's family. If you and I end up making our relationship permanent, you can consider him family, too. A brother."

She blanched.

Damn.

"So this dinner party's a family gathering," she protested. "I'll be the only outsider. You don't want to spend your time babysitting me."

"You'll be fine." Thoughts ricocheted around his mind. He needed to do something to salvage his brilliant scheme. But what? "If you're worried about having no one to talk to, bring Madhubala along." *Double damn.* What had he done? To his relief, Seema looked mildly surprised but didn't comment.

Chapter 9

The sky was a bright blue, with the waters of the Arabian Sea beneath reflecting the same vivid hue. Boats chugged along, giving passengers ample time to gawk at the large arched structure of the Gateway of India as well as the iconic Taj Mahal Palace Hotel.

The breeze ruffling Adhith's hair brought with it the stench of rotting garbage. Hip resting on the quay wall, he threw pieces of bread to the waiting pigeons, their throaty coos mimicking the erratic vibrations in his chest as he watched the woman approach.

Madhubala. Or Madhu as her niece had called her. Grey cotton hoodie, jeans washed white, sneakers, black tote on the left shoulder. Plus, the square-rimmed spectacles. Long, straight hair in a ponytail. As she got within hearing range, he asked, "Is this the Madhu Rawat uniform?"

She didn't bother dignifying his remark with a response. She didn't even seem to notice the trouble he'd taken with his attire. Every situation demanded its own approach, and he'd been determined to keep the mood of the afternoon breezy and friendly. Hence, the short-sleeved cream shirt, khaki pants, and brown loafers. His usual sporty cologne.

"You called me at my job," Madhu snapped, her tone still as low and measured as he remembered from the tea stall. "Three times. The company doesn't appreciate it when employees take personal calls during work hours."

He'd Googled the number and made three calls over three days. Adhith finally growled at the clerk at the other end of the line, asking if he were delivering the messages. Madhu still hadn't come to the phone, only having the clerk tell Adhith to show up at the Gateway of India on Saturday afternoon.

He'd planned to invite her to dinner. Instead, she'd picked one of the most crowded spots in the city on a guaranteed-to-be-packed afternoon. There would be no privacy, no opportunity for them to get to know each other. He consoled himself with the thought the Gateway—the arch built in the early 1900s to commemorate the visit of the British king—was also one of the most picturesque spots in Mumbai.

Adhith tossed the last of the bread pieces to the birds. "I'm sorry, but it was the only contact info I could find online for you. The accounting company seems too strict. I'd have thought they'd even let you work from home."

"You'd have thought wrong. Plus, people I want to talk to already know how to reach me."

Grinning, Adhith asked, "Is this where I'm supposed to slink off, tail between my legs?"

Her eyelids flickered, the thick lashes brushing against the glass pieces of her spectacles. "Tell me why you wanted to see me."

Dusting the breadcrumbs off his jeans, Adhith gestured towards the Taj. "We can sit and talk. Also, I'm hungry."

"I didn't come here to socialise with you, Verma. I agreed to meet you only to make sure Seema's all right."

"She's fine," he said, distracted by the movements of Madhu's lush lips. "Call me Adhith. Or Adhi, like the rest of my friends."

Nostrils flaring, she asked, "What is *wrong* with you? We're not friends. We're never going to be friends. The only reason I'm here is to make sure you don't end up hurting Seema. Otherwise, I stay far away from the likes of you."

A splinter of hurt lodged in his heart. "'The likes of me'? What would that be?"

"Privileged, entitled, careless of other people."

A buzz started in his brain. All he'd wanted was a chance to start afresh with Madhu before he figured a way out of the mess. Except, she'd already written him off as scum.

"Judgemental, narrow-minded, stubborn," he snarled, uncaring of the curious looks from the other visitors to the monument. "I'm a man. Therefore, I must be bad. Nothing I say or do is going to convince you otherwise."

"I never said anything about hating men," she spat back. "Contrary to what you seem to believe, I enjoy male company. But rich, arrogant brats are not my type."

Adhith bared his teeth. "I never offered myself to you, so neither of us has to worry about me not being your 'type.'"

Madhu stilled. A red flush worked its way up her neck. "Do you have something important to tell me, Verma? If not, I'm going home."

Shit. The party.

Seema was already reluctant to attend. Given her and Vikram's reactions to the mere mention of each other's names, Adhith was damned sure something had happened between them. Vikram would've refused to take things any further. Not just because of his best friend. Also, because of his laser-like focus on his career. Adhith had a feeling she'd eventually agreed to attend the party only to make Vikram jealous. If she thought better of it, she'd back out.

Adhith couldn't afford for her to do anything of the sort until he figured out an alternate way to stay clear of the political swamp. He'd managed to keep their interactions limited to polite nothings so as not to give her a reason to decline. He also needed Madhu to accept the invitation so Seema couldn't claim the awkwardness of being the odd one out as an excuse.

Right now, Madhu saw no reason to work with him. They'd met twice, and each time, he'd behaved like a madman. "Can we start over?" he asked. "Please?"

She wheeled around and strode towards the street.

"Wait." Adhith followed, matching stride for stride. "I do have something—excuse me." An elderly gentleman in a *taqiya*—Muslim skull cap—stood in the way, smartphone in hand. An equally elderly woman had her hands wrapped around his elbow, her black *hijab* fluttering in the wind. The pungent odour of spices permeated the surrounding air.

Adhith skirted the couple. His shoulder brushed against the man's arm. A dismayed "hoy," followed by a thud.

Adhith pivoted. The phone lay on the ground, the protective glass shield shattered. He went down on his haunches and picked it up. *"Maaf karna,* Uncle," Adhith apologised. "It was an accident."

"My phone," the old man wailed. "Do you realise how much it cost?"

Adhith had a fair idea. Under the cracks on the cover, the icons were still lit. He touched one, and the phone keypad came on. "It's working, but the screen protector needs to be replaced." Handing the phone to the woman, he craned his neck to spot Madhu. The grey hoodie was still visible. "Tell you what—" He dug out his wallet from his back pocket. "Here's my card. Take the phone to a repair shop, and I'll pay the bill."

"Yeah, yeah," said the old man. "Fake card. We've heard things like this happen all the time in Mumbai."

Keeping Madhu's hoodie in sight, Adhith said, "Fake? I swear to God— here—" He took out a few notes from his wallet.

"You think that will pay for a new phone?" the old man asked, incredulously.

"This phone's still working." Adhith peered through the crowd. He couldn't lose Madhu. She wasn't going to give him another chance to talk. "All you need is a new screen protector."

"That's what *you* say," said the old man.

"Uncleji—" A sniffle from the old woman. Adhith sighed. Any attempt to persuade Madhu would have to wait. "Why don't we go to a repair shop and get it done?"

It took him fifteen minutes to cajole the suspicious old gent and his wife into a taxi. The woman's relative silence lasted only until the car door slammed shut. In the half hour it took them to reach the electronics store, she learned everything from the name of Adhith's long-dead mother to the caste of both his parents. When he refused to put a number to the salary he earned, he was interrogated on the kind of home and car he owned. Finally, she wanted to know if someone was looking out for "suitable girls" on his behalf. Laughing helplessly, he tucked the two photographs back into the lady's hands and firmly declared he'd find a wife on his own schedule. When the taxi rolled up to the glass-walled showroom, she told him twenty-eight was old enough to be "settled."

The young salesgirl quickly and efficiently replaced the screen protector, demonstrating for the couple their device worked fine. The old man asked the salesgirl to take a picture of him and his wife with Adhith.

Within minutes, the couple was settled into another taxi. The old lady extracted a promise from Adhith to join the family meal if he were to saunter by the city of Surat at any point. "Bohra fish curry is the best," the old man said, smacking his lips.

As the taxi squealed away from the curb, a low voice asked, "Do you do that with everyone you meet?"

Adhith spun in surprise.

Madhu, her back resting against the glass wall, her thumbs hooked on her pockets.

"What the—" Adhith shook his head. *"How?"*

A bead of sweat trickled its way down her temple, but she made no move to wipe it off. "I was waiting for the bus when you showed up with them at the taxi stand."

On the road, cars and buses and motorised rickshaws continued to screech past, their distorted images on the glass panels behind Madhu. Horns blared.

Exhaust fumes—thick and dark—swirled around them, adding stink to the muggy heat.

His eyes, nose, throat... everything stung. Coughing into his shoulder, Adhith asked, "So you what? Followed me?"

"More or less."

"Why?"

Madhu shrugged. "I'd thought you were alone back there, and I wanted to make sure..."

He gawked. "What did you think I was doing? Using a network of old people to trap women into doing my bidding? You seem to believe I'm the world's biggest cad."

Face tightening, Madhu said, "I was confused... that's all. So I got into the cab behind yours."

With loud whoops and excited yells, a group of young men and women walked by. Adhith moved closer to Madhu, letting them pass behind him. The sweet, intoxicating smell of her perfume teased his nostrils. Muscles bunching, he forced himself to focus on the reflections on the glass wall. Tourists, lugging rucksacks on their back—white, black... all Brits, if the accent were any indication.

Once the noise died down, Adhith asked, "How did you know where I was headed?"

"I didn't. I asked the driver to follow you." Unexpectedly, she giggled. "I've always wanted to say that: 'follow that car.'" The mirth, the excitement, the *joy*. Adhith savoured the tiny sound. Eyes dancing, she continued, "I got into the store right behind you."

"I didn't notice," he murmured. How was it possible?

"You were so focused on the couple... I heard you tell the salesgirl what happened. I want to know... why didn't you walk away?"

"It was my fault. Plus, why leave things on a bad note? Why not take a negative and turn it into a positive?"

"Not only their phone. Everyone in that tea stall on Grant Road knew you."

"I've been going there for years."

"So has your friend. He doesn't feel obliged to help them."

Adhith sighed. "Not everyone's the same, Madhu. I've known Vikram a long time. He can be awkward around people, but he always has *my* back."

She stared. "Fixing your mistakes, loyal to your friends... ambitious, calculating... I can't get a handle on you. Where do you fall on the moral spectrum?"

He had to laugh. "Do you have to fit people into boxes? Good, bad, ugly?"

"How else do you decide if someone's friend or foe?"

"What did you decide about me?" When her lips parted on an answer, he raised both hands. "Wait, you don't need to say it. The first time we met, you pointed a weapon at me. Which, I think—" He took a deep breath. "—says it all."

With a short laugh, she asked, "Did it scare you?"

"Hell, yeah." Warily, he eyed the tote on her shoulder. On the reflected image of the purse, he imagined the shape of a gun. "Do you have it with you?"

"Always."

She would've *had* to keep herself armed. Forget about escaping the redlight district. She'd helped another girl avoid the same fate. The men who ruled the streets would never forget what she'd done. Which explained why while her movements were minimal, her body always appeared coiled. She was always watching out for danger. Rescuing Seema had come at immense personal cost to Madhu.

"You're amazing," Adhith said. "What you did for Seema..."

Madhu's eyes lit with love. "Yeah, well... we're family. There's not much I wouldn't do for her... what did you want to talk to me about, Verma?"

"Hmm? Oh, yes. The party." He'd forgotten. "I... ahh... wanted to invite you myself."

"What party..." The pleasant look on her face faded. "Oh. The wedding anniversary dinner with your friend's parents. Seema said something about it... I'm not going... I don't know if *she's*—"

On a groan, he asked, "What now? If Seema mentioned the party, she must have told you I asked her if we could start over. Also, I thought I'd convinced *you* I'm not such a bad guy."

"You could be the world's nicest man, and you still wouldn't be right for Seema."

"Why not?"

Madhu shoved off from the wall, a finger pointed at his chest. She opened and closed her mouth a couple of times. Cars continued to speed by. Pedestrians hurried down the footpath. Waiting for her to come up with a reason—a *single* reason—Adhith counted the images bobbing along the glass wall behind her.

A flurry of honks. Vehicles squealing to a halt. A blurred form at the window of a taxi. Frowning, Adhith tilted his head. Vikram's brother-in-law, the dumbass, was back in Mumbai? It would be the third time in as many weeks.

Madhu snapped, "Verma, you—"

Holding up a finger, Adhith turned on his heel. All kinds of cars crowded the road, including taxis. Adhith looked up and down, trying to spot the dumbass's smirking face.

Tone irate, Madhu asked, "What are you—"

Striding towards the stalled vehicles, he said, "Wait right here. I'll be back."

The shrill whistle of a traffic cop. The phut-phut-phut of a motorcycle. Buses and cars revved up, speeding past Adhith.

"Something wrong?" asked Madhu, coming up behind him.

Eyeing the moving cars, Adhith shook his head. "I thought I saw someone, but he lives in Delhi, not here." Turning to her, he begged, "Show up at the party, please? Seema's worried about being left alone."

If Seema's behaviour were any indication, she'd already changed her mind about Adhith. However, he needed her at this party, or his entire strategy would fall apart. Once she showed up, he'd have to figure out what next, but if she didn't show in the first place, his political future would be in jeopardy. He couldn't allow her any excuses to decline the invitation.

"Fine," Madhu said. "For Seema."

Struggling to hide his elation, Adhith agreed, "For Seema."

Chapter 10

The metallic clatters of the chaiwalla's tumbler holder reverberated around the office each time he set down the contraption, echoing past the closed door into the manager's room. More than a week after Vikram made a mess of things with Seema, more than a week after he complained to California about monitoring employee activity, HR was calling back. As the lady droned on over the speakerphone, a pulse pounded hard behind Vikram's eyebrow, sending sharp pain zigzagging through his head.

Across the desk, Adhith and the accountant were silent, but they were all aware what HR's denial meant. An intruder had accessed their systems. There was a breach of security in one of the world's largest cybersecurity firms. On Vikram's watch.

Disaster. Absolute, unmitigated disaster. His entire career was in the toilet, circling the drain. With sweaty fingers, Vikram pulled the keyboard towards him and typed in a request for an emergency conference with the regional CIO stationed in Singapore. As the HR woman was hanging up, a message popped up on the monitor.

"Adhith, Britto," Vikram snapped out an order. "Clear your schedules this afternoon for a conference call with the Singapore office. Be prepared to stay late. We're in crisis mode."

"Can't we tackle this on our own?" asked Tiger Britto Prabhu, the accountant. "Do we need to involve Singapore?"

"We don't have a choice," Adhith muttered. "We don't even know it's limited to India. If the problem's company-wide, the bigwigs need to be notified."

Vikram nodded, guiltily hoping that would turn out to be the case. If the intrusion happened from India, he'd be held responsible.

How the hell did it happen? The defences he'd erected were hard to beat. The walls morphed at the first nudge from any unknown source. An attack should've been easily repelled. Even if the hacker tunnelled through the external barriers, he should've lost himself in the labyrinth of bland nonsense between the external and internal walls. Or found himself dead in the water from some of the counterstrike mechanisms. If he somehow crossed the moat and scaled the rampart, he should've found the internal systems as challenging to penetrate. The passwords were continually changed, delivered to employees' phones only when they requested access. Any employee trying to connect to an unauthorised external server would trigger multiple alarms. The hacker still managed to stroll through every part of their operations.

Who *was* this dude? Vikram made a mental note to send out feelers to the hacking communities around the planet. He also needed to contact his former professors at IIT Bombay to see if they'd heard of any new prodigies on the scene capable of such feats. He had to do it carefully. Hackers were notoriously secretive, so they were not likely to talk, but academics were a nosy lot, prone to gossip. They couldn't be allowed to know what happened in the India division of the company. *If* it indeed started in the India division. Vikram fervently hoped it hadn't. He couldn't afford such a major slip-up on his record. "Don't talk to anyone about this. Not even your families."

With his tie, Britto wiped the sweat beads from his upper lip. "There was nothing stolen. The hackers were only monitoring employee online activity."

"It's not going to matter," Vikram said. "If we couldn't protect ourselves, how can we claim to protect others? The company's shares will drop to the bottom. Not just us, every business we provide security for will be dragged into the mess. Big as we are, we'll crash stock markets everywhere."

"Jesus," whispered Britto. His doting parents had given him the moniker "Tiger," but no one called him by the name. Anyone less predatory was hard to imagine with his short frame, shirt buttons straining over an ample belly, rounded eyes, and thin combover. A forty-something bachelor, Britto cared for his aged father and mother at home. He belonged to the Konkani Catholic Association and regularly attended mass.

Vikram was not even remotely religious, but he fervently hoped Britto lit a candle this Sunday. They needed all the help they could get to navigate their way out of this catastrophe. *Vikram* needed all the help he could get. Of the three of them, he was the one who stood to lose the most. When the dust settled, Adhith would still have his political career. Britto's primary responsibility in the office was as administrator, so he was not likely to come under much scrutiny. *Vikram* would be done for. No company, no client would ever again hire him to manage digital security.

Faces sombre, Adhith and Britto padded out of the room.

"Adhi, got a minute?" Vikram called. Adhith was a master at spinning awkward situations. He could help Vikram devise an escape strategy.

Holding the door open, Adhith asked, "What's up?"

Clear-toned laughter interrupted Vikram's train of thoughts. His gaze went past Adhith to Row Three where a woman currently chatted with the chick from Row Four. Seema had her swivel chair turned away from the monitor and was gesticulating wildly as the other woman leaned against the partition between cubicles, holding a pile of folders.

Abruptly, Adhith said, "We'll talk after the conference." Without waiting for Vikram's response, he strode back to his office. Correction—he practically *ran*.

Vikram cursed under his breath. His roommate of four years didn't even want to talk. Adhith couldn't have failed to notice the inappropriate attraction Vikram harboured for Seema.

How the hell was Vikram supposed to stop himself when she glowed like a light-emitting diode? Not only the dark brown curls cascading down her back or the rose-tinted cheeks or even the long legs made sexier still by the six-inch heels. The force of her spirit startled the universe into gaping in admiration. The sharp intellect could rival that of his best analysts. Vikram had taken to closely studying her downtime activities. There was one particular tool she built... surprise was followed by a mild case of envy he hadn't been the one to think of it.

Seema returned his admiration of her intelligence. She heard the music in the firewall he'd written. In her clear voice, she'd cooed about his drive to succeed. Shared her lunch with him and called him "macho."

God, she was driving him nuts. His career was on the line, and here he was slobbering over her.

The girl from Row Four turned towards the manager's room, her smile faltering as she saw Vikram watching them. Hurriedly, she plunked the folders on Seema's desk, muttering something. When the girl left, Seema swivelled her chair towards him. It was more than a week after their argument, and he'd been careful to stay clear of her, but whenever they accidentally ran into each other, her eyes shot furious sparks at him. There was no tenderness left in her gaze, no attraction in her demeanour. Seema had been all angry goddess since the fateful night.

What the hell was she getting mad about? It wasn't as though she were dying of a broken heart. In a few days, she'd already picked up where she'd left off with Adhith, Vikram's best friend.

The best friend who'd already claimed Seema as his girlfriend before Vikram met her. *Or not.* The friend who wanted to marry her. Or not. Why the hell was *Adhith* getting mad when he couldn't make up his mind? Was the rest of the world supposed to wait around until he decided what to do?

Vikram had no right to castigate either of them. When he first started the job at Imperium, he'd enjoyed some semblance of social life. Women were kind about his unconventional looks but not about his reluctance to spend time or money. After the first couple of disasters, Vikram swore off romance until he had enough of himself to spare. He should've remembered his vow before drooling at Seema like a chimpanzee with a dental problem. He should've remembered Adhith.

Damn her. Nothing had gone right since she sashayed out of the bathroom and into his life. She'd destroyed his peace of mind, ruined his sleep, and messed up his equation with his only friend in the world. Now, this thing with the security breach. *No,* Vikram corrected himself. Nothing had gone right after he returned from California. He couldn't blame her for things she wasn't responsible for. Seema Rawat might be able to tempt him and frustrate him to the point of madness, but she had nothing to do with the hacking.

***

Vikram was not in a good mood. He'd spent two hours at the gym, but Adhith didn't show. They needed to brainstorm solutions to the hacking problem, dammit. Adhith was avoiding his best buddy because of Seema.

The click of the key was all the sound Vikram made when he opened the door to his parents' duplex flat. It was dark and silent. Both his parents were early-to-bed types and would've retired a precise thirty minutes after dinner. The air conditioner seemed to be off, but the gentle breeze coming in through the open windows kept the living room comfortable. The full moon hung in the starry sky outside, bathing the furniture in its silvery glow.

Since Vikram hadn't shown for dinner, food would've been left in the fridge for him, but he planned to head upstairs for a much-needed shower. The cotton tee and gym shorts were sweat-soaked, not to mention the sodden sneakers. At the window, the sheer curtains fluttered. The breeze gusted for a couple of seconds, drying the sweat on his skin. Coolness. Blessed coolness. The pressure within his skull receded a little.

Tossing the gym bag on the sofa, he went to the window and leaning out with his hands on the sill, stared into the night. High-rises abounded, but the streets were well-lit and lined with trees. There were parks, art galleries, fine restaurants. From the fourteenth-floor flat, Vikram enjoyed an unobstructed view of the dark waters of the Arabian Sea where pinpricks of light bobbed up and down. Boats, taking riders for a romantic night on the ocean from where they could marvel at the glittering city.

This was one of India's wealthiest pin codes. The slums weren't too far away, but they might as well have been on a different planet as far as the affluent residents of Cuffe Parade were concerned. Here, there was no rotting garbage on street corners, requiring gagging passers-by to cover their nostrils with handkerchiefs. No beggars carrying emaciated children on their hips, knocking on the windows of stopped cars. Cuffe Parade was nothing like Grant Road.

Seema easily morphed into a small-town girl, newly arrived in the city. She'd handled the EU client's local representative with aplomb, but both Adhith and the EU client had been prepared to be charmed. Not so Vikram's father and mother. How would she cope with being put under the microscope by doyens of Mumbai high society like his parents? Hell, Vikram was born into this world and hadn't yet figured out how to navigate it—didn't even want to. Adhith managed to fit in, but he was made of different stuff. *Political* stuff. He wasn't going to be much help to her, in any case. He'd want to see how she'd do under pressure.

Seema was smart, though, much better tuned into social cues than Vikram. She'd probably pass the test with flying colours. Except, this dinner would be a job interview for the position of Mrs Adhith Verma. How could she fail to see the fact? How could she not realise how insulting it all was?

Perhaps, she did know. Perhaps, she'd decided having Adhith as husband was worth the effort. Why not? Even if there were conditions attached to his plans, he did want to marry her. Unlike Vikram, who'd nipped the idea of a relationship in the bud. What she wanted to do was anyway up to her, not him. Vikram swallowed hard. Insane ideas about tests for marriageability aside, Adhith was a nice man and would make her a great husband. Vikram needed to move on and find a way to keep Adhith's friendship.

A scuffle behind Vikram drew his attention back to the living room. A deep cough. His father. Vikram didn't bother turning around. Dr Joshi had probably forgotten to get water for the night. He had his shortcomings, but bothering domestic help for trivial things during off-hours was not one of them, a trait shared by his wife. Those who worked for the Joshi couple were well-paid and well-treated.

"You stayed late at the gym today," commented Vikram's father. "Something going on?"

Puzzled, Vikram turned. "How do you—did Adhith call here?"

"No one called. You have your pattern." Clad in his usual white kurta-pyjama, Vikram's father padded to the window. There was a glass in one of his hands, and his other hand was cupped, holding something in the palm. He tossed whatever it was into his mouth and followed it with water. "BP pill," he explained. "I always forget the evening dose."

His father needed medicines? When did he get so old? Mom had been hennaing her hair for years, and Dad had been bald for as long as Vikram could remember, so there was no grey on either to indicate the passage of time. Dad was also several inches shorter than Vikram, with girth expanding over the decades.

"What pattern?" Vikram finally asked.

"All of us have those. When I need to think things out, I like to drive."

"In *Mumbai?*" The unruly drivers, the blocked roads, the honking... on the other hand, Dad's habit explained the need for BP pills.

"To Lonavala."

The family owned a home in the hill station on top of a grass-covered mount overlooking Lonavala Lake. It was one of the ancestral holdings. The Joshis of yore had made their money flattering royalty and later, working for the British Empire, but most of their wealth had been in the form of gold and land, of which the Lonavala property was a part.

Around the time of India's independence, there were widespread riots targeting Maharashtrian brahmins. A lot of the Joshi property was either

141

looted or destroyed. The incident caused Vikram's great-grandfather—the old man whose portrait bore a startling resemblance to Vikram—to see the need to diversify.

Starting with his investments in private hospitals and pharmaceutical companies, the Joshis owned stock in a variety of businesses all over the world. Not to mention the rentals in and around Mumbai and other big cities. The Joshi Trust was flush with money and supported the entire extended clan, but said ancestor also taught his family to downplay their wealth, and their abodes tended to be modestly sized despite being fitted with every luxury. Certain pieces of property—like ancestral land and jewellery—were kept out of the trust and passed from eldest son to eldest son, including the Lonavala house, where Vikram's father went to work out life's little glitches.

"You have your own ways of sorting out problems," continued Dad. "The computer, the guitar, the gym... it's been your pattern since you were a boy."

So that's how he'd guessed Vikram had things going on. "Issues at the company," he said. "I did my usual two hours at the gym."

"With Adhith."

Vikram muttered, noncommittally. He wasn't about to reveal all the complications Seema brought into their lives when the Joshis were gearing up to judge her worthiness as wife to Adhith.

"Before Adhith, it was your nanaji," mused Vikram's father.

The comment grated. "Nanaji liked having me around. Nobody else wanted to talk to him." Or to Vikram.

"Your nanaji—" started Dad. The tone was unusually hard for the soft-spoken cardiologist. "He marched to his own drummer."

Gritting his teeth, Vikram asked, "Was it enough reason to pretend he didn't exist?"

Of course, it wasn't the reason. Nanaji had been a Parsi guitarist, with no money or lineage to make him worthy of the aristocratic Joshis. Moreover,

Parsis migrated from Persia to India only a few centuries ago. And Naniji—Vikram's maternal grandmother—came with Muslim and fishermen ancestors. She'd died years before Vikram's mom met his dad.

Dad puffed out a breath. "Son, the dynamics between a parent and child can be delicate. Especially, when the child gets old enough to make her own decisions. Your mom made a couple of choices her father didn't agree with. He considered it a betrayal."

"Wouldn't *you?*" Vikram asked, incredulously. "She met you and immediately acted like she was better than everyone else. How could a simple guitarist compete with the Joshis?"

"Careful," said Vikram's father, firmly. "You might be talking about your mom, but Rattan's my wife. I won't put up with anyone insulting her. Be it her father or her son."

"Pratap, please," said Mom's voice. A click. White light flooded the room. Tying a sash around her printed caftan, she walked to the two men. "What's the point of getting angry with Vikram when he wasn't around for any of it?"

"Your father's words," exclaimed Dad, a hand to his forehead. "From our son's mouth. Eleven years after he died, the old man's still making you pay for your disobedience."

Ignoring her husband's frustration, Mom smiled tremulously at Vikram. "Betay, I... *we've* been wanting to talk to you a long time."

"Would be a first," muttered Vikram.

"Wouldn't it?" she agreed. "Since you left for IIT, this is the first you've stayed home more than a couple of days at a stretch."

"The seventeen years I lived here weren't enough?" Vikram mocked.

Frowning, Mom asked, "What do you mean? You were too young... it didn't seem right... he was your grandfather, after all. The timing always seemed wrong."

"There was never *any* time, right or wrong," Vikram said, bitterly. No one was ever interested enough in him to make time. "Mom, I'm sorry you heard what I said. I'm sure you had your reasons for keeping away from Nanaji, but the fact remains he was terribly hurt."

Dad said, "She's trying to explain—"

"I don't want to hear any explanations. Not about your gripes with Nanaji. Besides, I have problems from this century to deal with before digging up stuff from the past."

The senior Joshis fell silent, ruefully contemplating Vikram. To Vikram's surprise, his father laughed. Tone conversational, Dad said, "You know, for all your protestations of loyalty toward your nanaji, you're a Joshi, through and through. Not just your looks. Your stubbornness. My God! If I were the superstitious sort, I would've believed you were possessed by my grandmother's ghost. Once the old lady got an idea into her head, you'd have had to split her skull open and physically extract it before she'd admit she was wrong. You remember, Rattan?"

"Do I ever?" said Mom, breathing in horror. "She was the one I had to impress before any of the other Joshis dared acknowledge our marriage."

Acknowledge? It sounded like they'd eloped or something. How could it be? In their wedding pictures, the couple was surrounded by all the Joshis from the aforementioned tyrant of a granny to the infant son of a distant cousin.

"Including her husband," agreed Dad, grinning at Vikram. "Your great-grandfather." The man who glared at the world out of the portrait hanging over the living room fireplace in Lonavala. Vikram's *doppelganger.*

"You see?" Mom asked Vikram, her voice eager. "There were so many things—"

"Let it go," said Dad. "He's not in the mood to hear what we have to say."

Clutching his elbow with her hand, Mom said, "But—"

Dad continued, "Rattan, Vikram's busy. He has issues to deal with at work. Once he's done, I'm sure he'll find time for us." He nodded at Vikram. "Goodnight, son."

Chapter 11

"Vikram, you discovered the attack, so California wants *you* to work on it," the CIO's voice came over the phone. Vikram cradled the receiver on his shoulder and continued to type in commands on the keyboard. Headphones connected to the landline, Adhith sat in the chair across the desk and listened in. His laptop was open in front, hiding his expression from Vikram. "They're still trying to figure out who to assign to help," said the CIO. "It has to be someone one-hundred per cent trustworthy."

Some*one* as in one other person. This was life-or-death for the company, but they could afford only a small team comprised of Vikram, Adhith, and this third person from San Jose. The bigger the team, the greater the chances of leaks. They urgently needed to get the hacker before the news got out.

Who *was* the S.O.B? None of the hacking groups around the world had reported back to Vikram on any new prodigies on the scene, but hackers were a secretive lot. Also, every generation was getting younger and younger. At twenty-eight, Vikram was already one of the ancients of the community. This particular punk could well be just a boy, trying to make his name by taking out one of the celebrities. The hacker's pattern didn't suggest it, though. In any case, Vikram Joshi wasn't about to go down to some young punk with a hankering to be the new champion.

"Product-related applications have already been separated from the operational programs," Vikram muttered, half to himself. "Whoever wants to cross the firewall will only be able to do so after retina scan." The first defensive step.

The funny thing was the hacker hadn't even wandered by the company's key products. Which was what made Vikram believe the punk wasn't after glory. He acted as if he merely wanted to check what the employees were up to when they were supposed to be working. It did make Vikram's job a little easier. Chances were the hacker hadn't encountered the extra layers of security, so he didn't know he was being tracked.

"Good," said the CIO. "The next step should be to minimise exposure. Go section by section and isolate all operations programs. Within a couple of days, we should eject him from our systems."

Vikram grunted. "His interest seems to be in the drudge work going on behind the scenes, so any attempt to secure those sections will tell him we're on to him. Afterwards, he'll make sure he's digitally and physically out of our reach. Then, he'll be free to leak to the press what he did here. We'll be finished, and he'll be safe." This was the conundrum Vikram grappled with.

"We need to find him before we tip him off," the CIO mused. "We have to make it all appear to be routine company activity, so we *don't* tip him off. Not a small order, but we must do it. And we have to make sure he doesn't talk."

Shoving fingers into his hair, Vikram said, "Even if we manage to shut *him* up, it will still leave us the problem of media leaks from whomever hired him."

"*If* he was hired by someone," said the CIO.

"I don't see what else it could be," Adhith said. "The hacker hasn't been inside our product. He hasn't introduced any malware. He's spying on us so he can tell the world Imperium was not able to secure its own house."

Vikram continued, "If what happened to Imperium becomes public, we won't have much credibility left in the cybersecurity business."

"Options?" asked the CIO.

Tone hard, Adhith said, "We *have* to find him and get him to tell us who he's working for. We'll threaten public shaming, not just criminal prosecution. If we go down, they'll go down, too. Him and whichever company hired him. When they're exposed as responsible for a digital attack of this kind, *they're* not going to have any credibility left as a cybersecurity company, either. Who will trust them? It will stop them from talking to the press."

Vikram smiled in relief. Adhith might not have shown up to brainstorm solutions to their problem, but he'd been thinking about it all the same. He hadn't abandoned his buddy.

The CIO hissed. "So you both agree this was done by one of our competitors? In this day and age!"

"Corporate warfare," said Vikram. "There are no limits to what some people will do if they believe they won't get caught. We've seen it before. Bank fraud, IP theft, political corrupt—" He coughed, not daring to look in Adhith's direction. As if messing around with his girlfriend weren't enough of a deal-breaker, Vikram *had* to rub Adhith's father's crimes in his face immediately after he came up with a way out of the cyberespionage problem.

"True," mused the CIO. "What's our plan of action for finding him?"

Attention drawn back to the problem at hand, Vikram said, "We ran tests on our intrusion detection software. No signs of forced entry." Whoever the slippery bastard was, he was good. "I'm considering—"

With a snap, Adhith closed his laptop and slipped off the headphones.

Vikram swore, silently. "Sorry, Tim," he said to the CIO. "Gotta go. The EU client's walking in." Before either the CIO or Adhith could react, Vikram hung up. In two bounds, he was across the desk and at the door, blocking Adhith's way. "Oh, no," snarled Vikram. "You're staying right here and talking to me."

Adhith wrapped the power cord around itself and stood. "I'm meeting Britto to go over the financials for the EU project."

"Britto can wait. I need to tell you something. What I said before... I didn't mean to."

Adhith's eyebrows drew together in confusion. "Oh, the stuff about politicians. I know you didn't say it on purpose."

Vikram let out a relieved breath. "Good. I was worried... uhh..." He mauled his hair, trying to devise a way of asking Adhith not to give up on their friendship without sounding as melodramatic as a sitcom *bahu*, the put-upon daughter-in-law who seemed to be the central character of every damned television show on Indian cable. "Never mind," Vikram finally said, stepping aside.

Adhith tucked the laptop under his arm and headed out. At the exit, he swung back. He barely made eye contact before directing his regard at the desktop computer. "Bro, I've been thinking a lot about... about what you said. Corruption in politics and such."

The hesitation in his voice, the wavering gaze... very unlike the friend Vikram was used to seeing. "And?"

"I can't do it," Adhith confessed.

"You already told me all this. You dragged Seema into the mess so *you* could stay out of it."

"It's not all. Even if I manage to stay out of Papaji's circle and win a seat in the parliament on my own, I'd still know everything. Any time I voted for or against a project, I'd still know how it would benefit him... and *me, eventually.*"

Vikram didn't know what to say. It wasn't only Minister Verma. Through his network, Vikram and Adhith also unearthed some dubious connections between other politicians, corporations, and criminal enterprises. Over the years, the thought occurred a few times to Vikram he was complicit with corruption on a monstrous scale, but he always shoved it to the back of his mind, telling himself there was nothing he could do. Not only because Adhith's father would be the first to go down in an investigation.

For one, the watchdogs appointed by the government were undoubtedly aware of the minister's pattern and what it implied, and *they* hadn't done anything, which meant they were all in it. For another, if Vikram tried to make the information public, the minister could and would retaliate by punishing him and his family. Vikram didn't even want to imagine what forms the punishment might take. The son of a powerful politician who once killed a celebrity bartender in full view of three-hundred people had been acquitted of the crime as not one single witness would admit to having seen anything. The Joshis might be wealthy, but the minister and his ilk *ruled* the country.

As the minister's son, Adhith was in a different situation, and he knew it. His love for his father so far prevented him from doing anything, but now...

"I need this dinner to be over and done with," Adhith brooded. "Afterwards—" The phone rang. The landline. With a dismissive glance at it, Vikram waited for Adhith to continue. "You'd better pick it up," he said. "It's probably Tim." The regional CIO. At Vikram's hesitation, Adhith added, "We'll talk after the dinner. I swear, we will."

The door was closing behind him when Vikram picked up the receiver. "This is Joshi," he barked. Damn the CIO. The man could've given Vikram five minutes before calling back.

"Vikram?" queried a female voice, tone tentative.

"Yeah. Who's—*Anju?*"

✦✦✦

Phone held to her ear, Seema kept an eye on the men and women walking past her spot at the entrance to the office building. With Vikram's loo no longer available for private conversations, this was the place she'd chosen. Everyone who crossed the doors was in a hurry to get somewhere and paid no attention to one more woman talking on her device. Getting away from the office was the tricky part. It was tea-break time, so hopefully, no one would notice.

Cringing in humiliation, Seema had reported to the bureau her auntie met with the suspect under investigation to make sure he didn't break Seema's heart. After the initial storm of fury, the SSP—senior superintendent—was calling back with the bureau's decision.

"I'm grateful for the second chance," Seema mumbled into the phone.

"Get this clear, Rawat," the SSP said, her angry voice almost vibrating in Seema's ear. "This is not a second chance. The only reason we're letting you continue is taking you out and inserting a new officer will take time and make Verma suspicious. Do you understand what happened could bring down our entire investigation?"

The bureau had senior agents working the case, infiltrating the businesses and charities connected with the finance minister. Seema didn't know who it was, but she'd been told there was a mole in the minister's office in Delhi. Seema's role was limited to stealing data from Adhith's devices, but if she found enough evidence implicating him and his father, IB could even pull out the rest of the team. If she didn't destroy it all, instead.

Tone brooding, the SSP continued, "I recommended you for this mission only because of your technical skills. Nothing else. You were told not to do dumb shit. We should've said it to your *auntie*. And now... all those officers... all the time we've put in..."

With a loud honk, a taxi came to a halt in front of her building. Tourists piled out, petting the stray dog who welcomed them with a volley of barks. Trying to ignore the ruckus, Seema said, "It might work out for the best. Adhith Verma seems to be... umm... serious about me."

She refused to feel guilty about it. The cold, calculating bastard had invited her to the party only to see if she'd fit in with his circle. That part was crystal clear. He was limiting himself to polite friendliness until she proved herself worthy of being his missus. If Seema had truly been in love with him, she'd have been crushed.

"As I said," Seema went on, "Adhith invited Madhu and me to the Joshi party. Since we've gone as far as meeting each other's families, I'm sure I can persuade him to invite me to his flat soon." Hell, Seema could've done *that* weeks back by agreeing to sleep with him, but she needed to give the bureau *something* to keep them happy.

"A party with the suspect's friends," muttered the SSP. "And your auntie. My God."

Seema winced. "It *is* a family event, so if Madhu refuses, everyone's going to wonder why." This was the real reason she'd agreed to go.

"Whatever," said the SSP, her eye roll obvious even over the phone. "Take Auntie to the party. Let her eat, drink, be merry. Keep her away from the investigation."

"Yes, sir—"

A loud beep. The woman had hung up.

Heading back to the office in the lift, Seema scowled at the phone. If she had something to show for her efforts so far, she could've told the SSP to shut it.

There was a yellow banner flashing across the top of her phone. The spyware she'd installed on Adhith's device had intercepted another communication. Clicking it open, Seema groaned, eliciting curious looks from the other passengers in the quiet lift. Yet another message from Adhith, the fashion plate's tailor in Bangkok.

Adhith read five newspapers religiously, set Google news alerts for his father's name, subscribed to *Men's Health* and *Maxim*, and paid to watch boxing matches. While Sun Tzu's *The Art of War* and Chanakya's *Arthashastra* were his favourite nonfiction reads, Adhith also gorged on the *Game of Thrones* series—*A Song of Ice and Fire* saga as he insisted on calling it in his online book club.

Unlike Vikram, whose only social media presence appeared to be WhatsApp, Adhith maintained accounts on Facebook, Twitter, and Instagram, all set to private. Tinder, too, under a fake name, but it hadn't been used in a while. He also kept a Tumblr blog, not shying away from the socio-political hot buttons of the day.

There were texts and emails from his father, the minister, from Vikram and other friends, from the gym, and a couple of former girlfriends. Appointment reminders from his salon. The greatest number of messages were from the tailor in Bangkok who made shirts to order. Plain old designer clothes weren't enough for Adhith. He got his custom-made and monogrammed.

Seema was getting worried both the income tax department and the Intelligence Bureau were wrong. It didn't look like Adhith Verma was involved in his father's corruption. The only thing criminal about his activities was the money he spent on haircuts and mani-pedis and clothes, but the government had yet to pass laws making metrosexuality illegal. She still needed to check his home computer before she closed the file on her part of the investigation. Even if she hadn't nabbed herself a criminal, she'd have still played an important role in the mission.

When she got to the office, she was careful not to look in the direction of the manager's room. It was ridiculous to be still furious with Vikram over one stupid cab ride, but she couldn't help it.

Tucking the phone into her tote, Seema turned the computer back on. The bureau's orders were to collect data locally, which meant using only her clean phone and her work terminal. The information from the computer was transferred to IB using the phone, then erased. Even the call history was automatically cleared several times a minute. In any case, the phone could not be traced. If Seema got caught, there would be no evidence linking her to the bureau. Since she wasn't planning to get caught, she always kept her phone within reach and turned off her computer when she left her desk. She didn't dare risk anyone accidentally happening on her extra-curricular activities.

"Psst."

Startled, she swivelled her chair both ways. All around her, Imperium employees continued with the day's work. No one was looking at her. Neither the jerk nor the fashion plate was to be seen. The accountant was at his desk, munching on a candy bar while he peered into his monitor.

"To your front," hissed the same voice. Beaming at Seema from above the partition between cubicles was a rounded face, a giant, red dot—*bindi*—between the brows.

"What's up?" asked Seema.

Handing her a slip of paper, the owner of the head withdrew.

Seema took one look and whimpered in dismay. An offer of discount with the bindi-wearer's cousin, the wedding caterer.

In less than two minutes, Seema was in Row Four, confronting Payel, her Bengali friend. "*You* did this. You told everyone about Adhith's party."

Payel stayed in her chair, unperturbed. "Yaar, this is super news. I couldn't keep it to myself."

Seema gritted her teeth. "Yesterday, someone emailed me a list of wedding organisers. Britto says his mother thinks I should pick up a couple of Mysore saris for my trousseau. I haven't even met the woman! Everyone here's acting like I'm marrying Adhith. It's just a party. Not even *his* family's party."

"Everyone here knows Adhith and Vikram sir are almost brothers," soothed Payel. "Meeting the Joshis is like meeting Adhith's family. That's why we're giving you advice. We all think Adhith's going to ask you to marry him. Don't wait too long to say yes. The site visit for our EU client is coming up, and Brussels would be lovely for a honeymoon. Plus, your travel expenses will be covered by work."

There was a plate of banana fritters on Payel's desk, the remnant of the morning snack. Grabbing a piece, Seema stuffed the whole thing into her mouth to keep the frustrated moan from escaping. Payel's laughter followed Seema as she stalked back to her desk.

Her problems didn't show signs of ending. There was an email from the EU client's India representative, Gerrard Peeters—a.k.a. the ghoul. From hitting on her, he'd done a 180 to drooling over her romance with Vikram. Peeters had sent several messages telling her how lovely Brussels would be for a honeymoon. "Why not turn your site visit for the project into a romantic holiday?" the latest missive urged.

A few weeks back, Seema led a sheltered life. *Very* sheltered, thanks to Madhu. No men. Whatsoever. Now, Seema was juggling two fiancés—soul brothers—both of whom were supposed to romance her in Brussels in the near future. In present-day Mumbai, the two men were avoiding her. Vikram, because of their disaster of a cab ride; Adhith, because he didn't want to risk a relationship until she passed his damned test.

At least for the sake of her sanity, Seema needed to finish her mission and get out. The only thing remaining was to check Adhith's home device, but she didn't know how she was going to do it. She entertained herself for a few minutes with the visual of an intrepid, young cryptanalyst in a sheer chiffon sari, dancing seductively to lure the minister's son into her lair. She'd then point her Glock at him, forcing him to reveal his secrets.

Vikram Joshi's accusing face popped into her mind. *Go away,* she ordered the image. *Why should you care who I sleep with?* Seema shuddered. No, she couldn't do it. Someday, she'd find someone better than Vikram, but the fashion plate was not going to be it.

Somehow, she had to get to Adhith's home computer and extract data without sleeping with him. Then, she'd resign from Imperium. She'd disappear from the lives of everyone she'd met there, including Vikram. He wouldn't care. He'd made it clear there was no place for her in his future. Just as well. It wasn't as though Seema could've stuck around.

Even if Vikram forgave her lies *and* decided she was more important than his career, the bureau would immediately suspect her of betrayal. Once Adhith got to know of her real qualifications, he and his father might figure out what she'd been up to. She'd be facing danger from all directions. As her lover... husband... whatever... Vikram would be, too.

Seema shot a glance at the manager's room. As if on cue, the door swung open, and Vikram stepped out, peering in the direction of the office entrance.

Scooting her chair back, Seema followed his gaze. So did a few others in her row.

A short, slim chick with dark brown hair tied in a bun. Not beautiful in the conventional sense but elegant. Features so sharp they could've been sketched with a fine pencil. Skin so clear it was almost translucent. Pale blue jeans, light pink tee, sports shoes. Seema coveted those jeans, but she knew the brand. It was beyond her bank account. The red alligator-skin purse hanging from the chick's shoulder would've cost Seema two years' pay.

The chick smiled at Vikram and walked straight ahead to where he waited, not bothering to acknowledge a single other human being in the office. Hands on his shoulders, she went on tiptoes. With Vikram bending to accommodate the considerable difference in their heights, she planted a kiss on his cheek.

Seema hissed.

Both Adhith and Britto rushed to meet the chick. It was evident Adhith already knew her. After barely a minute's chitchat, Vikram wrapped an arm around her shoulders and led her out, not even looking in Seema's direction.

How could he look? He wouldn't want the snooty princess finding out he'd gone slumming the week before. *Fool,* Seema berated herself, tears pricking her eyes. There was a dull throbbing behind her brow. She'd actually believed a man like Vikram Joshi could be interested in her. Her fingers curled into fists.

"Seema," shouted a voice.

"Huh... Br... Britto." Damn. Vikram's henchman had caught her staring. Pretending nonchalance, Seema leaned back in her chair. "Did you need something?"

The henchman snapped, "I need you to stop being nosy and pay attention to what you're supposed to be doing."

"What do you mean?"

"You didn't read my email, did you?" asked Britto, puffing up. "Change in company policy on accessing product-related applications. From now on, retina scans will be needed to access core areas."

A shock went through Seema. "Why?"

"In case you haven't noticed, we're a cybersecurity company," said the henchman.

"Yeah, but retina scan? Kind of overkill, don't you think?"

The henchman huffed. "Vikram always tests things out in our own office. No one else has ever complained. What's *your* problem?"

"Nothing at all." A test? That was it?

✳✳✳

"Pick a restaurant," Vikram said, dodging a couple of salwar-clad ladies speed-walking their way down Marine Drive's promenade.

Black tetrapod rocks lined the walkway on its ocean side, thwarting the high tide from lashing the coastline. Cars and buses zoomed along the road, beyond which were the office towers forming the Mumbai skyline. The roar of the ocean and the honks of the vehicles mingled in a rhythm peculiar to seaside cities. Wind gusted into the shore, whipping Vikram's red tie around and billowing his shirt into a white cloud. He didn't bother swatting it down. Any respite from the humid heat was welcome. Monsoon was supposedly days away, but the sun thumbed its nose at the experts, continuing its tyranny over the residents of India's west coast.

"I don't feel like lunch yet," said Anjali, kicking a stone with her sneakered foot.

Vikram stopped himself from asking why she dragged him out for lunch if she didn't—you know—feel like eating. Wasn't she *supposed* to eat on time? He eyed her up and down.

She had the same sharp looks as their mother, and like Mom, Anjali was vertically challenged at barely an inch over five feet. With her short, skinny stature and the current lack of makeup on her face, she looked about sixteen. If Vikram didn't already know, he'd have never guessed she was pregnant.

"I'm hungry," he complained.

With a sisterly sigh, Anjali gestured at something. Heavily laden basket slung around his neck, a man with a tanned leathery face was headed towards them. "I'll get you some *chana*," she said. "Okay, Vicky?"

Holding paper cones warm from the spiced chickpeas, they wandered further down the promenade. Chewing on tangy chana, Vikram said, "I haven't heard that name since I was five or six."

She laughed. "You wouldn't let us call you Vicky after you started kindergarten." Meditatively, she added, "You were so excited to go to school with me."

The stories about pregnant women were correct. They were weird. Anjali didn't seem to remember she was strolling down Marine Drive. Instead, she was on a trip along the memory lane. "Life's taken us both a long way from there," said Vikram.

Anjali pointed to the parapet separating the promenade from the tetrapod rocks. "Let's sit for a few minutes." Dropping down next to her, Vikram fidgeted on the scalding hot concrete seating. "The dust will show on the black fabric," she noted, apologetically.

He didn't give a damn about the dust. If he stayed on the concrete too long, his skin was going to peel away when he took his pants off. "So what's up? What are you doing back in Mumbai?" He was pretty sure she hadn't flown two-plus hours merely to have lunch with him. Actually, he couldn't remember them ever having lunch together. Just *them*, not the Joshi family.

"The anniversary party."

"It's on Friday." This was Tuesday. "Don't you have to work until then?"

"I thought Mom might appreciate some help with the arrangements, so I took a couple of days off."

What arrangements? The party was at The Oberoi. The event manager was taking care of everything. All they had to do was show up, looking reasonably clean. "What about the—" Vikram coughed. "—your husband? Is he here, too?"

"He left for Tokyo last week. There's a conference going on."

Oh? Maybe, the stupid party wouldn't turn out as bad as Vikram imagined.

Anjali went on, "He's taking the flight to Mumbai on Friday morning."

Damn.

"Anyway, I didn't want to stay in Delhi all by myself," she said. The dumbass's parents lived in Dubai with one of his older sisters. "So I thought I'd spend some time with my own family. You, especially."

Confused, Vikram asked, "Why did you want to go for lunch if you didn't feel like food? You could've told me to show up on time for the family dinner."

"At home, we won't get a chance to talk one-on-one."

Was it why she'd called on the landline? When Vikram was at work, he didn't pick up calls to his cell phone from his family, figuring they knew how to reach him at the office for emergencies. He wouldn't have taken Anjali's call, either. They wouldn't have had their "one-on-one." What *was* with the Joshis and their newfound desire to reconnect? "What do you want to talk about?"

"Life in general. As you said, we've both come a long way. Vicky, do you ever... have you ever... I mean, are you where you thought you'd be at this age?"

"Sure," he mumbled. "I already knew things weren't gonna be easy. If I keep going at this pace, I'll get where I want in another five or six years. Ten, at the most."

"Have you ever... you know... looked back at some point and felt you made the wrong decision?"

Seema's image flashed into his mind: her smile, her clear voice, her hurt and anger. Ruthlessly, he shut a mental door in her face. "No, I haven't. What's this about, anyway? You have everything you wanted. Perfect career, perfect husband, perfect life."

Anjali flushed. "I was only making conversation. Not complaining." She stood, leaving the packet of chana on the parapet. "See you at home, Vikram."

The first thing Vikram saw when he returned was the note sitting on his desk. Stunt Raju, the stunt director friend of Vikram's nanaji. Since Nanaji's death, the stunt director called every few months, asking about the unpublished memoir gathering dust in the back of Vikram's cupboard. Following his graduation from IIT, the calls from the stunt director became more frequent. *"Just go through the papers,"* he would plead.

Vikram had been fond of his grandfather, but he wasn't going to waste any time perusing the old man's prurient fantasies. He'd first tried lying to the stunt director about having read the whole damned thing but easily got caught in his falsehood. Afterwards, Vikram plainly stated he had no intention of publishing, reading, or even glancing through the papers. There was no way the book would ever see the light of the day. Not unless the publisher possessed a death wish. The families of the women mentioned in the dozen or so pages Vikram *did* read would offer *supari*—a kill contract—on anyone who dared publish such salacious stories. The refusal didn't stop the stunt director. This was his first call to the office, though.

Vikram returned the call, thinking *this* had to be an emergency of some kind. Only, it was the same old drama about the memoir.

"Both you and your mother need to see those papers," the stunt director said before hanging up.

Dr Rattanbai Batliwala Joshi was oblivious to the existence of the memoir, but if she knew, she would've wanted it burnt to ashes a long time back. Vikram frowned. *He* should've destroyed the stuff. He would. After he destroyed the cyberspy.

***

Argh. Seema could just... just *kill* Vikram. Him and his princess and his retina scan rule. She couldn't think of anything else all the way home. In the privacy of her bedroom, Seema dialled the number to the SSP at the bureau. The lady needed to be updated on the new security policy at Imperium.

"Hey." Gayathri poked her head through the door. Seema scrambled out of bed and tossed the phone to the side table, only half-listening to her flatmate. "...night cruise," said Gayathri. The e-zine she worked for was sponsoring a moonlight boat ride. If Seema wanted, she could meet Gayathri and her friends at the Gateway of India and join the party. "It will be fun," Gayathri cajoled.

"You don't need to twist my arm," Seema said. She needed reprieve, even if only for a night.

A quick shower. Seema pulled on a cute dress. Not mind-bogglingly expensive like that of Vikram's princess, but still, cute. A little bit of makeup. The Glock 26 was strapped to her thigh, concealed under the folds of her outfit. She was ready.

"Meow." The cat was on the ledge of the living room window. He had a habit of wandering around, jumping from windowsill to windowsill, peering into the rooms until he found Seema.

"Meow to you, too." She rewarded him with the chin tickle he so loved.

Her phone buzzed.

"I'm on my way, Gayathri," Seema muttered, digging into her tote. Or it could be the Uber taxi. A red ribbon flashed across the top of the screen. Seema's heart slammed against her chest wall. The alarm. Someone had tripped the alarm she'd written into her hacking tool. "Oh, God, oh, God, oh, God," she mumbled. Did she forget to shut down her office computer? Was something running on it?

Not stopping to think, she ran out of the flat. Luckily, her ride was pulling up just as she erupted into the street.

Climbing into the taxi, she said, "Change of plans. Get me to Nariman Point as fast as you can, and I'll pay you double your charge."

***

"Vikram saab," called a voice.

Eyes still glued to the monitor, Vikram said, "Hmm?"

"It's 6:45, saab."

With a start, Vikram looked up. The afternoon watchman was at the door to the manager's room, baton in his hand. It was almost time for him to close the office. Once Vikram left, the guard would have only fifteen minutes to check every nook and cranny before locking the front door for the day.

"Sorry," said Vikram. "I didn't realise it was this late." He'd been going over the company's operations systems thread by thread, trying to figure out how the intrusion happened.

They needed to camouflage the search to avoid tipping off the spy. So no round-the-clock teams. Simply shift work as though they were going on about routine company business. Between Adhith and Vikram in Mumbai and the young engineer based in San Jose, they had to find the hacker.

Picking up his phone, Vikram typed.

Code Master: Got to close up shop for the day.

Cyber Ninja: Roger that. Already been on it since oh-five-thirty. NJ out.

Despite the precariousness of their situation, Vikram was forced to grin. NJ, the young American, fancied himself a digital soldier and used a lot of military lingo in their conversations. The kid was sharp and tenacious. He would keep the work going from the other side of the planet where the day was starting.

Vikram powered down his laptop and tucked it into the bag. "Gimme one more minute," he said to the guard. Juggling the EU project and the cyberattack was tough enough, but add to those the visit from Anjali and the call from the stunt director, Vikram was drained. In the latrine, he splashed some water onto his face and debated going straight home versus making a detour to the gym.

Muffled voices, raised in surprise, sounded outside. Puzzled, Vikram turned off the tap to listen. The sounds weren't close enough to be coming from the manager's room. *The cubicle maze.* It emptied out at precisely five. Even Adhith and Britto, the accountant, left before six. One of the voices had to be the guard, but the other...

"Oh, yeah?" said a female voice, clear in tone. "It's *my* desk..." She rambled on.

Padding out of the room, Vikram's eyes fell on the woman standing with her back to him, arguing with the guard. With extreme willpower, Vikram kept his jaw in place. Seema, clad in a flirty dress, exposing her smooth legs to a couple of inches above her knees. The brown suede belt cinching her waist matched the ankle boots on her feet. The usual large tote was on her left shoulder.

Was this the outfit she wore earlier to work? It was a wonder anything got done in the office. He could only be grateful he'd avoided her all day, or there would've been no doubt left in anyone's mind as to the horny thoughts parading through Vikram's brain. Now, here she was, barging into his space when there was no one left as buffer.

Well, no one if the guard magically vanished. Vikram would be alone with Seema. There would be no one in the office to witness it if he moved those curls to the side to plant a kiss on the silky skin of her nape. No one would see if she turned in his embrace to offer him her lips. If she wrapped those long legs around his waist, letting him carry her to the manager's room. No one would hear his whispers of love or her sobs of pleasure. No one would be around to watch them shatter in each other's arms.

No one except their consciences would remind them she was nearly engaged to his best friend.

'Seema?' Vikram called, thankful he wasn't panting in raging lust. "What are you doing back?"

She spun around. Her large eyes widened. Expressions flickered across her face. Then, all colour leached out. "Vikram? You... it's *you*... I didn't know you were still here."

"It's not the first time I'm working late," he said, noting she was scared. Not embarrassed. Not nervous. Plain scared.

"It's almost seven, so I thought—" she attempted.

"Why are *you* here at seven in the evening?"

"I... umm... I thought I locked my credit card in my desk."

Vikram goggled. "You came here all the way from Kurla to look for it? It would've been safe enough until tomorrow."

"I'm supposed to meet someone nearby," she said, tucking a curl behind her ear. Her gaze skittered towards her desk. "Since the office was on the way, I decided to pick it up."

She was definitely jittery. Still, her explanation sounded plausible.

"I told her we're about to close up," complained the guard.

"It will only take a couple of seconds," Vikram urged. "Let her unlock the desk and get the card."

The guard nodded. "She already checked the desk, and there's nothing in it. She was also trying to check something on her computer."

"The activity on the card," she said. "I can check from home." She turned towards the exit.

"Let me grab my laptop," Vikram said. "I'll walk with you."

"Why?" she asked, tremulously.

Vikram could've understood anger. Annoyance. He could've even stomached indifference. But fear? Why would she fear him? "I need to talk to you about Friday's party," he said, ignoring the guard's curious stare.

In less than five minutes, the lift doors closed, leaving them cocooned in the tiny space. Buttons lit up on the panel. Twenty, nineteen, eighteen... Seema kept her eyes firmly fixed on the doors as though prepared to bolt the moment they opened.

"I hope you're not worried I'm going to mess it up for you," Vikram said, tone subdued. "I haven't mentioned anything to Adhith."

Her head swivelled towards him. "By God. You seem to believe I live to attach myself to one or the other of you. Say what you want to your friend. I don't care."

"You don't?" Vikram jeered. "Is it why you agreed to put yourself through—"

"The test?" Seema completed. The sneer still on her face, she continued, "Yeah, I know it's a test. You had me feeling guilty. When you said the fashion plate wanted to marry me, I felt horrible about... I didn't want it on my conscience. Guess what? If he can put me through that *insult* to find out if I'm worthy enough to be his missus, I have nothing to feel guilty about."

Confused, Vikram asked, "You *know* it's an insult, you're angry with him, but you're still going to the party? Why?"

"Maybe, I want to see how the one per cent lives. Or I could be on the hunt for other prospects. What is it to you?"

The lights on the panel continued to blink on and off. Twelve, eleven, ten... "Seema, don't be like thi—"

"'No women,'" she quoted him, her chest heaving with rage. "Lies. All lies."

"You're wrong," he said. "I meant exactly—"

"Oh, yeah? Who is she?"

"—what I said. Huh? Who?"

"As if you don't know! The snooty chick you went to lunch with."

"Anju?" The lift didn't stop on any of the floors. At this time, there was little chance anyone else was in the building. The lights continued to blink on and off in succession.

"Whoever. You told me... you *told* me you didn't have time for women."

"She's my sister."

"You told me you couldn't afford—"

"Anju—*Anjali*—is my *sister*," he said, loudly.

With a ping, the lift stopped on the ground floor. The doors whooshed open. "What?" asked Seema, slight confusion in her eyes.

"My sister. The one who's married to the dumbass."

Dazedly, Seema exited the lift and walked out into the sultry heat of the dusk. In perfect tandem, they marched to the bus stop. All through, she didn't say a word. Neither did Vikram. He was too busy savouring her jealousy.

In the two minutes it took them to get to the bus stop, the hot pink of the sky gave way to purple, then to glittering black. Horn blaring and headlights blazing, the red vehicle rolled to a halt. When Seema climbed in, Vikram followed, laptop bag on his shoulder. Surprisingly, there weren't many passengers, and they were able to sit together. The bus jerked forwards, throwing them back against the seat.

"Your sister's supposed to be pregnant," Seema blurted, sounding strangled. The wrinkled woman in the seat in front turned to smile at them, drawing one end of her sari closer over her grey head. "This chick didn't look pregnant," Seema accused.

Vikram clucked. "She just got pregnant. Women don't balloon up in a day, you know."

The old lady cackled. "He's right. It takes nine months."

Frowning, Seema snapped, "Who asked you?"

With an indignant sniff, the old lady turned back.

"Your sister," Seema mumbled. Eyes flashing, she added, "I wasn't upset or anything... I just... I felt like a fool."

Mentally patting himself on the back for not smirking, Vikram held up both hands. "I get it."

"No one likes to be made a fool of. That's all."

"I understand."

"S.P. Mukherjee Chowk coming up," called out the khaki-clad conductor. "Next stop, Old Custom House."

Smart card for the bus in hand, Seema stood in a hurry. "I'm getting out here."

"Custom House?" Vikram yelped, heaving himself up. He dug out his own smart card. "We're on the wrong bus."

"*We're* not," Seema squeezed past him to cling to one of the steel bars. "You are."

"Well, I'm supposed to go to Cuffe Parade. Why did you make me get on this one?" Brakes screeching, the bus jerked them back and forth. Vikram grabbed the closest steel bar to keep from falling flat on his face.

"Me?" asked Seema. "I didn't ask you to go anywhere. You wanted to talk about the party."

"Can you two please go home and continue the argument?" asked the conductor, tone insultingly polite. "The rest of us have places to get to."

"We're not together," Seema announced. "He doesn't want to marry me."

"Marriage?" Vikram exclaimed. "We haven't even gone out for coffee."

"Good for you," interjected the old lady. "Find a nice girl. *She's* indecent. See the way she's dressed."

Seema pivoted to the old woman, baring her teeth in a hiss.

The old woman screeched with laughter. *"Chudail,"* she said, calling Seema a witch.

"Dayan," snarled Seema, upping the insult level by calling the old lady a monster.

"Aey, chokri," called a voice, disrespectfully addressing Seema as a broad. A skinny lad stood from one of the back seats, his pencil-thin moustache trembling in outrage. "Don't speak like that to my grandmother." There were four or five more young men in seats near him, watching the scene with anticipation.

"Are you getting off the bus or not?" shouted the conductor.

"We are," said Vikram, keeping a wary eye on the gang at the back. He grabbed her smart card and waved both his and hers in front of the validator. "Let's go, Seema."

Seema had drawn herself to her full height and was facing down the young men. Her entire figure quivering, she opened her mouth. Before she could unleash the full force of her impressive vocabulary, Vikram swept an arm around her waist and hauled her towards the door.

Oh, sweet God. The softness of her form in his arms. The warmth of her against his chest. Her curls tickling his nostrils.

"Let go of me," she grunted, ramming her elbow into his lower sternum.

Goddammit. Tears sprouted in his eyes. She had great upper body strength. "I'm trying to help you." He managed to get them both to the top of the steps and muttered in her ear, "Those goons are itching for a fight."

Even Vikram—with all his social ineptness—could see the danger. Unfortunately, Seema was too incensed to care. Her bottom squirmed against his crotch. Her right breast was perilously close to his fingers. Almost weeping in mental agony, Vikram closed his hand into a fist, refusing to even *think* about shifting it up an inch.

A sharp pain shot up his leg. Vikram yowled. The heel of a boot was on his left foot. Her lower body strength wasn't too bad, either. "Stop mauling me," he bellowed. They tumbled down the steps, somehow managing not to fall on their faces.

"Chudail," the old woman shouted after them.

Before Seema could respond, the bus squealed away from the curb, taillights fast disappearing into the dark night. Not that it stopped her. Wriggling out of Vikram's hold, she ran to the next lamppost and stuck her tongue out at the vanishing vehicle.

Ignoring the curious stares of those waiting at the brightly lit bus stop, Vikram laughed. Hands on his knees, he guffawed.

Pivoting, she marched towards him. "You couldn't take care of those puny twits? What's the point of having all those muscles if you're not prepared to use them?

"Heh? There were *five* thugs back in the bus and only one of me." He whooped in hilarity. "You're a mathematician. What were the odds?"

"You might as well have not been around," she ground out. "If they'd actually attacked, I'd have been alone."

Laughter petering off, he asked, "You think so?" When she didn't answer, he said, "I'd have killed every one of them if they laid a finger on you."

"Really?" she jeered. "I thought you didn't care for the five-to-one odds."

Steadily, he said, "It wouldn't have mattered. Not even if the odds were hundred-to-one."

She subjected him to an unblinking gaze. "Hundred-to-two."

"Huh?"

"The odds. A hundred of them and two of us."

The idea of her defending him against the thugs should've been comical, but it wasn't. Vikram was damned sure Seema would've stayed at his side. "Rajni Kanth," he teased. The actor's stunts sometimes defied the laws of physics and biology.

Eyes crinkling in mischief, Seema balled her left hand into a fist and swung at the air by Vikram's jaw.

"Whooaa." Arms flailing, he pretended to topple backwards from the force of her blow.

She reached out and grabbed him by the shirtfront, acting as though she were holding him upright with one hand. As he shuddered with amusement, she snorted. Her sputters turned into gales of laughter. Together, they howled in mirth.

The passengers waiting for the next bus chattered among themselves. Pedestrians shook their heads in bemusement and skirted the couple laughing insanely in the middle of the footpath. On the road, taxis sped by, headlights glaring. Buses, bikes, and rickshaws careened past. Finally, the laughter slowed into occasional gurgles.

Silly grin still on his face, Vikram looked his fill of her. "You did it on purpose," he accused, playfully. "I saw you with the EU client. You can restrain yourself when you need to. So what happened in the bus?"

The joy on her face slowly faded, replaced by confusion, followed by worry. Abruptly, she said, "Gimme my smart card. I have to go."

At least the peculiar fear hadn't returned. Handing her the card, Vikram tucked his into his pocket. "Where—"

She turned away, her movements unusually clumsy.

"Seema?"

Back to him, she dug into her tote and brought out her phone. "*Seven* missed calls. I had it on vibrate. Damn. I'm so late."

"Late for what?"

Without answering, she made her way through the crowd.

He jogged to keep up. "Where are you going?"

"Gateway of India," she said, texting as she walked.

"Gatew—" Vikram put things together. Her dress, her nervousness, the romantic destination. "You're meeting Adhith."

She faltered. "No."

"Then?"

"None of your business."

In two long strides, Vikram was facing her, jogging backwards. "Adhith is my friend. Which makes it my business."

"Nice excuse."

"It's no excuse. Why else would I want to know who you're meeting?"

"You tell me." She kept on walking.

Vikram bumped into someone. More than one someone. Ignoring the annoyed shouts and angry curses, he kept walking backwards, facing Seema. "As you said, don't imagine I'm jealous or something."

"Why would you be?" Seema snapped. "No time for women, remember?"

"*I* remember. Merely making sure you do, too."

Seema huffed, flinging a hand above her head. "How could I forget?"

Vikram's backside collided with something hard. A jolt of electric pain went up his spine. At this rate, he was going to be black and blue by the morning. Cursing, he turned to find one of the Victorian lampposts around the Gateway.

The well-lit monument loomed against the night sky, glowing golden in the star-spangled darkness. Despite the late hour, crowds thronged the place.

A buzzing sound. Seema glanced at her phone and screeched, "They *left?*"

Alarmed by the tone, Vikram asked, "Who left?"

"Gayathri and her friends," Seema wailed. She dropped the phone back into her tote. "My flatmate. The e-zine she works for is sponsoring a night cruise. She invited me. We were supposed to meet here and go to the ship. There's supposed to be music and dancing and *everything*. But I was late."

"A cruise?" Vikram asked, incredulously. So much moaning over such a trivial thing. "Of the Mumbai shoreline? You've lived here all your life!"

Seema glared. "Unlike you, mister, I didn't have the money to go on cruises. I've never been on a ship. Not even on a little boat."

She had to be joking, being her usual melodramatic self. After her rescue by her auntie, she'd lived a stable life. There surely was money for *some* entertainment. "C'mon." He chortled.

"You're laughing at me?" she spat, immense hurt written on her face.

Shit. She wasn't kidding. He straightened. "I'm so sorry... I didn't mean... there will be other cruises."

"Which part of my life seems funny, you rich jerk-face? The part where my loser father tried to sell me to a pimp?"

"What?" Vikram knew her aunt rescued her from the redlight district, but he never realised... he should have...

"The part where I ran through the streets in the middle of the night to escape them?" Seema went on, fury radiating from her.

"Oh, my God, Seema. I didn't know." Vikram reached out, trying to gather her into an embrace.

Shrugging loose, she stepped back. "I didn't mean to tell you—" Her breath came in short, sharp spurts. "*Nothing's* going the way I planned." Eyes wide, she blinked. Her lashes suddenly sparkled.

Tears? Vikram couldn't stand it. "I'll kill the bastard," he promised.

She held up a hand, as though she'd reached the limits of her tolerance.

"Or I'll beat him until he begs for death. Then, *you* can kill him."

A small sob, quickly stifled.

"I will. I promise I will." He needed her to believe it. Anything to erase the sadness from her eyes. "Afterwards, we'll go on a cruise."

With a start, she stared at him. "Lemme get this straight. You and I are going to kill my loser father and go on a cruise?"

"We might have to be happy just beating him up," Vikram allowed. "Or the cops won't let us go anywhere."

"Have you gone mad?" Seema asked.

Reaching out, he took her hand and held it to his heart. "Listen to me, carefully. I *will* take you on one of those cruises."

Biting her lip, Seema mumbled, "You don't get it. It's not about the—"

Vikram tugged her closer. With his free hand, he cupped her cheek, his thumb wiping away the offending moisture. Her skin glowed under the golden light from the lamp. Sea breeze softly whistled around them, riffling through his hair, rustling her dress. The floral smell of her was in his breath. Her body heat penetrated his shirt, doing strange things to his heartbeat.

"We *will* go on a cruise," he whispered. "I'll bring my guitar. We'll dance until you're too tired to move another inch." Bending down, he kissed her tenderly on the mouth. Soft, warm honey. One tiny sip, and Vikram was giddy, as though he were drunk.

A muffled gasp of surprise. When he withdrew, she stayed perfectly still, her gaze pinned on his face. Vikram wasn't sure how long they remained in the pool of light thrown by the lamp, eyes locked on each other.

A shrill catcall broke their trance. Seema tugged her hand loose and looked wildly around. Before Vikram could say a word, she ran. She didn't respond to his shouts, his calls for her to stop. She didn't even turn back to check.

He gave chase. The people, the lights, the vehicles... all blended into a polychromatic tunnel. Brakes screeched to his left. Honks, yells, a piercing whistle. By the time he got to the other side of the road, she was inside a bus, speeding away. In less than ten seconds, she vanished into the night.

Chapter 12

Stupid, stupid, stupid. Seema Rawat was criminally stupid. She stumbled into a seat in the moving bus and wondered despairingly if she could mess up her life any worse.

As soon as she'd seen her computer still powered down and Vikram working late, she remembered the retina scan and had known it was he who tripped the alarm. Seema's mouth went dry. For the first time since signing up for the investigation, she fully comprehended the danger. Vikram was Adhith Verma's best friend. *They* might be innocent, but Minister Verma was not. Once the minister learned of the digital break-in, he'd figure out what Seema was up to, and it wouldn't be long before he sent his thugs after her and Madhu. When she blabbered, Vikram stared, mild confusion in his eyes.

Seema's thoughts came into sharper focus. Vikram's face held no trace of awareness of her perfidy. Either he accidentally set off the alarm, or he knew about the hacking but hadn't managed to ID the hacker. Given the retina scan policy, the latter was most likely. She was safe for now. Seema was almost back to breathing normally when he asked her to wait so he could ride with her to the lobby.

When he returned to his room to pick up his laptop bag, she cursed herself. She might be safe, but her career was disintegrating before her eyes. She knew—she *knew*—how skilled he was. The Indian government couldn't penetrate the defences he built, for God's sake. Vikram Joshi wasn't counted among the all-time greats of the game for nothing. He might eventually ID her as the culprit. Before that happened—before the minister heard about her— she needed to disappear. She also had to let the bureau know she'd botched the investigation. Both the Intelligence Bureau and the income tax department would deny any connection with Seema.

Her future as a cryptanalyst would vanish into thin air. She'd never be able to find another job. Not with the income tax department refusing to acknowledge she was ever employed by them. Or worse, if they informed other employers what a miserable failure she'd been.

Madhu. Oh, God. Madhu would have to be fired, too, to prevent the minister from tracking Seema through her family. Until someone else proved Minister Verma's corruption, the Rawat women would have to spend their lives on the run, hiding from him. Seema had set out to prove her worth as an independent adult, and she'd destroyed Madhu's life along with hers.

Stop, you damned fool. Think. If Seema could clean up any tracks she might have left, she could stop Vikram from ever IDing her. Then, she could quit her job at Imperium. Without completing her investigation, her career wouldn't be taking off as she imagined, but both she and Madhu would be safe. Their jobs would be safe. If she miraculously managed to extract data from Adhith's computer before erasing her tracks, she could even claim success.

"Let's go," said Vikram, back from the manager's room with the laptop bag on his right shoulder.

She trailed along to the lift. There would've been no excuse for him to accompany her any further than the lobby, but she *had* to respond to his oh-so-magnimous claim of silence about their cab ride. She couldn't help it. The memory of his female visitor had been gnawing at her mind all afternoon—the visitor who'd turned out to be his sister.

Seema proceeded to make matters worse by spending a cho-chweet-she-could-barf evening with the villain's handsome sidekick. The part about her father slipped out because Vikram Joshi was so damned adorable and made her want to spill her guts. She'd been horrified ten seconds after saying it. Any personal information could be used to track her.

When Vikram vowed to beat her father to death, her heart melted. He promised to take her on a cruise and play the guitar while she danced to his song. The kiss. Oh, God, the kiss. His warm hand, cupping her cheek. The fierce tenderness in his eyes, the shuddering breath, the softness of his lips against hers.

She gaped at him like an idiot, wanting nothing more than to drag his head back down and unleash her wild desires. Her hands itched to tear his shirt off and have her way with him. Seema longed to fill her lungs with his scent, to taste the salt on his skin. If they hadn't been in a public place...

She ran.

It took her three buses and three hours to get to Madhu's flat in Panvel. Twelve years ago, when Seema first arrived at the two-bedroom, Madhu had only been renting it. Within six months, she took out a bank loan and bought it. She claimed it was an excellent investment. Indeed, it more than tripled in value over the following decade. The flat was the one place in the whole world where both Madhu and Seema could relax their guard. With deadbolts and safety chains on the door and alarms on every window, the place was a mini-fortress. Seema had lived there until she was sent on this covert mission.

Madhu couldn't have believed the excuse about taking a few days off because of not wanting to be alone in the flat when Gayathri was at her parents' home in Lucknow. Madhu didn't say anything, though.

Seema spent her sleep hours reviewing options. The easiest way out would be to erase any tracks and abort the mission before returning to her real job at the income tax department. If she still wanted her glory, she'd have to get to Adhith's computer before her exit. She'd have to do it before Vikram managed to ID her. Either way, she'd be out of the lives of Adhith Verma and Vikram Joshi.

First things first: Seema checked the alerts in place for searches in governmental records for her or Madhu. If Vikram got suspicious of the Rawat women, the fake accounting company would be his next target, so she reinforced the digital traps the bureau set around the server. The second any of her alarms were triggered, she'd have to run, taking Madhu with her.

Unfortunately, she still couldn't think of a way to access Adhith's computer at home. The longer she stayed around to try, the higher the chances of discovery and greater the chances of danger to her and Madhu. As the sun came up, aborting the mission was seeming like the more reasonable option. Seema would be stuck in the same boring job, but she and Madhu would be safe.

Thanks to Vikram and the delicious kiss, Seema had a readymade excuse for quitting—the love triangle she found herself in with *two* of her bosses. She'd have to admit she was a failure, to both Madhu and herself. That she'd started out as the hunter tracking a thief, but now, she was the spy being hunted.

When she heard the first sounds of the morning outside her window, Seema staggered to the kitchen for her chai.

Madhu poured out two cups, adding milk and sugar to each. "I'm also staying home for the next three days," she announced, casually. "I've missed having you around."

Groaning mentally, Seema resigned herself to an interrogation. As soon as Madhu announced she wanted a carrom game, Seema knew her grilling was about to begin. By the time they set up the board, boyish sounds were echoing into the flat from the park next to the building. With school out for the summer, the kid brigade was about in full force, playing cricket. Seema chanced a glance across the dining table. One eye closed and tongue poking out between her teeth, Madhu was studying the carrom board.

Thwack. Swish. Plop. On the board, three pieces fell in, including the red queen. "Yes," hissed Madhu, pumping a fist high in the air.

Seema chuckled. "You're more like me than you wanna admit." Or she would've been if she hadn't been saddled with a rebellious preteen at an age when her mind should've held only dreams of her own glorious future.

Madhu arched an eyebrow. "Which means I can usually tell when you're trying to distract me."

Damn it.

"Out with it," said Madhu. "What happened?"

"Nothing," muttered Seema. Everything. "We might have been wrong," she blurted out. "About Adhith, I mean. I haven't found anything incriminating, so far."

Madhu admitted, "I've also been considering the possibility, but you still haven't had a chance to look at his computer."

Seema winced. "What if we stop the investigation here?"

"I *knew* this had to be why you came running home," Madhu continued. "You've taken this fake romance too far. Verma might be innocent, but he's still not the right man for you."

"Heh? It's not about him. I—"

"Seema, think for a minute about what you're saying!" Agitatedly, Madhu gathered the carrom pieces and arranged them in the middle of the board. "Even if you do complete the investigation and clear him, IB won't approve of any liaison between you two. Imagine what will happen if you stop it halfway through and hook up with him? Also, the minister will be a big problem."

Seema groaned. "There you go again. Madhu, the fashion plate is not my type. I like 'em a bit more masculine."

Fingers spinning the striker on the game board, Madhu looked away. "Verma seems manly enough."

"He gets manicu—argh. Who cares? I don't want him."

"You were talking about sleeping with him," Madhu, her tone snappish.

"It was a stupid joke, okay?" Seema shouted. "I don't know if the bureau has other officers willing to do it, but I'm not. You'd have to put a gun to my head for me to sleep with Adhith Verma."

"Why are you going with him to the dinner party?"

"I *already* told you I have no other option. Until I do a scan of his computer, I can't afford for him to get suspicious." Seema *did* have another option. Once she covered her digital tracks, she could call Vikram and have herself a melodramatic scene about her messed-up love life. She could announce she was quitting Imperium. She had to do it. It was the only way to keep both her and Madhu safe and save their jobs.

"Which brings us back to the problem we started with. How are you going to get into his flat without him thinking you *are* ready to sleep with him? Tell IB there's no more *you* can do. They can send someone else if they want. And no hanging around the place afterwards to romance Verma. Get yourself back home."

Bewildered, Seema started, "Isn't that what I—" Even when she heartily agreed with Madhu, she was misinterpreted. Madhu believed Seema wanted to quit because she was harbouring a crush on Adhith Verma and hoped to get together with him afterwards.

She'd have to explain. She needed to come clean about the whole mess, or she'd spend the rest of her life hearing what a mistake she'd made with Adhith Verma. She'd never again be trusted even with tax audits involving anyone younger than seventy. Taking a deep breath, she opened her mouth to speak.

Madhu continued, "You have to face facts. Verma is not likely to just let you into his flat without wanting something in return."

Seema arrested. A new option occurred to her. What if she didn't wait for him to let her in? The bureau could do warrantless electronic surveillance and wiretapping, but they were reluctant to consider physically breaking into his flat because any evidence thus collected could get thrown out of court. If she broke in and found *no* evidence, it would help them close this part of the case and move on. There would be no legal repercussions. Seema would get reprimanded, but she'd have proved something at least to herself. She'd probably keep her job at the income tax department.

In the unlikely event of her finding something, she'd be fired, and the bureau would send another officer to legitimately extract the same information. Seema wouldn't get the glory she dreamed of; she might even lose her job. But she'd get to keep her self-respect. She wouldn't be a total failure. Madhu's job would be safe in either case. Seema would be risking nothing except her own future.

Excitement built. Biting her lower lip, Seema studied Madhu. Nope. The less Madhu knew, the better. She would not agree to Seema's plan. Casually, she said, "Believe me, Madhu. I have no romantic interest in Adhith. I asked about quitting only because I thought there was no way to get information from his computer. I just thought of a new... umm... technique." Seema fluttered her fingers over the game board in a typing motion. "My professional skills will be enough to get me access. Give me time until the dinner party. I'll complete the investigation."

Calculating rapidly, Seema drummed the table with her fingertips. Yup, the dinner party was the best place to make her move. Adhith was going to find an adoring girlfriend at the party, one who refused to leave his side for anything—at least not until she copied the keys to his flat.

Mentally, Seema reviewed the shopping she'd have to do. Clay, baby powder, lead weights from the tyre shop, propane torch... all the equipment she remembered from her education in the slums. Usthaad—the mentor of her old gang—had just started tutoring the twelve-year-old pickpocket in the more rewarding games of lockpicking and key casting when Madhu dragged her out of the slums. Usthaad had been one-eyed, having sacrificed his left orb in an accident involving a propane torch. *Hmm.* If Seema were to do it herself, she was going to need safety gear.

With narrowed eyes, Madhu studied Seema. "You're very confident all of a sudden."

"Oh, I am. Not to worry, boss. Everything's under control."

The suspicion on Madhu's face did not abate. "Somehow, I *am* still worried."

A loud ping startled both women. On the table, Seema's phone vibrated. Looking at the message, she frowned.

"Something wrong, already?" asked Madhu.

"The spyware I installed on Adhith's phone," muttered Seema. "It alerts me whenever there is new communication. It seems he has an appointment tonight at the women's shelter on Grant Road. Isn't that the one you—"

Madhu sat up. "Yes."

"I wish you'd trusted me," Seema mumbled. "Instead, you poked your nose into my investigation, and now, Adhith is out there, looking for information on you."

On *Seema*, most likely—to make sure she didn't have anything else in her history that could damage him and his precious father in the public eye. She didn't think it had anything to do with the company's probe into the attack on their systems, but if it did, sooner or later, they would trip the digital alarms she'd set last night.

Face red, Madhu admitted, "I made a mistake. I'll fix it. No one at the shelter is going to tell Verma anything about me or you he doesn't already know."

Chapter 13

Adhith paused by the blue door at the end of the hallway and glanced back at the director of the shelter.

She turned from her conversation with the secretary and pushed gold-rimmed glasses up her nose. "Sorry, Mr Verma. Give me one more minute." Her short, curly hair was liberally sprinkled with grey, and her salwar was beige cotton, but the warm smile on her face more than made up for the lack of adornment.

"No problem," said Adhith. When he called for an appointment to tour the facilities, they indicated they'd be happy to let the minister's son come by anytime he wanted, but he asked the director to pick an hour most convenient for *them*. It was after ten in the night, but work never stopped for the ladies who ran the place.

The front entrance of the two-storey building had been unpretentious as was the tiny office where he'd met the director. From there, he followed the woman to this hallway. There were closed doors on either side, and no explanations were offered on what lay behind. The walls were covered with artwork clearly drawn by childish hands.

Vaguely, Adhith wondered if his jeans and navy tee and the leather sandals were too informal for this visit. The director appeared surprised when he introduced himself. Had she imagined a kurta-clad politician showing up at their doorstep? He *would've* costumed himself thusly had politics been on his mind when he scheduled the appointment.

The muttered conversation between the director and the secretary stopped, and the secretary—a young woman in severe need of a better haircut—returned to the front office.

"A friend of mine will be here in a few minutes," said the director. "She doesn't travel this way often, so she called to check if she can drop off some papers. Will it be all right if she joins us?"

Adhith shrugged his indifference.

"Over here is our after-school care centre," the director said. "The women's section is upstairs. We don't allow male visitors there. If you want, we can make you another appointment to meet the ladies in the office during the day."

"Whatever you're comfortable with is fine by me."

At a mild push from the director's fingertips, the blue door at the end of the hallway opened. The only light was from moon rays filtering in through the two barred windows on the far wall. Each rhythmic whir of the ceiling fan was accompanied by a whoosh of warm air in Adhith's face. A click. Dull yellow light replaced the darkness.

A dozen young boys slept on cotton sheets laid in a row. Most of them were clad only in shorts. "These children are all seven and under," whispered the director. "Girls the same age are in a different room. Those over seven need more space, so they have four rooms allotted." There didn't seem to be anything else to see, and she turned the light off.

Backing out into the hallway, Adhith asked, "Their parents?"

"Sex workers. If not for places like this, they'd be tucked under the cots while the moms entertained customers."

Shocked, he asked, "With the kids watching?"

"Some of the more concerned moms drug their children."

"Concerned? To drug them?"

"Believe it or not, yes. If not, they're likely to run around and start in the business earlier than intended."

"Start—" Rage, dark and thick, rushed into his head. "They're *babies."*

From the other end of the hallway came a familiar voice, "Welcome to the other half of the world, Verma."

He spun. "*Madhu?*"

A thick folder in her hands, the woman in the wine-red hoodie and black leggings marched to the director, her red booties making no sound on the concrete floor. "Sorry I'm late. Traffic. I completed your application for tax exemption renewal."

"Thanks," said the director, glancing between Adhith and Madhu. "You know Mr Verma?"

His mind teetered from the combination of angry disbelief at the director's words and confusion on seeing Madhu when he was least expecting her. "Are you having me followed?"

"I was about to ask you the same," she snapped back. "Why are you here?"

Worriedly, the director said, "Madhu, he—"

Not taking his eyes from Madhu, Adhith held up a hand. "I wanted to see if I could help in some way, so I asked to visit. Is it a problem?"

Eyes spitting fire, she said, "Hell, yes, it is. You chose this place on purpose."

"Shh," said the director. "The children are sleeping."

"You give yourself a lot of importance," Adhith said to Madhu.

"See?" Madhu hissed, shoving the folder in her hands into the arms of the confused director. "You knew about my connection to this place."

"The fact they rescued you? Yes, I assumed this was the NGO you mentioned. They're in the right location and would've been open back when you were fourteen. It doesn't give you veto over who visits them."

Flushed and sweaty, Madhu shouted, "You—"

"Shh," said Adhith, finger to his lips. "The children are sleeping."

There was a muffled gasp from the director which sounded suspiciously like a strangled laugh.

Gritting her teeth, Madhu fell silent. From the tote on her shoulder, she pulled out a bottle and gulped water.

He could almost *see* the raised hackles. Back in college when Vikram chose to hang out at the Verma residence in Uttarakhand than go home for vacations, they'd been on safaris at the Corbett Tiger Reserve. They'd once spotted a couple of tigers mating.

The restless tigress pacing, roaring, guzzling water. The male and female circling each other, sparring. He had to prove his worth before she signalled her willingness. Before she let him grab her by the scruff of her neck. At the end of coitus, she swiped at him, forcing him to take evasive action. But she welcomed him back, again and again. The cats had a glorious time, startling the forest with their roars of satisfaction. The guidebook said they'd be at it more than a dozen times a day for close to a week. True *jungle mein mangal*— jungle joy.

Adhith blinked, dragging his mind back to the hallway at the shelter. What the bloody hell was he doing? As though Madhu didn't occupy enough of his thoughts already, he had to fantasise about jungle sex with her?

"I swear," he said, a hand to his heart. "I wasn't trying to do whatever it is you're imagining. I don't know if you remember the waiter at the teashop where we met. His sister is a maid here. He told me about a government grant which never came through, and I thought I'd check things out in person before offering to intervene."

Adhith didn't reveal he'd drawn the waiter into a conversation about the NGO, hoping to learn more about Madhu Rawat. Even with all the other messes in his life he'd yet to sort out, there was a compulsion within him to learn what made her tick. If she wouldn't cooperate, he'd go to others who knew her. Finding that the waiter's sister worked for the shelter was a surprise.

In their difficulties with the grant, Adhith saw a way to get his foot in the door.

"Yes," said the director, eagerly. "I was hoping to talk to you about the grant. I had no idea that's why you asked to visit."

Adhith nodded at her, pasting a smile back on his face. Out of the corner of his eye, he watched Madhu take a deep breath, trying to compose herself. Fists clenched, she ground out, "I'm sorry. It seems I misunderstood your intentions."

In the most sickeningly sweet tone he could muster, Adhith cooed, "It's all right. Even the best of us make mistakes." He closed his left eye in a slight wink, making damned sure she got his mockery.

Temper sparked back in her coffee-coloured irises, but she was in no position to start another fight. Not when she'd come across as the bad guy in the last one.

"I'm glad you're here," said the director. "You understand the finances of the grant better—"

"I'm an accountant," Madhu interrupted, her words tumbling over each other. "I *should* understand finances better than other people."

The director frowned. "Heh? I guess you *are* an accountant, but you work for the Inc—"

"Don't worry," Madhu said, tittering. "My company's not going to charge you for it."

"Your *company?*" said the director, looking thoroughly confused.

Adhith snickered. "I think she made a joke."

Madhu glared. "I was merely reminding everyone I'm an accountant, working for *G.K. Financial Services.*"

The director rolled her eyes. "I got it. You're an accountant, working for... er... *G.K. Financial Services.* Mr Verma is the son of the finance minister. The shelter could use help from both of you. *If* you can refrain from provoking each other for an hour or so."

When they returned to the tiny front office, strains of the latest Bollywood hit song drifted in through the window on the left. Raucous male laughter accompanied the music. "A card club," said the director, gesturing Adhith to one of the chairs across her desk. "No choice but to ignore them."

The secretary brought in a tray laden with spiced chai and chocolate biscuits. From the chair next to his, Madhu helped herself to a number of pieces, munching on them with relish. He bit back a grin. On the day they met, she'd ordered kebabs, coated with spices and dripping grease. Now, the sugar-laden cookies. The tigress didn't believe in dieting.

They spent the next twenty or so minutes going over the programs run by the NGO, including this after-school care. "The private donations cover the food." The director leaned forwards with her elbows resting on the wooden desk. "But we need part-time teachers. The children need help with their homework. Also, we urgently need to add a couple of rooms to the building. There are too many children to cram into the space we currently have."

Hooking an ankle over his knee, Adhith rested the folder on his lap. "What exactly is the problem with the grant?"

"It came through," said the director. "On paper."

He flipped through the pages. "Do you mean it wasn't enough?" His eye snagged on a number in bold. "Twenty lakhs should've kept things going for a while."

At the sudden silence, he looked up. The director was exchanging glances with Madhu. "The Ministry of Women & Child Development handed over the administration of the grant to a third party," said the director. "They're in charge of all the hiring, the purchases, etcetera. We were told building an extension to the current structure was out of the question. All we got were two twelfth class graduates for ten thousand each a month."

"What?" exclaimed Adhith. "It's outrageous. Did you report it?"

"Yes," said the director.

"And?" Adhith prompted.

"Nothing happened," said Madhu. "The money for the grant was issued by the *finance* ministry, and they'd put out tender for its administration. The company won the contract with the same numbers."

"They were the lowest bidder?" Adhith asked, incredulously. "It's not possible. Something's wrong."

"That's what we believe," said the director. "I'm hoping you can check into it for us."

"I will," Adhith said. "I'm familiar with the company. I don't understand what they hope to gain from this kind of petty thievery. Twenty lakhs is pocket change to them."

Madhu set her glass of tea on the desk. "It's not only those twenty lakhs. The same people run a number of grants around the country."

Thus raking in crores of taxpayer money, part of which they funnelled to corrupt politicians like the finance minister. Unable to face the women, Adhith closed his eyes. Incredibly fatigued, he said, "Let me see what I can do. I'm going to need the financials on your organisation... details of how it's run, etcetera."

"I have copies from the grant application," said the director.

When she left to get the papers, Adhith closed the folder and tossed it onto the desk. He slid down in his chair, resting the back of his head on the wood frame. Outside, the card club switched to a different song, its tempo faster. "What am I going to do?" he muttered, moving his foot in time with the beat.

Madhu shifted in her seat, not saying anything in response.

"Tell me," he started. "Have you ever felt like you were at a fork in the road? When you can see both outcomes, and neither one is pleasant?"

"Yes."

That was quick. Turning his head, he studied her. Staring at him from behind black-rimmed glasses were the same almond-shaped eyes he remembered from their two previous meetings. The same lovely face, the same ponytail, the same intoxicating scent. Gorgeous woman, made all the more fascinating by the strength of her character—by the steel in her spine.

"Seema," he said, realising. "She was your fork in the road. What happened? Did you have a boyfriend who objected?" He didn't really expect an answer; except at their first meeting in the tea stall, Madhu had not volunteered any personal information.

"Does it always have to be about a man? No, there was no boyfriend. Not at the time, anyway. I got a lot of advice from a lot of different people. Even the NGO. They offered to place Seema in the same orphanage I lived in. I couldn't do it to her."

Bemused but gratified Madhu was finally opening up, he asked, "Why not? You obviously did well there. Also, you could've still visited." It couldn't have been easy for a twenty-four-year-old to take on the responsibility for a preteen girl. The decision altered the trajectory of Madhu's life.

"Yes. But Seema and I are temperamentally different. She prefers to forget the bad. All she remembers from her time in this neighbourhood is the fun she had." Madhu smiled to herself. "Seeing the world through rose-coloured glasses... Seema actually has a collection of red and pink sunglasses... anyway, she needed someone to watch over her, make sure she wasn't dragged back into the muck. Whereas I... after my parents died, my brother told me what I'd have to do if I wanted to eat."

"Bastard," Adhith growled. His hand itched to thrash the piece of shit to death.

"Don't give him all the blame," said Madhu. "You haven't heard the whole story. My father used to work at this shelter, doing odd jobs for them. The director at the time knew what was going on with me. She tried to get me out."

"The courts don't let NGOs take kids away from their families," Adhith said. "Not unless there is proof the family is unfit."

Shaking her head, Madhu said, "It didn't get to the courts. I refused to go."

After a couple of seconds, Adhith asked, "Why?"

"It was the home I'd grown up in. My brother was the only family left to me. I helped his wife around the house. His daughter—Seema—slept on my cot at night. When it rained, she and I used to count the drops dripping through the crack in the roof. That's how she learned her numbers."

"You were a child, Madhu. Even for adults, it's natural to want to stick with the familiar. Your brother was a grown man. Your flesh and blood."

"Intellectually, I know all this. It doesn't stop me from wishing I could go back to that day and make a different choice."

"So you decided to keep Seema with you," Adhith mused. "You were worried she'd make the same mistake as you... but out of naïveté, not fear of loss."

"More or less... anyway, when I got hungry enough, I thought 'how bad could it be?' I knew girls from the neighbourhood who did it. Some were younger than me. *I* escaped the business until the ripe old age of fourteen only because my parents were alive until then. Also, the other girls seemed to be doing okay." Madhu took a deep breath. "They *were* okay. As long as they went along with whatever the customer wanted. As long as the pimp and the agent got their money. The possibility of disease didn't even occur to me."

On her lap, her fingers twitched as though with minds of their own. He'd been arguing with her just minutes ago, but Adhith couldn't help but offer his hand to the tigress. Madhu took it, gripping it tightly.

"The first customer wasn't bad," she said. "A college student. Neither of us was sure what we were doing. The second... a teacher with a penchant for beating up bad girls."

Adhith sat up. Bringing their linked hands to his heart, he murmured, "I wish I'd known you then."

"You'd have been six or seven," she said. "What would you have done?"

"I don't know. Something..." *Anything* to keep her safe.

Madhu continued, "I remember the shock of the first blow. It was on my face. The pain, the terror. I screamed, but no one came to check. I fainted for a while. When he left, I tried to stand. Ended up falling on my face. I couldn't even breathe. My chest hurt. My leg hurt. If I could just get out the door, my pimp would be there. He could get help."

Closing his eyes against hot tears, Adhith kissed her knuckles.

"I was underage. Neither the pimp nor my brother dared take me to the hospital. I remember thinking I was going to die on the floor. I remember hearing Seema cry in the next room. She was two. Her mother was screaming at her to shut up."

"Seema's mother wouldn't help, either?"

Madhu laughed, the sound bitter and sad. "That woman? She was the one who collected the money from the customers. I didn't even bother asking."

"How did you get to the shelter?"

"I decided my brother and his wife were not going to be the last people I saw. The only one left who cared what happened to me was the director of the NGO. If I died, I wanted her to be holding my hand. If I lived, I'd ask for her help. So I limped and crawled until I got *here.*" Madhu looked around the small office they were in.

"You lived."

Inclining her head, she said, "I had broken ribs and a fractured knee, neither of which would've killed me. The hospital ruled out every possible STD. When I was released, the NGO sent me to the orphanage. Being orphaned and poor got me in the hospital, so I decided I needed to be able to take care of myself. The nuns at the home sent me to school. After that, the director of the NGO offered to pay for college, but I got scholarships. She helped me get a job at the Inc—doing income taxes for the accounting company. She's retired but still insists I call her once a week. The lady you met is her daughter; she was a brand-new teacher at the time. They saved me."

"You saved yourself," he corrected. "They helped."

"Perhaps. When I left, I never imagined my brother would try to sell Seema... his own child... someone in the neighbourhood heard about the plan and called the NGO. The women here helped me get her out. But there *have* been girls who died. *Boys* who died. Because of places like this shelter, there have been some like me and Seema who escaped. Verma, if you're the nice guy you claim to be, help them. Please."

There it was. The reason she'd opened up. She'd assumed the fork in the road he was talking about was ambivalence about helping the NGO. Adhith couldn't find it in himself to be annoyed. With a smile and a final pat to her knuckles, he laid her hand back on her lap. "I'll make sure the shelter gets the money."

Even if he had to pressure his father into signing over campaign funds, he'd do it. Papaji might take credit in the media, but Adhith didn't care. The next Madhu who needed a safe place to stay would have it. The next wounded tigress would have a place to heal.

As for the fork he'd actually been talking about, he'd have to decide. Soon. The only way he could have the political career he wanted was by forcing

Papaji out of business. His father or his future—Adhith's conscience wouldn't let him have both.

Fifteen minutes later, they were walking out of the shelter, Adhith holding one thick binder containing all the info on the NGO.

"Let me take you home," he begged, standing in the pool of light thrown by the streetlamp. "I know you have the gun and everything, but please... for my peace of mind."

Around them, the night continued. Temperature dipped slightly, bringing mild respite from the summer heat. Buses and cars crawled, honking irately at the pedestrians blocking the zebra crossing. "I'm going to Seema's place in Kurla. It's less than an hour on the bus."

"Stubborn woman," he accused. "Fine. I *am* going to stay with you until you get on the bus. Also, text me when you get to the flat."

Madhu smirked. "How did I survive all these years without you?"

As they ambled down the footpath, he asked, "Who told you I was here? Are you really having me followed?"

She laughed. "Nothing as exciting. Someone connected with the shelter heard about your visit and alerted me."

"I'm glad." When she looked up, he added, "Gave me a chance to talk to you."

A light flared in her eyes. At his slow smile, her gaze skittered away. His heart soared. Tone trying hard for primness, she said, "*I* had to put up with that god-awful noise, masquerading as music."

The tigress was pretending disinterest. They were in a public place, so he'd have to play along. "You don't like Bollywood music?"

"Are you kidding me? I *love* it... but the card club's songs can hardly be called music."

"Music, like beauty, is in the eye of the beholder. There wasn't much of a melody, but the beat was decent. I can easily see myself drunk and dancing to it."

"Do you have to spin everything into a positive? I bet you'd have joined them if you could."

"Would've been fun," he admitted. "Life's more pleasant when you find something to like about people. They tend to like you back. It means you have to tolerate each other's song choices."

She hmphed. "The cabaret numbers from the black-and-white movies are the best. Nothing from today comes even close."

He grinned. "I can see you in one of those scenes. Evening gown, diamond jewellery, fur stole..."

"I don't have a gown," she exclaimed.

"Twirling your way across the dance floor..."

"I do like to dance," she mused.

"Teasing me... tempting me..."

Her steps faltered. "Verma, you... Seema..."

They were at the bus stop, and Madhu peered down the road for her ride.

"Look at me," he demanded, urgently. She wouldn't turn in his direction, but she couldn't hide the tremor in her breath or the quivering of her lips. If they weren't on the street, if the damned folder weren't in his hands, he'd have circled his tigress, sparring with her. Back and forth they'd have swiped and jabbed until they went insane from longing. "You told me I wouldn't be right for Seema even if I were the nicest man in the world. Well, I have news for you. I don't want her. What's more, I don't think she wants me, either." He was damned sure she'd agreed to go to the party with him only to rub Vikram's face in it, to goad him into forgetting his vow of no women.

"It doesn't change anything," Madhu said, voice hoarse.

"Yes, it does," Adhith insisted. "I can't do anything about it until the damned dinner party is done." He didn't dare cancel the plan. Papaji would be relieved his son broke it off with Seema and would immediately pressure Adhith to throw his hat into the political ring. Announcing he'd developed a thing for the auntie instead of the niece would call a screeching halt to his father's schemes, but Adhith couldn't do it to Madhu. He'd been willing to use Seema but not Madhu. "There are a few things I have to sort through. Afterwards... Madhu, I haven't been able to stop thinking about you. I need to figure out—"

"It's not only about what *you* need. *My* feelings are important. I don't feel the need to figure out anything."

"Gimme a break. I've lived long enough to be able to tell when a woman's indifferent to me. You, Madhu, are far from it. What you are is scared. I'm not sure why. If it's the age thing, I don't give a damn, and neither should you. If you thought Seema had feelings for me, I could've understood. I assure you, she doesn't. In fact, she..."

Adhith shook his head. Vikram and Seema could sort out their own problems. Neither Adhith nor Madhu needed to interfere. He frowned, guiltily hoping the other couple didn't sort it out before Friday. All of them needed to get through the dinner party, where every guest would be under the assumption Adhith and Seema were nearly engaged.

Mentally, he groaned. They were trapped in an impossible situation. He couldn't beg out of the party without his father thinking he'd broken it off with Seema. If the Joshis endorsed her, Papaji would immediately start the media spin of her bio. Once the love story of the girl from the slums and the minister's son was splashed across the newspapers, Madhu would nix any romance with Adhith.

He couldn't imagine a scenario where the Joshis ended up outright hostile to Seema, but if they did, his father would give him space and time to emotionally extricate himself from the unsuitable relationship.

Unfortunately, Adhith had a strong feeling Vikram wouldn't want his family disapproving of Seema. He didn't seem to want to act on his feelings for her, either. Vikram had a one-track mind. He was a twenty-first-century Vishwamitra, the mythical king who'd renounced romance for his career.

Adhith straightened on a sudden thought. Fearing the king's self-denial would give him magical powers to rival the immortals, the chief of the demigods sent the divine temptress, Menaka, to seduce Vishwamitra into abandoning his penances. With help from the God of Love and Desire, Menaka succeeded. Adhith grinned. Calculating rapidly, he announced, "I've got it."

"Got what?" Madhu asked, irately.

"A way for me to convince you to take a chance on me." *And* save his political career. In his mind, Adhith readied the arrows of love he was about to fire into Vikram's heart. Driven crazy by his passion for Seema/Menaka, if Vikram were to publicly announce his feelings, they could muddy the waters long enough for Adhith to escape Papaji's clutches and sort out his relationship with Madhu. *The dinner.* Yup. That was the best place to make a move. "Don't worry, my love," Adhith cooed at Madhu. "Everything's under control."

She arrested, staring at him with wide-open eyes. "People have *got* to stop saying that."

"What do you—"

The phone rang in his back pocket. "Damn," he said, trying to balance the heavy folder in one hand while he pulled out the device.

Tyres screeching, the bus slid to a stop two feet from them. "I have to go," said Madhu.

He nodded. "See you Friday evening."

The phone stopped ringing. Adhith waited until the bus disappeared around the corner to check caller ID. By then, there was a ping, signalling new voicemail.

Device cradled on his shoulder, Adhith listened to the message from one of his former schoolmates who was now a deputy commissioner in Delhi Police. "Hey, Adhi. I checked on your friend's brother-in-law as you wanted. He's at a conference in Japan. You couldn't have seen him in Mumbai."

The dumbass sighting near the Gateway of India when Adhith was talking to Madhu. He'd followed it up only because Vikram hadn't shown up at the Colaba flat as he usually did when the brother-in-law was in residence at the family home. It got Adhith worried the Seema mess inflicted more damage to their friendship than he realised. Anyway, it turned out to be his imagination. The dumbass had not been in Mumbai.

Chapter 14

Vikram watched the scrawny man in the blue, flowery shirt and skinny pants making his way down the aisle between rows two and three. The stainless-steel drink carrier on his shoulder brushed against one of the cubicle partitions, causing the tumblers in it to clink, but he didn't turn around. Bath rag wrapped turban-fashion above his ears, he nodded along to whatever song was flowing through the headphones. The chaiwalla was done for the morning and was headed out.

Calling him into the manager's room for a private conversation was impossible. Every eye in the cubicle maze would be on the closed door. To Vikram's guilty imagination, it seemed there were funny looks on the employees' faces these days. Every one of them appeared to be accusing him of messing around with his best friend's girl—of leading her on and breaking her heart.

He desperately wanted to talk to Seema. They needed to thrash this thing out. For it to happen, she had to show up at the office instead of texting the accountant on Wednesday morning she was taking casual leave for three days. Something about an old collegemate falling down stairs, breaking all four limbs *and* her spine. Miraculously, said friend was still alive and coherent enough to ask for Seema's help until Friday's party. Also, the friend was an orphan with absolutely no one else to take care of her. The outraged accountant approached Vikram, but what the hell was he supposed to say when he knew Seema was staying away because of him? In the end, he asked Britto to wait and see if it became a recurring problem, but Vikram needed to know she was OK.

He tried calling, but she didn't pick up. On Thursday, he knocked on the door of her Kurla flat. No answer. The building manager said Seema's flatmate was in Lucknow to visit family. The manager had no idea where

Seema was. Today was Friday. Vikram needed to talk to her before the party at night, where she'd be on Adhith's arm as his girlfriend.

Vikram considered asking the Bengali chick, Payel Biswas, for Seema's whereabouts, but going to her would start gossip in the office. The one other person Vikram knew Seema interacted at length with was the chaiwalla, who was right now disappearing into the lift outside the entrance to the office.

Catapulting off his chair, Vikram strode through the cubicle maze, getting to the emergency stairwell as quickly as he could. Twenty-one floors to the lobby. He could run fast, though, and the lift would undoubtedly be delayed by stops along the way.

Thundering down, Vikram crossed a couple of electricians, nearly knocking them off their stepladder. When he exploded out the exit, the chaiwalla was nearing the glass doors at the main entrance. "Hold on a second... man," Vikram shouted. *What the hell is his name?*

One of the security guards by the doors scooted his chair back until he was in the chaiwalla's way. The chaiwalla tugged off his headphones. "What, saar? I already gave you your tea and samosa." When the guard gestured with his eyes towards Vikram, the chaiwalla turned, his equipment setting up a loud clatter. Around them, men and women continued to walk in and out of the entrance. "Vikram saar?" the chaiwalla exclaimed. "You want a samosa? I thought you were on a diet."

"No, I'm n—" Was it the excuse Vikram gave? "I mean, I *am* on a diet, and no, I don't want a samosa. Look... uhh..." *Dammit, what is his name? Something Malayali.*

The chaiwalla's eyes narrowed. "Dulquer Salmaan."

The name did ring a bell. Heaving a sigh of relief the man didn't take offence, Vikram made a note to himself never to forget it again. "Listen, Dulquer Salmaan—"

"I prefer to be called DQ," said the chaiwalla, a glint in his eyes.

"Sure. DQ, I need to ask you something." Vikram searched his mind for a way to introduce the topic. Why would he need to contact Seema behind her fiancé's back? "I'm planning a birthday party for Adhith. A surprise party."

"You want me to cater it?" asked DQ, eagerly. "I've been thinking of starting a catering business. My wife's an excellent cook as you can tell."

"No. I mean, yes. Why not? Adhith likes your food. We all do. But—"

"My neighbour's son is studying hotel management. I can get him and a couple of his friends to do the serving." DQ pulled a phone from his pocket, once again setting up a loud clatter with the drink carrier and the tumblers.

"Uhh... okay. But—"

"The venue, you'll have to arrange."

As though Vikram weren't in enough trouble with the real party that night, he had to fake a second party. "First, I need to talk to Seema," he said, words tripping over each other.

"Duh. Seema madam is Adhith saar's fiancée. Of course, you need to talk to her before arranging the party."

"*There's* the problem. She's been off these three days, and I don't know where she is."

"Isn't she supposed to be attending your parents' party tonight?"

"I can't talk to her there," Vikram said, triumphantly. He was good at this. "Adhith will overhear."

DQ ptchaaed. "*Call* her."

"I did. She's not picking up. I... uhh... might have been a little tough on her. Sloppy work, etcetera." Silently, Vikram begged Seema's pardon. Her work was anything but sloppy. In fact, if it hadn't been for their personal entanglement, he would've recommended her for the firm's work-study programme in the U.S. She was blessed with talent, which needed to be nourished. "I thought... uhh... *you* could call? I'll give you her phone number."

DQ waved the phone under Vikram's nose. "I have the number." It hadn't occurred to him to wonder how an entry-level analyst could refuse a phone call from the boss, personal problem or not.

Vikram could hear the ring. *Pick up, pick up, pick up*, he muttered in his mind.

"Hello," came a faint, female voice.

Yes!

"Seema madam?" shouted the chaiwalla, as though he expected the wind to carry his words from Nariman Point to wherever she was. "This is Krish—" His gaze flickered to Vikram. "This is Dulquer Salmaan. DQ."

There was a squawk from the phone. Vikram gestured with his fingers, asking for the device. Holding it to his ear, he moved a couple of steps away. "Don't hang up," he whispered, urgently. "This is Vikram. I need to know... are you all right?"

Silence.

"I'd tell you I'm sorry, but only if it—" His eyes went to DQ and the security guards, all of them staring in his direction. "—was something that didn't seem right to you." Kissing her had seemed the most natural thing in the world to him. "If *you* feel there was nothing wrong about it, I'm not sorry."

"Really?" came the clear, sweet tone. "Not even a bit? What about your future as the cybersecurity king? What about your best friend?"

"I don't have all the answers, okay? I've got to talk to Adhi." Adhith already knew something was going on. He'd said they'd talk after the dinner party. If Vikram didn't go crazy by then.

Seema screeched, "You'd better not mess up my life any more than you already have."

"I'm not doing it on purpose," he said. "I don't want to screw up Adhi's plans. It's not just me and him who need to think this through. You have to decide who you—" Vikram eyed the chaiwalla and the security guards. "—what you want. The original idea you had before I came into the picture or something else?" Casually, Vikram wandered to the other end of the vast lobby, out of earshot of the eavesdroppers.

"How is it any of your business? *You* don't want to be the 'something else.'"

"Forget what *I* want. It seems to me you're not sure about the original idea. Don't do anything you're going to end up regretting the rest of your life."

"Lemme tell you something, mister. Just because I showed an interest doesn't mean my life revolves around you or your friend or any other man. Maybe, I'll set up my own company and beat you every chance I get."

Confusion instantly overcome by sheer pleasure, Vikram laughed. "See? This is what I lo—" Seema had her unique vantage point, something which helped her thumb her nose at the irritants in her life. With or without all the pain-in-the-butt people crowding her space, Seema Rawat would be an awesome force. Plus, there was the sharp intellect camouflaged by the histrionic exterior. "I'm not going to just stand around and let you beat me," Vikram teased. "You *could* put up a good fight. I've been going over the work you did for our EU client. Also, some of your independent research."

She'd been hired in an entry-level analyst position as befitting her bachelor's degree in math and three-month certification in cybersecurity, but her talent surpassed her formal education.

"You're gifted, Seema," he continued. "In fact, I have questions about one of the tools you made. I'm going to present it to the bosses in San Jose. We should incorporate it into—"

"Vikram Joshi," Seema snapped. "Don't change the subject. We're talking about your habit of kissing women and refusing to marry them."

"I don't," he howled. "It was only y... I didn't say I won't... we didn't even talk about marr... women? As in more than one? I swear to God, I haven't done anything of the sort before."

"What do you mean? Are you a virgin?"

"No! I'm—" How did they get onto the topic of his virginity? "You're driving me nuts."

"How many women?"

"Do you honestly expect me to answer such a question?"

"More than hundred or less than hundred?"

"Heh?" Vikram guffawed. "First of all, what do you think I am? A stray cat? Secondly, imagine the question with roles reversed."

"I'd have called you a Neanderthal," Seema admitted, instantly. "The answer's zero."

"What answer?"

"You know, the number of men..."

Everything around Vikram vanished, leaving him standing in a fluorescent green tube. Ones and zeroes rained in sheets along the walls. There was no sound, except his breathing. When he shouted her name, it echoed back at him. Then, he heard a whisper. From somewhere in cyberspace, she called to him. He thundered down the electronic tube. There. A shadow ahead of him. Laughing uproariously, he chased her. Once he caught her, it was she who spun around and dragged his head down for a kiss. Warm, sweet honey. God, she was delicious. He needed to have her. All of her. He didn't care they were in a passageway. He didn't *need* to care because no other life existed in their virtual reality universe. Them. Just them. Laughing, playing, loving. Vikram closed his eyes. "You're going to drive me nuts," he repeated.

"Vikram saar," shouted a voice, from across the lobby.

Damn. DQ, the chaiwalla.

"I've got to go," DQ bellowed. "Gimme my phone."

Holding a hand up, Vikram said into the phone, "DQ wants his device back, so I've got to make this quick. Until I kissed you, I thought I could handle the idea of you and Adhi. Right now, I have no clue what I'm going to do, but I'm not sorry about kissing you. I'm afraid I'm going to keep doing it until you stop me. What's more, Adhi knows how I feel."

Seema hissed.

"I didn't tell him," Vikram added, quickly. "He knows me too well not to have figured it out. He's the one who said we should talk after the party. If I lie, he's gonna figure *that* out, too. I'll have no choice but to come clean. About what's in my mind... not about..." The kiss. It would remain a memory he treasured.

"Don't," she begged. "Please, don't do anything stupid until after the party. Once it's done, everything will return to normal. The way it was before I—everything will be back to normal."

"What's this about the party? Everyone wants to wait until after the party."

"Promise me," she said.

"Fine. Nothing until after the party."

"Vikram saar," yelled DQ.

"One more minute," Vikram hollered across the lobby. His own device was in his pocket, but if he now called her on it, they'd never stop talking. Not until someone blew up the entire planet. Into the chaiwalla*'s* phone, Vikram whispered, "Got to go. Dulquer Salmaan wants his phone."

"Don't hang up," she said. "Which tool?"

"Huh? Oh..." Vikram told her. "Incredible design," he enthused.

"Isn't it?" she said. "I got the idea from the latest HIV research. Something administered at regular intervals—"

"Like a virus scan."

"Like a virus scan," Seema agreed. "Instead of just scanning, it activates—under controlled conditions—both the immune system and anything new it sees."

"Saar, I need my phone back." The chaiwalla was only three feet from Vikram now.

"DQ, please hold on a couple of seconds," Vikram implored.

Seema heard it and laughed. "You don't need me to explain how the tool works. I'm sure you've already taken it apart and studied it."

"Yes, I have," said Vikram. "It's *ingenious*. I want to present it to the big bosses. No matter what you decide about... the other stuff, I'm going to make certain your tool gets to them."

"Sure," she said, tone suddenly deflated. "Vikram, whatever happens, I want you to know what you said means a lot to me."

"You're not discussing any party," complained the chaiwalla. "You're talking about work. No wonder she didn't want to take your call."

"Vikram," sang Seema. "Tell Krishnan I'm going to twist his ear if he does it to you again."

"Who?" asked Vikram, swatting away DQ's grabby hands. The drink carrier got Vikram on the elbow, sending shock waves shooting down to his fingertips.

"Your DQ. His real name's Krishnan. Dulquer Salmaan is an actor. *He's* kind of a cutie." On a peel of laughter, Seema hung up.

Phone gripped tightly in his hands, Vikram turned to face its owner. "Krishnan," he ground out.

The chaiwalla grinned. "She told you, heh? Too bad. I was planning to have you call me DQ in the office."

"Just for the stupid trick you pulled…" Vikram tried to think up appropriate retaliation.

In a sudden move, Krishnan swiped the phone from Vikram's hand. "If you'd paid attention the first five thousand times I told you, you'd have known I was lying."

When Vikram headed back to the office, he felt light-hearted enough to whistle, but when the lift doors swished shut on him and the only other passenger, his misgivings returned.

It was too late for Vikram to change his mind about Seema. Adhith knew of his friend's feelings and still showed no signs of being willing to back out of the dinner. Once he introduced her to his social circle, their identity as a couple would be established. No matter how ambivalent his feelings were in the beginning, he now seemed certain of wanting to marry her.

Everything in Vikram urged him to claim Seema for himself and damn the consequences. He'd even betray his best friend, humiliate him in front of the world. If Seema pushed, if she dared him to follow his heart, Vikram was afraid he'd do it. But she seemed to be weighing the man who wanted her against the man who needed to be browbeaten into acknowledging her. Vikram didn't know what he was going to do if she decided to marry Adhith. Vikram would be part of the *baraat,* the groom's procession. He'd have to dance at the wedding. With the rest of Adhith's friends, Vikram would have to shower the couple with flowers and drink to their happiness.

The lift swooshed up, not stopping on any level. Only the button for Vikram's floor was lit. Vaguely, he wondered where the other passenger was headed. A woman in jeans and a cotton hoodie, an oversized tote on her right shoulder. Her face was turned away, but the blurry reflection on the steel panel showed a pair of glasses on her nose.

What if Vikram had to peer at Seema from a distance, mourning lost chances? What if he shed a tear or two when her first child was born, wishing it were his baby she was nursing? What if his arms ached to hold her, night after bloody night? What if he, bereft of senses, one day begged to make love to her?

What if she let him?

Slumping against the back wall of the lift, Vikram groaned. He needed to leave Mumbai. Anything else was asking for trouble. He'd request a transfer to the San Jose office. Corporate had been wanting him to move there, anyway.

"Are you feeling ill?" asked the woman in the lift, her face still turned away.

"Huh?" Oh. The groan. "I'm fine. I was only... er... thinking of something unpleasant." It would be temporary unpleasantness. Yup. Once Vikram put ten thousand-plus kilometres between him and Seema, things would return to normal. "Everything's under control," he muttered.

The woman straightened. "I'm beginning to hate those words."

Irritably, Vikram said, "What does it have to do with y—" The phone rang in his pocket. An American number flashed on the screen. "Vikram Joshi," he barked into the device, ignoring the strange woman and the sudden gasp she made.

"Vikster," came the excited voice of Cyber Ninja, Vikram's American associate in the mission to capture the cyberspy. "We have a problem."

"Tell me," Vikram said, instantly alert.

"Our spy knows we're onto him."

Shit. All Vikram needed now was for his career to take a knife to the gut like his love life. "How?"

"I don't know. His online fingerprints don't look exactly the same as before."

Heat flared behind Vikram's eyes. "He's covering his tracks. NJ, no more shift work. You, me, Adhith... all three of us are going to be on this round-the-clock."

"All hands, battle stations," agreed Cyber Ninja, tone sombre.

With a ping, the lift stopped on the twenty-first floor. When Vikram hurried out, he was still on the phone with NJ, but he noted the woman stayed inside. The panel above the external doors showed the lift making its way back to the lobby.

"Weirdo," Vikram muttered.

Chapter 15

Adhith waited by the large steel gates guarding the Oberoi while security officers searched his Toyota, making sure there was nothing in it to pose any threat to the hotel or its occupants. Next to Adhith, Vikram was silent, his eyes fixed unblinkingly on the building.

It was only a bit past four in the afternoon, but thousands of yellow bulbs already lit up the hotel, making it glow golden against the bright blue sky. Behind the thirty-five-storey structure, the waters of the sea seemed a seamless extension of the heavens. The sounds of the city continued around them—the honks, the chatter, the disco music coming from one of the taxis. And of course, the ever-present exhaust fumes. The streets thrummed with life.

But Adhith's thoughts were of death. His mind was on a November night in 2008, when the world had been in a celebratory mood over the election of the first black president of the United States. The internet was abuzz with excitement over Twitter, the new messaging app. The students at IIT Bombay were in the throes of their semester exams.

Vikram and Adhith were in their hostel room, poring over study material. There was a commotion outside. Without warning, their door was thrust open. "Did you hear?" asked a classmate. "Shootout at Leopold Café."

"Heh?" asked Adhith, confused. The café was actually one of the most popular *bars* in Mumbai. He and Vikram were planning to go there after the exams.

In the same excited tone, the classmate hurried on, "My brother was outside when it happened. Thank God he's safe. He says it must be one of the gangs."

Even before the classmate finished speaking, another one shoved his way into the room. "It's not a gang," he said, voice trembling. "Check Twitter. There are gunmen at the Taj and the Oberoi."

Adhith's stomach dropped. "Terrorists?"

The second classmate nodded. "They're all over South Mumbai."

A clatter. His chair falling to the floor, Vikram stood. "My parents." When he ran out, Adhith followed.

"No, no, no," said the security guards at the door, pushing back the crowd of students. "You cannot leave. It's not safe." The resultant roars of objection were ignored.

Every phone in the building was occupied, but Vikram took out his brand-new iPhone 3G. He called his parents' home number, the hospital they worked at, their cell phones. "All circuits are busy," he parroted the message. Pale-faced and trembling, he muttered, "God, please God."

"Hang on," Adhith said. "I'm calling Papaji."

Dr Pratapchandra Joshi was part of the emergency medical team, but Minister Verma's secretary managed to track him down. Adhith's father kept in constant contact with the Joshi parents, calling Vikram back to reassure him they were okay. Anjali Joshi—not yet the dumbass's wife at the time—was ordered by the minister to stay put at the medical college in Delhi instead of hysterically running home.

It took a couple of days for the situation to be brought under control. By then, Islamic terrorists had succeeded in killing more than a hundred people with gunshots, grenades, and fire. Bombs exploded in taxis. In addition to the café and the two hotels, the busy Chhatrapati Shivaji railway terminus and Nariman House, a Jewish community centre, were hit.

More than a decade had passed since the horrific day. "Do you remember?" Adhith asked, eyeing the rebuilt hotel.

"I haven't been able to forget," Vikram said, not even asking what Adhith was talking about. "It's strange. We've been here many times since then, but I get a... sometimes, I can still smell the blood. I don't know how to explain it."

Adhith nodded in perfect understanding. When he remembered all the lives lost, his stomach always dropped the same way it did when he first heard the news. "Look at the city now. We beat the bastards."

When Adhith and Vikram were finally allowed out, they ran to South Mumbai and found a people in pain. The man on the street was terrified what the next day would bring. All of India remained scared of what waited around the corner. The economy, which had already taken damage in the global crisis following the fall of Lehman brothers, slowed. Then, anger took over. Determination to defeat the cowardly enemy.

"Mumbaikars kick butt," Vikram said, fierce satisfaction in his tone.

The city had roared back to business. Within a couple of years, all the establishments targeted were rebuilt—bigger, better, more secure. When the Oberoi reopened its doors, Adhith and Vikram scraped together enough money for vodka at the Eau Bar. It was one way of thumbing their noses at the terrorists. Unfortunately, the staff politely showed the two nineteen-year-olds the door, telling them to return when they were of legal drinking age.

Still, it was the day Adhith decided he was making Mumbai his home. Whether he represented the small town back in Uttarakhand or if he worked in New Delhi, Mumbai would remain his city. Its people were his family. Its success, his triumph. Now, he was back at the hotel, once again on the verge of making an important decision.

Neither he nor Vikram needed to scrounge for cash to pay for drinks or worry about being carded for age, but neither had the luxury of time. The cyberattack came at the worst possible point, when both their lives were a complete mess. Once the party was done, they had to return to the office to continue their work. If either survived the evening with sanity intact.

Adhith intended to force a showdown with his best friend over the elephant in the room—a.k.a the Seema in the office. The timing had to be exactly right. He didn't dare bring it up before the dinner. If Vikram broke down and admitted his feelings for her, he wasn't likely to let Adhith continue to claim her as his almost-fiancée in front of the Joshis. Papaji would conclude Adhith was free to pursue his political career. If he waited too long, the Joshis might give their stamp of approval to the match between him and Seema, and Papaji would get his press team involved. It would mean, *"Sayonara,* Madhubala."

Using Madhu instead of Seema in the scheme was out of the question. Adhith's heart wouldn't let him do it. Madhu was... important. If whatever was between them progressed as far as marriage, there would be no tests of her fitness for the role of his wife. He'd be *begging* her to take a chance on him.

The more Adhith thought about it, the more he was certain Vikram was the only one who could save the day. This evening, Vikram was going to be prodded into announcing his intention to fight his best friend for Seema's love. It would create enough mayhem in the two families, giving Adhith time to chalk out an escape route.

"You can go ahead, sir," said the guard checking the Toyota. The security officers were satisfied neither Adhith nor Vikram was a threat to their establishment. The safety measures were one of the aftereffects of the terrorist strike.

Both Vikram and Adhith waited until they were inside the air-conditioned lobby before pulling on their blazers. Because of their work at the multinational, they needed business wear frequently, or Vikram would've never thought of keeping such sartorial essentials on hand. Of course, his black suit and equally black shirt were clearly off-the-rack, as was the red tie. Adhith's suit of the same colour was custom-made with his initials monogrammed into the right cuff of the silvery-grey shirt. He'd discarded his black silk tie in the office. The evening called for the casual chic of an open collar. The shoeshine boy who'd commandeered the street corner by the office building made sure both men sported gleaming black dress shoes.

As a smiling woman in a black and gold ensemble led them to the poolside dining space, Adhith eyed his best friend, walking in stoic silence, giving every appearance of a man being led to his execution. *You brought it on yourself, bro*. If Vikram was less than honest about his attraction, Adhith was shamelessly using Seema to escape Papaji's plans. *She* was using Adhith to make Vikram jealous. None of them was blameless.

Mild breeze sneaked under Adhith's collar when they approached the door leading to the pool. The cool air from the sea filled his lungs. Jazz music greeted them. The Oberoi hostess moved aside. "Beautiful," Adhith breathed, taking in the view.

The sky was a gorgeous blue with tufts of cottony clouds floating along. The geometrically shaped pool held no swimmers, and except for the palm trees and shrubs, the deck had been cleared to make space for the event. Hidden lighting cast a golden glow over the whole area. A tuxedoed band sat to the far left, leaving the ocean view on the right unobstructed. Dressed in formal wear, the few people present were gathered near the musicians or clustered at the bar on the near left. Sandwiched between the two were circular tables—covered in dark yellow cloth—the golden plates and gleaming wine glasses on them currently empty. Vikram's parents were next to the band, talking to another couple.

Adhith said, "Let's not spend more time here than we have to. We need to get back to work."

Vikram nodded. "We'll get some food and get out." Neither had taken time for lunch, what with working all day on the hacker problem. Plus, he wouldn't want to watch his best friend and his girl as a couple any longer than absolutely necessary. "Adhi, I've been considering the possibility it might be an inside job."

"Inside... the hacker?"

"We haven't been able to find the entry point. No matter how good he is, he should've left some evidence somewhere of how he got in. We haven't found any. The only remaining possibility is it was done from the inside."

"Maybe." Adhith mulled the idea. He'd have to give it serious thought after sorting out their love lives. Tone carefully casual, he said, "We'll put in two or three hours here and get back to work. It should be more than enough time to convince your mom Seema is unsuitable."

"I agr—*what?*"

"Vikram, Adhith." Whiskey glass in hand, a tall, skinny man waved to them from the bar. Elegantly dressed and salt-and-pepper hair beautifully styled, he was one of Dr Joshi's three younger brothers. The gentleman was a dermatologist who lived in Los Angeles with his partner of many years, a plastic surgeon.

Voice low and urgent, Vikram asked, "What do you mean 'unsuitable'?"

"Later," Adhith muttered, striding towards the dermatologist, leaving Vikram to follow.

A second man turned from the bar. Caucasian with a dapper beard and a yarmulke—the Jewish cap—on his head, he was the only male in the crowd wearing a Nehru jacket instead of a regular suit. The plastic surgeon. His face lit when he saw them approaching. "You still haven't taken care of the nose, Vikram? You should've come to our place when you were in California. I could've fixed it for you. Free of charge."

"I'm happy with it the way it is, Uncle Rob," said Vikram, a hand held up to ward off imaginary knives. "Adhi, I want to talk to—"

"Didn't know you two were going to be here." Adhith nodded at the plastic surgeon. "How are the kids doing?"

"Henry's somewhere around." The dermatologist gestured with his head towards the crowd around the band. Henry Asher-Joshi, Vietnamese in origin, urologist in training. "Maya got back from her Haiti medical camp on time, so she came along. I don't know if you heard... Mohini's moving to India. She wants to do her undergrad in Indian dance forms."

Vikram snorted. Adhith managed not to howl in dismay. Maya—former Jewish orphan and current medical student—was perfectly fine. Mohini, the third of the Asher-Joshi brood, on the other hand... the toddler rescued by the

American military from Kandahar had harboured a mega crush on Adhith from the time she laid her eyes on him at the age of twenty. *He'd* been the twenty-year-old. She'd been ten, in India to attend her Anju *Didi's*—her big sister's—wedding. As if Adhith didn't already have enough women to juggle!

"She was heartbroken when she heard about your engagement," said the dermatologist, a twinkle in his eye. "The younger two are at summer camp. They're not going to be happy when they hear everyone else was here, and they missed out."

The other two Joshi brothers were doctors, as well. The one with the pencil-thin moustache was a cancer researcher at Harvard and married to a colleague. They were the other couple talking to Vikram's parents. Their twin sons were both well into adulthood. Of course, the sons were doctors. The bespectacled young men were watching the boats on the ocean with the rest of the Joshi cousins.

The youngest of Pratap Joshi's brothers—a trauma surgeon and two-time divorcé with no children—served as an army medic for twenty years. He now worked for Doctors Without Borders. From the gossip Adhith picked up, the surgeon's current romantic status was best described as multiple—a woman in every nation he visited, one even in Kabul. Of all the Joshi men, he was the best looking. An Indian version of Harrison Ford in his forties. He was alone at a table, fiddling with his phone.

Both his former wives were with Anjali and her husband, moving between the remaining guests grouped around the band—friends and colleagues of the Joshis. Adhith recognised them from previous events. Less than thirty, altogether. No Seema or Madhu yet.

As Adhith surveyed the cluster, Anjali's gaze went towards the bar and fell on her brother and his friend. With a delighted smile, she hurried over, followed by her husband. Before the pair got close, Vikram said in a fierce whisper, "We need to talk."

"In front of the dumbass?" Adhith muttered back, tilting his head at the approaching couple. Ignoring Vikram's frustrated growl, Adhith smiled at Anjali. "Looking good, Anju."

The claret-coloured cocktail dress brought out the glow in her cheeks and the reddish sheen in her dark brown hair. She preened. "Thanks, Adhi. You always say the right things."

"So Adhi," said the dumbass. "Where's your girlfriend?"

"Her name's Seema," Adhith supplied. Out of the corner of his eye, he saw Vikram open and close his mouth in panic. Adhith suppressed a grin. "She'll be here soon." *With Madhu.*

He couldn't wait to see her. All day, he'd been imagining what she'd be wearing. A cocktail dress like Vikram's sister or semiformal Indian clothes like some of the other women present? If the shapeless hoodie and worn jeans hadn't been able to conceal the sheer glamour of Madhu's face and form, what would she look like in something designed to show off her figure? Whatever she wore, Adhith hoped liked hell she didn't change her perfume. The fragrance always set his blood on fire.

"Vikram," shouted someone. Galloping through the crowd came the cousins.

"Adhi," squealed Maya, throwing her arms around his neck. He tried his best to ignore the sulky glances directed at him by her sister.

"Adhi, betay," came Vikram's mom's voice. Dr Rattanbai Joshi nudged her niece aside to wrap Adhith in a hug. "Where's Seema?"

"She wasn't working today, so she'll come straight to the party," Adhith said, smiling.

"We've all been dying to meet her," said Anjali. "The woman who captured Adhith Verma's heart."

"I'm going to tell her what a nice boy you are," said Vikram's mom. "That reminds me... thanks so much for the lovely roses you sent."

Right behind her was Vikram's dad. "Red roses," he said, tone stern. "Save those for your own girl. Rattan's taken."

Adhith grinned. "Pratap Uncle, with you around, the rest of us don't stand a chance."

"Speak for yourself," called out the plastic surgeon, beloved of the dermatologist for the last twenty years. "Women adore me. I simply don't happen to adore them back."

"Robbie," chided the trauma surgeon, wicked gleam on his face. "They love your knife. Not your dic—"

"Ladies present," snapped Vikram's mom.

The trauma surgeon held up both hands and bowed deeply.

"Not only that, we're expecting *Seema* tonight," continued Rattan Joshi. "We don't want to give her the wrong impression." Turning to Adhith, she added, "Right, betay?"

At Adhith's side, Vikram gulped. He had to be remembering the exact same thing as Adhith. Seema and her "PhD level cursing."

Tone smooth, Adhith said, "Of course, Auntieji."

Rattanbai and Pratapchandra Joshi moved onto their other guests, leaving their son and his friend with the younger Joshis. "Vikram Bhaiyya," said one of the twins. "The hotel's letting us use the pool after dinner. Let the parents go back to their rooms, and we'll have our own party."

"Sounds like fun," said Vikram. "But we can't stay. There's too much work."

"It's Friday night," whined Mohini, stomping a foot.

"We have work," Adhith firmly agreed. The hacker issue wasn't going to solve itself.

"Count *me* out, too," said Anjali. "I can't stay awake past nine these days."

Sulkily, Mohini said to the rest of her cousins, "C'mon, guys. Let's go and talk to the event manager. He promised to have swimsuits brought in." They trailed off, leaving Vikram and Adhith with Anjali and her husband.

Vikram's fingers closed around Adhith's elbow in an iron grip. "Let's get beer." Holding a hand up, Vikram asked the bartender for their preferred brands.

"*I* will take a menu," said Anjali, sighing. "Let me see what kind of non-alcoholic drinks you have."

"Anything to eat?" Vikram asked the bartender.

"Dinner will be served early, sir," said the young man. "So no *hors d'oeuvres*. We do have peanuts if you want."

"I'll take some, too," said Adhith. After shovelling cornflakes into his mouth in the morning, he hadn't taken time for food. Neither had Vikram.

Waiting at the counter, Vikram demanded in a voice only loud enough for Adhith to hear, "Explain what you meant about Seema."

Adhith shrugged. "There's nothing *to* explain. You were the one who told me about Seema and her cussing. Your mom's not going to like it."

"Seema's not going to cuss at my parents. When she wants to, she can behave like a princess. Also, I thought you'd decided to give it a chance."

Adhith looked around to make sure Anjali and her husband were still busy with the drink menu. "Since when did you become such an expert on Seema's behaviour?"

"I... uhh..." Tugging at the knot in his tie, Vikram glanced away.

"Go ahead," Adhith muttered, suppressing the twinge of sympathy in his chest. Vikram deserved it for not being honest with his best friend. "Tell me I have no reason to make sure she embarrasses herself tonight."

"Excuse me," Vikram called to the bartender in a loud voice. "I changed my mind. Make mine a lemon drop shot, please."

Watching Vikram's imagination fill in the blanks, Adhith said, "Mine, too."

If they'd been in a comic book, Adhith would've been a supervillain, playing mind games with Vikram's straight-arrow superhero. Tonight, the villain was going to play the God of Love, saving the hero from his own stubborn stupidity. Even if they both needed to get dead-drunk by the end of the evening, Vikram was going to admit he'd tumbled into love with Seema.

"Oooh." Anjali looked up from the menu. "Shots."

"Coming right up," said the bartender, turning to the bottle rack.

Raising the tiny glass holding chilled Grey Goose vodka, Adhith said, "May this evening be all we hoped for."

Vikram downed his drink and grabbed a sugar-coated lemon wedge, sucking on it. "May we all survive to see the morning."

Nodding gravely, Adhith tossed the vodka straight down his throat and snatched a lemon wedge from the dish to soothe the mild burn.

The dumbass laughed. "I didn't know you were planning to go to war. Or I'd have stayed in Japan."

Eyeing his brother-in-law, Vikram said to the bartender, "Keep 'em coming."

As he followed his second drink with another sugary piece of lemon, Adhith said to the dumbass, "Speaking of your conference in Japan... I thought I saw you here a few days back. Did you fly out of Mumbai or something?"

The joviality instantly vanished from the dumbass's face, replaced by dismay. "I... from Mumbai?"

"What?" asked Anjali, shock in her tone. "That's silly. You were not in Mumbai, right?"

"No, no," soothed the dumbass. "I was in Tokyo. I wasn't anywhere near Mumbai."

"Maybe, you have a lookalike," Adhith continued, bewildered by the melodramatic reactions. "Somewhere by the Gateway of India."

"The Gateway?" echoed Anjali, her eyes suddenly stark against a pale face.

Expression puzzled, Vikram asked, "Anju? Are you okay?"

"She's pregnant," snapped the dumbass.

"Gateway?" Anjali parroted. "Are you sure?"

A hand cupping her elbow, the dumbass said, "No, he's not sure. How can he be? I wasn't in Mumbai... Anju, why don't you sit for a while?" As he was ushering her to the table farthest from the bar, she kept turning to stare at Adhith.

Chewing on peanuts for the next five minutes, Adhith leaned back against the counter and smiled at whomever he happened to see, but out of the corner of his eye, he kept watch on Anjali and the dumbass. Vikram also stayed put at the bar, his gaze darting between his sister and the door to the poolside space.

Ten minutes passed. The sickeningly-in-love couple was still arguing. Turning around, Adhith called to the bartender, "One more."

"Sure, sir," said the bartender. He glanced at Vikram. "You, too?"

"Go ahead," Vikram said, morosely.

Gulping his third shot of the evening, Adhith asked Vikram, "What's going on with Anju and the dumbass, bro?"

"You tell me," muttered Vikram. "I didn't even know you'd seen him in Mumbai."

"I thought I made a mistake. Like I did with Seema." He sucked on the lemon wedge. Good God, the thing was *sour*.

Vikram hurled the piece of fruit in his hand to the wastebasket on the other side of the counter. Lurching, he gripped the edge to regain his balance.

"Hey, Adhi," called the cancer specialist. "Your guest is here."

Adhith wheeled around towards the door, staggering a little. Damn, the vodka was strong. He was already feeling the buzz after three shots.

A vision in silvery-white slammed into his senses. Madhu. Her hair was down to her shoulders, gleaming under the lights. The glasses were still on her nose, but the eyes behind them were lined. There was nude gloss on those full lips. Long earrings dangled from her delicate lobes, and a string of small white stones sparkled around her neck.

Her *choli*—a spaghetti-strap blouse—barely did the job of covering her beautiful breasts. A gauzy white sari with silver embroidery was draped chastely across her tummy and chest, but through the translucent fabric, Adhith could see the curve of her waist, her belly button, and a hint of rounded hips. The embroidered cloth covering her long legs glittered and swished as she strode towards him. With each step, white strappy sandals and red-painted toenails peeked out below the hem. Her usual black tote was gone, a small, silvery wristlet taking its place. Vaguely, Adhith wondered what she'd done with her gun.

Madhu came to a halt three feet in front of him. "Verma," she said, her tone low and firm as always. The same sweetly intoxicating scent drifted to his nostrils.

There was a dark blur next to Madhu. Someone said something. His name? He didn't want to turn. He didn't want to see or hear anyone except her.

"Thanks for coming," he stuttered.

"I almost didn't. In fact, I was on my way to your office to tell you, but—" Madhu's gaze wandered past Adhith.

He turned to check what she was looking at. A fuzzy shape blocked his view. Impatiently, he put out a hand to push the person aside. Something jangled and clinked. Slim arms slid up his chest and around his neck. A curvy form plastered itself against his torso. Warm lips pressed against his cheek. Startled, Adhith took a step back. The woman clung to him. About to lose his balance, he gripped her by the hips.

"Hello, darling," cooed Seema, fluttering her eyelashes.

***

Vikram was just regaining his balance when he heard Cancerwalla Uncle call, "Hey, Adhi. Your guest is here."

Adhith pivoted, almost toppling sideways in his hurry. A low growl escaped his chest.

Vikram couldn't bring himself to turn and greet the latest arrivals. Thoughts battled for dominance in his brain. Adhith was planning... what, exactly? To lead Seema into making a mockery of herself in front of the Joshis and their guests? To humiliate her in front of Vikram's parents for an attraction she hadn't intended? Adhith could've simply broken it off with her, but a break-up wouldn't get the manipulative sonuvabitch what he wanted, would it? Reprieve from his father's plans.

Adhith was still standing right next to Vikram, not saying a word in welcome to his almost-fiancée. "Bastard," Vikram snarled under his breath. He wasn't about to let Seema be shamed at his own family event. "Gimme one more," he said to the bartender.

It would be Vikram's fourth drink in less than half an hour, but he needed the fortification. He was about to take on Adhith Verma and the entire Joshi contingent. Hell, if he had to, he'd take on the whole bloody city of Mumbai for her.

Around Vikram, chatter peaked. The party surged en masse towards the new arrivals. No, not as a whole. Anjali and the dumbass were still at their table, arguing in low tones. It *looked* like an argument. The dumbass's face was red, and Anjali... Vikram frowned. Her eyes. She wasn't exactly crying,

223

Just staring vacantly as though she couldn't see anything. As though she'd been blindsided by someone she trusted.

He knew exactly how she felt.

"Here you go, sir." The bartender slid the shot glass towards Vikram, pouring a measure of vodka into it.

Vikram tossed the drink down his gullet and chased it with another wedge of sugared lemon. His face puckered in defence against the sharp tartness.

"Hello, darling," Seema sang, her voice as clear as always.

Vikram spun, and everything seesawed once. The pool, the deck, even the blue sea beyond.

Smooth, slim arms were wrapped around Adhith's neck. A ridiculous number of metallic bangles of light to dark coppery hues decorated both wrists. There was a hint of her curls to one side of his head and a smacking sound as she kissed his cheek. Over his shoulder, one thickly lashed eye caught Vikram's gaze and blinked.

"Seema, my love," he shouted, and in one move gripped her right arm and twirled her around.

Her knee-length, black halter dress swirled as she pirouetted into his chest. The bangles jangled. Her purse slipped off her shoulder and fell to the floor with a thud. Her light brown eyes were wide open, and her peach-painted lips formed a surprised "O" as her body slammed against his. Breath whooshed out of her in a soft gasp—from him, too.

His hands spanned her tiny waist, his fingers closing around soft fabric. Dear God. She felt so good plastered against him with her generous breasts crushed against his torso. Her hands gripped his shoulders. Her toned legs tangled with his. Something hard pressed into his thigh, but Vikram was more interested in the mouth hovering mere pixels below his. Her floral scent tickled his nostrils.

"Vikram," snapped an astounded voice. His mother.

He didn't look away from the gorgeousness in his arms. *"Ji,* Mom?" he queried, asking what she wanted.

"What are you doing?" ground out Mom.

Seema squirmed in his embrace. "Have you gone mental?" she hissed, pushing against his shoulders. "Let go of me."

"In a minute," he soothed, his thumb rubbing circles on her midback. He turned his head to his left to deal with maternal outrage. It wasn't only her. The rest of the party was staring in shock. The band played on, switching to the instrumental version of some old song, but no one else made a sound, not even Adhith who stood there with a smirk on his face. Behind him was a woman in white, her nostrils flared and eyes angry. Seema's auntie, Vikram presumed. She seemed familia—

Tone ferocious, Seema muttered, "Let me go, you crazy jerk."

He'd have to tell her the whole story. When she heard what Adhith had in mind for her, she'd understand Vikram was only trying to save her from embarrassment. "For now," he agreed, loosening his hold. "But we gotta talk." *In private,* he finished with his eyes, blinking meaningfully to make sure she got the message.

When Seema shrugged out of his arms, uneasy murmurs rose among the guests. Mom smiled awkwardly at Seema. "Sorry, betay. I don't know what came over Vikram. He's usually not—"

Seema didn't respond. Glaring at him, she brushed a tendril back from her shoulder.

Her *bare* shoulder. The dark brown hair was held back in an intricate braid with the lighter streaks luminescent under the yellow bulbs. Except for the coppery studs in her ears and the crazy number of metallic bangles on her wrists, there was no jewellery.

She was dressed like a figure skater—the top half of her body was well defined by the halter dress, but the flared skirt extended to an inch above her knees. *Pity.* Vikram would've loved to see her in an actual skating outfit with the hem barely covering her bottom.

"As you might have guessed, I'm Vikram's mom," Rattanbai Joshi said to Seema. "Let me introduce you to everyone else." An arm around the younger woman's shoulders, Dr Rattan Joshi extended her other hand to the woman in white. "You must be Madhubala."

Recovering her shiny black purse from the floor, Seema gave Vikram one last glare and followed his mom and Madhubala into the crowd of guests. Adhith accompanied the three ladies.

"Whooaa," said Seema, teetering on her black stilettos. Fingers clutching Adhith's blazer, she regained her balance. He caught her by her upper arms.

Vikram gritted his teeth. There was an unnecessary amount of touching going on. From *her* side. What was the need for her to put her hands on Adhith's thighs? Even her auntie, Madhubala, was annoyed. Seema needed to be told what her almost-fiancé was planning before she embarrassed herself any further.

As soon as she stood, they were intercepted by Traumawalla Uncle. Bending down, he picked something up and handed it to Adhith. "Your wallet." He peered at something on the floor. "Is that your car key?"

"Heh?" Adhith patted his pant pockets. "I guess they fell out. Thanks." Tucking the wallet back in, he scooped up the key.

Madhubala Rawat took a step forward, a frown on her face. "Seem—"

"Hello," said Traumawalla Uncle, blocking the lady's path. "I'm—"

When Adhith first heard Vikram refer to his uncles as Skinwalla, Cancerwalla, and Traumawalla, he'd gone into fits of laughter. The Parsi practice of naming people by their occupations tickled Adhith into snickers each time he met one of the Joshi brothers.

Right now, Adhith didn't look even mildly amused. Visibly irritated, he squeezed himself into the space between Madhubala and the trauma surgeon, a known womaniser.

Keep going, Uncleji, Vikram cheered. If Adhith were kept busy running interference, he wouldn't have time to put his nefarious plan into action. Vikram stayed where he was, keeping Seema in sight. She was chatting with his father, one hand on the purse hanging on her left shoulder. It wasn't as big as the monstrosity she brought to work but was still large enough to hold her phone and half-a-dozen others. It was shiny—as shiny and smooth as her legs.

He wished she'd turn ninety degrees to the right so he could study her calf muscles. He was fascinated by how toned they were, but they wouldn't stay in such good shape if she continued wearing those skyscraper heels.

"Stop staring at her," someone hissed in Vikram's ear. "You've already created enough of a scene." Dr Henry Asher-Joshi fell between Anjali and Vikram in age. Henry was the oldest of the five kids of Uncle Robbie and Skinwalla Uncle.

"I'm not staring," Vikram muttered. "I've got to put my eyes somewhere, don't I?"

"Put them someplace else," suggested Henry, sharply. "The auntie, maybe. *Everyone* at the party is staring at her. Even my dads."

Vikram gave said auntie a quick once-over. "She's all right."

Henry gawked. "It's all you have to say?"

Vikram shrugged. "This is Mumbai. There are beautiful women everywhere."

"You think she—" Henry gestured in the general direction of Madhubala Rawat. "—is something you'd see on your commute? How much did you drink?"

"Four shots," admitted Vikram. His head *was* floaty. "C'mon, Henry. Your parents are in the beauty business."

Henry snorted. "Sonny boy, what you see there ain't fake."

"Who cares?" Vikram muttered. "She doesn't glow."

"Huh?"

Vikram craned his neck, trying to locate Seema, again. She'd moved on from his father. There she was, talking to Uncle Rob. She ran a finger over the bridge of her nose and laughed, the tinkling sound mingling merrily with the music made by her coppery bangles. Uncle Rob said something, and they both looked towards Vikram.

"They're talking about *my* nose, aren't they?" He resisted the urge to hold up his hands and hide the broken appendage.

"Vikram, you—" exclaimed Henry. "Never mind."

A loud shout went up at the door as two waiters rolled a giant cake in. To the accompaniment of hoots and whistles from the guests, it was set not too far from the band.

The three-tiered yellow-and-white cake, the tuxedoed musicians, the deepening blue of the sky, tinged pink by the sunset to come... the music, the chatter, the laughter... the muggy warmth, the salty sea breeze, the euphoria... the evening was made for romance. For lovers to laugh and tease and whisper in each other's ears about the night waiting for them.

Except, Seema was with someone else, not Vikram—with a man who was leading her into disaster.

"Everyone, please sit at your tables," called out the dumbass, clapping hands.

When did he return to the scene? Vikram turned a 180, looking for his sister. She was at the back of the crowd, her face still wan. There was a smile on her lips, but it seemed forced.

"Saale saab," called the dumbass. "You're up here with the rest of the family." The table closest to the band. "You, too, Adhi. And your guests." Of course. Mom would need to study Seema at close quarters.

Vikram practically ran to the table. "Excuse me," he called out, pushing aside a sari-draped form in his path, sending her spinning.

"Oww," squealed the woman.

"Sorry," Vikram called, not bothering to stop. He needed to get to his parents' table. No way was he going to leave Seema boxed in by enemies.

Escorting both former wives to their table, Traumawalla Uncle jumped out of the way and yelled, "What the hell, Vikram?"

"Not now," Vikram said, keeping on jogging.

Adhith was pulling out chairs for the Rawat women, preparing to seat himself between them. Seema was clinging to him, her fingers clutching his blazer as though for balance. Anjali and the dumbass were on Madhu Rawat's other side. Vikram's mom was approaching the chair next to Seema's, leaving him the spot between his dad and the dumbass.

There were ten more feet to go between Vikram and the table. And one waiter.

Nine feet, eight...

"Beamer coming," Vikram shouted, hoping like hell the waiter was as cricket-crazy as the rest of India and would know there was a ball (or a human) headed straight for him.

Seven... six...

Heads turned towards Vikram, including his mom's. Gaping at her son, she stilled, her hand on the chair next to Seema's. The waiter took one look, realising there was no time to get out of Vikram's way. Hurling the bottle in his hands towards the pool, the waiter ducked. The perfect way to escape a cricket ball—but a human? Not so much.

The bottle spun through the air and splashed into the pool. "Champagne," someone wailed.

Five... four...

Vikram's elbow crashed into the table on his left, sending cutlery clattering and plates bouncing. Someone screamed. At the main table, Seema turned to check on the commotion, her eyes widening in confusion.

Three... two...

He grabbed a chair and spun it around. Slamming the heels of his hands on the back, he vaulted across the crouching waiter.

One... zero!

Vikram landed inches away from his shocked mother. Seema—and everyone else at the table—was gawking, open-mouthed. The vodka sloshed about in his stomach. His head felt as though it were separated from the rest of his body.

"Mom, Dad." Willing all body parts to settle down where they belonged, Vikram straightened his cuffs. "I forgot to wish you a happy anniversary." He planted a quick kiss on his mother's cheek and oh, so casually grabbed the chair next to Seema's. Plunking himself in it, he said, "Let's get this party started."

Both Rawat ladies were looking at Vikram as though he'd gone stark, raving mad. So were his parents and Anjali. The dumbass smirked. Vikram couldn't blame any of them. He *had* acted kind of crazy. A snort came from between the Rawat women. Adhith. His face was red as though he were barely stopping himself from laughing out loud.

Vikram nodded. *Wait until the end of the evening, meray bachchey.* They'd see who had the last laugh.

The hotel staff scurried around, straightening chairs and picking cutlery off the floor. A lad appeared with what looked like a butterfly net and fished the bottle of champagne from the pool. The Oberoi hostess glided to the main table, the smile on her face slightly strained. "Are we ready?"

"Ready or not," said the dumbass, "let's start. Or saale saab might act out more than he already has."

With a frown, Seema turned to peer at the dumbass.

"My friend—" started Adhith.

The arrival of the waiter stopped him from saying whatever he intended. While the hotel staff topped everyone's glasses, the hostess led the guests of honour to the cake. The band played "The Anniversary Song" as Rattan and Pratap Joshi cut the cake. When they fed each other the pastry, there was the same love in their eyes Vikram had seen since boyhood. While the first course was being rolled in, two waiters cut the cake into slices to be later served as dessert. Cancerwalla Uncle stood, drink in his hand, and toasted his brother and sister-in-law.

"Yeah, yeah," shouted Uncle Rob. "Let's get to the smooch."

"I'm not about to say no," shouted back Vikram's dad right before twirling his wife into a dip and soundly kissing her.

Clapping enthusiastically with the rest of the guests, Seema said, "Oy, Vikram. Your parents are cool."

Savouring the sound of his name on her tongue, Vikram sipped champagne.

"They're wonderful," gushed the dumbass. "I'm lucky they consider me their son."

Under the table, Vikram's fingers curled into a tight fist. The comment shouldn't have grated, but it did. There was nothing he could say in response without looking like an absolute jerk. A feathery touch landed on his knuckles. Even without having heard the soft tinkle from her bangles, he'd have known it was Seema. Gratefully, he inclined his head just a bit in her direction.

Across from him, Anjali was staring at their parents, her eyes forlorn. Vikram frowned. From the time she heard from Adhith her husband might have been in Mumbai, she'd been quiet. What was going on with those two?

Dinner was served as soon as the embracing couple returned to their seats. White tomato soup was followed by salmon and lobster appetisers. Then, it was salad, sorbet, mustard chicken, and Arabica lamb chop. Vikram managed to hold himself back from falling on the food like a ravenous beast. From the look on Adhith's face, he was struggling with the same intense emotion.

There was plenty of conversation all around the table. Mom leaned in one direction or the other to speak to Seema across Vikram. Neither he nor Adhith said much, but even when Seema excused herself to go to the latrine, Vikram kept his ears open for any attempt by Adhith to embarrass her.

The only other person not contributing much to the fun was Anjali. Oh, she was keeping Madhubala Rawat entertained, talking about movies and music, but there was none of the animation Vikram was used to seeing on his sister's face. He took a sip of the red wine, making a mental note to speak to Anjali sometime in the coming week.

"Dessert," exclaimed Seema. "I got back in time." As she pulled the chair out, it scraped the stone floor. "Excuse me, Vikram. There's..." She crouched and came back up, holding something. "Anyone lose their keys?"

Vikram checked his inside pocket. "Not me."

As denials went around, Adhith leapt from his chair. "Those are mine."

"Got a hole in your pocket?" Vikram asked. "First, your wallet. Now, your keys."

"I guess," Adhith muttered.

"Seema," called Madhubala Rawat, sounding uneasy.

"Yes, Madhu?" Seema asked, her enormous eyes wide open and fixed on her relative.

"You... I... we should leave soon," said Madhubala.

"Leave?" Vikram's father dug into a slice of the anniversary cake. "This early?" It was past seven, but the midsummer sun was only beginning to sink into the sea. "We have dancing after dinner."

"Let's wait until after sunset," said Seema, her words rushed.

"We should have a special dance for the other couple of the evening," announced Dad.

Seema gulped. Adhith raised a hand, shaking his head in unwillingness.

"Why not?" cajoled Vikram's father. "Make it a night to remember. You can tell your children and grandchildren the story."

Over my dead body. Gritting his teeth, Vikram turned towards the waiter—the same one he'd knocked down—and raised a finger. "I'll take more wine, please."

"Another drink?" asked the dumbass, smirking. "How many now?"

Not enough to make up for sharing a table with him.

Vikram's mom was on his other side and took his hand in hers. "Are you all right, betay?"

Forehead puckered in concern, the dumbass said, "He's not going to be all right for long. Saale saab, if you do this every day, you're going to pickle your brain."

Seema stilled.

Without a word, Vikram tugged his fingers loose from his mother's. Carefully, he picked up the snowy white napkin from his thigh and wiped his mouth. What could he say—what denial could he issue—that wouldn't brand him an alcoholic exactly as the dumbass implied? Especially, when the rest of his family stared at him with the same concern?

He didn't dare look at Seema. He didn't want to see the same thoughts on her face he saw on his family. Rough and unpolished Vikram, so different from the other Joshis. Unfit for company. Best ignored.

Voice carefully pleasant, Adhith interjected, "No need to lay it on so thick. Vikram's hardly a drunk."

"He is *not* a drunk," snapped Seema, her clear tone lashing across the table.

"With all due respect," said the dumbass, "you two are hardly qualified to diagnose alcoholism."

Baring her teeth in a hiss, Seema said, "With all due respect, you're a little prick."

***

Seema seethed. She didn't have the time to start a fight. She needed to copy the rest of Adhith's keys and close the book on her investigation, but she couldn't ignore it when Vikram's brother-in-law was making him sound like a total loser. Vikram Joshi, the smartest man she knew, the nicest, kindest man she'd ever met, a loser?

His family was decent, yet none of them seemed willing to defend him. Adhith said something, but the fashion plate's words were a pathetic excuse for a rebuke. Poor Vikram. They were all gawking at her. If the sudden silence surrounding them were any indication, so was the rest of the party.

"Excuse me?" asked the dumbass.

"You heard what I said," responded Seema, stabbing at her cake with a spoon.

Vikram laughed, smothering his mirth with a cough. On her other side, Adhith muttered something about it going better than he expected. Madhu moaned, both hands covering her face. Anjali paled.

"You seem very fond of our Vikram," said the dumbass, tone honeyed. "Maybe, we shouldn't have been surprised by what he did earlier."

For a second, Seema contemplated straddling Vikram's thighs and planting a smooch on his mouth to flip the bird at everyone around. Well... she'd been longing to do exactly that since the delicious kiss at the Gateway of India. Given the way he'd been acting all evening, they'd end up rolling on the floor, tearing each other's clothes off. Carefully avoiding the sight of the tempting thighs on her left, she said to the dumbass, "You need to get your mind out of the toilet."

"Oh, God," said Vikram's mom, clumsily dropping her fork into her plate. "Pratap."

Pratap Joshi had been gaping at Seema. "Heh? Oh... cut it out, both of you. Seema betay, when you're a family, you tend to take a lot of freedom you otherwise wouldn't. No one's calling Vikram a drunk."

Family! She and Madhu were a family. They'd hurt each other plenty of times over the years. Seema had called Madhu a bitch to Gayathri. As though the guilt and shame gnawing away at Seema's conscience weren't enough, the universe visited retribution in the form of Vikram Joshi's arrival. That day, she'd sworn never to inflict hurt on Madhu ever again, not even if she wouldn't hear of it. If someone else dared attack Madhu, they'd first have to kill Seema.

Vikram's parents were smart people. Why couldn't they recognise the dumbass's venom for what it was?

"You know what?" said Pratap Joshi, heartily. "Dessert's done, and it's time for dancing."

Oh, goody. Time to stare goofily into the fashion plate's eyes. On the other hand, dancing *would* be better cover for checking the last of his pockets. Better than falling into his arms or against him for the umpteenth time. The first key Seema got hold of obviously belonged to Adhith's car. Since she didn't need it, she dropped it and the wallet on the floor for him to find.

Next, she'd gotten a bunch of giant office keys, not something you'd expect to open a flat door. Still, she couldn't take a chance, so she'd escaped to the loo to make imprints in the clay she carried in her purse. "Finding" them under the chairs had clearly caused auntie-alarms to go off in Madhu's brain. Before she insisted on leaving to keep her niece out of trouble, Seema wanted to finish the job. She was working against the clock. Yup, dancing with Adhith was a very good idea. She did need to be careful not to let him feel the gun on her thigh.

Vikram's dad stood and waved the hostess over. With a bright smile, she announced to the party the dancing was about to commence. "Woohoo," exclaimed the lead singer. The drummer set the cymbals crashing, punctuating the excitement.

Seema fluttered her eyelashes at Adhith. "I'd love to dance with you."

Was it her imagination, or was he having a panic attack? He shot a glance in Madhu's direction. Seema frowned. Did he have hang-ups about romancing her in front of her family? Why? It wasn't as if Madhu was old and staid. She was only thirty-six. Freakin' gorgeous, too.

In fact, if Seema read the signs correctly, that forty-ish uncle of Vikram's wanted to get to know Madhu. *We'll see.* The man had already gone through two wives for God's sake. Also, even if he'd been as virtuous as... as... well, whoever... it wouldn't matter. He was a Joshi. All members of the family were out of bounds for Madhu. For Seema, too. *Finish your job and get out,* she ordered herself. She stood, flirtatiously smiling at Adhith.

"I... ahh..." Face red and sweaty, he tugged at his tie. Once again, he looked towards Madhu.

Had Madhu said something to make sure he didn't take it any further with Seema? Seema thought she'd been convincing about her utter lack of romantic interest where Adhith was concerned, but Madhu was a tad overprotective. Her face was also red and tight, as though... dammit, she knew what Seema was up to. That had to be it.

"I'll dance with you," Vikram said, knocking his chair down in his hurry to stand.

To whirl around the floor in his arms. To laugh with him and tease him with whisper-light touches. Smiling sweetly, Seema said, "The first dance should be with my boyfriend, right?"

Vikram flushed. "He doesn't want to." Under his breath, he added, "Seema, we have to talk. Adhith—"

"Oh, yes, he does want to," Seema insisted, tugging at Adhith's arm.

"Please, Seema," Vikram mumbled, both hands clutching his hair. "Don't go. At least, not until we've talked."

"Please, Seema," Madhu said. "Don't do anything stupid."

"Madhu," chided Vikram's mom. "I understand you've had to be careful as women living alone. But it's just a dance. That, too, with a man who wants to marry her." Madhu's face darkened even further. Vikram growled, the animal sound and his tousled mane giving him the appearance of an enraged lion. "She'll be all right," soothed his mom, smiling at Madhu. "Plus, you'll be sitting right here."

"Not if I can help it," said a male voice. "Dance with me?"

Seema turned to find the handsome trauma surgeon next to the table. Vikram's uncle, the former army medic who now worked for Doctors Without Borders. "No," she said.

"No way," said Adhith, a nanosecond after Seema's own refusal.

"Huh?" Puzzled frown turning into amused grin, the trauma surgeon said, "I was asking *Madhubala.*"

Seema nodded. "I know. The answer's still no."

Flinging her napkin to the table, Madhu stood. "Yes."

The trauma surgeon's head swivelled between the two women. "You're answering for your auntie?" he asked Seema, puzzled look back on his face.

Ignoring him, Seema said, "Please, Madhu. Don't do anything stupid."

With a nasty little smile, Madhu asked, "Wasn't that *my* line?"

Seema glared. "Okay. You've made your point, but what's with the attitude?" What was going on with Madhu?

There was a gasp from Vikram's mom.

"Madhu," muttered Adhith, eyes wild.

What was going on with *him*?

Standing, he announced to Madhu, "He has a girlfriend in practically every city."

"I do not," exclaimed the trauma surgeon, visibly angry. "You mind your own business, punk. Dance with your fiancée."

"No," said Vikram, firmly. "She's dancing with me."

"*Who's* dancing with you?" asked his father, bewildered. Other than him, only his wife, daughter, and son-in-law were still in their chairs, all equally confused. "Seema or Madhu?"

The five people standing paid him no mind.

"If she doesn't know how to dance," came another voice, "you can dance with *me*, Adhi." Pouting at the fashion plate stood the green-eyed brat who'd been giving Seema dirty looks ever since she set foot into the gathering. Her tie-and-dye silk dress was cut low where it should've been high and high where it should've been low. Chunky platforms were on her feet.

"Which cousin are you?" Seema asked.

Nose in the air, the brat said, "Mohini. Adhi and I have known each other for *years*."

"Through Vikram," Adhith added, hurriedly. "It's all. I swear."

The fashion plate didn't look like he appreciated childishness, however pretty the package. Seema opened her mouth to say she believed him.

"Why would I care?" Madhu asked, showing every appearance of a woman goaded beyond her endurance.

What?

"What?" asked the trauma surgeon, Vikram's uncle.

Bestowing a dazzling smile on the surgeon, Madhu said, "Let's dance." She dragged him to where the band was. The dumbass and his wife followed them, neither appearing overjoyed at the experience. The rest of the Joshi cousins were already there, swaying away to something jazzy.

"Madhu, wait," Adhith called, jogging behind her and the trauma surgeon. "I just need some time." Seema sprinted after him. Just as he got to the dance floor, she pounced, catching the back of his blazer in her fists. "What are you—" Adhith struggled, bringing his hand to the back and trying to tug her grip loose. "Seema, let go of me."

On the dance floor, Madhu yanked the trauma surgeon's hand to her waist and proceeded to stomp around with none of her usual grace. Her angry eyes were turned determinedly away from her niece. The dumbass and Anjali were waltzing with him talking and her gaze fixed far away.

"Seema," said Vikram, his tone urgent. She couldn't see him without turning around. "You can't dance with him," he pleaded.

"I want to dance," Seema said to Adhith, trying to keep the flirtatious smile on her face and her balance on the stilettoes *while* making sure he didn't escape her clutches.

"So do I," said the brat, appearing next to him.

"Go away," Seema hissed.

"You go away," sniffed the brat. "He doesn't want to dance with you."

Incensed beyond imagination, Seema bellowed, "I want to dance with my boyfriend!"

The song being played by the band came to an end. A collective hush fell over the crowd. Every head turned towards her. Towards the tableau at the edge of the dance floor. "All right, my fair lady," the singer said over the microphone. "You want to dance with your boyfriend. What song would you like us to play for you?"

"I don't know," Seema yelled back. "Something with some pep to it. Something Indian?"

"How about something even more local?" asked the singer.

"Whatever," she said.

"Oh, God," Adhith said, his voice strangled. When he finally turned to face her, it was with exasperation and resignation in his eyes. And puzzlement.

Seema didn't dare look at Vikram, at the hurt she might have inflicted on him.

The rosy evening was the perfect backdrop for an outdoor dance. The drummer tapped the sticks together. The sounds of a banjo flowed over the audience. A remembered rhythm. A fuzzy memory from her childhood.

"Navrai Majhi Laadachi, Laadachi Ga," crooned the singer. "Avad Hila Chandrachi, Chandrachi Ga." A roar went up from the audience. Most recognised the wedding song of Marathi brides.

"Our girl has been so loved and indulged," the skin specialist translated for his partner, "she might even demand you get her the moon."

One hand at his hip and the other held to the side of his head, the bespectacled cancer specialist danced. He and his wife were immediately joined by his brothers. Even Vikram's parents were pushing their chairs back. The younger Joshis copied the movements of their elders.

Seema's heart pounded in time with the rhythm. Her feet itched to hop, skip, and twirl with the beat of the folk song—to swing her hips from side to side. The singer had chosen this song in honour of her and her supposed fiancé, but the man she wanted to marry was not the one in front of her. *Snap out of it, Seema.* She had a job to do. As rumbling drums joined the rapid twangs from the banjo, she clutched Adhith's lapels, keeping a careful inch or two between their bodies. They staggered, nearly toppling to the floor.

She heard Vikram's anguished "Seema, why are you doing this?" but didn't turn.

Her hand slipped into the inside pocket on the left of Adhith's blazer. Metal. One smooth move, and the keys were in her grip. The bangles masked any sounds. Her hand slid down his torso until she reached the pocket hidden in the folds of her dress. There. The keys were now with her. Only the inside pocket to the right of Adhith's blazer remained to be checked. With her previous hugs and falls, she'd already gone through the rest. He'd returned his wallet and office keys to his pant pocket.

Adhith regained his balance and stood, holding her away from him.

"Don't embarrass me," she hissed.

"You're doing a pretty good job of it all on your own," he said, huffing in irritation. "I don't get it. You like Vikram, and he likes you. If you're trying to make him jealous, don't bother. He's already crazy about you."

Seema didn't get it, either. Why had Adhith wanted her to go with him to the party if he thought she was in love with his friend? Why was he chasing Madhu? But none of it mattered. "Dance with me. Everyone's looking at us."

"Including Vikram," Adhith said, grimly. "He's going to kill me for this, but you've left me no choice. If I don't dance with you, my father's going to wonder why."

"What do you mean—"

Without answering, Adhith twirled her into a wrap. Even while rocking with him, Seema didn't have to worry about keeping a couple of inches between them. *He* took care of it. What the hell was going on with the fashion plate this evening? Was this the same guy who'd been pushing her to spend the weekend at his apartment?

Her gaze caught on an approaching form. Oh, dear God. Vikram, with murder in his eyes. Stopping directly in their path, he nodded at Adhith. "My turn."

A sudden, firm grip on her fingers. Everything spun. "Whooaa," she screamed, landing against Vikram's chest for the second time in one night. "Let go of me, you... you... *insane man.*"

"I'm sorry, but I need to tell you something, and you're not giving me a chance to talk..." His hands slipped down her arms, ending at her hips.

The gun. He was going to feel the gun.

Swatting at him, she yelped, "What are you *doing?* You can't touch me like that in public."

He twirled her, and her back against his chest, they swayed side to side. "...in private."

For one blissful moment, she imagined them alone on a beach, hiding from the guests at their own wedding. Bare feet squishing wet sand, they'd dance to the faraway music from the party. Their breaths would be jittery, their touches trembling, their kisses heated. If only they weren't who they were. Not Seema Rawat, income tax officer-turned-IB agent. Not Vikram Joshi, the cybersecurity expert determined to bring her down. Her heart heavy, Seema said, "You can't touch me like that in private, either."

"What are you talking about?"

She *had* to get back to the job she was supposed to be doing. Peering through the crowd, she looked for Adhith. The dumbass and Anjali were in her line of vision. Vikram's sister pried her husband's hands off her waist and strode away. Angry expression on his face, he stalked off in the direction of the bar. Adhith came into view. He was waylaid by the brat.

"I have to go." Seema shrugged loose from Vikram's hold. Unfortunately, she found her hands caught, her arms stretched backwards. One small jerk, and she was back in his embrace, his fingers splayed on her belly, his warm mouth against her ear. Her toes curled.

"Oooh," someone said.

"Vikram Bhaiyya," howled someone else, clapping. One of the twins.

A third person called his name, sounding annoyed. Rattanbai Joshi, Vikram's mother.

Vikram paid no heed. "You can't go," he whispered, his lips tickling Seema's earlobe. "I need to tell you—" He groaned. "Listen to me, Seema. Marriage to Adhith is not gonna happen. You don't love him, anyway. So why are you doing this?"

"First, you say you don't have time for women," Seema muttered. "Then, you say you don't know what you're going to do. So how does it matter to you what *I* do?"

"Are you punishing me for it?" he asked, tone fierce. "If you are, you'd better stop soon. I'm warning you. There's only so much more I can take."

"What do *you* mea—" Her heart stilled. She'd been puzzling over his crazy behaviour. *Had* he decided he wanted her for himself? Panic. Pure panic. What was he trying to say? She didn't want to hear it. She didn't dare respond. She *couldn't*. Not in a way that wouldn't break both their hearts. "Let go of me, or I'm going to put my heel through your foot," she said. "You won't be walking for a month."

"Didn't you hear what I said?"

Seema threw her head back, her skull striking Vikram's face.

He staggered. "My nose... Seema, stop. We're gonna fall." His left shoe skidded forwards in his effort to balance himself.

"Got ya," she muttered. In one smooth move, she bent down and grabbed his leg.

"Stop," he shouted. His hold loosened as he teetered about.

A scream came from across the poolside space. Then, another. And another.

Everyone around Seema and Vikram swivelled in the direction of the sounds. Startled, Seema let go of Vikram's leg. There was a thud behind her as he fell on his butt. The music came to a discordant end with the banjo hitting a false note. A few feet from Seema, Madhu was staring at something on the floor, fingertips held to her mouth.

"Adhi," Vikram shouted. "What's going on?"

Seema sprinted. She shoved everyone out of the way, ignoring every annoyed snap. Vikram followed right behind.

Next to Madhu's feet was the trauma surgeon, half sitting and half lying down. There was no visible injury on him, but his hand nursed his jaw. Fists clenched and eyes angry, Adhith loomed over him. The brat in the tie-and-dye caftan was the one doing the screaming.

"Madhu?" asked Seema, her pulse pounding in alarm.

Without saying a word, never moving her fingers from her lips, Madhu stared at Seema.

"What happened?" Vikram asked Adhith.

"Your uncle," said Adhith, his words reverberating with rage, "doesn't know how to behave with women."

"All I did was dance with her," said the trauma surgeon, his protest barely audible over the brat's screams.

"Mohini, can you please—" Vikram snapped.

One of the twins clapped a hand over her mouth, cutting off the shrill noise.

"What is going on here?" asked Pratap Joshi, pushing his way through the onlookers. His wife was with him.

"He punched me," informed the trauma surgeon, glaring at Adhith. "Just for dancing with his fiancée's auntie."

The fashion plate? He'd risked getting his knuckles bruised?

"Why?" asked Vikram's dad.

"Because—" Adhith started on a shout, but stopped, looking wildly around.

Madhu closed her eyes, her face bright red.

"Because *he* wanted to dance with her," completed the trauma surgeon. "I said 'No, wait for the next song.'"

Forcing her cousin's hand away from her face, the brat said, "*I* want to dance with Adhi."

"Aarrgh," screamed Rattan Joshi. "All *I* wanted was a nice family get-together. Instead—" She flung her arm up. "I get this... this comedy show."

Her husband grunted in agreement.

She turned to Adhith. "You... what is wrong with you? You told your father you want to marry Seema, but you're starting fights over Madhubala? What about Mohini? This is the twenty-first century, betay. You can't have your own harem." Vikram's mom pivoted to Madhu. "I can't blame you for Adhi's behaviour, but you wouldn't let your niece dance with her own fiancé. You told her it would be stupid. What is *wrong* with you? This is the twenty-first century." Nostrils flaring, Rattan Joshi spun to face her son. "What is wrong with *you?* I don't care what century this is. *You can't make love to your friend's fiancée on the dance floor."*

"Or anyplace else," her husband added. As one, the whole crowd turned to him. "Just making it clear," said Pratap Joshi.

"*Almost*-fiancée," Vikram muttered.

"What?" asked his mother.

"Making it clear," he said. "Like Dad did."

On a sudden mewl, Vikram's mom leaned against her husband's shoulder. "This party's over."

Seema bit back a yelp. It couldn't be over. She had one more pocket to check.

Fingertips steepled, Adhith said, "Auntieji, I'm so sorry—"

On a loud howl, Seema rushed towards him and grabbed his lapels. "How could you do this to me?" she screamed.

He staggered back with a startled gasp, but she didn't let go. Fingers clutching his blazer, she shook him, sobbing loud enough to bring the roof down if they'd been indoors. Now that she had the keys, his left pocket would be empty. Her left hand slipped under the right lapel. The cotton of his shirt was under her palm. The thicker fabric of his blazer was on top of her knuckles. Empty. Seema closed her eyes in relief. Almost done. All she had to do was make imprints of the keys she already had.

"Seema, stop," Adhith begged, his hands at her elbows, tugging her loose.

A pair of masculine arms wrapped around her waist, pulling her away from the fashion plate right in the middle of a melodramatic shriek. Vikram. Again. "I was trying to warn you," he bellowed.

"By pawing her in front of everyone?" shouted his mom. Turning to Seema, Rattan Joshi said, "Can you please stop screeching? I thought you were... but you're a fool. *Show some self-respect*, young lady. How many times are you going to throw yourself at a man who clearly doesn't want you?"

When Vikram let her go, Seema crept back, keeping her eyes on the floor. She didn't have to pretend to be ashamed. Right at the moment, she felt about two inches tall. Right at the moment, Seema fervently wished she could tell Vikram's mom she wasn't the idiot she was pretending to be. Instead, she mumbled, "I need to go to the loo."

Make the imprints, slip the keys back into Adhith's pocket, and leave. It didn't matter what Rattan Joshi thought. Seema would never see any of these people again. She'd never again see Vikram.

She longed to say something memorable to him. Kiss him a second time before she left. Fiercely willing her tears to damn well stay inside the ducts where they belonged, she stalked to the table and grabbed her purse before walking away from the party.

Chapter 16

Heels clicking on the white marble floor, Seema hurried towards the ladies' room. The noise from the party receded.

With each step, her purse bumped against her hip. In it was the equipment she needed. A dozen two-inch aluminium cases which opened like staplers with clay cakes on each half to make imprints of both sides of a key. There was also a small bottle of baby powder to make sure she didn't leave any residue on the metal.

Afterwards, Seema would somehow slip the keys back into Adhith's pocket. "Finding" them after "finding" the rest of his stuff would arouse suspicion.

Fingertips to the door, she pushed into the ladies' room. Running water. *Dammit.* Someone was inside. Not that she couldn't use the privacy of the stall to make imprints, but the countertop would be easier.

Seema saw the image in the mirror before the actual person. A short, slim woman, wearing a claret-coloured dress. Her dark brown head was bent over the sink. Both her hands were on the faucet. Vikram's sister, Anjali. Was she sick or something? Pregnant women threw up a lot, didn't they? "Are you okay?" Seema asked.

Anjali's head jerked up. Eyes wide, she stared at Seema.

"Anjali?" Seema called, mildly concerned at the pallor on the other woman's face.

In a sudden move, Anjali pulled her left hand behind her. With her right hand, she turned off the water. "Yeah. Just needed a break."

"I understand," Seema said. *Liar.* But everyone was entitled to a harmless lie or two. Especially, when fighting with a spouse.

She didn't know what made her look at the floor. Perhaps, it was an accident. Perhaps, she had keener hearing than she realised, enough to pick up the plop of a drop on the marble tiles. Perhaps, it was instinct born of a childhood in the slums, which told her something was very, very wrong.

Red dots decorated the marble next to Anjali's shoes. Another dot joined the rest. *Red dot, red dot, red do—blood?* Seema's heart slammed against her ribcage. A gasp. When Seema looked up, Anjali had her left hand up, a knife gripped in red-coated fingers. Blood spurted rhythmically from her wrist. She switched the blade to her right hand.

"Don't come near me," Anjali said, hoarsely. "I won't hurt you. Go into the bathroom, and I'll lock you in. Someone will find you—and me—sooner or later."

Seema opened her mouth to say something... *any*thing, but only a gurgling sound came out. She couldn't see anything except the gushing blood. And Anjali's pale face.

"Go," Anjali said, swaying.

Her hand darting to her thigh holster, Seema took one step forward.

"I said, 'Go into the bathroom,'" Anjali ordered, but her voice was weaker than it had been seconds ago.

The woman was intent on dying. What would be the point of aiming the Glock at her? By the time standoff was done— "You'll bleed to death," Seema mumbled. The red dots on the floor coalesced to form a small pool.

With a crazed laugh, Anjali asked, "Are you really this dumb? Of course, I'll die. That's the idea."

The scent of warm iron pierced Seema's nostrils. Muscles clenched in her belly, forming a hard knot. Hand to her mouth, she gagged.

"What are you doing?" asked Anjali.

"I'm gonna throw up," Seema said, lurching to the washbasin.

One step. Two steps. With a loud scream, she whirled around and lunged. Before Anjali even realised what was happening, Seema's fingers closed around the arm with the knife. In a split second, Seema was behind Anjali, yanking the suicidal woman's right arm behind her back. The strap of Seema's purse slipped off, sliding all the way to her wrist. The knife fell from Anjali's fingers, landing perilously close to Seema's foot.

Again and again, Seema screamed, "*Help.*" She hadn't seen any of the hotel staff on her way here from the pool, but she hoped like crazy *someone* would walk by and hear her.

The top of Anjali's head barely reached the middle of Seema's chest, but bloody hell, the woman put up a fight. "Let go of me," Anjali shrieked, kicking backwards.

The kitten heel struck Seema's shin. "Oww. Stay still, you little *princess*. I'm trying to save your life."

Anjali struggled even more, holding her bleeding left wrist as far away from Seema as possible. "I didn't ask you to save me," Anjali said. "Go away. I won't tell anyone you ignored me while I was dying."

"How could you?" Still holding Anjali's right arm behind her back, Seema hooked her free arm around Anjali's left elbow. "You'll be dead." With a grunt, Seema wrenched the arm to the back, slipping her hand down to the bleeding wrist. Warm wetness seeped through her fingers. *"Help,"* she screamed. *"Somebody, help."* Another kick landed on her leg. Ignoring the sharp pain shooting down to her toes, Seema tightened her grip on the wound. "Dammit, the bleeding's not stopping." Her left foot slid, colliding with something light. The wastebasket toppled over, its contents strewing across the room.

Seema and Anjali teetered together on the marble floor, their feet slipping on the puddles of thick, red liquid. Blood smeared both women everywhere. Hair, face, body, limbs.

"You know what?" Seema mumbled. "I have a better idea." She went into a half-squat, her kneecaps striking the back of Anjali's knees. Vikram's sister collapsed forwards. Still holding onto her wrists, Seema dropped to the floor. Somehow, she managed to sit on Anjali's right arm. Now, Seema could use both her hands. Anjali floundered about like a fish. The strap of Seema's purse was caught under Anjali's hip. Tugging it out, Seema tied it tightly above the knife wound. Damn the bangles. They clinked and clanked and got in the way.

"I can't see," Anjali sobbed, voice suddenly terrified.

"What—" Hands holding the crude tourniquet tight, Seema twisted around. Anjali's eyes were wide open, her head turning from side to side. There wasn't enough hair on her face to be blocking her vision. "Are you fainting?" Seema screeched. "Don't you faint on me. You hear me, princess? *Don't faint.*"

Weeping hard, Anjali said, "I'm scared, Seema. I think I'm gonna die."

"No way," said Seema. "I *will not* let you die." She had to keep holding the tourniquet tight enough to staunch the bleeding. She couldn't go anywhere. Eyes darting to the door, she screamed, "*Help.* Someone. *Please.*" The door stayed closed.

"Stay with me," Anjali wept.

"I will," vowed Seema. But she needed to get help. One fist holding the tourniquet tight, she reached for the purse with the other and tugged the zipper open. The phone slipped out, as did the rest of her equipment. When Seema finally opened the messenger app, the phone was coated with blood. She pressed a knuckle over Vikram's name.

Ring... ring...

"Pick up," she muttered. "For God's sake, pick up."

Anjali's sobs were getting weaker and weaker.

A click. "Seema, where are you?" came Vikram's anxious voice. "We need to talk."

"Vikram," she screamed. "Get over here before she dies."

"What?"

"Your sister," Seema babbled. "She cut her wrist."

With one last shudder, Anjali became still.

***

The next few minutes were a blur for Seema. Flipping Anjali's body over, finding a reassuring pulse on the other wrist, not knowing what to do to keep her alive. Seema dragged the unconscious woman onto her lap and stayed on the floor, shouting threats at God not to let her die.

She kept the purse strap wrapped tightly above the bleeding wrist. Her clay staplers were scattered all around them. Whatever she could reach, she scooped back into the purse. The phone was close to her shoe, but she didn't pick it up. The WhatsApp call was still on. Vikram bellowed, telling her he was on his way. She could barely hear him over the panicked screams in the background.

The door burst open, letting a couple of hotel employees in. Taking in the scene in one glance, the man turned to the woman. "Get an ambulance. Now."

"Seema," shouted Vikram, his voice coming simultaneously from outside the door and over the phone.

"In here," she shrieked, her voice hoarse.

He exploded in, followed by his parents and the dumbass. Screaming "Anju," all four rushed towards her.

Other voices joined the crowd in the ladies' room. The rest of the Joshis. Madhu and Adhith, too.

Someone lifted Anjali's body away from Seema's lap. The dumbass. Cradling his wife's form against his chest, he shouted, "Call an ambulance." Her blood smeared his face and body. "Oh, God, Anju. Don't die. Please, don't die."

Squatting around them, Vikram and his parents shouted her name over and over and alternately yelled for an ambulance. All three were sobbing, holding onto her, holding onto each other. Blood-slick fingers clutching the back of Vikram's blazer, Seema muttered incoherent prayers.

"Move," someone snapped at her. The trauma surgeon.

Face pale and drawn, he knelt to check Anjali's wrist, the purse strap still wrapped tightly around it. "The bleeding has stopped," he announced, his fingertips now on one side of her neck. "Pulse is still palpable. Breathing's a little rapid but nothing to be alarmed about. She probably fainted from blood loss and pain. The wound is easily repaired. What she needs is transfusion. Fast."

Even before he finished speaking, there were shouts at them to make room for the ambulance people. Seema scooted back, and with a hand gripping the edge of the countertop, she heaved herself up. Her knees were wobbly. Brushing the sticky curls back from her face, she watched Anjali's body being strapped to the stretcher.

One of the emergency medical technicians belted a wide, blue tourniquet above the wound and cut the purse strap with a pair of scissors. The purse fell to the floor, and Seema lurched to pick it up, barely avoiding having her hands trampled. Her phone... she couldn't see it. It was probably already smashed to pieces under someone's shoe.

As the Joshis followed the stretcher out the bathroom door, Seema's gaze collided with Madhu's anxious eyes. Adhith was next to her, yelling orders into his phone. When Vikram brushed past, Adhith said, "Bro, the blood's going to be ready as soon as she gets there."

The Joshis were clearly loaded, and almost all of them were doctors, but none had Adhith's clout. A single phone call from the finance minister's son set the system on alert blood was needed for a V.I.P patient.

Shit. The minister. The investigation. Seema needed to make imprints and return the keys to Adhith before he checked. She also had to find the bureau's phone. If it got into outside hands... it couldn't be tracked, but IB would prefer not to take the risk.

"Are you all right?" asked Madhu.

Seema nodded, looking at the floor. Bloody footprints, one of Anjali's red suede shoes, her knife, the contents of the wastebasket strewn all over, a couple of pieces of medical equipment... "My phone—"

Adhith soothed, "We'll ask the hotel staff to look for it. Seema, you can't go home in a cab all covered in blood like this. Let me get Vikram to the hospital. Then, I can drop you and Madhu off."

Shaking her head, Seema said, "I need to—"

"Seema," shouted a hoarse voice. Vikram.

One of the ambulance men came hurrying back in. "Are you Seema? The patient wants you with her."

"She's awake?" asked Madhu.

"Barely," said the ambulance man.

***

In the confines of the ambulance, Seema crouched by Anjali's hip, holding onto her hand. Cut ends of the strap knotted together, Seema's purse hung on her shoulder. The only other people allowed in the vehicle were Anjali's husband and her mother. They squatted next to her head, one on either side, stroking her hair and pleading with her to hold on. Anjali came awake twice during the ride. The first time, she looked blearily at each of them and whispered to Seema, "Don't leave."

"I won't," Seema promised.

The second time Anjali opened her eyes was when the ambulance screeched to a halt, and the doors opened. "Rishi?" she called.

"Right here," croaked the dumbass. His pretty face was splotchy with tears.

"I'm so sorry," Anjali said.

Within minutes of getting her into the hospital bed, Vikram and his father came running. Adhith had driven them there. Madhu was with them.

When the IV line was inserted into her arm, Anjali moaned. Anxiously, she scanned the crowd surrounding her, relaxing only when she saw Seema. Voice drowsy, Anjali explained to the room at large, "She's not a fool."

The dumbass took the chair by the bed, blood bags hanging on the IV pole between him and his wife. On the sofa to the right, Rattan and Pratap Joshi held onto each other. Vikram sat on the windowsill to the left of the bed, his gaze never leaving his sister. There was a second room in the deluxe suite into which Adhith herded Madhu and the remaining Joshis. He walked in and out a couple of times, bringing coffee and water for Anjali's parents.

Purse hanging on her shoulder, Seema slumped against the wall opposite the bed for as long as she could, sliding to the mosaic floor only when her legs gave out. She kicked her stilettos off and settled her bottom on the cold tiles. When Adhith moved a chair next to her, she held up a hand, declining the offer. Tired as she was, she'd fall out of it.

Dammit. The keys. She had to make imprints and return the originals to Adhith before he found out they were missing. Barefoot, Seema padded to the bathroom and cleaned the blood off her hands as best as she could before getting around to the task of pressing keys into clay. When she returned to the room, Adhith wasn't there. She couldn't afford to wait until he checked on the Joshis again. "Let me make sure Madhu's okay," Seema said.

Vikram's mom sat up, her gaze going to her daughter.

Seema smiled, reassuringly. "I'll be back in a couple of minutes."

The air conditioner was on full blast in the companion room. With more than ten people crammed in, they needed it. In one corner, the brat was perched on a footstool and sobbing. The rest of the cousins and their parents were sitting on the bed and the chairs, leaning against walls, or pacing. Adhith and Madhu were talking by the window. They hadn't spotted Seema yet.

A few patches of dried blood stained his pants and silver-grey shirt, but Madhu's white and silver sari was still spotless. Trembling mildly, she wrapped the free end of the sari around her upper arms. Adhith shrugged off his blazer. With a tender gaze, he draped it over her shoulders. The look on her face just as open and vulnerable, she smiled back at him.

Oh, Madhu, Seema muttered, closing her eyes in sudden realisation. She had her explanation for the scene from the party. Why him? Of all the men who'd begged Madhu for a friendly glance, why Adhith Verma? A diplomat, a businessman-philanthropist whose mother took an interest in the women's shelter on Grant Road, a best-selling author... the businessman was the only one who'd gotten within ten feet of her, but when he made noises about sending the then fifteen-year-old Seema to some fancy boarding school in Dehradun, Madhu threw him out on his ear. Madhubala Rawat rejected all the eligible bachelors clamouring to worship at her feet, only to fall for the one man who should be off-limits.

"Hey," Seema called, purse on her shoulder and her left hand tucked into the pocket of her flared skirt. Her fingers closed around the keys. When she got to the couple, she stumbled forwards, clutching the blazer on Madhu for support. The bangles on Seema's wrists jangled. Madhu staggered. Somehow, they managed not to tumble to the floor in a heap. Seema slipped the keys back where she'd found them. "Sorry," she said, letting go. "My legs fell asleep."

Madhu's eyes narrowed. "What are you..." She huffed. "Are you all right?"

"I'm fine," Seema said. "Madhu, I'm going to stay here until I know Anjali's okay."

"Wait here until morning, please?" Adhith begged Madhu. "It's not safe for you to wander around at night when you don't even have your—" He glanced at her silver wristlet.

The gun? Since Seema's Glock was strapped to her thigh, Madhu stashed hers in the Kurla flat before leaving for the dinner party. Seema had planned to stay in the flat after and not return to Panvel, and Madhu would've picked up her weapon before continuing her way home. But Adhith *knew* Madhu carried a gun? How far had things gotten between them? In what... three, four meetings?

"*I* want to make sure Anjali's okay, too," Madhu said. "I'll call a taxi in the morning."

"Could *you* take her to Kurla?" Seema asked Adhith. "And... umm..." Guard Madhu until she had her gun back? Nah, awkward thing to say even if he knew about it. "Madhu can send me fresh clothes with you."

Adhith nodded.

When Seema limped back to the patient room, there was a nurse at the bedside, changing blood bags. "Her colour seems better," the nurse muttered.

Thank God. Seema let herself collapse to the same spot on the floor she'd occupied before. A form dropped down next to her. Vikram. In silence, he shrugged off his bloodstained blazer. Before he could wrap the blazer around her as Adhith did with Madhu, Seema held up a hand in refusal. She couldn't even bear to look at him. When this investigation was over, both Rawat women were going to be left devastated.

Tossing the blazer to the side, he wrapped his arms around her. Inside her chest, her heart squeezed, painfully. She knew she should push him away. She couldn't. She just couldn't. He clung to her, letting his head rest on her shoulder while his breathing steadied. They stayed that way for hours. Through the constant beeping of the monitors on the wood-panelled walls, the nurses in white dresses wandering in and out, and the quiet conversations between the hospital staff and the Joshi parents.

Anjali woke up more than a few times. Her eyes always went to her silent husband first. She fretted when she couldn't spot Seema sitting on the floor. When Seema stomped away the numbness in her legs and hobbled over to the bed, Anjali gripped her fingers, whispering, "You wouldn't let me die."

Just before dawn, the staff physician came in to let them know Anjali's vital signs were stable. The pelvic ultrasound showed a strong, healthy heartbeat. Both the mother and the baby would be fine. A collective sigh of relief went up.

Adhith persuaded the Joshi brothers and their families to return to the hotel, but Anjali's parents refused to leave her side even to rest in the other room. Her husband hadn't said a word after they got her to the hospital, and he didn't appear to have heard Adhith's suggestion of getting some sleep, either. Red-rimmed eyes fixed on his wife, he stayed in the chair by her bed. Neither Vikram nor Seema budged from their spot on the floor. Adhith continued to walk between the two rooms, comforting the Joshis with his presence and making sure Madhu was fine. When morning brought light outside the window and the chatter of the hospital staff outside the door, Seema was still on the floor.

With a small scream, a fiftyish woman, clad in a cotton sari, came scurrying in. There was a duffel bag on her shoulder. When she ran to the bed, Rattan Joshi stumbled up from the sofa. "Kusum." Holding onto each other, the two women sobbed. "Anju's going to be fine," said Rattan, voice trembling.

"Kusum used to be our nanny," Vikram muttered to Seema. "Now, she supervises things at home."

"Here you go," Adhith said, from the door. He was holding a plastic bag. "The hotel staff found your phone."

"Madhu?" asked Seema.

"At your flat in Kurla." Head inclining towards the plastic bag, he added, "She put some clothes in there for you. I picked up Kusum on the way back."

258

***

In the bathroom attached to the companion room of the deluxe suite, Seema took a deep, gulping breath. What a rough night it had been, but it was over. Anjali was going to be all right. Amidst all the tumult, Seema managed to finish the job she'd set out to do.

Seema pulled the bangles off and threw them into the wastebasket. They'd served as her cover and were no longer needed. She stripped off the bloodstained cocktail dress and the thigh holster before taking a quick shower.

Pulling on clean jeans and a loose cotton shirt over fresh underwear, Seema grinned. Madhu had thoughtfully included Seema's special belt and her inside-the-waistband holster. The Glock went back on, nicely concealed under the shirt. The dress was a total loss. She rolled it up and started to stuff it into the plastic bag. She paused, eyeing the paper sack with the Oberoi logo on it.

Seema took her phone out from the paper sack. A spider web of cracks extended across the front. There were pieces of metal protruding from the sides. The device looked irreparably broken. Plus, it could not be tracked. The bureau would still not want her tossing it out with the waste where anyone could find it. Grimacing, Seema slipped it back into the paper sack and tucked it into her purse.

The strap of the purse might be cut, but she hadn't lost any of its contents in the struggle with Anjali. The fake *aadhaar* card—her phoney national ID—given by the Intelligence Bureau, the credit cards, even the cash. She hadn't brought the company-provided phone to the party. Considering everything, one phone wasn't a big loss. Seema frowned, mentally picturing the contents of the purse. Something *was* missing.

With unsteady fingers, she zipped the purse back open. Cards, paper sack with the broken phone, clay staplers... in one quick sweep, she counted the staplers. Eleven. Heart pounding painfully in her chest, she counted again. Eleven. Not the twelve she'd brought with her.

Quickly she opened each of the staplers to check. There had been five keys in the set she first lifted from Adhith. Three keys in the second. There should've been eight used moulds and four unused. The unused moulds were all accounted for. The missing stapler had a key imprint. Grabbing the paper sack, she pulled out the ruined phone. There. At the bottom of the sack was the missing clay stapler.

Her head swam. The white lights in the bathroom suddenly seemed too bright. The smell of the disinfectant too strong. She could hear her own harsh, raspy breaths. *Calm down.* Adhith wasn't the one who found the phone. The hotel staff did. An employee of a high-end hotel wasn't likely to know what a clay stapler with a key imprint meant. Could Adhith have seen it? Madhu. Oh, God. He'd taken her home. If he saw the clay stapler and recognised it for what it was...

Seema's hands were shaking so badly it took her three tries to unlock the door. The second bedroom was empty. They were all there in the other room. When she crept to the connecting door, Anjali was still on the bed, sleeping quietly. Her silent husband was stretched out on the chair. Vikram's parents were on the sofa, with Kusum. Vikram and Adhith were by the door, talking.

If Adhith knew what the clay stapler meant, he was going to march her straight to his corrupt father. "All done?" Adhith asked, tone still friendly. "Let's get some breakfast."

Seema glanced between him and Vikram, trying to think of a way to decline the offer. She couldn't shoot her way out in public without destroying the mission. Nor could she scream out the truth. "I don't want to be a bother."

"Bother?" Adhith's eyes crinkled. "I've known Anju almost as long as I've known Vikram. They're my family. You saved her life. Trust me, buying you breakfast is no bother."

"You already had to go to the hotel to get my phone back," she protested. "Then, to Kurla to drop off Madhu."

Adhith ptchaaed. "We were in Kurla when the hotel called. All I had to do was stop there after I picked up Kusum."

Hope. Thready hope he might not have seen the key imprint. He wasn't acting like there was anything wrong. "They had the paper sack waiting for you?" she asked, keeping her tone casual.

"At the reception desk," he assured her. "They handed me the sack as soon as I walked in. No trouble, at all."

"Go, betay," said Vikram's mom. "The nurse gave Anju a sedative. Get something to eat before she wakes up, again. Vikram, you should get some food, too."

Chapter 17

Jogging back to the car from the lobby of the Oberoi, Adhith had opened the paper sack given him by the hotel staff to check on Seema's phone. The metallic glint at the bottom of the sack almost went unnoticed. The aluminium lid first made him think it was cheap makeup. Only the garish green stuff coating the edges made him take a closer look. The stuff stuck to his fingers. "Clay?" he muttered to himself, puzzled. He turned halfway back, thinking the hotel mistakenly placed some child's lost toy in the sack. Curiosity made him pry the two halves apart. Surprise stopped him in his tracks. *Key impression?* The clay gadget was no toy. What was Seema doing, copying keys? He needed to think about this.

When he got back to his car, Kusum was still in the passenger seat where he'd left her. "They're all going to need fresh clothes," she fretted, bouncing the duffel on her knee. The plastic bag given by Madhu was next to her feet. "How far is it to the hospital?"

"Only a few minutes." Handing over the paper sack, he asked, "Kusum, can you put this in the plastic bag?"

Waiting behind a red BEST bus at the traffic light, Adhith drummed the steering wheel with his fingers. The gadget need not be Seema's, obviously. It could even be Anjali's, but the idea of the Joshi princess copying keys was laughable. Seema, though... her childhood in the slums... it could belong to a third person. Only one way to find out. He'd have to ask her.

Outside the car window, the city streets were humming with the sounds of taxis and buses and bikes. Mumbaikars had been begging for the monsoon to bring relief from the heat, but the blazing sun and the salty ocean kept them sweating. Within the car, the cool draught from the air conditioner washed over Adhith. His mind replayed the events of the night before.

The tension over his father, the stupidity of involving Seema in the scheme to get away from politics as usual, falling for Madhu when he was supposedly dating her niece, manipulating Vikram into blurting out his feelings... Anjali... what could've prompted her to... none of the Joshis was yet in a state of mind to ask why, but Adhith asked himself the question over and over. She'd been smiling and happy until he mentioned seeing the dumbass next to the Gateway of India. That had to be the key to the—

Keys, keys, keys. The whole evening revolved around keys, literal and metaphorical. First, Adhith lost his wallet and car keys. Then, the office keys fell from his pocket. Finally, the key impression in clay. He sat up. Twisting to the side, he dug the office keys out from his pants. The plastic bag with the Oberoi paper sack in it was next to Kusum's feet, but Adhith remembered the clay imprint well enough. The key to the supplies cupboard. A perfect match.

A loud honk. "Green light," said Kusum.

Pulse pounding at his temple, Adhith slipped the bunch back into his pocket and followed the vehicles snaking down the road. *Seema.* It had to be Seema. She'd gotten the keys from him to copy the one to the supplies cupboard. That's why he kept losing them all evening.

Why the hell did she need access to the supplies? Even if she thought she needed it for whatever weird reason, all she had to do was ask. Their accountant, Britto, was in charge, but he'd been begging for some help with administrative duties. He'd have been happy to let Seema handle office supplies. How did she lift the keys in the first place?

Mind whirling, Adhith followed Kusum into the lift. It didn't make any sense. Yeah, Seema's background was sketchy, but she'd grown up poor, not a pickpocket. In any case, the only reason for her to copy the key would be to steal something from the cupboard, but what was she hoping to find there? Printing paper and stapler pins? The office petty cash was usually locked in the strongbox under Britto's desk.

Adhith shook his head, angrily. Was he actually considering the possibility of Seema stealing from the cash box? He'd never do so with anyone else. No wonder she'd lied about her past. She must know she wouldn't get the benefit of the doubt if and when something went wrong.

But she *had* been trying to copy the key. Secretly, when she had no need to. Hell, even if there was a good reason to steal something, she could've easily lifted *Vikram's* keys. Crazy as he was about her, he might not have noticed even if she'd *rammed* her hands into his pockets.

The lift pinged. Adhith halted outside the doors and let Kusum run on ahead to Anjali's room. He took the office keys from his pant pocket. Why from him? Perhaps, Seema thought he had access to something Vikram didn't. The only things Adhith could think of were his car and his flat. Did she make copies of all of those, as well?

Adhith peered at the rest of the keys in the office bunch. He couldn't find any trace of clay on any of them. The car key was electronic, so she wouldn't be able to copy it. He dug into the inside pocket to the left of his blazer. The keys to his flat. No trace of clay there, either. There *was* a tiny, red dot, almost invisible.

He snarled. She *did* copy them. After the encounter with Anjali. There was no other way blood got on something tucked into his inside pocket. What was Seema planning? A robbery? They'd trusted her, made her part of their circle, and she was going to reward them by stealing? Fury galloped through his veins. He thundered down the corridor, ignoring the curious looks from a couple of nurses he passed. It was only the sobbing from the room that prevented him from exploding in to haul Seema up by her scruff.

From the door, Adhith studied the scene inside. His eyes went to the pale form lying quietly in the bed. The monitor beeped at regular intervals. Kusum and Rattan Joshi were holding onto each other, sobbing. Anjali's father and her husband were still in the same spots they'd occupied all night.

Vikram was sitting on the floor, his back against the wall and legs stretched out in front. His left arm was wrapped around Seema's shoulders. Legs tucked under her, she was curled up against his side. Vikram was whispering in her ear. Her French braid from the evening before had come loose. Dried blood streaked through the curls. Red patches were all over her. On the black, halter-neck dress from the party, her face and arms and legs... her stilettos, discarded on the floor, were also caked with blood.

Anjali... her husband and her parents... her brother, who was trustingly cradling the traitor in his arms... Adhith couldn't make a scene here. Taking a deep breath, he held out the plastic bag. "Here you go. The hotel staff found your phone."

Seema stirred. "Madhu?"

No, Adhith refused to believe Madhu was part of her niece's schemes. The NGO wouldn't have trusted her to go over their accounts if so. Also, she'd tried again and again to warn him away from Seema. This had to be why. Madhu was worried Seema remembered only the fun side of her life in the slums. Seema was no longer a naïve twelve-year-old. She was an adult, responsible for her own bad decisions. Madhu was the naïve one, believing her niece's behaviour to be anything but criminal. "At your flat in Kurla," Adhith said. If she let him, he'd take her far, far away from Seema and her toxic presence. Head inclining towards the plastic bag, he added, "She put some clothes in there for you."

As Seema disappeared into the other room with her purse and the plastic bag, he realised how she'd made the copies. At the party, she'd taken a few trips to the latrine. On returning, she'd let him "find" the keys.

Vikram heaved himself off the floor and padded to the door. "Adhi, I forgot to call Cyber Ninja."

"The kid in San Jose? He texted me when he couldn't reach you. I told him there was a family emergency. He's been sending me regular updates on the work. I'll head over to the office in a couple of hours so he can take a break. Work from here if you can. If not, we'll manage."

"Family emergency," Vikram muttered, raking his fingers through his hair. His black blazer was thrown carelessly on the floor, and his tie was nowhere in sight. Patches of dried blood were on his black shirt and pants, too, but not as much as on Seema. "I never imagined... if Seema hadn't been in the right place at the right time..."

She'd been in the latrine to make copies of Adhith's home keys. If she hadn't run into Anjali, Seema would've been long gone. She'd returned the keys to his blazer sometime after. It was the only way to explain the drop of blood.

Why had she helped Anjali? Even if Seema couldn't bring herself to ignore a dying woman, she didn't need to agree to go with Anjali in the ambulance. Nor to sit in her room all night. Why had Seema stuck around, risking exposure?

Taking care to keep his tone light, Adhith updated Vikram on Cyber Ninja's progress.

When Seema returned from her shower, her face was pale. Could be the events of the night, of course, but Adhith didn't think so. She'd seen the gadget in the paper sack and was worried Adhith figured out her game. "All done?" he asked. "Let's get some breakfast." She was going to answer his questions.

Silently, she glanced between him and Vikram, fear and misery mingling in her eyes.

You don't want Vikram finding out, do you? Why do you care what he thinks of you? Adhith had believed she attended the party to make Vikram jealous. But no. Seema went there to rob Adhith. When Vikram tried to save her from being embarrassed, she made it clear she didn't want him or his help. So why this anxiety at being exposed as a criminal in front of him? Seema was going to answer every one of Adhith's questions. He had to lure her out of the hospital room before asking. Neither Vikram nor the Joshis needed the added trauma. Pretty words came easily to Adhith. He didn't have any difficulty thanking Seema for saving Anjali. No problem issuing a pleasant invitation to breakfast.

"You already had to go to the hotel to get my phone back," Seema protested, his friendliness turning the panic on her face to confusion. "Then, to Kurla to drop off Madhu."

Adhith dismissed the pitiful objection. "We were in Kurla when the hotel called. It was easy to stop there after I picked up Kusum."

"The hotel had the paper sack waiting for you?" Seema asked, tone carefully casual.

"At the reception desk," he said. "They handed it to me as soon as I walked in. No trouble, at all."

Hope dawned in Seema's eyes. Hope he hadn't seen the clay gadget.

Say yes, he urged. Once they were out of earshot of the Joshis, they'd have a blunt conversation.

"Go, betay," Vikram's mom said to Seema. "...Vikram, you should get some food, too."

Adhith cursed in his mind. How was he going to interrogate Seema with Vikram around?

***

They ate breakfast in silence. None of them was in the mood for light chatter, and no one wanted to talk about the near tragedy.

Holding the cup of coffee to his mouth, Adhith went over the first time he met Seema: salwar-clad woman, folder clutched to her chest. Her sweet voice telling him she was from Sarkhagat, a small town in Himachal Pradesh. She'd targeted him from the beginning, studying his background and using it to lure him. *Why? To rob my home? What do you want from there?*

Whatever she wanted, she'd drawn the line at sleeping with him. The shy smiles... the coy rejections... *of course!* She lifted the keys *because* she didn't want to sleep with him to get into his flat.

Again, what did she want from there? What merited so much effort on her part? Three months was a long time to invest in robbing the home of a twenty-eight-year-old IT professional. There were easier targets. Vikram, for one. She'd seen how far he was willing to go for her. If she were merely after cash, besotted fool Vikram was, he'd have let her right into his parent's duplex. The Joshis preferred tasteful luxury to ostentatious displays of wealth, but Seema surely got how rich they were.

No, this was an operation meant to trap *Adhith*, not any other IT professional, not any other well-to-do bachelor, not Vikram. Adhith Verma, son of India's finance minister, was Seema's target. Political takedown? Journalist? Or something infinitely more sinister? India had many enemies.

If she were working for a foreign power, she was going about it all wrong. So far, she'd made no attempts to infiltrate his father's circle. In fact, she'd been reluctant to attend the party when she thought his father would be there. What self-respecting spy would need to go to such lengths as lifting his keys to copy them? Why wouldn't the agency provide her with a master? Or help her stage a break-in? Also, what the hell did she expect to find in *his* flat as opposed to Papaji's residence? Espionage was low on the list of probabilities.

Tabloid reporter or political rivalry was more likely. Gossip about Adhith joining the *ganda dhanda*—the dirty business—of politics ran rampant in Delhi circles even before the parliamentary seat opened in Uttarakhand.

Her flatmate worked for an e-zine. Madhu, when she first met him, said something about being a political reporter. Chances were Seema Rawat was one of the yellow press, looking for dirt on him. Bringing down the son of one of India's most powerful politicians would make her career. But a political rival would pay much, much more than a tabloid, enough for her to ignore the lure of the Joshi wealth.

Whatever the motive behind the months-long preparations, she'd risked it all by saving Anjali's life and by sitting in the hospital room all night.

Adhith set the coffee mug back on the table and bit off a piece of the delicately buttered toast. Perhaps Seema was not the sort to ignore a dying woman. Forgetting all her schemes and staying by Anjali's side went beyond basic human decency. Seema did it because Anjali was Vikram's sister. *You didn't plan on falling in love with him, did you?*

Seema was still prepared to go through with her scheme and make her escape, or she wouldn't have been all over Adhith at the party when she clearly harboured feelings for Vikram. She'd have never lifted the keys. She needed to be stopped—not just from her criminal activities but from causing any more emotional devastation in the lives of the people who cared about her. Vikram, Madhu—

Adhith bit back a curse. Madhu wasn't involved in her relative's misdeeds, or she wouldn't have been trying so hard to talk him out of a relationship with Seema. Still, there was no question Madhu knew about it, and she loved Seema more than what was good for her. She'd be crushed if Adhith were to haul her niece to the cops for theft.

First, he had to extricate Madhu from the mess, physically *and* emotionally. He needed to show her there was no choice but to let Seema face the consequences of her actions. In the meantime, he had to make sure Seema didn't break into his flat with the keys she'd copied. If he changed the locks, she'd know he knew and would bolt, persuading Madhu to go with her.

"I'm also going to work from home for a couple of days," Adhith said to Vikram. "Less distraction while I focus on our... ahh... internal project." He'd almost blurted something about the hacker problem in front of Seema. As though they hadn't already given her enough chances to destroy their lives.

Vikram nodded. "Britto can deal with the EU client. It's all fine-tuning now, anyway. The senior analysts can take care of the technical side."

If Adhith weren't listening carefully, he might have missed Seema's whimper of frustration. She couldn't raid Adhith's flat while he was in it.

❋❋❋

Settling into his living room sofa with the phone held to his ear, Adhith asked Madhu, "Why didn't you wait for me at the Kurla flat? Weren't we supposed to do lunch?" When he realised she'd left, his heart quaked in worry for her safety until he remembered seeing her black tote in the flat. Madhu had her weapon back.

Still, he needed to talk to her. The only contact info he had on her was her work number, but this was Saturday, and she'd be home. He considered asking Seema for her auntie's personal number, but he felt bloody awkward about it even if she didn't know he was trying to break the bond between the women. In the end, he begged Vikram to have Seema tell Madhu when *she* called that Adhith found one of her earrings in his car, so could she call him, please? No one would've bought the convoluted story after the drama he created at the party, but Adhith didn't care.

"*You* thought we were going to have lunch," Madhu said, her low tone mildly mocking. "I never agreed. Plus, I couldn't go to lunch in that fancy sari."

"Excuses," he scoffed. He kept one eye on the numbers and letters scrolling down the laptop on the coffee table. There was no one else in the flat, and the TV was off, but there was no quiet to be had. Even on the eleventh floor, there were always sounds from the streets. "You were at Seema's flat. You could've borrowed something from her cupboard."

On a peel of laughter, Madhu said, "Our styles don't exactly match."

"No," he agreed. "You have a touch of sophistication which she lacks."

"Is that so? Which is more sophisticated? My hoodie or my jeans?"

"You may sneer," he said, grandly. "Sophistication has just as much to do with attitude as with clothes. Whether you wear your ridiculous hoodies or the sari from yesterday, you look classy. You were gorgeous in the sari... try other outfits. Expand your horizons a bit."

"Are you giving me fashion advice?"

Tone lowering to a husky murmur, he said, "You should let me dress you."

"Don't you already have a job? Besides, I thought you wanted to get into politics. Stay out of women's fashion."

He laughed. "You don't understand. If you let me dress you, I'd put everything on you myself. Piece by piece."

A pause, followed by a gasp.

"Silk and lace, first," he said, picturing her clad only in bra and panties.

"It wouldn't work."

"Why not?" In his mind, she was lounging on her bed, wearing barely there underwear while she talked to him on the phone.

"Because I insist on equality in all things."

"Huh?"

"If you get to dress me up, I get to dress you up, too."

He snorted. "You want me to wear a hoodie? Not in my lifetime."

"Oh, no. A hoodie wouldn't suit you... you weren't wearing a tie yesterday."

"A tie? What's so unworkable about it?"

"Just a tie. Nothing else."

In a nanosecond, he was hard as a rock. On the bed in his imagination, he joined her, wearing only a tie. "Bloody hell, Madhu. You can give as good as you get. Why did you leave the flat? If you were next to me..."

She groaned. "I shouldn't have... you have to stop calling me."

"Why? I know Seema acted a little crazy yesterday, but trust me, she doesn't love me any more than I love her. Which I don't."

"It's not about who loves whom, and it's not about who's older than whom. I *am* past the age for casual flings. I don't get into relationships in which I see no future."

"Who said it would be casual?" Adhith countered. "I'm serious."

"Oh, God." Madhu sighed. "Serious? You had qualms about marrying Seema because she grew up in the slums. Were you asleep when I was telling you about my life there? I was actually a—"

"Survivor," he completed.

"See? You're already trying to pretty it up. This is why it wouldn't work between us."

"*You're* making it sound worse than it was. Tell me something. Those kids at the shelter... would you call any of those girls a prostitute?"

"Damn you."

"Why are you calling *yourself* one? You *know* it's not true. Madhu, credit me with enough intelligence to see what you're doing. By saying the word a few dozen times, you're hoping to drive me away. Well, it won't work. Not when I know how you feel."

"You do?" she asked. "Funny. I don't remember that conversation."

He guffawed. "Some conversations don't require words."

"So you don't need to call me," she said, triumphantly. "Let your imagination do the job."

"I called you because I can't stand not having you around." Also, because they were facing a dire situation involving her relative with criminal tendencies. "Madhu, have dinner with me? At my flat, I mean. We have to talk about Seema."

"What about her?" Madhu asked, tone guarded.

"She... I don't know how to... she did something at the party... it's bothering me, and I need to discuss it with you. In private."

Madhu's angry huff was audible over the phone. "*Seema* did something? What were *you* doing? And your friend, Vikram? Hell, I have no idea what *I* was doing there."

"It's not about—Madhu, you've known Seema since she was a child. I'd like to think you're beginning to know *me* as well. Do you believe Seema would've put up with Vikram's antics if she didn't feel anything for him? Do you believe I'd have let it happen if I didn't know how both of them feel?"

A sharp hiss.

"Yeah, she's in love with him. She still—" Adhith gritted his teeth. "She's making choices which are not going to end well."

"Don't you worry. We'll both be out of your lives as soon as Anjali leaves the hospital. Seema promised Anjali she'd stay, but it won't be forever. I'll make sure Seema knows you don't want her sticking around to bother you."

"It's not about what happened at the party." It was, kind of, but Adhith was not about to accuse Seema of being a pickpocket over the phone. "Also, you're going to walk out of my life? You're going to be fine never seeing me, again?"

"Verma—"

"You don't think you'll remember me every night the rest of your life? Because *I* will. Even if I find a hundred other women to love, I will always remember how you felt in my arms."

Tone faltering, Madhu said, "We never got that far."

"Doesn't matter. In my mind, I've made love to you a hundred times. Tell me you haven't done the same."

A tiny sound, almost like a sob.

"We need to talk about this before all our lives are ruined. Only, I don't want to talk in a restaurant. We can't do it over the phone, either. If you're not comfortable coming to my home, I can meet you wherever you live." He'd pay someone to stay in his flat and stop Seema from raiding the place while he was gone. "Please, Madhu. I refuse to lose you."

"Do you think either of us has a choice? The future's not promised to anyone."

"We have the present. We have tonight. What we do in the here and now will determine the future."

"Tonight," Madhu whispered. "We have tonight."

***

Heart pounding, Adhith waited for the doorbell to ring. At seven sharp as agreed, Madhu was on her way up.

He'd used the hours after her call well, getting the building manager's sister to give the flat a quick clean. The manager was a retired soldier and a bachelor. He and his widowed sister lived rent-free in one of the basement apartments and in addition to the duties of their employment, did work on the side for the residents. Adhith focused his energies on the hacker problem while the woman swept and mopped and washed every dish.

When Adhith first met Madhu in the teashop on Grant Road, she'd been nibbling on kebabs, and she'd pounced on the chocolate biscuits at the women's shelter. Papaji's secretary knew one of the chefs at the Souk, the Taj Mahal Palace Hotel's famed Mediterranean restaurant. For the finance minister's son, they delivered a platter with lamb skewers and lobster and chocolate pie along with a bottle of Yeni Raki, the Turkish wine.

At 5:30 PM, Cyber Ninja called. They compared notes on the hacker's pattern. Most known troublemakers in the world of cybersecurity possessed signature moves, but this particular S.O.B's method didn't match any of the ones the team already checked, and there were few prior attacks left to analyse.

NJ was still trying to track the hacker through the trails he hadn't yet managed to obscure. As soon as the watchman called saying he'd sighted Madhu walking in, Adhith asked NJ for a few hours' quiet time while he took a break.

The round mahogany dining table to the left gleamed under the yellow lights. Buttery candles in glass jars sat in the middle. Dinnerware, silverware, wine glasses, the bottle of apéritif... everything was ready, even the music on his computer.

To his right, the living room windows overlooked the Arabian Sea. Dusk was a gloomy purple today, not the mind-blowing shades of orange and pink it had been for weeks with the red sun sinking into the sea. Still, an ocean view was an ocean view. Romantic.

A chime rang through the flat. His pulse skittered. He was in lousy shape. If they couldn't work through the Seema situation, he didn't know what he'd do. He *had* to persuade Madhu to leave her relative aside and live for herself.

Tugging the door open, he stood for a minute, drinking in the sight of her. With her disinclination to dress up, he'd thought it best to limit himself to jeans and a black shirt. She'd shown up in a printed, wraparound maxi and a cropped white tee. Her hair was down as it had been at the party. Glasses still perched on her nose, and the oversized black tote was on her shoulder.

"Aren't you going to invite me in?" Madhu asked.

With an embarrassing stutter, he stood to the side. The first thing her eyes went to was the dining table. "No reason to go hungry while we talk," he said, closing the door behind her. He waved towards the sofa, brushing past Madhu to get the bottle of wine. God, there was the perfume again—sweet, soft, seductive. What the hell was it? He'd never smelled it on any other woman. When he handed her a glass of the milky white wine and settled next to her on the sofa, he saw the beads of sweat on her upper lip. Adhith couldn't help it. He laughed. To her raised eyebrow, he responded, "You're as nervous as I am. I thought you didn't love me."

Taking a quick sip of the wine, she mumbled, "I don't." Her gaze was fixed on the tote she'd laid on the coffee table.

Adhith set his wine glass next to the purse and twisted towards her. "Look at me and say it."

It took her a few seconds, but Madhu did turn to face him. "I don't... I'm not sure how I feel..."

"Aren't you?" he challenged, his tone as low as hers. Sweet warmth filled his chest at the yearning in her eyes. "Madhu, I'm serious about us. I lo—"

A clatter. The wine glass in her hand was on the table, tumbling to its side. The white liquid spread over the dark mahogany. Madhu's warm hand cupped his cheek. She was so close her breasts brushed against his chest with each trembling breath. Her mouth grazed his.

Groaning, Adhith wrapped his arms around her, gathering her against him to savour the softness of her lips, the bitterness of the wine giving way to the pepperminty taste on her tongue. The sweet seduction of her scent.

Her fingers dug through his hair, slipping down to his shoulders, kneading his back. His muscles flexed under her touch. Blood rushed to his crotch.

"Madhu," he murmured against her neck. His hands slipped under her cropped tee to stroke the silky skin. "We need to talk."

"No," she whispered. "We have tonight. Let's not waste it."

"Are you sure?" Sliding an arm under her knees, he lifted her into his lap.

"I'm sure, or I wouldn't have come here."

Food forgotten, wine forgotten, he carried her to the bedroom. Touching, kissing, peeling every bit of clothing off each other. In the soft glow illuminating the room, Adhith tried to prolong their enjoyment, to savour each new patch of her skin he exposed, but Madhu refused to stay still. She circled him, nipping at his lip and collarbone, running her fingers over his shoulders and back, digging her nails into the tops of his buttocks, rearing against him with a growl.

"Tigress," he whispered, fiercely. *His* tigress.

With an answering growl, he grabbed her by the scruff, rewarding her mischief with sensual caresses until violent shudders racked both of them. Their breaths were loud and harsh in the silence of the room. The air conditioner was set to near-freezing levels, but her skin was slippery with sweat. His, too.

When she shoved him onto the mattress, Adhith wasn't aware of much else except the need to touch her and have her touch him. More teasing, fondling, driving themselves insane. He heard pleas and demands, sobs of pleasure and roars of triumph, but for the life of him, he couldn't have said which of them was making the sounds.

Looming over her on his hands and knees, he found himself unable to look away. He couldn't stop smiling in joy even as they rolled around in madness.

Finally, there was ecstasy as though his heart took wing.

He must have fallen asleep. A crash, reverberating through the room, rattled his brain. He jerked up, heart pounding. Madhu had been spooned against his chest. With a gasp, she scrambled into a sitting position, her eyes going to the window on their left.

Lightning forked through the dark sky outside. Another thunderclap. The windowpanes shuddered. Rain lashed against the glass. "Monsoon?" he asked. "It's here?" Throwing his head back, he laughed in joy. "Will you look at that?"

Holding the bed sheet to her chest, Madhu laughed with him. "You sound ready to go and dance in the rain."

"*You* have no umbrella. You're going to have to stay here until the storm's done." Neither mentioned the possibility of a taxi.

Batting her eyelashes, she asked, "What if I get bored?"

Adhith leered. "Oh, I think I can keep you entertained."

Rain continued to pelt the city. Thunder roared. Lightning flashed. The storm separated them from the rest of the universe, cocooning them in the flat. They sampled the cold food, drank Turkish wine, and danced to the old cabaret songs she liked. When she cheated at an arm-wrestling contest by flashing her cleavage at him, he chased her into the bedroom.

The rain slowed to a drizzle, but the sky remained dark. The feeling of blissful solitude—of being the last man and woman on earth—remained. They made love again and a third time, right before dawn.

As they floated back to reality, Adhith mumbled, "What *is* your perfume? It's been driving me crazy since the day we met."

"Almond oil. I rub a few drops into my hair after washing it."

He turned on his side to run his fingers through the tresses spread out on the pillow. "I'd imagined something more exotic. It's damned... what's the word... captivating. Like the birth of a new star or the colours of the sunrise."

Her eyes drifting shut, Madhu sputtered. "Poetry?"

"For you, anything." Adhith glanced towards the window. "Wanna watch the colours of the sunrise?"

Madhu's eyes snapped open. "No." She turned to bury her face in his chest. "Verma, I... I don't want this night to end."

In one quick move, he pulled the bedsheet over their heads. "Let's just stay in here."

"Forever?"

"Forever," he promised, gathering her to his heart.

When Adhith woke again, he was alone in bed. Tepid sunrays streamed in through the window and struck his face, making him blink. The loud singing coming from the bathroom broke off, and in less than a minute, the door opened, revealing Madhu covered only by a towel.

"What a view to wake up to," he said, lazily. "Now, come back to bed."

"Can't. I promised Seema I'd drop by the hospital with new clothes."

Adhith managed to keep the pleasant expression on his face from slipping. Seema. He'd wanted to talk to Madhu about her niece, but the issue had utterly escaped his mind. "Have breakfast before you go."

Eggs, milk, and sugar whisked to a froth, and slices of bread dipped in the mixture and fried in the pan. Bombay toast—the Indian version of French toast—was ready.

"Perfect," Adhith exclaimed, sliding a plate in front of her and drizzling a spoonful of honey on the bread.

Taking a bite of the toast, Madhu closed her eyes. "Mmhmm. If you're going to use honey, use a little less sugar. Or it becomes a bit much."

Adhith bared his teeth. "Next time, you do the honours."

She raised an eyebrow. "Touchy, are we?"

"Hell, yeah. After I started living here, I took a cookery course. I bet you don't have certificates in Indian and international cuisines from the Palate Culinary Studio."

She plopped a couple of sugar cubes into her tea. "No, but I have a *degree* in raising a teenager. Believe me, Seema wasn't quiet about her likes and dislikes."

Perfect cue. "Madhu, you told me Seema only remembers the fun part of her life in the slums. Has she ever gone back there to visit? Does she still have friends there?" It had to be how she learned to pick pockets.

A nanosecond passed before Madhu put the cup of tea back on the table. "Gone back there? Not unless she did so in the last few months. Friends? Again, not unless she's recently managed to reconnect with them. Why do you ask?"

"Ahh... I was wondering... what exactly did she find fun there? She had no real family in the place. Her father—your brother—was worse than useless. There was no mother, no siblings."

Madhu smiled. "Seema made her own family. A group of boys she hung out with. There was a mentor, too. A one-eyed man. He was basically taking care of her... feeding her, clothing her... I don't think she knows it, but he was the one who contacted the NGO when her father and the pimp made the deal about starting her in the business."

"Why didn't this mentor call the police?"

"Verma, you pal around with the kid from the tea shop on Grant Road, and you still don't get it? For one, few of the residents trust authority of any kind. With good reason, too. The cops they've encountered, the politicians who promise to help... everyone takes advantage of their powerlessness. You saw what happened to the money which was supposed to go to the NGO. For another, Usthaad—the mentor I was talking about—was not exactly a saintly character. Let's just say he taught the kids the skills they needed to survive on the streets."

Adhith got his answer as to how Seema had lifted the keys. "Did it ever become a problem for you? The... ahh... survival skills?"

Madhu's face paled in realisation she'd said too much. "Seema and I came to an understanding. She promised to follow all my rules. She never broke the law."

Adhith noted nothing in the denial covered Seema's life in the slums. "She's an adult now, but you're still watching over her," he stated, chewing on sweet, crunchy Bombay toast. "It's how *we* met. You were worried she was about to make a mistake. Where do you draw the line? At what point do you decide enough is enough and cut her loose?"

Madhu jerked up. Confusion clouded her eyes, followed by hurt. "A mistake is not the same as breaking the law, Verma," she said, her voice rising. "Seema is not a criminal. Anyway, I don't see *you* disowning your father."

His father? Why would Adhith disown his father? For his corrup—Adhith coughed. "Excuse me," he mumbled, scooting the chair back. "It went down the wrong way. Let me get some water."

In the kitchen, he turned on the tap and stood with one hand on the faucet. The hissing water masked the sound of rapid breathing. There was a lead weight in his upper abdomen. Why did she mention his father in the conversation? She couldn't be aware of the bribes Papaji had taken. As far as the public knew, he was a model politician. It was the reason he was given charge of the nation's treasury.

"Verma," called Madhu. When he turned, she was at the door. "I'm sorry about snapping at you, but it's been an issue before. Whenever there's a guy who's interested, he wants Seema out of the picture. I didn't think I'd hear it from you."

Madhu seemed to have forgotten her remark about Minister Verma. Maybe, it meant nothing. Maybe, Adhith was paranoid. He *had* been thinking about it quite a bit lately. "Seema being in your life makes no difference to me. Except, she's no longer a child who needs your constant attention. She must face the consequences of her actions. It's time you stopped fixing things for her. If you don't accept the fact, it's going to end up destroying both of you."

"Is this because Seema asked me to get her fresh clothes? I'm not playing maid for her. She wouldn't dream of asking me to. You already know Seema's staying in the hospital because of... all of you are lucky it was she who found..." Madhu paused, the angry reverberation in her low voice giving way to faint satisfaction. Almost meditatively, she added, "Seema dropped everything to... she saved Anjali's life."

"I'm grateful to her for it," Adhith said, immediately. It didn't mean he'd let her burglarise his home.

Steely resolve now on her face, Madhu said, "Seema's flatmate is out of town, so she asked me for help. Considering the circumstances, you and your friends should be *jumping* to run errands for her; I don't understand why you're acting like a jealous jackass, instead."

"No, I didn't mean—" Bringing up what Seema did with his keys was out of the question in Madhu's current mood. "Maybe, I *was* jealous. I don't know. I'm sorry for upsetting you." Turning the tap off, he went to Madhu and took her fingers in his. "I'm staying home to finish a project," he muttered. "Will you return after visiting Seema?"

"Tomorrow is Monday," Madhu said, eyes skittering. "I have to work."

"Please, don't stay mad at me. I'm sorry—"

She shook her head. "It's not that. I can't commute to my job from your flat. A woman in my position has to be careful."

"I understand." With her past, every small misstep would be seen as evidence of her loose morals. Adhith wasn't about to limit himself to weekends to satisfy society's sense of propriety, though. He'd be climbing the walls from unsatisfied lust. As it was, he was barely holding back from throwing her over his shoulder and carrying her back to bed. "We have to figure something out. Soon. Now that I've got you, I'm not about to let go."

A smile crept onto her face. Damned if it didn't look forced.

He kissed her knuckles. "I'll call you tonight."

"I can't give you my number," she said, quickly. "As I said, I have to be careful."

Eyes narrowing, he studied her. Did Madhu forget *she'd* called him the day before? He already had her phone number.

Reaching up, she kissed him. "I should go," she murmured against his lips.

His hands came up to grip her shoulders. He deepened the kiss, taking his time, leaving his taste on her tongue. "One more thing before you do."

"What?" she whispered.

"Repeat after me, 'I love you, Adhi.'"

A quick breath. "I... Verma, I—"

"Nuh-huh. Not Verma. Adhi." Eyes boring into hers, he demanded, "Say it. Or do you need me to say it first? I love you, Madhu. So very much. Now, it's your turn."

"I love you, Adhi." Her beautiful eyes glinted with the sheen of tears.

Crying? Why, by God? She surely was over her qualms about the age gap and about him first dating Seema, or she wouldn't have accepted his invitation. Was it because of their little tiff?

Shrugging loose from his hold, she said, "I have to leave now." Madhu whirled, and grabbing her tote from the coffee table, she strode out. She didn't look back, didn't give him a chance to ask more questions.

***

"I'm sorry, NJ," Adhith muttered, phone cradled on his shoulder. From the sofa, he could see the remains of breakfast on the table, but he couldn't afford to spend even a few minutes clearing it. He'd already taken more time off than intended. "You've been doing most of the work on this."

"Vikster logged in from wherever he was," said Cyber Ninja, a.k.a NJ. "We're good. It's looking like whatever we do, this bastard's not going to be found."

"Nothing," Adhith huffed in frustration, tapping away on his laptop. "Absolutely nothing. Who *is* this guy?"

Vikram had mentioned something about an inside job, but before Adhith could bring up the theory, NJ spoke, "The one possibility I can think of is the FBI. Or some other intelligence agency."

"Heh?" Adhith guffawed. "Why not an alien invasion? They could be studying us from outer space."

"Go ahead and laugh. I bet Vikster won't. FBI has some top-notch hackers working for them, and he knows it. Those are the kind of people who could break into a system like ours."

"I'll tell you why you're wrong," Adhith said. "They have no reason to hack us. Imperium has done work for the U.S. government. The FBI has already vetted us."

"Some other agency?" NJ argued.

"FBI or CIA or MI6 or whoever... why would they wander around our support systems instead of getting into the core product?"

Voice grumpy, NJ admitted, "I can't explain it."

"Got to be one of our competitors." Or an inside job, as Vikram said.

"What happens if we don't get him?" NJ asked.

"It's the part *I* can't answer." Forget the hacker. There was nothing about the last two days Adhith had an answer to. Why did Anjali try to kill herself? Why was Seema copying his keys? Why would Madhu say what she did about Papaji? Why were there tears in her eyes when she left? "NJ, I need to make another call," Adhith said. "I'll get back to you in ten, fifteen minutes."

"Roger that. NJ out."

Scrolling through the call list, Adhith paused at the number from the day before, the one Madhu called from. A landline. She'd have gone from his flat to Seema's Kurla flat to pick up clothes. From there, to the hospital. There wouldn't be much time for chatter with Anjali needing constant reassurance. Madhu would've left almost immediately. She should've gotten home by now, wherever it was. He pressed "call." It rang. And rang. A hitch in the third ring. Adhith frowned. Call transfer?

A click. "G.K. Financial Services," said a bland voice.

"Huh?" Her work? Madhu went all the way to her work on a Saturday to call him? "I got the wrong number. Sorry."

Leaving the laptop and the phone on the coffee table, he went to the living room windows and stood looking out through the glass panes. The sky was still grey and cloudy with barely any sunlight peeking out.

The number he used wasn't the same one on the accounting firm's website. He knew because he'd called the listed number before the party to invite Madhu. Yesterday, she'd either returned to her work just to make the call to him, or she'd routed the call through the firm. Why so much secrecy? Because of her niece's stupid behaviour? People didn't go to such lengths to cover up a burglary into the home of an IT manager—a burglary which hadn't yet happened. Adhith already knew there was more to it—Seema was after dirt on him—but... irritably, he scratched the back of his neck. "NJ and his zany theories."

Because of the American, Adhith was back to thinking along the lines of international espionage. If Seema were a foreign spy, she was thoroughly incompetent. Any self-respecting intelligence agency would've recalled her for making zero efforts to infiltrate Minister Verma's circle. In fact, she'd been reluctant to attend the Joshi dinner when she thought Papaji would be there.

Seema focused all her energies on the minister's son, instead. Even if she believed there was something in Adhith's flat to interest her employer, why would a spy simply not stage a break-in instead of making stupid moves like copying his keys? Or use some kind of a master key? Plus, there was Seema's behaviour *after* she lifted the keys. Adhith couldn't believe an intelligence agency would put up with one of their spies risking discovery to help the sister of their target's best friend. She'd have been removed from the scene by now.

Seema was surely acting on her own. What could she be hoping to gain from it except gossip to sell either to the tabloids or to an unknown rival who didn't want Adhith succeeding in politics? The theory didn't explain the time she'd spent on this. Three months was an eternity in both politics and journalism, and the story would've already been scrolling through TV screens as breaking news. Madhu's extreme efforts to maintain secrecy was another confounding factor.

Huffing, Adhith returned to the sofa. He wished he could talk it over with Vikram, but not when Seema was involved. Not after Adhith made it seem he would drag Seema's reputation through the mud to avoid marrying her. Vikram wouldn't believe any of it. He might even warn her.

Adhith slumped back into the pillows, reviewing what he knew. One, Seema spent a lot of time and energy on him. Two, Madhu got involved because she was worried about Seema. Three, Madhu was in love with him. He was sure of it. Four, there had been heartbreak in her eyes when he forced the confession out of her. Five, despite being in love, she'd made sure he couldn't contact her. If she chose not to call back, there was a good chance he'd never see her again, which explained the anguish on her face.

Seema's preparations pointed to a high-stakes operation involving Minister Verma, not his son. The grief on Madhu's face could also be explained by the same scenario. She couldn't contact him when his father was the target of her traitorous niece's employer. Except, Seema deliberately kept away from Papaji. Other than when they talked about the Joshi dinner party, Adhith couldn't remember her ever mentioning his father. Madhu actually talked about him more times than—

Why would Madhu suggest Adhith had any reason to disown Papaji? If she knew about his dirty deals... *did* she know? How could she? She was an accountant—an accountant who'd gone into her workplace on a weekend to answer a call from her beloved, making sure he couldn't track her. If she knew about Papaji, she was no ordinary accountant, and Seema couldn't be an ordinary analyst.

Like NJ about the hacker, Adhith could see no answers about Seema Rawat. Like with the hacker, espionage was one of the possible motives behind Seema's actions.

Picking up the phone, Adhith called NJ back. "Bud, let's say you're right about the CIA or whoever. Throw out some possibilities why they might send a hacker after us. Forget the part about what he did once he was inside. Why would he be assigned to Imperium to begin with?"

"The FBI, not CIA," corrected NJ. "The CIA is not supposed to spy on American citizens, and most of Imperium's chief executives are American. *We* get spied on by the FBI. Both agencies investigate crimes against the U.S."

With a short laugh, Adhith said, "In India, we have RAW and IB. RAW does all the international work while IB deals with—"

Everything around him whirled. Everything *within* him whirled. Intelligence Bureau, the agency tasked with gathering information within India. The agency rumoured to be keeping an eye on every union minister. The agency authorised to do warrantless wiretapping. If they were investigating Minister Verma for corruption, his son, the cybersecurity engineer, would be prime target for surveillance.

NJ continued, "I just talked to Vikram. He wants us to review time zones—"

"I'll have to call you back," Adhith said, hanging up. He didn't know what the idea was behind reviewing time zones. It didn't matter, any longer. He knew who'd hacked them.

Tossing the phone to the sofa, he paced. Everything fit. It was IB or one of the other agencies, monitoring the activities of the minister's son. Right when a junior analyst named Seema Rawat was planning to break into his home. What were the odds?

"She's a cop," Adhith whispered. "Oh, my God. Papaji."

Chapter 18

Two hours. The psychiatrist had been counselling Anjali and her husband for two hours.

"How much longer is it going to take?" Vikram mumbled, glaring at the door between the two rooms of the suite. The blue armchair in the companion room was plush and comfortable, but he was finding it hard to focus on the data scrolling down the laptop on his... well... lap.

He wasn't expecting an answer. After the good doctor's first session with the patient on Saturday, the Joshis pleaded with her to visit on Sunday. Rattanbai and Pratapchandra Joshi were royalty in India's medical circles, so the psychiatrist agreed, but she told them firmly they'd have to vacate the premises until she was done talking to Anjali and the dumb—no, Vikram wasn't calling him the dumbass, anymore. Rishi was devastated by what almost happened to Anjali. The doctor requested Seema stay in the other room in case the patient needed a shoulder right after the session.

The Joshi parents said they'd go home for the duration of the doctor's visit and pick up some essentials, but Vikram insisted on staying. In no mood to make up excuses, he said he wasn't about to leave, and the doctor could try and make him if she wanted. With a knowing glance at Seema in her shorts and flimsy blouse, Anjali asked the doctor to let her brother remain.

Vikram was also in an old pair of shorts and a cotton tee, but unlike him, Seema looked good enough to eat. He hadn't been thinking about romance, though. He simply needed the comfort of her presence. Sadly, she didn't offer either. Ignoring the bed on the other side of the room, she'd collapsed onto the sofa and fallen asleep, leaving Vikram to his own mutterings. She'd slept only in snatches in the last two days—the same as Vikram and his parents. Also, Anjali's husband, Rishi. *They* had the obligation of love and family towards Anjali that Seema didn't.

Although with Seema asleep, Vikram was able to get some more work done. He'd been attending to it all Saturday, waiting for her to take a nap so he could focus on the hacker issue. He wished he could talk to her about the son of a bitch. She could've offered a fresh set of eyes on the problem, but Imperium would not appreciate one of their junior employees being told about this potential catastrophe.

Vikram's phone pinged. He almost didn't check, thinking it was Nanaji's stunt director friend again. In the twenty-four hours after he heard about Anjali's suicide attempt, the man sent five texts asking Vikram to *please* read the old man's memoir before there was any further damage done to his family.

With an exasperated sigh, Vikram picked up the phone. He'd already asked his mother to bring the papers from the cupboard in his room. He was going to read the damned memoir this afternoon. If there was nothing in there meriting the melodrama, the stunt director was going to feel Vikram's wrath.

Eyeing the ID of the caller, Vikram huffed. Back to the hacker problem.

Cyber Ninja: Yo, Vikster.

Code Master: What's the status on your end, NJ?

Cyber Ninja: Almost completed review of the hacker's activities.

Code Master: Nothing?

Cyber Ninja: Nothing.

Code Master: I'm finishing up comparison to all known prior hacks. Nothing there, either.

Cyber Ninja: I was telling Adhi it looks like a government hit.

Code Master: Adhi's back at work?

Cyber Ninja: Yeah, he was online this morning.

After having promised Vikram he'd apply himself to the hacker issue, Adhith went missing in action the day before. NJ was left mostly on his own with Vikram logging in whenever he got a chance. Then, there was all the drooling Adhith did over Seema's auntie. Vikram didn't know what was going on with his best friend these days. Soon, he'd have to corner Adhith and beat the reason out of him.

Code Master: Government hit? Like the CIA or something?

Cyber Ninja: Adhi found my theory funny, but I knew *you* wouldn't. It's more likely to be the FBI doing the hacking, though. Not the CIA.

Code Master: The FBI is capable of a lot of things, but what the hell are they doing monitoring our support systems? They already know we're the good guys. We've done work for the U.S. government.

Cyber Ninja: Exactly what Adhi said.

Code Master: *I've* been thinking about the possibility of it being an inside job.

Cyber Ninja: Ha! Even crazier than my FBI theory. Someone got themselves hired by us just to go through our systems?

Code Master: Why not?

Cyber Ninja: What's the motive? Our competitors wouldn't gain anything if they didn't show someone breached our walls. If the bastard's working alone, he won't get any glory because he didn't actually hack in. If it was for money, he hasn't gone near our core product. You just don't want to admit someone was able to break into our systems.

A giggle.

Vikram threw a startled glance in Seema's direction.

No. She was still asleep, dreaming of something, probably. She turned to sprawl across the sofa on her tummy, kicking off the fleece covering her. Her curls, damp and dark after her recent shower, were spread all over the pillow. Her blouse rode up until the black bra strap was visible, stretching across the smooth skin of her upper back.

Almost involuntarily, Vikram's eyes drifted down the curvature of her spine to the cotton shorts riding the tops of her rounded buttocks. Her long legs were bare, starting from the hem of the shorts to the tips of her red-painted toenails. God, her body was gorgeous.

Dammit. He had no business ogling her with his sister sick in the next room. Cursing the good angel on his shoulder, Vikram picked up the fleece from the floor and tossed it over Seema's legs.

Cyber Ninja: Vikster?

Cyber Ninja: Are you still there?

Code Master: Sorry. Got distracted. The hacker was still good enough to go undetected into every system except our product. He figured out we were onto him. He's managed to cover his tracks this quickly and this completely. If the attack ever becomes public, everyone in the business will be talking about him.

Cyber Ninja: So why hasn't he gone public, already?

Code Master: I don't know.

Cyber Ninja: It must be the FBI. Who else has the time and money to waste on just monitoring our activities?

Code Master: Again, no motive. Also, even the U.S. government cannot drop in from the sky. We haven't been able to localise the hacker's entry point. We haven't detected any communication with unauthorised servers. It's got to be an inside job.

Cyber Ninja: Hmm. How do we figure out who?

Laughter. Seema flipped over to lie on her back.

Vikram grinned. What *was* she dreaming about?

Code Master: See if you can pull the data on when the S.O.B was online. As in what hours of the day. The info will help us localise him to a longitude.

Cyber Ninja: He's been working 24/7 since he figured out we spotted him.

There were new changes in the hacker's tracks almost every minute. Plus, the wily bastard was making it seem the entire business was in on the cover-up, commandeering digital IDs of Imperium employees all over the planet to kick mud on his footprints as fast as he could.

Code Master: Even hackers gotta sleep sometime. I'm sure he's automated much of it. Remember, when he was actively spying, he was just an extra presence in the systems no one noticed. He didn't use any of the other profiles because he didn't want to tip anyone off. Which means he *couldn't* work all day or automate anything, or someone would've spotted the high after-hours activity coming from one region. For the same reason, he wouldn't have continued his tricks when signed in from outside Imperium. Which means he had to do his dirty work strictly during business hours and through his workstation. Now he knows he's been found, his priority is making sure we don't locate him, so he's doing whatever he can—automation, hijacking other IDs, etc. Let's review the time log on the hacker activity *before* he started covering his tracks.

Cyber Ninja: Or... if *I'm* right, the time log might point to the agency spying on us.

Vikram snorted.

Code Master: Just get on it, will ya? Hanging up, but I'll still be online.

The laptop stayed open, but Vikram's eyes kept wandering in Seema's direction. If he hadn't been stupid enough to reject her the first time around, he could've carried her from the sofa to the bed on the other side of the room. Sliding his hand up her thigh and belly, he could've made her giggle helplessly by tickling her navel with a fingertip. He just *knew* she'd be ticklish. He could've then continued his upward journey, culminating with his palm covering her lace-covered breast and their mouths fusing. Sunday morning loving.

Groaning, Vikram asked the universe if it were punishing him for his blunders. This wasn't the time or place to fantasise about sex. Staying in the suite was a mistake. Between worrying about what was going on with Anjali and drooling over Seema's sleeping form, he was going crazy. He should've taken his laptop and gone to the cafeteria.

The connecting door between the two rooms opened. The psychiatrist entered, the expression on her face grave but pleasant. "Give your sister and her husband a few more minutes before asking your parents to return."

Closing the laptop, Vikram slid it onto the coffee table. "Did she say anything about why..."

Behind the gold-rimmed glasses, the doctor's eyelids flickered. "*Anjali* will tell you."

On the sofa, Seema mumbled and sat up, offering Vikram a drowsy smile.

Nodding at her, the doctor said, "Anjali thanks you for everything you did."

"I'm glad she's all right," Seema said.

The doctor continued, "Seema, she's aware she's been using you as buffer. She's still hoping you'll stick around for her conversation with her family."

Seema blinked. "I don't mind, but..." She glanced at Vikram. "Your mom and dad..."

"They'd be grateful if you could," Vikram said, immediately. At this point, if Anjali demanded the moon, the Joshis—including Vikram—would try their best to get it for her. When Kusum brought him his laptop, he asked her to bring his guitar, too, and played it for Anjali as she'd once asked. He'd been rewarded with the love-drenched look in Seema's eyes, but no matter what anyone did, Anjali refused to explain why...

***

293

Vikram was baffled. So were his parents at what Anjali was telling them. Next to Vikram on the windowsill, Seema sat silently as Anjali announced her decision to file for divorce.

"I love you, Anju," Rishi wept, kneeling by the side of her bed.

"I know," she said, a protective hand on her belly. "I love you, too. Just not the kind of love which should've ended in marriage. I should've... *we* should've known better."

"Our baby," Rishi begged. "Please, don't do this. I swear I'll do whatever you want."

Anjali smiled. "You're always going to be the baby's father, and you'll always be my best friend, but if I use my stupidity to force you to change, you'll be in this bed in my place a year or two down the line."

"My family," Rishi whispered. "My God, my father's going to—"

"*We're* your family," Anjali said, tone firm. "This baby and I. If your parents can't accept you for who you are, it's their loss, not yours. Rishi, if you'll take one last piece of advice from an old friend... move from Delhi. Take your..." She swallowed hard. "...partner with you and move someplace where you can be yourself."

No amount of pleading from him would change her mind. "Go to him," she urged Rishi. "All three of us need to be at peace."

Go to 'him'? Vikram shifted. He'd vaguely expected marital trouble to be the cause of Anjali's attempted suicide, but there was no question in his mind the dumbass truly loved Anjali. Hell, he still seemed to, but...

After shooing her husband out of the room, Anjali turned to the sofa where her shocked parents were seated. "You heard enough to put it all together. When Rishi and I decided to get married, I already knew he was gay. His parents were vehemently opposed to what they saw as his perversion, and I... I thought Rishi was the perfect man. I thought I could make it work. Why wouldn't it, right? The perfect Anjali Joshi would have the perfect husband, perfect career, perfect life."

"Anju," Vikram muttered, painfully recalling their conversation by the sea. She'd been trying to tell him what was going on, and he'd blown her off. If only he'd listened...

Anjali smiled. "You don't have to feel guilty about what you said. That's what *everyone* believed, and I desperately wanted it to be true." She shifted, her chin dipping. "Rishi told me about a doctor he met in Mumbai. An anaesthesiologist, like me. I knew at the time. Something in his tone... but it was months before I could bring myself to confront him. The baby was supposed to put an end to everything. Then, at the party, Adhi said he'd seen Rishi by the Gateway when he was supposed to be in Tokyo." One tiny hiccup, and the sobs started. Her shoulders shook. With an indistinct murmur, her mother rushed to sit next to her on the bed. "I saw you and dad... you were always so proud of me. You didn't know how badly I'd messed up my life. So I did something even more stupid. If Seema hadn't come along..."

A loud ring. Startled, Vikram looked towards the sofa. His father turned the mobile phone off and tossed it onto the side table.

"The reality of death hit me when I started to faint," Anjali continued, voice hoarse from tears. "I wanted to live. I was going to have to admit to my family I messed up, but I wanted to live. I have no husband. There's a baby on the way. I'm going to have to go back to work, knowing everyone in the theatre is waiting for me to leave so they can talk about stupid Anjali Joshi who thought she had it all. I'm a failure, but I still want to live."

"My girl," whimpered Vikram's mom, gathering Anjali into a hug. His dad was now on the other side of the bed, holding her hand in his.

"One mistake doesn't make you a failure," said Dad.

"C'mon, Dad," said Anjali, sniffling between words. "You and Mom never believed I could do anything wrong."

"Probably," Dad acknowledged. "Because you were always so—"

"Perfect," completed Anjali.

He asked, "I didn't realise... my God... we set a lot of expectations on you, didn't we? Anju, even if you make a hundred mistakes, you're still perfect for us. You're our child."

"Oh, really?" asked Anjali. "Would you say the same about Vikram? No matter what Rishi said about Vikram, you agreed. A couple of days back, you were worried he was a womanising alcoholic."

"Is that what you've been thinking?" asked Mom. She glanced at Vikram. "You, too?"

What the hell was he supposed to say in response? Vikram focused on a piece of paper fluttering about the floor.

Sitting next to him on the windowsill, Seema fidgeted. "I should leave," she mumbled.

Shooting out his hand, he caught her fingers. "Please, don't."

She yanked against his hold. "I'm done playing buffer. Solve your own problems. I have enough of my own."

"I need you here," he begged, bringing their linked fingers to his heart. The three people on the bed were back to staring at Vikram. He gave them a weak grin.

"Yaar—" Seema flung her free hand up. "Okay, fine. Only, cut out the caveman tactics, or I'll pickle your family jewels."

Dad winced and crossed his legs. With the same aghast looks they'd worn at the party, Mom and Anjali turned to Seema. Unexpectedly, Mom laughed. "Vikram, your nanaji would've loved her."

"A nice poke in the collective Joshi eye," Dad agreed, smiling. Mirth fading, he addressed Vikram, "Betay, how could you think you weren't perfect for us?"

They actually expected him to believe it after the years of pretending he didn't exist? "Am I?" Vikram asked, bitterly. "Tell me, Dad. What do you know about me? When did you realise I didn't want to be a doctor? Do you know what I do for a living? Do you know anything about my future plans?"

"Vikram," Seema muttered.

Anjali scrambled out of bed, wobbling a little when she stood. "No, Seema. Don't stop him. This has been a long time coming."

Letting go of Seema's hand, Vikram stood and paced. Out of the corner of his eye, he could see Anjali hobbling to the windowsill to sit next to Seema.

"Mom, can you tell me what I was like at ten?" he raged. "At fifteen? Do you know what kind of food I like? My taste in women? Have you ever thought about me beyond the obvious fact I'm not your idea of a perfect Joshi?"

Pratap Joshi stood. "Vikram—"

"Let *me* talk." Mom walked around the bed and stood next to Dad. "You like a lot of sugar in whatever you eat, and I try very hard not to think about the kind of women you find attractive. You're my *son*. It's true we didn't really understand you. Vikram, your dad and I never used a computer until we were in our *forties*. Most of the time, we didn't have a clue what you were talking about. We still don't. Also, do either of us *look* like we go gymming? What's left, the guitar? To be honest, I was afraid of encouraging you because of—"

"Nanaji," Vikram completed, angrily. The old man taught him how to play.

Mom sighed. "I'll tell you what we do know. We knew you had trouble making friends in school. We realised you were getting teased at parties. We hoped if we kept taking you with us, you'd eventually understand how to navigate the world. After all, we weren't going to be around to guide you the rest of your life. When that didn't work, we tried keeping you away from it all. You simply got angrier. Nothing we did *ever* worked."

"You know why?" Dad asked, tone harsh. "Because of the bitter old man, your nanaji. He hated the fact Rattan married me."

Vikram snarled. "Yeah. Like he didn't have reason to. He wasn't good enough for the Joshis, either." He stalked to the door. "I'm out of here. Let's go, Seema. *We* need to discuss a few things."

Dad was at the door, blocking Vikram's way. Pratap Joshi was several inches shorter than his son, but at the moment, he seemed to loom over Vikram. "Sit," Dad snapped, pointing at the bed. "You're going to listen to what we have to say."

"Now, you care enough to talk to me?" Shoving both hands into his hair, Vikram plunked himself down on the mattress.

"I begged your nanaji to understand," Mom said, her eyes swimming in tears. "Yes, Pratap's grandmother was a snob and a half, and yes, she insulted your nanaji when she visited the 'bride's house.' You couldn't get any higher caste than the Joshis. The Batliwalas... lemme see... my father was Parsi, and my mother was part Gujarati Muslim, part Mangela Koli—the fisherman caste."

"C'mon," Vikram scoffed. "I've never seen any of the Joshis give you a hard time about being lower caste."

"Not your uncles," Mom acknowledged. "They accepted me, but the rest of the family..."

"I control the flow of money," Dad said, bluntly. "As long as I'm head of the Joshi Trust, no one will dare say anything. After me, it will be you, Vikram. Your mother will be safe, but do you really think they've stopped resenting her for marrying me?"

"So imagine what it was like in the old days," Mom said. "It wasn't just the caste issue. Your nanaji had no money except for the pension from the work he used to do for the Bombay municipality at one point. Pratap's grandmother was very insulting about it all, but my father gave back as good as he got. He called her every name in the book. I wasn't about to give up Pratap because of their quarrel. If I hadn't apologised for my father, I wouldn't have been allowed into the Joshi clan. The only reason they didn't kick me out anyway was that we'd already eloped."

"What?" came Anjali's startled voice.

"What?" echoed Vikram.

The phone rang a second time, vibrating on the side table. Turning it off, Dad waved his hands. "We didn't want to give anyone a chance to say no, so we did a court ceremony before meeting each other's families. After Rattan begged for forgiveness on her father's behalf, my grandmother arranged a temple wedding. But no matter how many times I apologised for my family, your nanaji refused to relent. If he'd accepted us, we'd have found a way to make things work. Lots of in-laws don't get along. They all survive. Your nanaji wouldn't give an inch. He wanted Rattan to throw me out of her life. When she wouldn't, he mocked her for making the effort to fit in with the Joshis. He refused to understand she was only trying to have a peaceful life."

"We hoped he'd give in once the grandkids came," Mom said, sounding defeated. "That obviously didn't happen. Instead, he took advantage of your insecurities and turned you against us. The only time we saw a smile on your face was when you knew you could visit him, so we couldn't even stop you from going. By that point, I'd given up on him. What you think of as my forgetting where I came from was my unwillingness to take any more of my father's taunts."

"We kept hoping things would get better once you got old enough to understand," Dad continued. "I don't deny my grandmother had her faults. Casteism was the least of it. Your Skinwalla Uncle didn't dare come out until after her death. The Joshis changed. My parents—your grandparents, Vikram—weren't terribly happy about your uncle's news, but they preferred to accept Robbie than risk losing their son."

Vikram's paternal grandfather had been a quiet man—a general practitioner. For as long as Vikram could remember, the old doctor and his wife lived in semi-retirement in Goa. They'd passed within months of each other when Vikram was fourteen, leaving Pratapchandra Joshi the head of the family.

While Pratap and Rattan Joshi were *bona fide* South Mumbai snobs, they'd never exhibited any other form of bigotry. No homophobia, whatsoever.

Dad went on, "Your mom and I hoped you'd see all this. We tried to make it clear whatever you wanted to do with your life was fine by us—computers, guitar, bodybuilding... all we wanted was for you to be happy. We hoped you'd understand we were not the monsters your nanaji made us out to be. Then, the old man died, and he became a saint in your eyes. What he told you became gospel, and once you left for IIT, you never returned. Until this summer."

Vikram jeered, "Nice story. Blame Nanaji now he's not here to defend himself. Why are you bothering, anyway? You don't need me for anything."

"Why am I bothering?" Dad bellowed, his colour an unhealthy red. "Because I can't risk losing *you* like we almost lost—" His face crumpled. "Like we—"

"Pratap," said Mom, clutching at his sleeve. "Your blood pressure."

He patted her hand. "What are we going to do, Rattan?" he asked, voice shaky. "Our son hates us because we didn't set any expectations, and our daughter tried to kill herself because we set too much."

"I swear it's not going to happen, again," said Anjali. Limping to her parents, she wrapped her arms around them.

"You're not going to lose me," Vikram said. Not to suicide, certainly.

Patting Anjali's shoulder, Mom said, "You don't have to take our word for it, betay. I peeked at those papers in your cupboard." She grimaced. "Some of it's... you should've read through to the end."

"What do you mean?" asked Vikram.

From the duffel on the sofa, she brought out a thick envelope. "Your nanaji's memoir. See for yourself."

***

Nanaji didn't have a phone for the longest time, so they'd written letters. Message after message after message from Dad and Mom, pleading with Nanaji to let bygones be bygones. Updates from Mom on her graduation from her course in obstetrics and gynaecology. A faded picture of Anjali as a newborn. A postcard thanking Nanaji for the traditional Parsi tray he sent after Anjali's birth, with paper, ink, pen, coconut, and *kumkum*, the red turmeric. There was a second postcard for the same after Vikram was born.

Having scanned each piece of paper, Vikram would look up from his seat on the sofa to the bed where Mom and Dad were going through some old postcards with Anjali. Seema was also on the sofa next to Vikram. She was intently focused on the pages in her hand, not paying the least mind to his emotional turmoil.

His parents were telling the truth. Vikram could hear the eager hope in the thank you cards Mom sent for the Parsi gift trays. The letters following expressed disappointment Nanaji hadn't shown up to the naming ceremony of her children at the temple in Lonavala. Later, she sent polite notes, thanking him for letting his grandson spend time with him in the two-room space he rented at the chawl.

Nanaji installed a phone around the time Vikram started school. There were only one or two letters after then. The last one was an invitation to Vikram's *munja* at the age of eight, the ritual signifying his official admission to the Joshi clan. There were a few receipts from the gym Nanaji and the stunt director took Vikram to. The old man had dug into the small pension he received from a government job he'd held a long time back. It didn't seem to have occurred to Nanaji he could've asked his very wealthy daughter to pay for her son.

Tossing the pages in his hand next to Dad's phone on the side table, Vikram slumped back into the sofa. Nanaji certainly loved him. There was nothing Mom and Dad could say to convince Vikram otherwise. Nanaji also very deliberately led Vikram to believe his parents had no use for anyone who didn't fit in, that they had no use for their own son. "Nanaji made sure I could defend myself," Vikram muttered. "He taught me to play the guitar."

On the bed, Anjali looked up from the postcard in her hand. "He left all this to you," she said. "We have to assume he meant for you to know what went wrong."

"I don't get it," Vikram brooded.

"I'd like to think he regretted what he did," Mom whispered. "He did ask his friend to make sure you read it."

Vikram grunted. "He could've told me. Or at least, asked his friend to tell me. Why all this drama?"

"He'd have lost you if he'd told you," Mom pointed out. "After his death, well... for one, Stunt Master Raju didn't know exactly what was in the memoir. Only that your nanaji wanted you to read it for the good of the family. For another, would you have believed it without proof? You didn't believe *me*."

Forget about believing, Vikram had outright accused his parents of lying. He'd brought his father to tears.

At his side, Seema giggled. "My God, Vikram. Your nanaji had some imagination." She waved a page under his nose. "Read this one. Is it even possible?"

"What—" Nanaji's sexcapades, of course. Swatting the paper away, Vikram snapped, "Do you mind? I'm having a moment here."

Seema tucked her legs under her. "Oh, please. Stop whining."

"*Me? You're* the one who's always going on about Britto giving you a hard time."

She snorted. "In case you forgot, Vikram Joshi... Britto's your henchman. It's my God-given right as employee to whine about bosses. *You* spent twenty-some years sulking because your dad and mom weren't telepathic to know exactly what you were thinking. Now, you're finding out your nanaji lied to you. Guess what? People make mistakes. Sometimes, they can't go back and fix what they did. It doesn't always make them bad people. If you want to see actual bad parenting, I could show you—" Abruptly, she halted.

Vikram remembered what she'd said about her father trying to sell her to a pimp. Before anyone could comment, Anjali said, "That's what Rishi used to say."

"The dumbass is lucky I didn't beat the crap out of him," Vikram said. "Instead of dragging you into his mess, he should've told his family to go to hell."

Tiredly, Anjali explained, "Don't you get it, Vicky? This is exactly what bugged Rishi. You find it easy to make pronouncements like that *because* you were born into our family. Mom and Dad would support you no matter what. Rishi had no one, except me. You were a part of the family *he* wanted, and you didn't appreciate them. I could've asked him to stop needling you, I suppose. For that, I'd have had to face facts."

"It's not as if *we* never heard what Rishi said," Dad admitted. "Anjali was happy with him, and I thought... I didn't want to become your nanaji."

Mom turned to Anjali. "We're always going to be with you, Anju. No matter how imperfect life gets, you're always going to be my precious baby girl. Please, don't... never again, okay?"

"Never again," Anjali promised, tears streaming down her cheeks.

On the side table, the phone rang, loud and shrill. Vikram reached for it. "No," shouted both Mom and Dad. Fingers hovering over the vibrating device, Vikram stilled.

"It's Minister Verma," Mom explained. "He's going to ask... you know... about Seema."

"We're not sure what to say," Dad confessed.

With her face flaming red, Seema tossed the pages in her hand to the sofa and stood. "I should go."

The ringing stopped. Outraged, Vikram asked, "After the last three days, you still don't know what to say about Seema?"

"Hold on," said Mom, scrambling out of the bed. "Let me call the minister back and tell him Seema is a lovely young lady, and Adhi would be lucky to have her as his wife."

"I... ahh..." Vikram stammered.

"Hand over the phone," Mom said, gesturing with her fingers. "I'm going to make that call right now."

Anjali giggled through her tears. Dad was practically convulsing with laughter. Seema's eyes were screwed shut, and her lips were moving silently as though she were begging the deities for escape.

"You don't have to," Vikram assured Mom, hurriedly moving to barricade the side table with the phone on it.

"Oh, no," she said. "I want to. Since we're such terrible people and all."

"Mom, please," he begged, his ears burning.

"I'm leaving," Seema mumbled, running to the other room.

***

"Gimme some time here," Vikram objected, settling his hip on the backrest of the armchair. The door to the patient room was closed, giving him and Seema privacy. "It's force of habit not to give them the benefit of the doubt. I need to process the new information."

From the sofa, Seema glared. She'd pulled on a pair of jeans in place of the shorts and was braiding her hair. Her purse with the broken strap was on her lap. A duffel bag with all her dirty clothes sat next to her feet. "Process faster," she snapped. "You're lucky they love you."

"I know." He was beginning to realise the fact. "We're going to need to heal as a family. Seema, about *your* father..."

"The loser?"

Vikram shoved away from the chair and went down on his knees in front of her. "The night at the Gateway... you were crying... and today, you said... my offer still stands. I'll go and beat the shit out of him. I don't want to see you crying, ever again."

"Thank you," she whispered. "It means a lot to me. I try not to remember unpleasant things, but you can never really forget, you know?"

"What's his name?"

"Why do you want to know?"

"So I can find him, obviously. He's going to pay."

"Are you the same man who dragged me out of the bus when I was arguing with those boys?" Seema teased.

Vikram grinned. "It's called being rational. No need to fight if you don't have to. When it's inevitable, you give it everything you have. Your father's going to get a thrashing for what he did. You might not care about it, but I do."

"Oh, Vikram," she said on a spurt of laughter. "If we had time... long story short, I was dumb enough to run away from Madhu twice. The second time, there was a pimp waiting at home for me. I made an excuse about needing to pee and went to the back of the shack." Her eyes went to the window and the dark sky outside. "It was raining," she whispered. "Somehow, I waded through the water in the streets. I was so afraid they'd catch up." With a sigh, she returned her gaze to Vikram. "Anyway, I escaped the loser and got myself to Usthaad's warehouse. *He* was a mentor of sorts to a whole bunch of kids in the neighbourhood. He called Madhu, and she took me back to her flat. After that, I never tried to escape. Madhu got the loser thrashed, so he never again tried to contact me."

"I'm still going to pay him a visit," Vikram said, firmly. "Him *and* the pimp."

Seema batted her eyelashes. "My hero." Cheeks pinkening, she added, "I have to get going."

"Why can't you stay until tomorrow?" Vikram argued. "The hospital's planning to discharge Anjali in the morning. Also, you need to sleep a few hours straight before heading to work."

Duffel in her hand and the purse with its cut strap knotted together slung across her torso, Seema stood. "Vikram, the princess doesn't need me any longer. I don't have any excuses left to—"

"Why do you need an excuse?" he asked, standing with her. "Isn't it enough to know I love you?"

"I... ahh... Vikram, please." Her eyes were fixed on her canvas slip-ons.

He reached out, stroking her cheek with a fingertip. She shivered under the mild touch. "There's no way you don't know it by now." He traced her jawline, running his thumb over her lower lip.

Her chest heaved in a shuddering breath. "I love you, too," she admitted.

One sudden move. The duffel fell to the floor, and Seema was in his arms, trembling in his embrace. Something hard dug into Vikram's abdomen. Her purse, probably, and whatever was in it, but he didn't care. He was drowning in the warmth of her body, the light, floral scent when he buried his mouth where her neck met her shoulder.

Her hands were running all over his back, digging into his hair. "Kiss me," she demanded.

Tiny, sweet kisses, teasing and tantalising. Deep, drugging kisses. There was her honey taste. He could spend a lifetime doing the tongue tango with her, blowing soothingly on her bruised lips. Drunkenly, he smiled into her eyes.

"Again," she said, yanking his head back down.

Sweet, wild madness. He couldn't stay two seconds away from her lips. Sucking, nibbling... his hands slipped under her shirt. One snap, and the bra strap came undone. When his fingers closed around a breast, she moaned into his mouth, her nails digging into his deltoids.

"Your parents," she murmured.

"They're not going to barge in," he assured her, unwilling to relinquish possession of the silky globe.

With a small laugh, Seema pushed against his shoulders, putting a couple of inches between them. "Madhu would have. By now, your butt would've met the back end of a broomstick."

"Marry me," Vikram whispered. "She can't stop me from making love to my own wife." *Twenty-four/seven.* They'd stop only to eat.

"Oh?" Seema shrugged loose from his embrace. "What about your career? Weren't you going to show your family what a genius you are?"

"None of it will mean much without you by my side," he admitted.

Fixing her bra strap, she glared at the duffel on the floor, seemingly arguing with herself.

"Are you turning shy on me?" he asked, amused. "Okay. As soon as Anjali's back home, I'll ask my mom to talk to Madhu. Let them fix the *rishta.*" The marriage arrangements would take time, but he could still see Seema at the office. Also, there was her flat in Kurla.

She picked up her duffel. "I really have to leave. There's an old friend who promised to do me a favour. I've already kept him waiting two days. Plus, I want to get back home before it rains." The thunderstorm of the night before had died down, but monsoon season was unpredictable. "Will let your henchman know I won't be in until Tuesday?" she asked. "I do need to sleep."

Walking with Seema to the lift, Vikram said, huskily, "I'll see you at work."

The lift doors swished open. A peculiar urgency on her face, she turned to him. "Don't forget me."

"Huh?"

She was already pushing her way to the back of the crowd.

***

Euphoria like Vikram never felt before washed over him. His family was in the other room, but he didn't want to go in there yet. Collapsing into the chair, he dreamed of Seema and their glorious future together. Of their days of joy and their nights of passion. There would be problems being married to a subordinate, but Vikram was very close to realising his dream of opening his own business. There, he and Seema would be partners.

If Vikram didn't catch the hacker, the new business would not have any clients willing to trust it with their digital security. His electronic devices were still on the coffee table. Vikram picked up his phone and goggled. *"Seventeen* messages?" Demands from NJ to call as soon as Vikram saw the texts, time differences be damned. Ominous mentions of big brother watching.

With a frown, Vikram dialled the number. In the middle of the second ring, NJ's excited voice said, "Vikram? Where were you? Never mind. I was right about the government hit."

"What?"

"Adhi called back after you hung up. He was asking questions about American agencies and said something about RAW and IB in India."

After waiting a couple of seconds, Vikram prompted, "And?"

"Don't you see? Adhi thinks the Indian government is spying on us. Before I even got a chance to tell him about the time zone thing!"

This was the reason for the urgency? Vikram made a mental note to ask Adhith not to encourage NJ's fantasies. Clients would not be impressed. "Anything so far on the log-in times?"

"I've been trying to tell you," NJ exclaimed. "Open the email I sent. The hacking activity happened exclusively on weekdays. Generally, between nine and five in the UTC + 05:00 and UTC + 06:00 zones."

"Which countries?"

NJ growled in frustration. "Russia, Kazakhstan, Uzbekistan, Tajikistan, Turkmenistan, Pakistan, Maldives, Australia, Azerbaijan, Armenia, Kyrgyzstan, Sri Lanka, India, Bangladesh, Bhutan, and Xinjiang province in China. Even some bases in Antarctica. How are we supposed to know which of these governments sent the hacker after us?"

"We'll get to your theory if mine doesn't pan out," Vikram said. "From the countries on your list, Imperium has offices in Mumbai, Sydney, and Beijing. NJ, did you email me the dates when the hacker activity peaked? Not just the general times?"

"Of course. Check your email."

Laptop open, Vikram downloaded the document and brought up a list of national holidays for the three countries. "Once we narrow it down to one place, we'll review office attendance."

If it were indeed an inside job, the hacker wouldn't have risked discovery by continuing his spying when logged in from outside. If he'd managed to go in every single workday, all employees of the particular office would need to be investigated.

The document popped up. Typed neatly were dates, starting from March. Monday to Friday activity, as NJ said. Nothing on weekends and a few other days.

Vikram froze. He didn't need to compare the dates with the national holidays of any country. He didn't even need to see the office attendance list. He knew exactly who'd been out sick from the Mumbai office on those days. "Seema?" Vikram murmured, disbelievingly.

Chapter 19

Seema had known her mother didn't give a damn about her only child even before she eloped with her boyfriend. The drunk loser who called himself Seema's father didn't care, either. Still, after she was rescued against her will from the slums, he called her at the flat and said he'd be waiting at the Panvel railway station. He probably did it simply to piss off Madhu, but twelve-year-old Seema grabbed the chance. She first escaped through the front door of the flat when Madhu wasn't looking. Before Seema even got to the railway station, Madhu dragged her back. Then, Seema waited until Madhu fell asleep before clambering down from the balcony.

When Seema and the loser reached Mumbai, monsoon was in full force. Her new jeans and shirt were drenched in seconds, and her teeth chattered, but she couldn't care less. She was almost back with the people who *did* care about her—with Usthaad and the rest of the gang on Grant Road. Lightning lit her way home. Splashing through the shin-deep water flooding the narrow streets, she followed the loser to their two-room shack.

The shadowy form of a man waited at the door, the darkness and the giant umbrella in his hand hiding his face. Without bothering to check the identity of the visitor, Seema waded in. Inside held almost as much water as the outside. The bulbs in the shack—one in each room—were lit. She came to an abrupt halt when she noticed the gaudy outfit lying on her cot in the inner chamber. Purple satin shorts? She'd seen other girls in the neighbourhood dressed in such clothes. Her loser father thought her dumb, but she knew what it meant.

Seema pushed open the connecting door between the two rooms, the wood and metal contraption almost falling apart under her touch. Only one of the men looked up. The loser was sitting on the wooden bench, knocking back moonshine straight from the bottle. He was still wearing his wet shirt and pants. There was a pile of cash next to him. The other man stared at her. He was short and skinny and dressed like the government-type men Madhu worked with, but his cold, calculating eyes sent a shiver snaking down Seema's spine. "What?" he asked.

Seema shook her head. She couldn't speak. Terror quaked her insides. For the first time in her twelve years of life, she was scared shitless.

"She doesn't care," said the loser. "She begged me to bring her back." The men laughed.

"I'm going to the chawl to pee," Seema blurted. For a fee, they could use the toilets in the nearby tenement building.

"Go in the back," snapped her father. "One week, and she thinks she's a princess."

Nodding jerkily, she splashed out the door and to the back of the house, her brand-new sports shoes waterlogged and weighing a ton. Seema pulled the shoes off and waded as fast as she could through the flooded lanes. There were no streetlights, and the moon was hidden by dark clouds. Rain fell in sheets, blinding her further. Even the dilapidated buildings lining the narrow streets on both sides were reduced to ominous shadows. But this was the neighbourhood she'd grown up in; she didn't *need* to see.

Breathing harshly, she tried to speed up. Her legs were so heavy. Seema wished like hell she'd thought to strip off the jeans before running out. The damned thing was soaked through and weighed her down just when she needed to put as much distance as she could between her and the men. In a minute or two, they would be chasing after her. The jeans needed to go. Her hands went to the fly. A sharp pain shot across her shin. A steel drum floated by.

A shout came from behind, an angry demand for her to stop. Not waiting to check, Seema squeezed into the space between two buildings. The stench of putrid garbage was much stronger here. The men couldn't squeeze through the tight space, but they'd be waiting for her on the other side.

At twelve, Seema was small and skinny and didn't have boobs yet. Grossly underweight as the doctor Madhu took her to proclaimed. Seema was also used to climbing the roof of the shack they called home. In the darkness, she patted the side of the building, searching for the pipes sure to be running along the wall.

Her hand struck metal. Thanking every deity she knew, she gripped the pipe with her hands and feet. With the first upward heave, she slid back down. Wet. Too wet. Plus, the jeans weighed a ton. Seema turned every which way she could in the narrow space, trying to peel off the wet denim. Pain shot down her right elbow as it made contact with the bloody wall. Ignoring her screaming nerve endings, she tugged at the jeans. Nothing. It was as though the rain glued the damned thing to her legs. With a desperate growl, she dug her hands into the ground—into the mud and God only knew what else. Smearing dirt all over her arms and the jeans, she tried again to climb.

She heaved herself upwards, gritting her teeth to stop the sounds of terror from escaping her lips. Her shoulders stretched so tight they threatened to pop out of their sockets. Her chest burned. The mud she'd smeared scraped her skin, leaving trails of fire on her hands. The denim rubbed her thighs raw. Seema didn't have to go all the way to the roof as she'd planned. To her left was the shadow of a balcony. Twining her right leg around the pipe to keep balance, she stretched out her left one. Somehow, she hooked her foot over the railing and scrambled across.

It was a chawl building, the balcony extending end to end. Curling into a ball behind a pillar, Seema waited. Water sluiced down her body and puddled around her. She tried her best to stay awake and watch for danger. At some point, her eyes must have drifted shut. When she woke, she was violently shuddering from being wet and cold. She didn't know how long she'd been asleep, but she couldn't leave. In the darkness, she couldn't be sure the men weren't still around. She didn't even dare ask for help from the tenants of the building. Who knew what kind of monsters she'd find?

It was near dawn when she made the trip back down. The rain hadn't stopped, but she could see enough to spot danger. Plus, there were a few other residents wading through the flooded lanes, making it unlikely the loser and the pimp would abduct her. They wouldn't want Usthaad or Madhu hearing what happened and calling the cops.

When Seema got to the old warehouse owned by Usthaad, she laughed in relief. Tired and cold, she could only croak his name. She banged on the shutters with a piece of wood she found floating around.

The next moments were filled with the clanking of shutters being raised, the shocked face of her mentor, and a rough blanket drying her off. She shivered in the warm breeze set up by the ceiling fan above the cot. Seema didn't remember falling asleep but woke to a female voice.

Madhu was there, talking to Usthaad. Seema kept her eyes closed, feigning sleep. *Usthaad* was the one to first contact the NGO about her? *He'd* gotten Madhu to rescue Seema from the loser and the pimp? And Seema stupidly ran back.

"I'd like to keep her," said Usthaad. "But—"

"I know," said Madhu. "The courts won't let you, and neither will the pimp. Seema's my responsibility, anyway. Not yours."

She was? Why? Her mother didn't care, and her loser father had no use for her except as a source of income.

"I need to make sure she knows there's nothing left for her here," Madhu continued. "After tonight, she's not going to trust my brother. But you, Usthaad... she's going to keep coming back for you."

"I'll make sure it doesn't happen," said Usthaad. "I'm more worried about your brother and the pimp following you."

"I can take care of both of them," assured Madhu. "The NGO's director is acquainted with the police commissioner. They might not be able to save all the girls here, but they've promised to help me save Seema. Trust me. My brother will pay for what he tried to do."

"And for what he did to you," said Usthaad, tone quiet.

What had the loser done to Madhu? Did he sell her, too?

"It took a broken knee and shattered ribs to teach me a lesson," said Madhu, grimly. "I won't let that happen to Seema."

Fear went through Seema. A murmur escaped.

"Seema?" called Madhu. "Are you awake?"

In fifteen minutes, Seema was dressed in dry clothes and waiting for the taxi. Madhu was silent at her side, but Usthaad was not.

"Don't return here," he raged. "I don't need your kind of trouble."

I know what you're doing, buddhe, Seema muttered in her mind, telling off the old man.

"She won't return," Madhu said. "She doesn't need to. We're family."

The child of the same brother who sold her to a pimp? *Why do you give a damn?*

***

Seema woke with a start. She was on the same cot at the back of the warehouse. There was the same high ceiling with the charcoal sketch of a naked woman and her gravity-defying boobs. The same hanging fan, setting up a warm breeze. Everything was the same. Except, the air reeked of hot rubber, and there were loud clanging sounds not too far from her.

In the time Seema had been away from Grant Road, Usthaad had gone legit, and the warehouse was now a tyre service centre. She didn't know because they hadn't talked in twelve years. When she called the week before, he'd agreed to do her a "small favour." She'd shown up two days late, but he didn't quibble. Seema brought the clay staplers out of her purse, assuring him

315

she wasn't up to anything illegal. The eye that was not covered with a black patch stared unblinkingly, but her former mentor still called one of his employees to get the copies made while she took a small nap. Usthaad's warehouse was the one place other than the flat in Panvel where she knew she was safe.

Swinging her feet to the floor, she sat up. Her canvas slip-ons were arranged neatly under the cot.

"Finally," said Usthaad, pulling up a wooden stool and seating himself. The *topi*—his cloth cap—fell off, revealing the bald head. As always, he was in a long-sleeved shirt and skinny pants.

"How long was I out?" Seema asked, eyeing the street beyond the open shutters. Clouds had dissipated by the time she got there, and nothing seemed to have changed. The sun was pretty much in the same position. Usthaad's employees were still making the same racket, working on the red Maruti car and the old Tempo van.

"You're late to work," Usthaad said.

Seema goggled. "It's *Monday?*"

"Two in the afternoon," he said, cheerfully. "I did try to wake you, but you threatened to chop me into little pieces and send me to China by Speed Post." Face softening, he added, "Madhu called on your phone. She told me what you've been up to. Under the circumstances, I didn't think your boss would mind."

Seema wasn't supposed to use her personal phone while on this mission, but she needed it until the bureau assigned her a new clean device, so Madhu had brought it along with the fresh clothes. Shaking her head, Seema said, "I already took the day off. Usthaad, you didn't tell her about—"

"Your reason for being here? I said you were visiting."

Seema heaved a sigh of relief. "Good."

Other than shoot her a curious look, Usthaad didn't probe. He did insist on feeding her chicken biryani before she left.

"I'd kill for some rain right now," Seema muttered, scratching at her sweaty collarbone. "What happened to the monsoon? Done in one night?"

On the other side of the cashier's desk, Usthaad rocked back in his chair. "You lived on Grant Road, Seema *bachchi.*" He'd always called her his daughter, an honour he hadn't extended to his other protégés. "You should know better than to label that little sample monsoon rain."

Seema's phone rang. With a quick glance at the ID, she cancelled the call.

"Madhu?" asked Usthaad.

There was no point in lying. "She'll have questions." Seema was certain Madhu knew why Adhith kept losing keys at the party. She hadn't been able to interrogate Seema while she'd been at the hospital within earshot of the Joshis.

"Madamji," called one of Usthaad's employees, holding out a bunch of keys. His expression was pleasant, trusting. Everything secured in her purse, Seema zipped it up.

The chair squeaked when Usthaad stood. "Let me drop you home."

"You don't have to bother," Seema said, quickly. She needed to pick up her new phone from the bureau's Mumbai office. "I'll be all right. These days, there's no one trying to hunt me down."

Plus, the Glock was tucked into the waistband of her jeans. The only time she'd slipped the gun into her duffel and worn something comfortable was when she napped, and she'd risked it only because Vikram was around. No matter who came barging in for her, she'd known Vikram would protect her.

Emotions battered at Seema: the grief of loss, anger at her fate, pain when she thought of the years ahead. She gritted her teeth. The black thoughts would have to wait until later. She'd already wasted enough time. As soon as

Adhith stepped out of his flat, she'd search the place and close the file on her mission. *Then,* she would mourn Vikram.

"As you wish," Usthaad said, settling back into the chair.

Seema took two steps towards the street before turning back. "Usthaad?"

"Yeah?"

"You never asked for proof the keys are for legit purposes."

Still relaxing in his chair, the old man shrugged. "You trusted me enough to know I drove you away for your own good. Or you wouldn't have been here, asking for my help. So I trust *you.* If I'm wrong... you're an adult now. Old enough to face the consequences of your actions. If I land in prison along with you, it will only be karma."

Seema laughed, mildly. "I wish Madhu had the same faith in me."

"Madhu loves you. All she wants is for you to be safe and happy."

"And I love her. I wish she *trusted* me."

"Do you trust her?"

Surprised, Seema stared. "Of course."

"Enough to accept her insight?"

"I always do... uhh... I..." Forget about accepting Madhu's wisdom. Seema constantly defied her. Even after acknowledging Madhu as family, Seema's adolescent rebellion never entirely dissipated, inviting fitting response from Madhu.

"Trust has to be a two-way street," said Usthaad. "Or it becomes naïveté."

***

IB was as bad as any other governmental agency. It took Seema hours of paperwork to turn in her old phone and get a new one. By the time she was done, dark clouds obscured the setting sun. Getting out of the bus, Seema tossed her personal device in her hand. Usthaad's words rang in her mind. She needed to try explaining her reasoning to Madhu instead of acting like a mutinous teenager. Before she lost her nerve, Seema dialled Madhu's number. Two rings.

"Seema, where are you?" asked Madhu, tone worried.

Taking a deep breath, Seema blurted, "On my way home. I was at Usthaad's warehouse."

"I know. Why?"

"He promised to do me a favour." A drop fell on Seema's nose. Then, another. *Shit*. She'd hoped to be inside before the rain restarted. Purse slung across her body and duffel in hand, she strode down the footpath. Around her, the city continued with its business. Honking cars and rumbling buses continued to their destinations. Men and women and children streamed along the street, popping open umbrellas.

Madhu asked, "Adhi's keys?"

"Yes."

"Explain."

"I don't have much time left to try anything else," Seema admitted. "One of my digital alarms went off."

Madhu hissed. "At Imperium?"

"Yes. They haven't... I don't think Vikram knows it's me yet. Or he wouldn't have been so... but he's good at what he does. It's not totally improbable he might track me down. I need to finish things, quickly."

"IB cannot use any evidence you get by breaking in. And I don't think Verma is involved in his father's schemes."

Seema almost smiled. Madhu had referred to the fashion plate as "Adhi" a few seconds back. "It's precisely the point. If I can tell the bureau Adhith's innocent, we can bring that part of the investigation to a close. I'd have done what I set out to do."

"Seema, I won't let you..." Madhu huffed. "You're a grown woman, and you deserve to be treated like one. You *are* capable of analysing probabilities and making decisions. But I love you, and I don't want you in danger, so I'm going to tell you this. If you get caught, you can't claim you were only trying to exonerate Verma. The whole investigation will collapse if you do. The bureau will refuse to acknowledge your existence. So why are you doing this?"

Gruffly, Seema said, "I love you, too. I don't think I've ever said it before, but I'm very grateful you found me when you did."

"There's no need for gratit—"

"There's every need. Intentionally and unintentionally, I made life difficult for you many, many times. Also, I don't want you believing I still resent being taken out of Grant Road." Swallowing hard, Seema admitted, "Except for Usthaad, I'd been pretty much on my own. It was tough to trust *any*one, but I realised a long time ago I could trust *you*. Instead of simply doubling down whenever you objected to something I did, I should've talked things over with you."

"I'm not blameless," said Madhu. "I've been treating you like the twelve-year-old you were when... you don't like to dwell on the negative, but you're smart, and you know right from wrong, or you wouldn't have done what you did for Anjali... which brings us back to my question. Why are you bent on breaking into Adhi's flat? You surely understand the risk outweighs the benefit."

"Because I don't want to be a failu—" Seema stumbled, barely managing not to fall. Phone to her ear, she stared at a couple of yowling cats nosing through the foul-smelling garbage piled at the end of the block. Anjali's words. The reason for her suicide attempt. Was what Seema doing any less suicidal? She'd "forgotten" her plan several times during the last couple of days. Did her subconscious already know what a damn fool idea it was?

Anjali had been worried about not meeting her parents' expectations, but like Vikram, all Seema was expected to do was stay safe and happy. Unlike

Vikram, there was no third party to be blamed for Seema's problem. She'd embarked on this quest to prove... what the hell *was* she trying to prove? The people she most cared about—Vikram, Madhu—already acknowledged her as an equal. The goddamned *IB* trusted her enough to put the nation's security in her hands. Well... in hers and her superior's and a few other officers' hands. Still... she couldn't betray their faith in her by going rogue.

"Are you still there?" asked Madhu.

"Yeah." Seema resumed her walk. Her building was only a few feet away. "I've had many lucky escapes—" A taxi screeched past, splashing muddy water on Seema. "Argh," she screamed, eyeing the brown splotches on her jeans and on the duffel in her hand. There were even a few on her blouse. Someone cackled. The beggar with the scraggly beard who frequented her block was chilling under the lamppost. Making a face at him, she wondered what he'd do when the rains started in earnest.

"Seema?" called Madhu, voice urgent.

"Stupid driver," Seema muttered. "I'm lucky he didn't run me over. Hold on. I'm at my building." When she shouldered open the front door, the lift was in the lobby. "I was about to say you're right. I'm going to call the bureau and let them know this is all we'll get from Adhith. I'm not breaking in when it could put the mission in jeopardy. Plus, how many more times can I count on dumb luck? He almost found one of my moulds."

"What do you mean?"

As the lift clanked its way to the fifth floor, Seema explained the clay stapler she'd lost at the Oberoi. With a ping, the lift stopped. Backing into the flat, she dumped the duffel by the door and turned on the lights. She smiled. The cat was waiting for her on the ledge outside the window. Strolling over, she extended a hand through the bars and tickled his chin. "Thank God, Adhith didn't see it."

"Seema, I... I think he did see it."

Her hand stilled. *"What?"*

"You need to get out of your flat. "

"What do you mean—"

"Trust me."

The cat shifted away from Seema's touch, his eyes darting to a spot behind her. *Too late.* One swift move. Glock in her hand, she wheeled around. "Call the bureau," she screamed into the phone. *"Now. "* Pointing the weapon at the two men, she said, "Tell them I have intruders in my flat. Adhith Verma and—" Seema took a painful breath. "—Vikram Joshi."

✸✸✸

"Sit," ordered Seema, gesturing with her phone towards the sofa to her right. The call was still on, but she hoped like hell Madhu was contacting the bureau on the landline.

"Seema," started Vikram. "Listen to—"

"Sit," she roared, pointing the gun at his traitorous heart.

The jerk-face was still in the tee and the shorts from the day before, the same clothes he'd worn when he declared his love. "Okay, okay. I'm sitting." Holding his hands up, he collapsed onto the sofa.

"You, too, Fashion Plate," spat Seema.

"Heh?" Adhith asked, stupidly. "Me?"

"Yeah, you. Get over there."

He eyed his jeans and black shirt. "Why are you calling me a fashion pl... can you point your pistol somewhere else?" Seema snarled, aiming the gun straight at his crotch. He practically leapt to the sofa. "Is this a family trait or what? Pulling guns on people!"

"Please, don't make her any angrier," said a quavering voice. Startled, Seema looked left, the Glock still covering the two culprits on the sofa. A man stood dressed in a white shirt and pants, a black blazer stretched over his ample form despite the sweltering heat.

"Who the hell are you?" asked Seema.

"Advocate R.P. Sharma. I work for the Joshi Trust."

"A lawyer?" Seema asked, incredulously. She eyed the jerk-face and the fashion plate. "You brought a lawyer with you to ambush me? What for? Anticipatory bail?"

"Madam," said the lawyer, adjusting the glasses on his face. "Your question demonstrates a fundamental ignorance of how anticipatory bail works."

"I don't give a damn," Seema snapped. "Sit."

He didn't need to be told a second time.

"How can you think I came here to ambush you?" Vikram asked, a ton of hurt in his voice.

"Oh, I don't know. Because you *broke into my flat?*"

"*You* broke into Imperium's systems," Vikram pointed out. "You didn't do too badly, either. The only reason I figured out you were the hacker is the suspicious activity happened during work hours in Mumbai only on the days *you* were around."

"*And* you were planning to break into my flat," Adhith said.

Seema bared her teeth. "There's a ton of difference between the two. *I* am—"

"Seema Rawat," Vikram completed. "Star student of the mathematics department at the Mumbai University. We got as much from Imperium's records. I first tried hacking into the accounting company you listed in your application with Imperium but didn't get anywhere. The head of the math department at MU is a friend of one of my old professors at IIT. According to her, you went on to get two degrees from the Indian Statistical Institute.

Somehow, you couldn't find a job despite graduating top of the cryptology and security class. Then, you were hired by the income tax department where your auntie works." Vikram smiled. "Neural networks are not as easy to alter as digital ones."

"Give yourself a medal," Seema mocked. He got lucky. The digital alarms she'd set around the fake accounting company were linked to the destroyed phone. That was the reason she hadn't gotten a single warning someone was tracking her. The bureau would've been alerted, but given that she'd concealed Vikram's discovery of the hacking attempt from them, they wouldn't have picked up on the urgency of the situation. They might have even dismissed it as routine background check on the woman Adhith Verma was considering marrying. One of the other analysts would've been told to keep an eye on it to see if it went anywhere. Seema's ego left her without backup when the villain and his sidekick—the jerk-face she'd fallen in love with—barged into her flat. "Once you worked it out, you got your friend and came here?" she asked Vikram, gritting her teeth against the hurt. "To get me for the cyberattack?"

Outside the window, thunder rumbled. The skies opened. Another monsoon storm descended on Mumbai. The cat meowed, squeezing his head and body through the bars. Swishing his tail, he settled on the floor to watch.

"Sure, you'd attacked Imperium," Vikram acknowledged. "'People make mistakes,' right? I went looking for your reasons, but it all seemed too well-planned to be a mistake. Still, I knew damned well you love me, or you wouldn't have stuck around for..." He'd refused to believe she'd intended to hurt him. A soothing coolness spurted in her chest, easing the raw pain of betrayal. Vikram continued, "The only thing which made sense was... uhh..."

"He was convinced this was a government hit," Adhith took up. "There's no other way you and Madhu could've concealed every bit of information we could use to track you. He thought it had to be about my father and me. By then, I was already going out of my mind. I'd seen your key imprint. Long story short, I also thought you were spying on me to get my father. Vikram and I discussed a few things."

"Vikram," Seema howled. "Why did you even take his call? Do you realise what he could do to me? To both of us?"

"Adhi is not going to take advantage of what I told him," Vikram said, firmly. "He's not Nanaji. Also, *I* contacted Adhi, not the other way around."

"What?" Seema nearly hopped in frustration. Vikram refused to believe she'd done anything wrong on purpose, but he'd extended the same benefit of the doubt to his best friend. He really didn't have a clue how to read people. Adhith Verma was the son of the finance minister, for God's sake, the corrupt bastard who'd stolen crores from the taxpayers.

"Seema," chided Adhith. "We didn't come here to... Vikram convinced me the only way to be free of my father's... ahh... legacy would be to end it."

Vikram went on, "Adhi's been trying to come up with a way out of this for the last few months. It's why he told his father he wanted to marry you. He thought it would stop the pressure on him to join politics. Unsuitable wife and all. For him, I mean. Not me. For me, you're *very* suitable."

"Bro," Adhith yelped. "She has a gun. Are you *trying* to get me killed?"

"I didn't particularly want you, either," Seema assured him.

"I knew Adhi wasn't about to hurt you," Vikram stated. "We talked. Then, we tried to call you. You didn't pick up your company phone, and your other phone..." Seema's work phone was at home in Panvel, and her clean phone—the only other number Vikram had—was crushed beyond repair.

"We thought you weren't picking up on purpose," Adhith said. "Because of the investigation, I mean. It's the reason we're here."

"How did you get in?" she asked.

"We didn't want to risk you refusing to meet us, so we bribed the building manager into letting us in," Adhith admitted. "We've been here since morning."

That was it? No elaborate schemes? No arrangements with a former burglar to copy keys? For a criminal, the fashion plate was hopelessly unimaginative.

"I want you to know I had nothing to do with the bribery," the lawyer stated. "If I were you, madam, I'd have the building manager fired."

"Where does *he* come in?" Seema asked, glancing at the lawyer.

"Adhi didn't dare contact his father's legal team," Vikram explained. "He couldn't be sure what they'd do. The only other lawyer-types we knew were Imperium's. And Sharma. He works for the Joshi Trust, so we asked him to help."

"They dragged me out of my office," corrected Sharma.

Vikram shrugged. "He's a securities lawyer... investments and stuff."

Seema's jaw dropped open. "What were you planning to have him do?"

"He's here only to make our offer official." Vikram stood. "Seema, this started with the three of us. You, me, Adhi. Let us be the ones to end it. We have a deal for your employer. You said something about the bureau. The Intelligence Bureau, I presume."

"Tell IB," Adhith said, "I can give them information on certain companies, plus a number of politicians. IB will get evidence of graft and corruption extending into every continent. You started investigating one union minister. Believe me, he's done nothing compared to the rest. You could end up with the biggest clean-up in the history of Indian intelligence."

"In return?" Seema asked.

"You will let my father resign and leave active politics," Adhith said, firmly. "There will be no prosecution. His name will not be mentioned anywhere in the public documents."

Seema laughed in derision. "You think the bureau will let him get away with the crores he's looted?"

"All those properties will be returned to the government," said Adhith. "He'll only keep what he legitimately made from stocks and such. Think about it, Seema. In return for my father's freedom, IB will be able to wipe out a large chunk of the corruption in the country."

"That's one helluva promise," Seema said. "Why should I believe it?"

Tone subdued, Vikram said, "For the last ten or so years, Adhi and I have been collecting information on the connections between politicians and businesses. Whatever he knows, I do, too. He... *we* will help you. Trust me?"

Even after finding damning evidence against Seema, Vikram refused to give up on her. Instead of seething in blind hatred, he'd gone searching for her reasons. Now, here he was, making himself vulnerable.

"I believe you." Keeping her eyes on Vikram, Seema tilted her head in Adhith's direction. "Do you think we can believe *him*—"

There was a squawk from the phone.

"Madhu?" Seema called, turning on the speakerphone. "Did you hear everything?"

"Yes, I did," said Madhu. "So did your senior superintendent. She's here with me."

"*What?*" asked Seema, taken aback. How did the bureau get to Panvel so fast?

"Rawat," came the SSP's impatient voice. "The minute we heard your auntie made contact with the suspect, we ordered covert protection for her. The bureau doesn't like risking civilians. The flat next door now belongs to IB. We actually thought *you* sent her to Colaba—"

"Seema," interrupted Madhu. "You can believe Adhi. He's only asking for the deal because it's his father."

The fashion plate simpered at the phone. "You don't know how much that means to me. Madhu, you gave me the strength to do this. *You* did what you had to do, personal costs be damned. Also, when Vikram said 'unsuitable,' he meant only Seema. Not you."

The SSP's groan was audible.

Tucking the Glock back into its holster, Seema called, "Sir?"

"Bring them into the office," said the SSP. "Let's see what they have."

"One more thing," Vikram said, his wary eyes on the gun. "Seema, you're fired."

Chapter 20

Nature waged war on the city in the form of a thunderstorm as Minister Verma announced his resignation in the conference room at the Sahyadri Guest House. Both his colleagues and the public were taken by surprise. Within a week, scandal rocked the government. Politicians and business leaders were led away in handcuffs. The stock market fluctuated, wildly. The president of India addressed the nation to reassure everyone the economic turmoil would be temporary. Over the course of one monsoon in Mumbai, India got rid of most of its unethical elite.

Minister Verma's name was nowhere in the list of those implicated. In fact, talk in the media was the minister resigned because he could no longer tolerate the corruption of his colleagues. There were rumours it was he who tipped off IB. The former politician became a hero to the public.

The media camped outside his ancestral home in Uttarakhand, but he refused to talk to them. He declined phone calls from colleagues, friends, and family. His beloved son, Adhith Verma, was not allowed admission to the house until today, six months after the minister left Delhi.

In the old Verma home in Bhikiyasen, a fire crackled under the living room chimney. A blanket spread over his legs, the former minister swayed back and forth in the rocking chair. As always, his kurta and pyjamas were pristine white.

"Papaji," called Adhith, leaning against the doorjamb. Winters in Bhikiyasen being only mildly chilly, his fleece pullover and jeans kept him pleasantly warm.

The motion of the chair paused. "Who let you in?" asked Papaji.

It was the secretary, the man who'd been with the minister since his days as a union leader. The secretary was scared his old friend was going into a decline. Adhith came running at the news, accompanied by the two people most dear to him. Vikram was in the garden, entertaining Adhith's pregnant wife, Madhubala, with stories of their youthful misadventures in the small town. Seema stayed in Mumbai to deal with some kind of wedding emergency. "I lived here a long time, Papaji," Adhith said. "I've snuck in and out of the house before."

The rocking restarted.

"Please, Papaji," Adhith begged. "Talk to me."

"There's nothing to be said. All the work I put in, everything I achieved... you destroyed it all in a matter of days."

In three steps, Adhith was by the chair, dropping to his knees. "Papaji, if I hadn't, they would've arrested you. How can you not see it?"

"They had nothing on me," Papaji spat. "Absolutely nothing... until *you* gave it to them."

"They would've gotten something at some point. This was the only way out for us. Also, Papaji, why would you even want to keep any of it? We have enough money to live comfortable lives."

"Comfort," Papaji snarled. "You don't understand a single thing, do you? Money isn't about clothes and shoes and all those idiotic things you like to buy. Money gives you control. You don't understand because you've never been without either. *I* have. As a union leader in this town, I've watched factory projects never take off, roads never built, schools tumbling down. Your ma died in pain because there wasn't any medicine in the hospital. You think any of that happens to rich people? Money gives them the power to get what they want when they want it. *Politics* is about power."

"Not for me. Sure, I like all the idiotic things money gets me, but if I must, I can do without them. Papaji, the stuff you talked about... bridges, roads, hospitals... that's not what you were doing. Somewhere along the way from Bhikiyasen to New Delhi, you started thinking only of yourself. You forgot the voters. *I* want to do those things for them. I still want to be the prime minister—"

With a bark of derisive laughter, Papaji asked, "You think it's going to happen? Everyone in the party believes I ratted them out. No one's going to support you. You have no money to run a campaign."

"Adhi won't have to worry about money," said Vikram. He and Madhu were at the door, both dressed in jeans and fleeces like Adhith. Madhu's hands were linked over her baby bump. "I had some saved for my business, but it's going for Adhi's campaign," Vikram assured Papaji. "The Joshi Trust will lend me the money *I* need."

Papaji glanced between Vikram and Adhith. "You think your friend's not going to want anything in return? You'll find out the hard way."

"Adhi's my buddy, Uncleji," Vikram said, tone easy. "I already got what I wanted from him. His friendship. All I want now is for him to win the state assembly seat from the Grant Road area. The people there need someone like him as the MLA."

The employees of the teashop were full-throated in their support of Adhith's candidacy. Seema convinced Usthaad to deploy his network to campaign for Adhith. The NGO couldn't officially get involved in politics, but the ladies they helped were well aware of his efforts to get funds released from the central government. They were aware he'd married one of them. All in all, there was a good chance Adhith would be an MLA come spring.

Papaji muttered, "MLA. After refusing a central government seat. He could've been an MP. A minister in five or six years. Prime Minister by his forties."

"I hope it happens," Adhith said. "If it doesn't, I'm fine with staying in the state assembly."

"I'm not," said Papaji. "I worked all my life to put you there. Now, you come here and tell me it doesn't matter to you? My hopes and dreams don't mean anything to you?"

"How can it be *your* dream when it's *my* life?" Adhith asked.

"Your life?" shouted Papaji. "The only life you have is the one I gave you. What are you without me?"

"Papaji," Adhith whispered, his heart breaking.

"I'll tell you what he is," came Madhu's low voice. "A wonderful man. A husband most women can only dream of. In a few weeks, he'll be a father. If you ever recognise him as a human being and not merely the stepping-stone to even more money and power, you'll know you raised a son to be proud of. For that, I thank you."

Papaji yelled for his secretary, asking the man to escort the unwanted guests out, including Adhith. Watching his father give strict instructions not to let him in even for funeral rites, Adhith crumpled inside.

He clung to Madhu on their flight from Dehradun to Mumbai the next morning. "I wish I could make it go away," Madhu murmured, rubbing her fingers over his chest.

"Let it be there," he murmured back. "It's the punishment I deserve for my duplicity. I lectured you on letting Seema face the consequences of her actions. All the while, I—" He glanced out of the window. "I'm still a phoney. If Papaji ever comes around—I can't give him up."

"That only means you're human."

With a short laugh, he teased, "What *you* said only means you love me."

A ping. The seatbelt sign came on. Adhith and Madhu drew off their fleeces, leaving them clad in jeans and cotton tees. It was December, but Mumbai weather was still hot and humid.

Across the aisle, Vikram closed his laptop and tucked it into his bag alongside his own light sweater. Walking out of the Chhatrapati Shivaji International Terminal, he laughed. "The last time I landed here was when I returned from San Jose. I was going to crash in the office for a couple of days. I didn't know..."

***

Vikram hadn't known at the time the rest of his life was waiting for him in the manager's personal latrine. This time, Seema waited for him at the airport exit. His fiancée was dressed in a white blouse and denim miniskirt. Her long, toned legs ended in sports shoes. After greeting Madhu and Adhith with quick hugs, Seema darted a deliciously wicked glance at Vikram.

Grazing her cheek with his mouth, Vikram muttered, "You wore this outfit on purpose. You *know* I'm crazy about your legs." As the other couple climbed into a taxi, Vikram glared at their backs. "Hypocrites," he grumbled.

After Vikram and Seema went to look at a two-bedroom in Andheri, Madhu almost had herself a meltdown, going on about the consequences of living together before marriage, especially for women. Adhith, the useless piece of shit, would only mumble he wasn't going to take sides, and he skulked out of the scene first chance he got.

Vikram insisted he'd defend Seema from anyone who dared say an unkind word, but his parents added their voices to Madhu's. Nuh-huh, no way. Not until he and Seema had their big, fat Marathi wedding. Eventually, they conceded the rest had a point. Flouting society's rules would lead to consequences in other arenas, such as their careers.

Then, Adhith made a song and dance about circumstances not being right for *him* to have a fussy wedding, and he and Madhu filed an application with the marriage registrar, barely waiting the government-mandated thirty days before getting hitched in a court ceremony. A couple of weeks later, they blithely announced the pregnancy. Oh, yeah, the baby was due in March, about six months from the day they tied the knot.

"You simply have to look the other way on some things," Seema's flatmate, Gayathri, advised an open-mouthed Seema. "Pretence is the glue which holds families together."

Vikram didn't give a damn about families and glue and whatever. He would've beaten the double standard out of the two-faced S.O.B he called a friend, but there was Madhu. Even Vikram knew better than to aggravate a pregnant woman.

He scowled at the couple in the cab. They were going home together while he and Seema—

"Forget them," Seema hissed, puckering her lips.

The crowd around... but Vikram couldn't help it. He needed a little something to keep him going until they got to someplace private. Bending down, he chanced a quick peck. Her fingers curled around his biceps. Breath jittery, she clung for a moment before pushing away. The mischief in her eyes was now clouded by longing.

As Adhith and Madhu's cab sped away from the curb, Vikram said, "If we'd done a court ceremony like them—"

"We would've broken your mother's heart," Seema said, her tone reflecting his frustration. "Two more weeks to the wedding of the year."

"Two more weeks," Vikram consoled, waving a taxi over.

Before the new year came around, they'd be married and living in the flat they'd rented. Their nights would be spent in each other's arms, and their days...

Both would be busy. Vikram was thankful for the faith his family showed, advancing the capital he needed to start Secure Systems, his new business. Also, surprised he wasn't more cheesed off at having to accept their help. Even if he *had* been resentful, it would've been small price to pay to help Adhith get started in politics.

As MLA, Adhith couldn't be part of Vikram's venture, but thanks to Seema's recommendation, he'd found someone who could be equally persuasive with clients. Seema's friend, Gayathri, was in charge of customer relations. Much to Seema's annoyance, Vikram lured Britto away from Imperium. When the accountant heard about her leaving the company, he'd danced in joy, but he was also honest and reliable. Britto danced a second time when he heard Seema declined any sort of role in the new business, saying it was *Vikram's* dream, not hers. She had her own...

***

In the backseat of the taxi speeding down Marine Drive, Seema rubbed her cheek against Vikram's shoulder. They were headed straight to his meeting with a prospective client, and he was busy looking over papers, but he still managed another kiss. The sweet warmth on her mouth was too quickly withdrawn. "Jerk-face," Seema accused, adoringly.

Vikram winked. "Count down the days, my love. I'm—" A sudden cough. The cabbie, making them aware of his presence. Vikram eyed the back of the driver's head, muttering something under his breath about the universe conspiring to keep them apart.

Giggling, Seema shifted away. *Soon,* her mind whispered. They wouldn't need to limit themselves to stolen moments and tiny, unsatisfying touches. She could kiss him whenever she wanted, touch him wherever, love him all night.

He'd be working as hard as he played, trying to make a go of the new business. Thank God the trust offered him enough money to quit his job with Imperium right away. He'd been so adorably flustered, explaining to the office staff how *he* ended up engaged to Seema. Since her part in the investigation remained classified, Adhith spun a romance novel, telling everyone—including their families—he'd only been pretend-dating Seema to force Vikram into making a move. In the process, Adhith met Madhu... blah, blah, blah. Vikram was still convinced the entire staff was staring at him in horror, accusing him of stealing his best friend's girl. The move from Imperium came in the nick of time as far as he was concerned, even if it meant he'd be working his butt off the first couple of years of their marriage.

Seema would also be busy. The Intelligence Bureau was pleased with her success. Sure, part of it was dumb luck as the SSP noted, but Seema's technical skills were unquestionable. *Imperium* vouched for it. They'd been miffed at IB for the intrusion, but it wasn't as though either party could go public about it. Plus, IB mollified Imperium by promising a contract for something or the other. The bureau also offered Seema a permanent job in their cybersecurity wing, provided she got accepted to the Indian Police Service training program. There was one more condition: Madhu had to keep her nose out of Seema's work. "Rawat," said the SSP. "You have what it takes to be a cop." On learning of the bureau's opinion, Usthaad—Seema's former mentor—guffawed until he almost puked out his guts.

It was only when the job was offered Seema realised how badly she wanted it. The civil services examination for admission to IPS training was months away, but she was already hitting the books. In her mind, she was stomping through the city streets, gun in one hand, handcuffs in the other. She'd be Assistant Superintendent of Police Seema Rawat. ASP Rawat. She'd have everything she wanted and then some.

Not just her. While not exactly what they'd imagined, a hopeful future was within reach for all of them, including Madhu. On the morning of her court wedding, Seema threatened to pepper the fashion plate's butt with bullets if he didn't keep his wife happy, but the warning was unnecessary. He turned out to be a doting husband, and there was a baby on the way. Seema could hardly wait for the next Rawat to make his dramatic entry into the world. He was already one lucky fella, starting out his life with Madhu as his mom. She'd be strict, though. But he'd have his dad to play dress-up with and Vikram Uncle and Seema Auntie to spoil him rotten.

Staring out the car window, Seema grinned at the urchins leaping from rock to rock on the seashore. Yup. Mumbai was indeed a puzzle of a city. It chewed up starry-eyed hopefuls on a daily basis and spat them out. On rare occasions, it allowed the wildest of dreams to come true.

Note from the author

Dear Reader,

Writers thrive on reviews. They help us figure out what worked and what fell flat. They help other readers make up their mind. Please do leave a comment on Amazon and/or Goodreads.

Sincerely,

Anitha

P.S. Do visit www.AnithaPerinchery.com for a bunch of other fun stuff.

Check out Anjali's story in *A Goan Holiday*

If you're in the mood for a historical thriller with angsty romance, take a look at the **One Hundred Years of War** series written under my pen name, Jay Perin. I call it *The Great Gatsby* meets *Succession*.

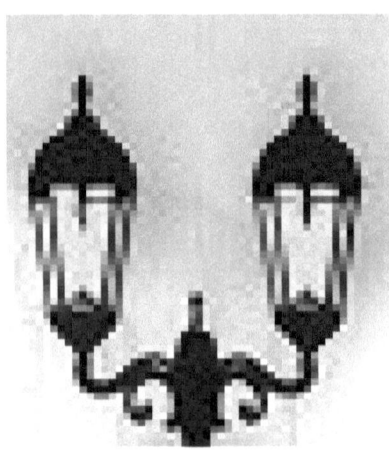

Pre(?Post)face and Acknowledgments

I was told by an oracle (book marketing tips on Google) I should place this section at the end so readers can get straight to the story. Here goes:

I read somewhere debut writers mention everyone on the planet, including their pets, and I won't be much different. I have many to thank and am grateful to Jesus for allowing me breathing room to explore my creative side.

My family: my long-suffering husband who had to tolerate my habit of disappearing into my thoughts in the middle of dinner while I worked out a plot glitch. There's a little bit of him in all my heroes. My three children who had to listen to the same song being blasted as the theme music until I typed, "The End." They still think I should make this a series and name the next *Two Tornadoes in Toronto*. My parents (here's where I cross my fingers and swear I've never actually been to any of the seedy places I mention in my stories), my brothers (including the cousins. They believed in me even when I didn't), and the extended family (aunt, uncle, mother-in-law) who probably chalked up the periods of radio silence to my natural grouchiness. Friends and colleagues who cheered me on.

My friends and beta readers: Amrita Talukdar who patiently read multiple versions of the same book. She sent enough angry-face emojis until I broke down and agreed to publish. It is my firm belief Preeti Gopal used to be an undercover agent. She gave me suggestions on how an Indian income tax officer might get recruited by the Intelligence Bureau. The ladies I tested out my zanier ideas on: Radhika Thampuran and Mamatha Prasad. My critique partners: Rebecca Chatterpaul-Johnson, Anna Skogerboe Gracia, and CJ Simone.

My editors/mentors/associates:

Michael P Lewis

https://www.goodreads.com/user/show/51908857-ts-media

I learned about the use of sensory detail from him. His bluntness in pointing out plot holes is something I appreciate.

Elizabeth Roderick http://talesfrompurgatory.com/ She did a fabulous job as developmental editor. I remember her telling me, "This is where I'd be tempted to toss your book out the window."

Chase Nottingham https://chaseediting.com/ I thought I knew how to write in English until I ran into Chase. He went through the whole thing line by agonising line, pointing out my crutch words and fixing my comma-heavy writing.

The mistakes in the manuscript may be attributed entirely to my inability to kill my darlings.

www.EbookorPrint.com The designer responsible for the beautiful cover.

A huge, heartfelt thanks to all.

Anitha Perinchery